THE
SURVIVOR

THE
SURVIVOR

ANDREW REID

MINOTAUR
BOOKS
NEW YORK

First published in the United States by Minotaur Books, an imprint of St. Martin's Publishing Group

EU Representative: Macmillan Publishers Ireland Ltd, 1st Floor, The Liffey Trust Center, 117–126 Sheriff Street Upper, Dublin 1, DO1 YC43

THE SURVIVOR. Copyright © 2026 by Andrew Reid. All rights reserved. Printed in the United States of America. For information, address St. Martin's Publishing Group, 120 Broadway, New York, NY 10271.

www.minotaurbooks.com

Designed by Omar Chapa

Library of Congress Cataloging-in-Publication Data (TK)

ISBN 978-1-250-39328-9 (hardcover)
ISBN 978-1-250-39329-6 (ebook)

Our books may be purchased in bulk for specialty retail/wholesale, literacy, corporate/premium, educational, and subscription box use. Please contact MacmillanSpecialMarkets@macmillan.com.

First Edition: 2026

10   9   8   7   6   5   4   3   2   1

For Lisa

THE
SURVIVOR

THE
SURVIVOR

CHAPTER ONE

SOUTH FERRY

At the entrance to the subway station, the stairs lead down from the street until they are swallowed by darkness. Standing four steps from the top, Ben Cross grips the railing tighter and watches as people walk past him and down with no hesitation at all: tourists straight from the ferry, personal trainers from sessions in the park, enough suits to start up a small but tasteful menswear store. Every one of them passes by and vanishes into the black as though stepping down and knowing that a step will even be there to meet your foot descending is the most everyday and normal thing a person could do.

Ben did it himself this morning, but that was a different Ben. One with a good night's sleep and a strong cup of coffee in him, and the promise of a new life waiting at the other end of the journey.

A lot has changed in the six hours since.

Someone bumps his shoulder, and Ben flinches at the contact. It isn't much, but his hands feel slick on the railing, like at any moment his grip could slip and send him tumbling down the steps. He is scared that

if he holds on any tighter, it will just make that fate even more likely.
The guy says something as he passes, but with all his attention focused
on the long shadow that swallows up the last few steps, Ben doesn't
catch the exact wording. Still, the rest of the stairs aren't crowded, and
the intent behind the bump is clear enough. *What are you doing just
standing there? Are you some kind of idiot?*

He doesn't have to do this. The subway is quick, but it's not
convenient—for him, at least—and it's not like he has anywhere to be
all of a sudden. A cab would be ideal—a box where he can sit and try
and make some kind of sense of the past half hour—but Ben can hear
the sound of distant traffic, and it has the same frantic energy as the
sound of a domestic argument two apartments over. All things considered, just the risk of sitting in traffic at seventy cents a minute feels too
rich for Ben's blood.

There are buses he can take, but every bus he has ever taken is its
own special brand of hell. The last time Ben was on a bus there was a
lady with a stroller full—or, briefly full—of cats.

He could always just walk.

Ben stops himself before he can entertain that thought any further.
It's almost a hundred degrees out, and the forecast is even higher. He's
wearing a suit that is meant to be dark blue, but right now feels like it is
one of those special kinds of black that absorbs 100 percent of the heat
that lands on it.

Ben can imagine what that walk uptown would feel like after the first
ten minutes. He can almost imagine how bad it would be after an hour.

The thought of free air-conditioning on the subway gets him down
two more steps, hand over hand on the railing, three points of contact
at all times, like a mountain climber, before the dark stops him again.

A friendly hand settles on his shoulder and gives him a shake. Not
hard enough to startle, more like it is intended to bring him back to
himself. A grounding. The effect is the exact opposite. It feels like the
steps are falling away from under him, and the past fifteen years along
with them.

You thought people would forget. It rises up through him, a column of heat building in his chest. *You thought you would forget*.

One of Ben's therapists told him once that people have bad thoughts all the time. That having them is part of living: we think of the worst things first so we can stop them from happening. Like driving your car over a bridge and entertaining for one brief moment the urge to yank the wheel to one side and drive clean through the barrier.

Ben never asked if everyone else's bad thoughts spoke to them like his do. Even when the voice isn't there, he can still feel it, like someone hanging on to his shoulder waiting to criticize him, to tell him how worthless he is.

"First step's always the hardest, right?"

The man's voice is deep, and has a little of the South in it. Ben had a lecturer from Charlotte who spoke the same way, and that association more than anything else breaks his train of thought, straightening him up to answer the man.

"I just—" Ben starts, and finds himself stumbling over the words. The black rectangle of shadow seems to tighten in on itself as he looks at it. "I think I'm going to take the bus," he says.

"That's your choice," the man says. "And a perfectly fine one." Ben doesn't look at the man—doesn't want the eye contact—but he can almost picture him exactly. Plaid shirt. Tan jacket. Jeans over a pair of well-worn boots. "But you came to the subway first. You going to let it beat you?"

"It's not beating me." Ben spits the words, the flush of embarrassment pushing them out fast and angry.

"Sure it is," the man says, his tone unrattled, hand still firm on Ben's shoulder.

There's movement, like he's pulling something from a pocket, and for a brief moment Ben thinks that it's a blade. That this is how he goes out: shanked by a country singer outside the New York subway.

"Might not know exactly what you're going through," the man says, "but I recognize it."

Ben looks down. The man's other hand is right there in front of him, held out at chest height, a single poker chip lying like an offering in the center of his palm. Looking a little closer, he sees what is written on the chip, three words forming the sides of a triangle. *Unity, Recovery, Service.* It's an AA chip, and the *XV* that stands bold on the face is there to show that the holder is fifteen years sober.

Ben wonders what kind of drunk the man could have been: the quiet type that hides it, with bottles in the toilet tank or taped under the workbench; or maybe something worse, constantly on the knife-edge, the instinct to violence honed keen by whatever he'd been drinking that day. There are only a handful of reasons to help a stranger out, and in Ben's experience the majority are acts of penance.

"You think I need help?"

"We all need help, son." The hand closes over the chip, whisks it away to be deposited back in whatever sacred pocket produced it. "But right now? It's your call."

Ben almost says something sarcastic about the fridge magnet motivational, but the weight of the man's hand holds it in check.

"You can take the bus," he says. "But if you do, then that's your fear making the choice for you." He laughs, low and throaty. "And who the fuck takes the bus, anyway? The bus is for crazies."

He gives Ben's shoulder a fatherly shake—*go get 'em, tiger*—and then the pressure is gone. As Ben turns to look at him the man is already past and on his way down the steps: broad shouldered, dark brown hair— too dark to be anything other than dye—thinning at the crown, his age showing in the cautious way he finds each step. Just as Ben guessed, he's wearing a tan jacket and denim jeans, but the boots are missing. Instead, he's got on a pair of chunky, faux-leather shoes. The kind of orthopedics you'd find advertised in a magazine aimed at retirees, built with the blunt functionality of a ball-peen hammer, available for the low, low price of forty nine dollars and ninety-nine cents for the pair, no postage required.

Ben wonders what it must have been like to find yourself sober at retirement age, and what it must have taken to stay that way.

Fifteen years. It feels like fate to share that number with him. Like Ben was meant to meet him, hear what he had to say.

That he was meant to take the subway.

Ben lightens his grip on the railing and takes a single step down toward the subway entrance, his left foot dropping like a dead weight as it drags in the wake of the right.

The man was wrong. The first step isn't hard at all. The second one, the one that comes after you commit yourself to and wake up to the fact that now you're going to have to follow through: that one is the real son of a bitch.

He takes the rest of the steps in a rush, tripping over his own feet, not giving himself the chance to think about anything other than keeping his balance. Before he can even start to panic, he's already there: the void at the bottom of the steps climbs in his vision like a wave crowding against a coastal shelf, impossibly tall and unavoidable and his heart does a jackrabbit leap in his chest—

And before the fear can seize hold of him, he's through.

Ben calms down once he's inside the subway station, because everything about the subway is designed to calm people down. There's nothing rational about it otherwise. Volunteering to make your way down a hundred feet below street level and climb inside a metal tube; to feel the whole thing shudder and jolt on a stop-start journey under a hundred million tons of city overhead. You'd have to be insane.

Everything from the way the space opens up toward the turnstile—after which you've paid, so even if you turn back it's no big loss—to the striplight brightness reflecting off of every tiled surface is designed to trick your brain into thinking you're not, in fact, a single structural flaw away from being buried alive. There are signs and countdowns everywhere, the sense of being in a hurry condensed to single digits, and any space that isn't dedicated to that distraction is filled with a poster for a Broadway show.

The air, though, is something they can't control. They can clean and sweep and polish every surface all they want, and it will never overcome the smell of the earth, the draw and push of the air moved by the trains as they pass, or the constant heat of the place: the collective effort of seven thousand air-conditioned trains venting constantly into the tunnels as they run. It's hot up on the sidewalk, but down here the heat mounts up against you like a wall, making your skin prickle with sweat.

There's a train heading north on the 1 that's due to pull out almost right this minute, and while he doesn't want to have to book it down to the platform Ben has a dim sense that if he hustles now, then he'll make it. The prospect of a victory—even a small one—puts the closeness of the ceiling (and the feeling that it is getting closer) to one side and he puts his head down and steps forward, hitting that perfect moment of flow where the crowd in the station seems to part and let him pass.

The rush of it carries him all the way down the escalator, the people ahead of him in a hurry, too, but a little too slow taking the steps to do anything but hold everyone else up. The people behind him huff and bump up against him, as though it is his fault they have had to stop, as though their disapproval will somehow magic the way ahead clear. He doesn't do anything about it. The voice in the back of his head tells him to angle his briefcase back, fake a stumble and swing the corner of it up at crotch height, but he refuses to acknowledge it. No point in risking his day getting any worse.

The conductor is leaning on the buzzer to let everyone know the doors are closing, and while Ben would normally aim for the middle of the train to improve his chances of getting a seat, there's just enough time to duck into the second car from the back.

Once he's on, though, the doors hang open almost twenty seconds longer before they close and the train gets rolling.

Ben doesn't pay it much mind. There's plenty of space in the car, even if he didn't need to rush to get on. It's a little over half full, and there are still enough places to sit. He plants himself on an empty seat in the front quarter of the car, and it occurs to him that half full feels plenty busy for the middle of the day. All the way through college he'd asked himself what kind of people had the time to walk around campus or sit on the subway in the middle of the day. Weren't they busy? Didn't they have other places to be?

The answer—for him, at least—is simple. He doesn't have anywhere else to be. Not now, and not for the immediate future, anyway.

Ben takes a deep breath and spreads his palms on the briefcase that was going to carry his future, and him along with it.

Fired on your first full day at work, he thinks. *So much for that fresh start, cowboy.*

The train shudders forward, jolting him in his seat, then picks up speed as it heads off out of the station and, without pause, into the darkness of the tunnel.

CHAPTER TWO

BROOKLYN

It is an immutable fact of the Universe that if you press the Snooze button more than one time when the alarm goes off, your day is destined to sit somewhere on the spectrum between *shit* and *worse*.

Even though she knows better, Detective Kelly Hendricks hits hers three times before deciding that enough is enough.

The resulting hustle to get out the door on time—eating breakfast so fast that she almost donated half to her shirt, drinking a whole cup of coffee hot enough that her teeth and gums would have grounds to sue, and her hair not so much styled as, simply, present—is enough to keep her from dwelling on it until it's too late. Down on the street, Hernandez is sitting in his beat-up Hyundai waiting to give her a ride. She steps down onto the sidewalk and he pops the passenger side door for her, and all at once she wonders, *Why the fuck didn't I call in sick?*

"You look peaky," Hernandez says. He has the engine running, but waits for her to pull the door closed and to hear the click of her seat belt before he starts driving. Kelly knows this, so she waits a beat, just long enough to annoy him but not so long that he'll feel the need to comment, before she sets the seat belt home.

"It's the suit," Kelly says. "Sales guy said I'd be getting men lined up round the block." She sniffs. "Didn't mention they'd all be morticians."

"Pale is in, I hear." He peels out from the curb and merges into traffic without signaling, the unmistakable aura of *cop* coming off of a gray import with two hundred thousand miles on the clock doing the work for him.

"I won't hold my breath," she says.

"You should. Lie down while you do it, maybe you'll get lucky and someone will try CPR."

"It's all fun and games until they zap you with a defibrillator."

Hernandez frowns out the side window at something Kelly doesn't see. He reaches for the radio but checks himself and accelerates to close the gap that's opened up between them and the car in front. "People pay good money for that."

"What was that about?"

"Nothing," Hernandez says. "Just kids. I swear I'm getting jumpy in my old age."

"You feel threatened by their youth," Kelly says. "They've got something you can't ever get back, and that scares the shit out of you."

He frowns again. "Aren't you, like, eight years older than me?"

"I'll pretend I didn't hear that." She keeps her tone light, but the jab still finds its mark. Kelly presses her fingers into her palms, not making fists, never anything so obvious, and stretches them out again, feeling the tension build in the tendons, then drain as she relaxes them. If it is meant to make her feel better, it doesn't work.

Eight years extra to climb the same height up the ladder, and only one bad day to fuck it all up.

"Where am I dropping you?"

"Cortlandt."

Hernandez puffs his cheeks out. "In this traffic? I'll drop you on the other side of the Williamsburg Bridge, you can hop the J line or something."

"Hernandez," Kelly says. "I am booked in for a full day of following the mole people around on the subway. I refuse to spend a second longer underground than I absolutely have to."

"What is this gig, anyway? Some kind of PR stunt, or something?"

"Something like that."

"Must be nice, getting to go around getting your picture taken instead of doing real police work."

It isn't a PR stunt. As much as Hernandez is trying to put a shine on it, there's no way in hell he can polish it up to resemble anything other than what it is: shit duty.

Someone at the commissioner's office dreamed it up, just for her. Cross precinct interdepartmental procedure and communications liaison. They might as well have printed her off a badge that read FUCKUP. Someone turns up at your precinct with enough words in their job title to fill half a paperback, you know that something has gone wrong in their career. *Detective* is one word, and everyone that hears it knows exactly what it means. *Patrolman. Sergeant. Captain.* No one is going to read any of those and need a ten-minute presentation to explain what the hell they are meant to be doing there. Kelly sometimes finds herself trying to parse meaning from it—*cross precinct interdepartmental procedure and communications liaison*—before remembering that it doesn't mean anything beyond her serving out her penance. A forced pilgrimage from one precinct to the next, to be paraded in front of every single serving police officer as a warning that this, too, could happen to you.

Still, it could have been worse. She could have ended up back in uniform.

She could have been fired.

"The subway has its own cops now?"

Kelly clears her throat, trying to cover the fact that Hernandez has been talking to himself while she was busy fuming. "Always has," she says. "NCOs, or neighborhood coordination officers. They're the contact point between the Transit Authority, the NYPD, and the public. Responsible for helping maintain a safe and positive atmosphere on one of the largest and busiest public transport networks in the world."

Hernandez grins at her. "Look at you, doing your homework."

"Just like to know who's going to be pissing in my Frosted Flakes before I have to take a bite, that's all."

"And what are they like, really?"

Kelly has done her homework on that, too. "Fucked is what they are," she says. "The city wants the trains to run, period. No stops, no delays, no issues. If a guy falls under the train or gets knifed on the platform, the first question they ask is how many minutes it's going to hold up service."

"Jesus," Hernandez says. "If you want to off someone, I guess do it on the subway."

"Yeah, and then you and I get to work on our migraines watching the security camera footage over and over."

"That's the truth right there."

They lapse into silence crossing over the Williamsburg Bridge. Kelly doesn't take in the view—too familiar to find it worth anything more than a glance—but something about the water always draws her eye. The way the city doesn't match, not like trees or sand would. Concrete and glass, pushed all the way up to the waterline, and only stopping there because nobody will sign off on the insurance for building skyscrapers on a pontoon. Not yet, anyway.

From this far away, the water looks like it could almost be clean.

The car slows, and Kelly looks ahead to where the traffic is thickening up. "What the hell am I going to talk to these guys about, Hernandez?" she asks. "It's not like there's anything we can learn from them, unless we plan on standing outside the precinct telling people how to get to Broadway."

"Maybe there's something they can learn from you," Hernandez says.

"I said it already, they don't have the time, the resources, the support—" Kelly stops talking as her brain stops reacting to what her partner has said and catches on to what he meant. For half a minute there she had almost taken the job seriously, like she was meant to find out about how other cops worked, look at it objectively through the lens of her own experience, and use it to make recommendations for improving her own precinct. That she was meant to be doing something useful, aside from serving as a cautionary tale.

Hernandez is grinning as he drives.

"Shut the fuck up," Kelly says.

"Look, I know it's shit, you know it's shit, and everyone that doesn't know or hasn't been told already will smell it before you're even in the door. Just treat it as a working tour of the city's worst coffee spots."

Kelly bites her tongue before she says something that she might regret later. Hernandez is trying his best, working all the angles to keep her spirits up. It's not his fault that every single one of them makes her want to scream and smash his head into the driver's-side window.

"You can drop me off at the J line," she says. "You don't have to drive all the way."

"It's fine," he says. "I'll drive you."

She said it with the intention of letting him off the hook, saving him from having to tolerate her self-inflicted bad mood, but he doesn't sound like he's relieved in the slightest. Instead, he sounds pissed.

"You following up on something after?" she asks. "When did we have that meeting with Vice booked? Was that today?"

Hernandez gives her a look. "Captain gave it to Nicholson."

"Nicholson?" Kelly tries to picture the guy trying to get through a meeting with Vice without saying something that will at best get him written up or—at worst—escorted to the nearest bathroom stall to have the number of teeth in his mouth adjusted. "But that's our case."

"Was our case," Hernandez says.

Kelly closes her eyes. "Fuck," she says. Wallowing in her own self-pity, she hasn't even thought that maybe there would be collateral damage. He isn't driving her just out of a sense of solidarity: he has nowhere else to be. "I'm sorry, Hernandez."

"It's fine," he says.

It obviously isn't.

Kelly pinches the bridge of her nose and forces herself not to audibly sigh. It wasn't supposed to be like this. None of it was. They both spent months building up their contact lists across Vice, Missing Persons, and Criminal Enterprise, pushing for cases and pulling down the kind of high-profile arrests that would see their names landing on the call sheet for the next Major Case Squad task force. Working with Hernandez, both of them feeding off of the other's ambition, her career had started to gain ground in a way she'd almost given up hoping for.

And then, at a medal presentation at One Police Plaza, one of the chiefs had come up behind Kelly and put his hand on her ass. She could have filed a sexual harassment complaint, and it would have been a coin toss as to whether that sealed or destroyed her career. What she did instead was grab him by his jacket sleeve and shiny dress uniform belt before executing a textbook hip throw that put him through an entire table of complimentary sparkling white wine. He broke three ribs and had to have surgery to remove the shattered stem of a wineglass from where it had been driven into his left buttock, an inch shy of going straight up his asshole. And while there were witnesses who testified that he had assaulted her first, and her union rep had gone to the wall for her, that moment of impulsive action was enough to kill both her and Hernandez's careers stone-dead.

"This is you." Hernandez eases the car out of the flow of traffic and pulls over. They have made better time than Kelly expected. He has cut across Manhattan with ease while she chewed over the past like she could do anything to change it.

"Thanks," Kelly says. She takes a deep breath. Olive branches aren't her thing, but Hernandez deserves some kind of effort on her part. "And just so you—"

"Jesus Christ," Hernandez says, cutting her off. "Get a load of the welcome party."

At the sidewalk, a uniformed cop in a high-vis vest is standing waiting for her. He looks pale and out of shape, listing where he stands like it has been a long-ass time since he has had to wear full regulation gear. He has his head ducked down to the level of his shoulders, already primed to apologize for the bright yellow vest he's holding.

"He looks terrified," Kelly says.

"You gotta tell him the story about the guy with the duffel bag full of dead rats," Hernandez says, all trace of bitterness gone. "Ten bucks says he faints or pisses himself."

"What if he does both?"

Hernandez's eyes go wide with the possibility. "Fifty bucks says he does both," he says. "But you don't hold back when you're telling it."

Kelly looks at the subway cop and grins. He'll do neither, probably, but fifty bucks is a small price to pay pouring oil on troubled waters. "Deal," she says, and they shake hands. She gets out of the car.

"Hey, Hendricks," Hernandez calls to her. "Don't get in any trouble."

She sees him off with a single, dismissive wave.

CHAPTER THREE

RECTOR ST.

Strange thing about the subway: once you're actually on it, things like claustrophobia don't seem to matter so much. It's not gone. Not entirely. But it is suppressed, like closing the door on a screaming argument. Ben read a thing about tinnitus one time, after nearly blowing his eardrums out playing with some old hi-fi gear: the more you focus on it, the worse it is. He can feel the fear there, at the corner of his mind, but if he doesn't turn toward it then the subway seems to do the rest. Maybe it's because you're submitting yourself to the power of a system so much bigger than the mind can easily comprehend. Like flying, where people not only endure being flung six miles into the sky by an invisible and poorly understood quirk of physics, but read books or even sleep while it's happening.

Or, Ben thinks, it's more likely because of *the rules*. There's no handbook as to what the rules of the subway are, much the same as there isn't a laminated card in every toilet telling you how to wipe your ass, but you know them anyway. Only madmen, babies, and panhandlers

break the rules: you don't talk to people, or touch them, or acknowledge their existence in any way shape or form except when getting the
fuck on the train, or getting the fuck off. With the weight of a city's collective neurosis weighing on you, something as simple as being afraid
doesn't get so much as a look in.

He takes out his phone and unlocks it, staring at the screen more
out of habit than an expectation of anything appearing on it. Three bars
of signal, even in the tunnel. It looks good, but then three bars on his
provider could truly mean anything. Three bars could be enough to
stream an HD movie, or it could be the number of people ahead of you
in the queue to speak to an old-timey switchboard operator in search of
a connection. He puts it away and looks down at the clasp of his briefcase, not because there's anything to find there, but it keeps him from
making any kind of eye contact with the other passengers.

Fired on his first day after orientation. The first Goddamn day.

It caught him on the blind side. The five days of mandatory orientation had gone like clockwork. Coffee with the other new hires, a
bad photo laminated into a new ID card, fire and safety orientation,
hooking up his phone to the company's intranet. It had been boring,
but boring was good. It felt like he'd found a space where he could fit
in, where no one would give him a sideways glance.

Then, on his first morning back after a weekend spent staring at
his phone and wondering if he should text one of the other new hires,
they fired him. He was at his desk trying to work out why the computer
wouldn't let him log in when security arrived. They told him it would
make everyone's day easier if he didn't make a fuss.

They didn't give him a reason, but then they didn't need to. Ben
knew why just from the look on their faces. He didn't make a fuss.

At least he was allowed to head out by a back staircase, instead of
being paraded past all the others. The guard that walked him down
asked for an address so they could forward his personal items on. It
wasn't necessary. He hadn't been in the building long enough to leave
an assprint in his ergonomic chair.

It wasn't fair.

They were the ones that headhunted him, for God's sake. Contract signed the day after he graduated. Ben had put all of his belongings—what few he had—and headed east the week after, signing the lease on an apartment and handing over his deposit while the engine on the rental van was still warm.

Not that he would see that deposit back now.

He slumps in his seat, hands limp in his lap, and lets his head fall back, his eyes closed in defeat.

He would have to give up. Go home. Back to the woman who'd once been his mom and Anne, the caregiver who looked after her. Always one room over, savage in her thin-lipped silence, clattering the dishes or dropping handfuls of laundry with a thump to let him know that she was busy and there'd be no discussion about his mom or any other thing while he was under her roof.

Ben came to New York thinking that it was the opposite of everything Anne cherished—the small-town existence, the long emptiness past the yard, the handful of neighbors all winnowed thin by hard living and age—and that it would mark the start of a new journey.

A dead-end journey, as it turned out.

Ben can feel his cell phone inside his suit jacket, the flat wedge of it against his arm, and thinks about all the other new hires.

They all went to a coffee place their new colleagues recommended to wait while their ID cards were made up. With the prices they had, Ben wondered if the company was getting some kind of kickback for sending customers their way. Still, faced with the expectant, movie-star smile on the barista's face, nobody was going to be the first to break ranks and order a glass of water, so they all sat down with their coffees and pastries and got their phones out to check the dent in their bank accounts before things went any further. To cover for it, they all swapped numbers.

They even included Ben, like he was part of the group the whole time, and not just hovering on the edge of it.

Maybe it was like a *Survivor* thing. Maybe they all been escorted out, and this was some kind of test.

Wishful thinking. You know why they fired you.

If the others know he was fired, then they might ask questions. Ben can only hope they will get the same spiel he was offered on the way out of the building: *"Just not the right fit for us, you don't connect with the company culture."* It is possible, however, that they'll get the truth instead. It's possible that one of them might remember that they have his number, and his name, and try to get a hold of him on it.

Ben decides to blacklist all of their numbers now, before any of them gets the chance. Better yet, he should probably take his SIM card out and crack it in half.

Ben gets his phone out in a scramble, swaying in his seat as the train decelerates, slowing to a stop. As he rights himself, he can see that he's too late. There's a message notification, although it's from an unknown number.

The preview shows the entire message:

> Tough day for all of us, huh?

He doesn't dismiss it straightaway. *All of us.* The way they marched him out, Ben thought it was just him, but maybe it isn't that simple. Maybe some of the others got canned as well.

The message was sent two minutes ago. He unlocks the phone to reply.

> Hey. Who is this? I didn't save your

He deletes it. They'll get hung up on the fact he doesn't know who it is, that it's his fault he didn't type in their name. He tries again. Straight to the facts.

> *Hey. What happened? Security tossed me out the back door.*

Ben stares at the screen after he sends the message, waiting for the reply. It's been a long time since he sent someone a text outside of an app. It feels weird not to know if they are typing a reply, or if his message has even been seen.

You taking the 1? the message asks.

Yeah. Ben replies. If they got fired as well, then there is still hope. If they are on the same train, then maybe they can meet up and compare notes on what the hell just happened. How about you?

While he waits for the reply, Ben wonders if it was downsizing that got them both. Maybe they can give him some tips on looking for a new job.

Maybe when they look at him, all they will see is a guy called Ben.

When the reply comes, less than a minute later, it isn't a message. It's a picture. Ben has to open up the thumbnail to make out what it is.

The man in the picture is somewhere on the far side of middle age: it's hard to judge with any more precision because he's lying down, and whatever wrinkles he might have had are smoothed away by the aid of gravity. Still, the state of his hands say that he's older, and of the type that runs to waste instead of thickening out. He's dressed in a white shirt and blue tie, and Ben would bet any money that there's a matching coat to go with the suit trousers he's wearing, upper thighs shiny from thousands of swipes drying sweat-prone palms.

A broad red line—a ragged, blooming arc—is stitched across his throat, the cut so high and so deep that it takes a second for Ben to register the sliver of white next to the man's jaw as bone. The spray of blood that has landed high on his cheek and spattered across his forehead looks black, like clusters of dead pixels in the image, but from the savage wound and the blood pooled underneath him, it's clear that the image isn't the one that is irreparably broken.

Ben's hands are shaking as he closes the image and types out a reply.

> That's not funny. Don't message me again.

They know. They know, and now his number has gotten out and someone at the company is sending him shit off the internet to fuck with him. There's a cold feeling to that realization that hangs somewhere between fear and anger. Anger that they'd do it, fear that they'll keep going.

The next messages come fast.

> Don't close your phone, Ben.

> Don't get off the train.

Ben types with his lips pressed tight together, hunched over the phone.

> How do you know I even made the train?

A pause. Maybe they are typing. Maybe they are gone.

> Because I'm here too.

Ben wants to sit up, to look around and maybe catch them staring, but instead he keeps his eyes on the screen. The next message isn't long in arriving.

> Do you remember me?

Ben frowns.

I don't know who you are. He tries to picture all of the new hires, tries to think which one of them would be the most likely troll. In his head, all of them are laughing at him.

> *You know who I am, Ben.*

He scrolls back up to the picture of the dead man, just to confirm to himself that it's actually what he saw, and not a kind of hallucination. The man is still there, with his head hanging on by whatever ragged flap his killer left him with. Still dead. It could be staged, some kind of special effects thing, but it seems pretty real to Ben.

> *Look around you.*

Ben lifts his head and looks down the length of the subway car, to the right and then the left. Nobody is watching him. At least half of the people are looking at a phone screen. No one even glances up. While he's looking, his phone vibrates again. It's another picture.

A man sitting in a subway station, waiting for the train. Ben recognizes him from his glance around the car. Heavyset, bull neck, and a linebacker's shoulders, his cheeks and nose an unhealthy shade of red that suggests someone too proud to take their blood pressure pill. He's sitting farther up, halfway between where Ben is sitting and the farthest door. His head is tipped forward, lurching with the motion of the train like he's close to falling asleep, but Ben knows that he's not truly asleep. It's more like a meditation: the moment they announce his station or someone messes with him, he'll snap right out of it.

He's getting off at Cortlandt, the next message reads. If he does, he dies.

Ben types his reply faster than he's ever sent a text in his life. Why are you doing this?

Ben stares at the phone, his guts turning to ice. How did they know he would be on this train? The way the door held longer than he thought it would: Were they blocking the door waiting for him to get on? Did he see them do it, and not even know that it was meant for him?

> *You know why.*

Ben knows why they are doing this, why they have picked him but he doesn't want to acknowledge it. It's just like tinnitus. If you don't turn back to look at it, then is the past really there?

A moment later, another message appears on his phone:

> *Do you think you can save this one? You're almost out of time.*

CHAPTER FOUR

WTC CORTLANDT

Ben holds the phone like it's something poisonous, his arm extending out away from his body, hand turned to drop it the instant it vibrates to send him another message. He can still see the words on the screen.

> *He's getting off at Cortlandt. If he does, he dies.*

Ben sits up and brings his arm back down, suddenly aware of how visible he is in the car, sitting on an open-facing seat, all by himself. It's some kind of sick prank. It has to be, and one of the other passengers is filming him to see what he does.

The speakers crackle as they come to life, and the conductor announces their next stop. *"WTC Cortlandt."* Ben flinches, the sound making the picture of a dead body jump into his head for a fraction of a second, but he shrugs it off. Doesn't take a lot of hard work to find a picture of a dead body on the internet and send it to someone. Ben stabs at the screen with his thumbs, angry at the other person for fucking with him, angry at himself for replying in the first place.

Go. Fuck. Yourself.

He sends it and blocks the number before they can reply. He doesn't even know if the message will reach them—maybe the network will have cut off the message the instant he sent it—but even if the last word only exists in his head, it still feels good to slam the virtual door in their face. A little karmic boost to balance the scales after security marched him out of the building, for sure.

Ben lifts the phone up as though it just buzzed in his hand, but there's nothing there. A phantom ring, like when he'd been waiting for the call after his interview and kept picking up the phone.

The texts have rattled him. He expected maybe a taunt, maybe some kind of threat to go to the press. But this is different.

The train reaches the subway platform, the close darkness of the tunnel coming away like a sticker being peeled away to reveal the platform and all the people waiting. Everything seems brighter compared to the darkness, the colors sharper, and Ben finds himself relieved by the sight of it. Life is going on uninterrupted, and not a single one of the people waiting to get on or get off give a single shit about the asshole that's been texting him. He could learn a thing or two from their example.

If he does, he dies. The words sour that sense of relief, like a band tightening around his chest, and he can't help but look down the car toward the man whose picture he was sent.

The man is awake now, and has come out of his seat to make his way to the nearest door. He's not steady on his feet, and Ben wonders if he has been drinking. When he reaches the door, he sways forward until he bumps into the back of the woman in front of him, and Ben sees her expression change at the contact, her face going tight at what is probably just one more humiliation in a daily life packed full of them.

The train comes to a stop and, as the people waiting to get off stand taller in anticipation of the doors opening, Ben almost gets to his feet, driven by the overwhelming feeling that this is not a prank at all, and that he is watching someone walk toward their own death.

The word *hey* dies in his throat unspoken, crushed by the thought that he would just be making an idiot of himself. What the hell was he going to say? *I got a text that says you're going to die?* It's one hundred percent guaranteed they'd be off the train before he could finish saying it.

Besides, it's just some asshole pulling a prank. It rattled him, that's all. Paranoia brought on by stress. Ben drops his shoulders, hoping that the change in posture might encourage his brain to relax and give him a break.

The subway car doors open, and all of the people waiting step off of the train. Ben tries not to, but still finds himself watching the man taking that first uncertain step, holding on to the open door to make sure he lands it, and then he's gone, walking down the platform and into the press and flow of all the other people getting off.

The doors close with a pneumatic hiss and the solid thud of rubber, the platform sounds cut to a murmur as the train seals itself off from the outside world. Over the sound of the conductor's voice, Ben catches the sound of something going *bang*. It sounds like someone has blown up and burst a paper bag, or a car backfiring. It sounds like it could be a thousand dumb, innocuous things, but Ben knows in his gut that it is none of them.

As the train shunts forward and begins to gather speed, Ben cranes his neck to try and keep the moving crowd of people in view.

He can see that something isn't right. Halfway down the platform, a group of people have slowed and are gathered around something. The movement of the train is too quick for him to catch it, but Ben does see that there's something large on the platform, something that could be a body. As the train picks up speed and they fly past, one image fixes itself in his mind. The woman who got off the train first, holding her phone up to one ear, looking down the platform in panic, her hand and coat sleeve covered in blood.

The train accelerates, and the platform is gone, replaced by the reflection of the car in the windows and, behind it, darkness.

Ben sits frozen in place, staring through the windows as if he looks far enough he can see back onto the platform. It was so fast, and yet the memory of her is still stuck in his head. Was there really blood, or did he see it because he imagined he would see it?

His phone drums against his leg as though vibrating, but when he looks the screen is dark, and the feeling is because his hands are shaking out of control. He flattens them against his thighs to smother the tremor, and his body answers with a rising nausea that forces him to swallow hard, his elbows jammed against his sides, jaw tight, holding it down, holding it in.

It was real. The body on the ground, the crowd around it, the woman's hand covered in blood. From the fingertips to the edge of her sleeve, like she'd dipped it in a pot of red ink.

Ben opens his phone up, scrolls back through the messages. This wasn't a prank. They weren't joking. The picture of the dead guy looks a hell of a lot more real to him now. He looks at the picture of the man that just got off, the man who is probably dead or dying on the platform right now.

He needs to get off the train. The next stop, be the first and only guy at the door and run like hell the moment it opens.

Don't close your phone.

How did they even kill him? Was there someone waiting for him on the platform? Or did someone step off the train for long enough to kill him and then use the confusion to get back on before the doors closed again? What if they are still there, a car or two ahead, waiting for Ben to bolt?

Don't get off the train.

He needs to get off the train, but maybe that would be the worst thing he could do. He needs more information. He needs to know what he is walking into. He needs to find out what they want.

The train bucks under him, like they are cresting a wave, and the feeling of his stomach dropping continues on long after the movement ends. He knows how he can find out why his mystery messenger—his mystery killer—is texting him. He just doesn't want to do it.

Ben opens up the caller's number and unblocks it.

He expects a flood of messages, but there's nothing. No rage, no accusations. If anything, it feels worse knowing that they've waited him out. He looks up and around: no one leaps out at him as a possible suspect. No one is holding their phone to film him. It doesn't mean that he isn't being watched, though.

They want him to make the first move.

Ben takes a deep breath in through his nose. It could all be a setup. A prank call. Some stupid stunt. He's heard about guys on the internet that pull sick shit like this all the time, pretending to kill themselves or staging kidnappings. Throw in the stress of losing his job, probably losing his deposit, and having to move back home, it makes it all seem even more real.

If he tells himself that enough times, he might even start to believe it.

Ben lets the breath out, steeling himself, and types out a message.

Who are you?

There's a brief pause before it sends, and it takes Ben a second to see that he has zero bars of signal. That it sends at all is a miracle. The answer comes back quickly, like they have pounced on his message.

You don't remember me? I remember you.

He frowns. I don't know anyone here.

> *Your first instinct is a lie. What a surprise. I know who you are. Where you came from.*

A lump forms in Ben's throat.

> *I know what you are.*

All of a sudden, Ben really wants to cry. His stomach cramps up at the same time, and as he leans forward, arm across his stomach, another message arrives.

> *Do not close your phone, block this number, or fail to acknowledge my messages.*

What is this? Ben types. Why are you doing this to me?

> *The next person is a woman. She usually gets off two stops from here. If she does, she will die. Do you understand?*

All Ben wants to do is throw his phone at the opposite wall. To stamp on it, snap it in half. To not be stuck in a metal tube feeling like he can't even breathe. He leans over the phone and types.

> *What do you want from me?*

> *Do you understand, Ben?*

> *I understand.*

> *She's three cars forward from you. Two stops, Ben.*

Ben waits for more, but nothing comes. He types again, to stave off the rising feeling of dread.

> *No picture? Who am I looking for?*

> *No picture. Call it the price of blocking me.*

Ben sways in his seat, the nausea rising through him. *I know who you are,* they said, but that's impossible. Nobody can know, not after all this time. It feels like the train is spinning somehow, so fast that he can't think straight. If they know who he is, then this is only the beginning.

A thought itches in the very back of his head. A tiny voice, reminding him that no matter how far away he goes or how much time passes, there is one secret still waiting. One hundred and fifty miles to the north, and about as far down underground as the train is now, lies the absolute truth of who he once was.

Sweat drips down from the corner of Ben's brows and onto the screen as he types. All he can do is play along, and maybe he'll find out how much they know.

> *How am I meant to find her?*

> *You'll figure it out. Good luck.*

CHAPTER FIVE

WTC CORTLANDT

The general feeling among most cops aboveground is that the neighborhood coordination officers are moles that scurry around on the subway trains picking up litter and telling people how to get to the Broadway show they're late for and, therefore, are not real cops. To Kelly, it doesn't feel like an entirely unfair assessment. Her handler—Officer Evan Rogers—is a prime example of the kind of guys she imagines populating their ranks. He's in his late thirties, bald, glasses, and even though he's got a big frame, he has the soft teddy bear look of someone who scraped through on the Cooper fitness standards and hasn't broken into a run since. Still, he surprises her with the admission that he used to be a beat cop.

"No shit," she offers, gesturing with her coffee. Showing her where to find the machine was the first thing on his list, and while she appreciates the gesture, it tastes like old dirt and motor oil and, even by a cop's standards, is undrinkable. "Which precinct?"

"Thirty-third."

Kelly tries not to make a face while she thinks about it. "Washington Heights, right?"

"That's the one."

Now would be the right time to offer some kind of anecdote or acquaintance that gives them a connection, but the thirty-third just finished clearing house after an Internal Affairs probe, so Kelly takes a drink of her coffee instead. It tastes like how she'd imagine licking a battery that just dropped out of a cat's asshole would taste.

"Yeah," Rogers says. "I guess it's better you hear it from me before anyone else: I'm the guy that blew the whistle on them."

"Shit." Kelly blurts it out, her brain too busy running a frantic reassessment of everything she has seen of Officer Rogers so far. She thought he looked soft because he was a rent-a-cop, his shoulders down and whole spine curved like he's ready to apologize for something that hasn't happened yet, but that's not it at all. He looks beat, like a fighter well past his best put back up on his feet to sway into one more punch. He had acted according to his conscience, and while it might have been the right thing to do, it would have put him in the crosshairs of every cop aboveground. No wonder he ended up down here with the moles.

"Well, no need to ask how you ended up babysitting me," she says.

"Yeah, I heard about that," Rogers says. "Something like you tried to make commissioner by challenging him to single combat?"

"Chief," she says. "Had him pinned but the review board said he got a shoulder up before the three-count."

"Heard you left him with a limp so bad he's started telling people it's an old shrapnel wound."

A warm feeling fills Kelly's chest at the thought. It almost feels like pride. "He wanted to party," she says. "He never specified how hard." She takes a look around the concourse and tries to get to grips with the flow of people making their way through the turnstiles. It's an odd station: the platform is above the level of the turnstiles, and that reversal makes everything else seem awkward to Kelly's sense of what the subway should be like. In her mind's eye, the people coming onto the subway should be running smack into passengers heading down from the trains, but somehow it all works out: they change course at the last second and stream past one another with a complete lack of interaction or physical contact that feels like a magic trick. "So how does it all work?" she asks.

Rogers contemplates the question. "Meant to be a whole department working on how to move people through a closed space," he says. "Boys with PhDs running computer simulations, coming down and measuring everything with lasers and survey equipment."

"You don't say."

"They did a whole presentation about it, about what they perceived would be trouble spots in and around the station." The way he says *perceived* suggests it isn't his choice of word, and that he wasn't best pleased to hear it the first time he did.

"I take it they're wrong," Kelly says.

"Wrong as they are about every other thing," he says. "It works because the scale is off. It's too big to fail."

"I don't get it."

"Look, you're stuck in traffic, a big long line of cars. Maybe an accident, maybe it's roadwork, whatever. The whole thing is barely moving, and who are you staring at the whole time?"

"The guy in front."

"Yeah. Now let's say he just cut in front of you after a half-hour wait, and you spend the next half hour staring at the back of his head. How are you gonna feel about him?"

Kelly can see where he's going, but she plays along anyway. "Like I want to split his bald spot open like a watermelon."

"Woah, easy on the bald spot." Rogers touches the back of his head self consciously. "But you're right. You get stuck with that one guy who was probably close to soiling himself thinking he missed the line forming and he'd never get to merge, and you are ready to hop out of the car and murder him."

"Right. Road rage."

"Except it doesn't happen on the subway. There's too many people, and they're all going way too fast to get mad. Four million people go through the system every day, are you going to pick a fight with all of them?" He shakes his head. "People get out of each other's way because it's too fast, there's too many faces. Nobody has time to really get up a good head of steam."

"Except it does happen on the subway," Kelly says.

"Yeah, sure, but a lot less than you think." Rogers shrugs. "That said, the boys up in Central would prefer it didn't happen at all."

"They want the subway to be a utopia? In this heat?"

"The MTA wants the trains moving," Rogers says. "That's all they want. No stops, no delays, no issues. If a guy falls onto the track, then maybe they'll stop the trains long enough to pull what's left of him off the rails, but otherwise trying to work any kind of incident down here is like pissing into a headwind."

Kelly can sympathize. There isn't a day goes by that a handful of requests land on her desk to let her know that investigating crimes is the least vital part of her job. The apartment needs to go on the market, the store can't stay closed another day, the insurance company is just waiting for a signature so can't you hurry it all up? Some kind of finance guy threw his Rolex—his *other* Rolex, the first having been taken off him at gunpoint—across the desk at her to press home the point about his time being valuable. The way she heard it was the desk sergeant made him fill out the release form a record number of twenty-three times, the twenty-second attempt invalid because he'd cried right onto the paper and the ink had run.

Rogers turns away from her, straightening up and lifting his chin so that he looks for all the world like a fucking meerkat trying to spot an incoming eagle. It would be funny but a fraction of a second later, she feels the mood of the crowd shift in a way that signals *danger* to every single one of her instincts and immediately follows suit.

It's one of the weird things about crowds. Pack enough people into an enclosed space together, you make a new kind of animal. Not a sentient one, as such, but it can still be capricious and sensitive to danger. Most likely there isn't an individual, aside from Kelly and Officer Rogers, who can see it yet, but something happening on the platform has just spooked the shit out of the crowd.

Slowly, like the first grains of sand before a landslide, voices pick up and echo against the walls of the subway. People start to move, coming down the stairs—even taking the escalator that's meant to be going up—and the radio on Rogers's belt bursts into life.

Kelly misses the distorted patter of the message, losing it against the growing noise, but Rogers ducks his head to work the mic and acknowledge it. He leans closer to Kelly before he speaks, keeping the words short.

"Shooting on the platform," he says.

Kelly nods once, keeping her expression neutral. Inside, the word *fuck* blows clean through her expectations of the new assignment like a cold wind, but she can unpack that later. Much, much later. "So much for bad coffee and being bored shitless," she says. She places the cold remnant of her coffee onto the shelf next to her and opens her jacket, clearing access to her sidearm.

Rogers gives her a hard stare. "Do not pull that weapon," he says.

She stares back, but his soft, tourist-friendly demeanor has evaporated.

"We need to get the emergency gates open," he says. "That's our priority."

It sounds a lot like the kind of subway bullshit he was just railing against, but she can see that he's right. The crowd isn't panicking, not yet, but they sure as shit aren't just standing around waiting to see what happens. They are streaming toward them, heading for the exits, and it's unlikely that there will be a polite queue to go through one by one when they reach the turnstiles.

A shooting is bad news. The shooter getting a chance to walk clean past them, doubly so. But a crowd crush is a lot, lot worse.

"What do you need me to do?"

Rogers is already pointing to one of the gates behind them, a glass-and-metal wall that is already shifting on its hinges as the electronic locks open. He unclips a flashlight from his belt and waves it in the direction of the crowd, and Kelly forces herself to walk—*don't run, don't set off a sprint by example*—to the gate and swing it open like she's inviting everyone to an attempt at the world record for most fare dodges in a single station.

The diversion works. Kelly didn't have a single doubt about it, because Rogers moved like it was a drill, knowing exactly where to stand so everyone could see him and yet still stay out of their way. He, or someone like him, has thought real hard about what they need to do in this kind of situation, and practiced it until every kink and error got smoothed out and running the numbers became second nature to everyone involved. It's the sort of policing that Kelly never really thinks about in her day-to-day work, where situations tend to be a lot more fluid, but there's something to admire in witnessing a contingency plan play out perfectly.

People stream through the gate, most of them already on their phones looking for a ride before the prices go stratospheric, more than a few on social media already, posting pictures as they walk. Kelly hopes that if there really was a shooting on the platform that none of them got close enough to take a high-res picture of someone on their worst and last day. She hops from one foot to the other, neck craned, keeping an eye out for guns or bloody clothes, anything that might give them an ID later.

By the time the bulk of them are through and Kelly has enough free space to duck back inside to regroup with Rogers, the subway station is silent and—to Kelly's eyes—darker.

"Did they turn the lights down?"

"Not all the way," Rogers says. He isn't looking at her, but is staring toward the escalators, which have come to a stop. His expression suggests that wasn't part of the plan. He leans into his radio.

"We got anyone on the platform, Central?"

There's a five-second hold, then through a burst of static the answer comes back: *"No staff on the platform."*

Rogers takes a deep breath as he switches the flashlight to his left hand and reaches down to unclip the holster at his hip.

Kelly isn't a subway cop, but she can read the situation easily enough. She doesn't wait for a nod before drawing her own weapon. The escalator is a metal-lined tunnel with steps that are too big to walk on easily and with exactly zero cover. If there's someone with a gun waiting at the top of it, then both of them will be like fish in a barrel. If one of them takes the steps, then the barrier dividing them will keep them from getting a clean shot while the other sucks a bullet.

"I guess we go and see what's what," she says.

Rogers nods, his face closed. They make their move, keeping far enough apart that anyone aiming at them will be forced to split their attention, and fast-walk toward the escalator.

CHAPTER SIX

WTC CORTLANDT

The shooter can't possibly be on the platform. It makes no sense for them to stay. They could have tossed the gun low, sent it out into one of the tunnels, and just joined in the general rush to be anywhere else but here. They could have even just put it in a pocket, or a bag, and trusted the fact that the platform was way too busy to stop everyone on the way out. There's no reason that they would stick around at the scene of the crime, waiting to get caught.

Kelly knows all of this, but she still hustles up the escalator like she's trying to catch a train, one hand light on the railing to keep her balance, the other rigid in front of her, aimed straight at the top, parallel to the angle of the steps, ready for an opportunity target. Fast beats quiet, and her footsteps ring out, echoing along the tunnel ahead of her. Rogers keeps pace on her right, not wanting to fall behind and risk putting her in his own sights, and she can hear what it is costing him in the heaviness of his steps and the ragged way he pulls in every breath.

When they hit the top, she takes in the view ahead. She can see

the victim lying supine, the soles of both feet facing her and the rest of
him hidden by the angle of a pillar, but no one else. Rogers touches her
shoulder to let her know he's got this direction covered and she turns
to clear her own left-rear quarter. The other end of the platform—the
shorter end, the wall terminating in a maintenance door that probably
leads to the guts of the escalator—is empty of people. No looky-loos, no
one with their phone out filming, no shooter.

Kelly can't shake the feeling that there's someone here, though. She
stares at the door long enough that Rogers starts to shift uncomfortably
next to her, wanting to know what she's looking at but not about to
drop his guard to find out.

Someone is here. She can feel it.

She turns back and gives Rogers the nod to move on. He's tight-
lipped, trying not to gasp for breath after double-timing it up the steps,
but there's no hesitation in his movement. They split up on either side
of a tiled pillar—too thin by half to be holding the whole city overhead
to Kelly's eye, but then she trusts the engineers to have calculated
it right—and start working their way down the platform toward the
victim.

The subway platform is a range master's nightmare. The long plat-
forms are lit so brightly that they draw the eye upward and along their
length; the tracks are too dark to make out detail, and looking too
long at one spot makes it feel like you can see shapes that aren't really
there. There's no covED: fixeder, except for the pillars, but they are
everywhere—too far apart to watch all of them at once—and with the
lights set vertically there are no shadows to help rule any of them out.

Empty of people, every noise seems louder. Every scrape and click
echoes clean off of the walls, making Kelly feel completely exposed. If
this was an exercise, it would be the perfect spot for an ambush, and
the correct move would be to pull back and wait for SWAT to fill the
place with smoke.

She glances over at Rogers, his gaze straight ahead. She can tell that he's looking at the guy on the ground, itching to get to him. If the victim is still alive, then there's no time to waste.

Kelly makes the first move, keeping her strides quick and even, staying flat-footed to keep her aiming from bobbing up and down, and stops at the first hint of cover that she finds. It's just a painted steel frame, there to hold up a poster for some show that finished its run before its advertising budget ran out, but it is better than nothing. She can just see the body from her side—an outflung hand, the rise of the chest, maybe part of his head—and it feels like they will get there fast. Two more hops forward, or even three to keep themselves safe.

Three seems like a solid choice.

Rogers comes up on her right, doing his best but his footsteps echoing clear across the platform, and she sharpens up as he passes and keeps on going, bringing her weapon back up into line, widening her gaze to catch anyone popping out of cover. He doesn't stop, doesn't have the same caution she does, and a spike of adrenaline hits as she imagines him stepping into a bullet.

"Rogers!" She breaks cover and hurries down her side of the platform, trying to catch up with him, but she can see that he has holstered his weapon, all his focus on the victim. She can hear him working the radio, asking where the fuck the EMTs are.

She clears the last pillar as Rogers rushes forward, his arms reaching out to try and save someone who—now that she can see him unobscured—is long past saving. There's more blood outside of him than in.

Kelly jumps as a figure steps out from behind the pillar to her right, their back curled, arms outstretched, both hands plastered red with blood. As they lurch toward Rogers, she aims her weapon, rear sight and front sight lined up clean on the back of their head.

"I couldn't save him," she says.

Kelly's breath explodes out of her as she lowers her gun, and the woman startles, turning to face her. She's dressed for some kind of office work—cream blouse, gray pants suit, Louboutins, more hair product than most salons can carry without a license for all the chemical storage—and all of it is covered in blood.

Rogers is standing now, giving a clear view of the body, and from the bullet wound almost dead center in the man's chest Kelly can guess what happened. When he took the bullet, it must have hit an artery, something close to the heart. Instead of getting blood around his body like it was supposed to, the frantic beat of his heart pumped it straight out of the hole instead.

It is one hell of a hole. Kelly wonders what kind of caliber bullet went through him.

The woman could have fainted, or run for her life, but instead she'd tried to help him, tried to plug the hole with her hands—both of them, by the looks of it—following him down to the platform floor and holding on in the hope that someone would be able to save him.

"It's okay," Kelly says. "You're all right." Half of it is Kelly reassuring herself. She tries not to think about how close she just came to blowing one side of the woman's head clean off. "Can you tell me your name?"

It takes her a moment to connect the question to a thought, and few more to turn that into a word. "Jo," she says.

"Okay, Jo. I'm Kelly," she says. "I'm a New York police detective. This is Officer Rogers. Can you tell us what happened?"

"I thought . . ." Jo is looking at her hands like they aren't her own. "I thought he was going to make it."

Kelly can imagine it. How it must have felt. To have that jackhammer pressure, the terminal beat of the man's pulse against your palms suddenly fade away, and to think for a fraction of a second that the bleeding had stopped. That you had done it.

Kelly's heart aches for her, but she has to press. There's steel in Jo, steel enough for her to try and hold a dying man together with her bare hands, and if there's a chance she saw the shooter, then Kelly has to take it.

"He was shot on the platform," Kelly says. "You were right next to him. Can you tell us what happened?"

Jo looks straight at her. "Where were you? Weren't . . . aren't you meant to—"

"We're here now," Kelly says, cutting her off. "And we need your help to catch the person that did this. Did you see who shot him?"

"I didn't . . . I—" She is struggling to speak, and her hands are twitching badly. She's struggling to coordinate her movements. Whatever resource she had that was holding the shock at bay, it is rapidly running out.

Rogers comes up next to Jo, blocking her line of sight to the body. He doesn't touch her, but he's close enough that if she needs to hold on to something, then he's there. "It's okay," he says. "Anything you can remember."

Jo shakes her head, gathers herself to speak. "It was so fast," she says. "There was a bang, and when I turned to see what had happened he was falling into me. There were people getting on the train, but I didn't see a gun."

It made no sense that the shooter would stay on the platform. Kelly had known that from the start. But she had expected them to walk out of the station, to blend in with the crowd. She hadn't realized that there was a third option.

"Call Central," Kelly says.

Rogers just stares at her, either because he didn't hear right or he hasn't connected all the dots.

"Call Central and tell them to get a hold of the conductor," she says. "I think the shooter got back on the train."

CHAPTER SEVEN

CHAMBERS ST.

If you get caught opening the door between the cars on the train, it's a seventy-five-dollar spot fine. More importantly, that spot fine will come with a full reading of the riot act from whatever transit cop or conductor catches you, along with being escorted off at the nearest station.

Two stops, Ben.

The seventy-five dollars is nothing. What Ben can't afford is losing time, or being thrown off of this train.

I know what you are.

Ben's stomach flutters as he peers through the window at the back end of his car and into the front of the next. It feels even tighter here, like the train car is narrowing down around him, tightening around him like a collar. He thought that maybe he'd be able to get some kind of idea what was in the next car, see if there are any uniforms or anyone that looks like they are working undercover. He doesn't have any metric for what an undercover inspector might look like, other than a feeling that anyone wearing khaki pants and a blue windbreaker by choice is probably a cop, but the effort is useless anyway. The view is almost completely opaque—the once-pristine piece of laminated glass now ruined with scratched graffiti and dust from the tunnel—so it's hard to get anything beyond a vague sense of the fact that there are people in the next car. At the very least, no one has reacted to him pressing his face up against the glass and acting exactly like someone who is about to jump between the cars, so Ben feels like he's good to go.

Unlatching the door brings a thrill of fear, the dread of a hand falling heavy on his shoulder, but when he pulls it open nobody tries to stop him. The truth is, nobody gives a shit. The only thing preventing people from opening the doors is their own conscience, and the simple fact that nobody wants to.

Ben steps out into the space between the cars, and instantly regrets it.

It had never occurred to him that someone could feel vertigo and claustrophobia at the same time, but staring down through the coupling at the track flashing past, the hot, stale air of the tunnel plucking at him like it wants to pull him off of the rear step, Ben feels it. The step across should be simple: it's no farther than a long stride to skip the coupling entirely and land safely on the other side. While he's taking the time to think about how easy it should be, the front cars slow up a fraction, and the space between the cars shrinks faster than Ben can react, only the rubber fenders that prevent them from clashing against each other stopping him from being crushed. He grabs at the handrail on the rear door on instinct, and when the cars separate again the motion hauls his arm straight, giving him the choice of crossing the gap or having his shoulder dislocated.

Ben hops across the gap.

Once across, he works the handle on the door and when it doesn't immediately give way he almost vomits at the thought of having to step back out and clear space for a door that opens outward. He jams his shoulder against it and shoves hard, feeling a seal peeling free under the pressure, the cracking sound quickening as the rubber peels free and the door finally gives way, letting him stumble into the next car.

Once he gets the door shut behind him, Ben takes a moment to wait for the trembling to pass. He never thought that he would be so relieved to cram himself inside a closed metal tube, and yet compared to the peak he just hit, the normal levels of fear the subway held for him feels like background noise.

The reaction to him coming into this car is even lower than when he left the last one. There isn't so much as a single person looks his way.

He keeps his head down and his briefcase tight to his leg as he walks the length of the next car. He needs to hurry, but he doesn't want to stand out, or give anyone any reason to stop him.

What if they're in this car? What if they're watching right now?

Ben risks a look. Nobody is watching him, or if they are, they're doing a good job of pretending to ignore him.

He doesn't know how the killer did it, but somehow they got to that guy at the station. Someone on the platform, one of the people that had been in the car with him all the time, Ben can't think how they did it, but it was just like they reached out from wherever they were hiding and there wasn't a damn thing anyone could do to stop them.

Ben didn't even try to stop the guy from getting off.

That's what really burns about all of this. He was right to treat it like it was a stupid prank—anyone else would do the same—but somehow he knew that he'd been kidding himself when he told himself that. Deep in his gut, he had always known it was really happening. He'd just wished it wasn't, and now someone is dead.

Ben checks his phone as he reaches the door at the far end. No new messages. A bar of service, at best. No chance of a picture, or a clue, or a change of heart.

You'll figure it out. Good luck.

The last message feels like a weight settling on his chest. Figure it out, or someone else dies.

The announcement comes for Chambers St., and Ben changes his mind about walking between the cars again. Less risky for his nerves to just step off the train and walk from one door to the next.

Don't get off the train.

Ben tries not to overthink it. They don't want him to bolt, that's all. They don't give a shit if he hops from one car to the next. All they care about is that he keeps playing their game.

As Ben straightens up from peering through the window at the front of the car, the door at the back end opens and a woman in an MTA uniform—the conductor—steps into the car. She fiddles with the door handle, checking it closely, and Ben realizes that he let it swing shut behind him instead of closing it properly. It never latched, and has been open ever since. He knows it's bullshit, but even so he can't stop himself from thinking that maybe there's an alarm in the cabin that lets them know the door has been opened, and it has been going full blast this whole time.

Whatever the truth is, it's obvious she's on the lookout for someone. Since Ben is standing in a weird place, right up at the door at the other end of the car, it puts him in prime suspect territory.

Moving back to the nearest exit will make him look guilty. Watching her come will make her look just as guilty, if not more. All he can do is go back to staring through the window into the next car as though he's late, and he's willing the train to go faster.

Don't think about her. Don't look back. Pretend she doesn't exist.

Trying to make out who he's meant to stop from getting off is almost impossible from the blurred view of the next car, but he tries to take a mental inventory of the space—clothes, bags, haircuts—so he can keep track of who gets off at the next stop and discount anyone who gets on.

Footsteps, heavy from the boots she's wearing, come up behind him.

"Excuse me, sir?"

Ben straightens up as he turns to face her. As he does, all of the tension in his gut forces itself upward and before he can even open his mouth he has his hand over it, fighting to keep himself from throwing up.

"Sir, you—" She starts to speak but takes in the look on his face and moves with the ease of a seasoned pro, stepping back and to the side to clear the way, anticipating the arc.

Ben holds it down, just, the acid burn climbing in his throat and catching in the back of his nostrils before he gets control of it, and the effort leaves him panting for breath. He has to do something, say something that will get rid of her, but all that comes out is a belch, deep from the base of his gut. It tastes like a stomach acid latte served with two pumps of fecal syrup, and at least one person in the closest seat crosses themselves at the sound he makes as it comes up.

"You look like you need some fresh air, sir," the conductor says. She doesn't touch him, but stands clear with one arm held out to mark the distance, the other at her belt. Ben wonders if she is going to mace him.

He thinks about the guy who just got shot on the platform. Word would have gotten to the train by now. Maybe that's why she's on the move. Maybe the door has nothing to do with it.

"What's happening?" he blurts it out. "Has something happened?"

"What?" The question startles her, and Ben takes advantage of her surprise.

"Why is the train so slow? I have . . ." He breathes hard, letting the mask drop. "I can't be here," he says. "I don't want to be here."

Something in her expression softens for a moment, before she puts her work face back on.

"Sir, I recommend you get off at the next station," she says. "Even if you have somewhere to be." She puts a hand on his shoulder with the ease of someone who has dealt with a lot of people in their time. "Drink some water. Get some fresh air. Speak to someone about getting a cab, okay?"

Ben nods. He has no intention of taking her advice, and lying is easier when you say nothing.

"I'm sorry about the delay, but I'm going to need you to move," she says. "Thank you."

Ben steps to the side to let her pass, and the instant he is out of her way she barrels past him, opening the door and heading through to the next car like the gap between them is nothing. The urge to be sick gets really intense as he thinks about it, the draft that comes in from the tunnel swirling around him and making his hairline prickle with sweat, but by the time the door clicks shut it is gone. Ben watches her through the window—walking fast, taking the bob and sway of the floor in her stride—and is relieved that she doesn't look back.

The train reaches the next station, and as the car fills with the light and sound of the platform beyond, people start moving in anticipation of arrival. Ben makes the mistake of catching a woman's eye as he heads back to the doors. She's old—her wrists look like they might snap under the weight of her hands—but her eyes are bright and intelligent, and as she holds his gaze she demonstrates the depth of her contempt with a single, slow shake of her head. He'd feel bad about it, but he suspects that once you hit eighty all you really feel is varying degrees of contempt for the world.

The subconscious effort to work out her age sets Ben to thinking. He doesn't know who he is looking for in the next car, but maybe he can narrow the field.

As the train comes to a stop, everyone getting off of the train straightens up, like the floor has just been electrified.

Ben lines up behind the other commuters waiting to get off, and the doors open. They step out onto the platform, the impatient shuffle of feet driving the group forward, and he's off of the train. Even though he's still underground, it feels as though the world has opened up around him.

You could just go, he thinks. *Just start running, and don't look back.*

Nobody has followed him off the train. Nobody is waiting for him on the platform. People swirl around and past him like he's just another thing in their way, completely anonymous, instantly forgotten.

A wave of dizziness climbs through him, the feeling starting somewhere down by his heels and heading upward, spreading out across his shoulders and finally up the back of his neck.

The dead body on his phone. The dead man on the platform.

The promise of another, in the next car along, in the next station.

It isn't his fault. He knows that. He'd be taking himself out of a dangerous situation. He could go right to the cops, and with everything he has they might even be able to catch the killers.

It would mean leaving someone to die, though. Someone Ben thinks he might be able to find.

The person on his phone thinks it is an impossible task. They don't want Ben to save anyone. They want him to fail, and for her to die while he watches.

They would burn her, too, if they could.

Ben tries not to acknowledge the thought. If he can find her, and he can stop her from getting off of the train, there's no promise that they'll stop. But it might throw them enough that whatever sick game they're trying to play falls apart before anyone else can get hurt.

He can't let anyone else die because of his past.

He has to try.

The loudspeaker on the platform announces the train's imminent departure, and Ben double-times it to the next car, just making it inside as the doors begin to close. He doesn't offer any apology to the man he shoulders on the way in. The next victim is in here somewhere, and Ben has just a few minutes left to find her.

CHAPTER EIGHT

CHAMBERS ST.—FRANKLIN ST.

The train is busier now than when Ben first got on. Almost every seat in this car is full, and enough people are standing that he can't get a good look down the entire length. He hoped that he'd be able to keep his search discreet, but he has barely started and already he has attracted a few glares for trying to push past people to improve his view.

Even so, he knows where to start.

Ben is looking for a woman. That cuts the number of potential victims in the car in half, probably more than that considering the cluster of guys who have parked themselves two-thirds of the way up the car, all taking turns yelling things at each other and braying into their phones. Even though they all probably dressed themselves independently, they look exactly alike: same branded hoodies and knit caps, the only difference being slightly different shades of blue-gray. Ben is willing to bet the instant the caps come off, they all have exactly the same haircut. One of them—a little shorter than the others—seems to be the one conducting the action, making sure that everyone in the car knows that he is the Man.

Ben marks him as someone to avoid. No dudes, and definitely no one from the New York Young Male Insecurity Chorus.

The guy who died at Cortlandt looked like he was counting down the days to retirement. Not just in how old he was, but how he moved as well. Like he could see the finish line, and he'd long stopped giving a shit about what anyone thought. Half asleep on the subway, lumbering from his seat like he was dragging himself up out of deep water.

The dead man in the picture on Ben's phone wasn't young, either. It was hard to gauge exactly, considering how carnage could draw the eye, but the wear on his pants and jacket was telling. It had an old world feel to it, like he'd been pulled forward in time from the days when traveling salesmen were a thing. Just one suit so you could fit the samples in your suitcase, and the cloth would slowly wear gossamer thin over the years and the miles, the accumulated effect of all the road dust a paradox, millions of tiny scratches polishing it up to a fine-looking shine.

Both of the victims were older. Not elderly, but both at the sort of age where you stopped chasing after your life and started trying to slow down what was left of it. Both of them were dressed smartly. One killed in his suit, and while the guy on the train hadn't looked like a picture of health, he'd still put on a shirt and a pair of shoes even if it was just out of habit.

An older woman, then. Not a tourist. Not dressed up, specifically, but still looking like the day has a purpose. No sweatpants, no Atlantic City souvenir T-shirt, no baseball cap.

Most likely traveling alone.

Ben starts walking the length of the compartment, trying to make it seem like he's looking for a free seat. There's always one hopeless pilgrim who feels compelled to check, which makes Ben's life easier. Everyone standing ignores him as he works his way past, and everyone seated either stares straight ahead, willing him to move the fuck on, or stares at their own reflection in the window until he has passed.

There's no luck as he makes his way down the train. Plenty of women dressed for business. Smart jackets, pencil skirts, heels and expensive bags, but every one of them is far too young to fit the age group he's aiming for. A handful of elderly women, staring off into the middle distance, clutching their bags two-handed like it's the only thing that is keeping them anchored. A few women are in the right age range, but their dress and demeanor has a distinct Midwest feel to it, and Ben feels like no one in their right mind would try to kill them. It's not like salt, opioids, and corn syrup aren't doing the work already, and besides they'd probably stop any murder attempt halfway through to take a picture, to have something for the folks back home.

"Hey, bro."

Ben's head snaps up and he finds himself standing in the shadow of Knit Cap and his posse who have—until this second—been huddled together in exclusion of the rest of the car. Now, they have opened up to form a rough semicircle, with their appointed speaker at the exact middle, and Ben as its focal point.

"You got your face in my video," Knit Cap says.

"I'm just looking for a seat," Ben says.

The guy just grins at him and, while his friends all keep their eyes locked on Ben, makes a show of turning and looking the rest of the way down the car. Ben follows his gaze, ignoring the waves of anticipation coming off of them, and catches a glimpse of gray-blond hair that makes his pulse quicken.

The group's speaker turns back, still grinning. "No seats left," he says. "Now fuck off."

"Look, I just want to get past—" Ben tries to slip past the outer edge of the group, but it's a mistake. The guy on his left drops his shoulder and shoves Ben back into place, while the rest of them tighten ranks. Ben can feel the panic rising in him as the space around him closes, and he knows they can see it, too.

"What'd you see, bro?" one of them asks. Then, to Knit Cap, showing deference. "He saw something." He backhands Ben's arm, looking for validation. Ben's whole body stiffens with fear. He wants to run but there is nowhere to go. "What'd you see?"

The same hand grabs at his elbow. "A seat!" He yells it, fear pitching his voice high.

"You calling me a fucking liar?" Knit Cap steps closer. He's rolling his shoulders as he comes, like a fighter warming up to the heavy bag. "You know who the fuck I am?"

"No." It's all Ben can find to say. They want him to back down, but he can't leave it now. Not when he's so close to finding the person he came looking for. "I have no idea who you're meant to be."

He feels sodden with fear, the weight of it too much for him to do anything but succumb to the inevitable. One or more of them is going to wind up and punch him, just for the sheer fun of doing it, and there isn't a thing he can do to stop them.

Kick his balls so hard you leave him with a cunt, coward.

The voice again. The stress and the fear make it loud enough that Ben starts, like someone has said it out loud. None of the men surrounding him react, though. The guy who backhanded him jerks his head at the others. "Check it out." When he points, Ben sees his hand close up. He has shaved his knuckles and the back of his hand: the line where he stopped is just visible inside his shirt cuff, a sharp line of coarse black hair contrasting the pale skin beneath. A crumbling DIY tattoo spells part of a name along the heel of his hand, something ANNE.

"Yeah I see it," another says.

"Fuckin' Worldstar."

"That's old-school shit." Not all of them turn to look, but the excited shiver of anticipation that follows it is shared by the group.

"Come on, bro." One of them grabs Ben by the elbow and pushes him forward, marching him ahead of the group. "We'll get you a seat."

They take turns pushing him past other passengers, all of whom have taken a sudden and intense interest in the dark walls of the tunnel going past outside. The group are getting more excited with every step—one asks them to wait so he can get his phone—as they drive Ben closer and closer to the woman he spotted. They couldn't possibly know that he is looking for her, or why he came, but they stop pushing and pull him to a halt right next to her.

She looks just like Ben had imagined. Older, old enough that she has stopped worrying about what kind of outfit is expected of her and is wearing exactly what she wants to: her long skirt is dark, but embroidered with flowers, and while the shirt she is wearing is plain enough, there is enough jewelry around her wrists and neck to lend it a decorative air.

She makes brief eye contact with him, just a flicker, before adjusting the oversized bag she's carrying in her lap—a dark blue duffel that doesn't fit with the rest of her look—and sets her gaze on a point somewhere in the middle distance.

The hands that are holding Ben in place turn him around, not gently, and he bites down on the rising urge to cry out as they bring him face-to-face with the passenger on the other side of the aisle.

The man in the aisle seat sits as though he has been welded there. He's maybe in his midforties, but his matted beard makes him look much older. He is wearing track pants and an army surplus coat, and it's possible they are the only clothes he has. He is maybe the only person on the entire train who looks up at the whole group, but it isn't really eye contact. His eyes are wide, the sclera yellow and mottled with blood, and his gaze is flicking back and forth at high speed, never really focusing on one face. It's like he isn't really seeing them as people, but more as one massive, threatening shadow.

"Man here wants your seat." The guy with a hold on Ben's arm gives him a demonstrative shake that jolts his shoulder hard. "Fifty bucks if you fight him for it."

The chorus of whoops from the others drowns out the homeless man's reply, but they don't need to hear it to catch his meaning. He shakes his head, some tremor in his neck giving it a bobbleheaded look, and turns his body away from them. He doesn't want any part of it.

The hand on Ben's arm grips tighter, frustrated at not being able to form a fist, but the swerve into rage is interrupted by Knit Cap.

"Hey! Hey! What did I say? You want content, you need to incentivize."

There's a quick, practiced flourish and a new-looking hundred-dollar bill, folded in half and held between finger and thumb, appears in front of Ben's face.

"Hundred. Cash up front."

Whatever is wrong with him, the homeless guy isn't crazy enough to ignore the money right in front of him. His head comes back around slowly, his eyes focusing first on it, then Ben. His beard twitches, his throat leaping as he works his mouth to speak.

"I'll do it," he says.

CHAPTER NINE

CHAMBERS ST.—FRANKLIN ST.

The sound of the men cheering on their new gladiator, urging him to stand and get started, is distant and muted. The noise is overwhelmed by something far more powerful: fear. It's like a yoke around his neck, the pressure and the weight of it choking him, filling his head with white noise and heat until he's barely aware of the homeless man in front of him, of the men waiting for their sport to start, the woman he was meant to be saving. It's not claustrophobia. That, he could always get a handle on, feel the shape and size of the fear, make a decision about how best to cope. This fear is different. It's like there's a well inside of him that has lain forgotten, and the cover has slipped, and he is drowning in what has come pouring out. It's in a place beyond panic, a place where Ben simply ceases to exist.

Go for his eyes. His mouth. How many of those rotten teeth will come out with his tongue?

The voice has its own sensation, like a vise closing on the fear, channeling down through his arms and legs like if he would just listen, then it will have something better to offer than fear.

It offers purpose.

Ben jerks away from the thought, the vicious impulse that wants to take control, and his legs go suddenly weak. The world tilts heavily around him, and Ben is dimly aware of someone letting his arm slip free of their grip.

"What the fuck, bro? Is he having a seizure?"

The press of bodies around Ben starts to peel away, as the group's appetite for chaos evaporates in the face of whatever is happening to him. They are going to drop him on the floor, return to their spot, and pretend that none of this has anything to do with them. Locked in the grip of his own terror, it is little comfort to Ben.

Someone moves into the space over him, and he can feel them touching his cheeks and forehead. He can feel the shift of tendons under their skin, the hard touch of a knuckle. Someone is checking to see if he's burning up.

You could snap that hand, if you wanted to.

Ben retches, and the hand is hastily withdrawn.

"Sit him down here." A woman's voice, brisk and commanding. "No, don't drop him. Sit him down. *Sit him.*"

The same hands that had forced him to this point reluctantly take hold of him and maneuver Ben so that he is almost sitting, then drop him into a recently vacated seat.

"Now go away, please."

"Look, lady, we didn't mean to—"

"I don't care. Go away."

Ben surfaces to find that he is sitting in the older woman's seat, and she is bending over him, waiting for him to come back himself.

"How are you feeling?" she asks. "Are you okay?"

Ben works his mouth, searches for the words, and settles on nodding his head *yes*. He's not sure about that, in all honesty, but a question requires an answer, and even though he's not certain what happened, at the very least nobody punched him. A *yes* seems appropriate.

"Was that a seizure? Do you often get them? Is there a medicine you need to take?"

Ben shakes his head. "No." He digs deep for the words. "No medicine." He doesn't think it was a seizure, but then he's not sure what one would feel like. He has a vague idea of shaking, but there was no time lost. He felt as though he was outside himself, cut off from his body, but he was present for all of it. "I don't have seizures."

She cocks her head, like she's weighing what he's saying to her to see if it's the truth. "Well, you might want to talk to your doctor about that. There's no fever, but you're shaking like you just ran a marathon." She clicks her tongue. "You feel like you wanna throw up?"

Ben absolutely feels like he wants to throw up, but he doesn't want to tell her that. "I'm okay," he says, and she sees right through it.

"Well, if the urge strikes you, let me know because I don't want it on my shoes."

The speakers in the car connect, and the driver's voice sounds out in the train to let them know that the next stop is due, that they will be briefly held up by a red light. It strikes Ben as strange how the sound can seem so tiny and distorted and yet at the same time fill the space as everyone goes quiet, spines straightening like prairie dogs as they strain to catch the words.

As the speakers go silent, the woman's face comes into sharp focus. Ben came here for a reason.

"Look," the woman says. "This is my stop. I need to leave you here. Will you be okay?"

"This is your stop?" It feels like all possible doubt is stripped away. She's the one the killer has targeted. It has to be her.

"It is. If you need a break"—she glances back down the car, toward the group who harassed him—"you should probably get off here as well."

Ben has been hoping that he'd find another way. That inspiration would strike, and he'd come up with some clever way to stop her from getting off the train. But he has nothing, and he is out of time.

"Don't get off the train," he says.

Her expression gives away her reactions: surprise and confusion, settling on sympathy. "Look. I know you've had a scare, and I'm glad I could help you, but I'm not the Good Samaritan."

"No," he says, "it's not that." Ben fumbles for his phone as he talks. "Someone texted me a threat, and I think it was meant for you."

She doesn't move, but he can feel her tense up when he says it. "What?"

"I got a text." Ben wants to look at his phone but he can feel her pulling away from him. If he breaks eye contact, he's certain that she'll bolt. "They said they were going to . . . they were going to hurt some-one in my car if I didn't stop him from getting off the train. I thought it was some kind of joke." Ben takes a breath, and in his head he sees the man fall. The people clustered around him. Someone running for help. "I'm serious." Ben looks straight at her and sees only doubt. "Please."

Her expression hardens. "What kind of scam is this?" She jerks her head at Knit Cap and friends. "Are your friends filming this?"

"It's not—" Ben says. "It isn't . . . they didn't say who they were tar-geting, but I put together the pattern, worked out who might be in danger. I was making my way down the car when those guys—"

"What do you mean, a 'pattern?'" Something changed in the wom-an's face as Ben was speaking, and he missed it.

"What?"

"You said they hurt someone," she says. "One person doesn't make a pattern."

She is very sharp. Ben doesn't have the space to think of a way around it. "He wasn't the first," he says.

"Show me your phone," she says, and shifts her grip on her bag so that she can hold out a hand to receive it. Ben unlocks the phone, opens the message thread, and hands it over without a word. As she scrolls back through the texts, the train reaches the station, and Ben doesn't need to see the screen to know that she has reached the picture of the dead man.

Ben is expecting shock—there's no way someone could look at that picture and not feel the floor drop out from under them—but there's something else in the woman's reaction. She doesn't recoil from the picture. Instead, she looks closer.

"I know him." She says it so softly that Ben almost misses it.

"You know who that is?"

She's looking at Ben now, pushing the phone back at him, and as their eyes meet she draws back suddenly so he almost loses his grip.

"I know who you are," she says. The train brakes, making her grab hold of a seat back to keep her balance, and Ben can see how hard she grips the seat to avoid touching him. "I can't believe I didn't see it."

"Please, don't get off the train." Ben starts out of his seat, but the movement spurs her into full flight.

"Don't you dare touch me!" She shouts it, lifting her voice for the whole train to hear. "Don't you dare!"

The group of men who were, until this moment, back in their protective circle, surge forward in answer to her cry. She grabs the nearest one by the forearm.

"Don't let him follow me." She says it loud enough for Ben to hear.

Every single one of their faces lights up as she sweeps past them. The people on the platform waiting to get on the train sense the violence waiting just inside the door and pause, not quite spooked enough to scatter.

Ben gets to his feet. "Please!"

She could still change her mind. There's still time to stop her.

As he moves forward, a hand catches hold of him. Not one of the group waiting to beat seven bells out of him, but the conductor who has come up behind him and now, with surprising strength, twists a handful of his suit jacket in her fist and lifts him up onto his tiptoes.

"I knew it," she says. "I should have maced you the instant I saw you."

Ben panics and tries to break loose of the conductor's grip. The woman is about to get a foot onto the platform, and if he's quick enough he just might be able to pull her back.

Knit Cap doesn't try to catch hold of Ben or help the conductor restrain him. He waits for Ben to slip loose and lets him run into a punch, a straight right that hits so hard it feels like Ben's nose is folding back inside his head.

There's no pain. Not at first. There's a strange feeling of hyper-awareness, as Ben's eyes focus on the man's hand as it closes on his shirtfront, spots of blood beading on the fabric, bright with the effort of trying to soak their way into fibers that have been pretreated to repel their advances.

"That's enough," the conductor says. And then, to Ben. "Walk. Rear of the train. Now."

Ben blinks, tries to speak, but he can barely breathe. His sinuses are swelling up, making him gasp for air like a fish pulled fresh from a lake.

"You heard her, asshole." Knit Cap's voice is ragged, like he can't hide his excitement. "Don't fucking try shit." He's not speaking for Ben's benefit, but to make sure that everyone else knows that he was allowed to do this. That it was justified.

A buzzing noise signals that the train is ready to depart, and Ben gets his head up just enough to see the doors close. Nobody has gotten on, the confrontation scattering them like birds. The woman is gone.

The conductor grabs hold of him and pushes him toward the back of the train.

CHAPTER TEN

FRANKLIN ST.

Even though no one wanted to look at Ben when he was jumping between the cars before, being walked to the back of the train by the conductor has turned him into the main attraction. Getting caught is the worst kind of failure, and there is a collective satisfaction in seeing someone break the rules and—from what it looks like—catching a punch in the face as their just reward. One guy tries to get a slow clap started, but even schadenfreude has its limits.

The pressure of all that attention barely registers. Ben's face is swollen from the punch he took to the face, and every step sends a jolt of pain through his nose. He can taste blood, and it feels wrong on his face, like the base of it has jumped sideways half an inch. It isn't broken, though—he knows what broken feels like, and it is an order of magnitude worse than this.

She got off the train.

Ben found her, based on nothing at all other than the fact that she existed, and even after all that he still failed.

"I know who you are." That's what she said to him. That was why she ran, more than anything else. She knew who he was. Where he had come from.

There's no such thing as coincidence. Not for someone like Ben. Whoever is doing this made sure that the woman and Ben were on the same train. They made sure that she would see him, and that the sight of him would compel her to run headlong into whatever fate they had planned for her.

Ben can sense the thread that links them together: the person on the phone, the woman he scared away, the man he didn't stop. It's like he can almost touch it. If he could just stop and think a minute, he is certain he could grasp hold of it.

Just who do you think got you fired?

Ben can't think. That woman is going to die out there. There has been no commotion, no alarm from outside the train, but that doesn't mean it isn't coming. He can't stop shaking, and his legs feel like they are about to collapse from the weight of knowing what's coming.

"Keep going," the conductor says.

She has him right at the back of the car, and Ben flinches away from the push she gives him before understanding that she is trying to get past to unlock the door to the rear cab. She works the lock and ushers him inside before closing the door behind them.

The cab is cramped, with most of the available wall space taken up by switches and panels that look completely unnecessary but are probably vital enough that Ben doesn't dare look at any one too long in case it spontaneously flips. Even so, it feels a lot bigger and more modern than Ben expected. Where he would have expected to see dials and gauges on the panel under the rear window, there is a LCD screen. There is even a comfortable-looking seat, and even though the swivel it is mounted on is bolted to the floor to keep it in place at the controls, there are electronic switches to change the angle and height of the back- and armrests.

"What's your name?" the conductor asks.

"Ben." It's surprisingly hard to get the word out.

"Okay, Ben. My name is Sarah, and it is my unfortunate duty to have to deal with whatever the fuck that situation was back there." She waits until he makes eye contact before continuing. "Now, are you going to give me any problems?"

Ben wants to tell her that he is the least of her problems, but he knows that it won't go well if he does. She doesn't want an explanation out of him. She wants compliance.

"No, ma'am."

"Ma'am." She rolls her eyes. "You can cut that shit out."

"Sorry."

Sarah unclips a radio mic from her jacket and speaks into it. "I'm at the back of the train," she says. "I've got him."

A tiny voice answers fast, the guy on the other end already talking before he starts transmitting. "—take it you didn't find Lee Harvey Oswald?"

"That's right, dipshit. He was posing halfway down the train with a rifle and a well-used copy of the subway map." The conductor addresses her words to the ceiling before actually replying on mic. "Look, you said Central wanted me to grab this guy, I grabbed him, now is someone coming to pick him up or not?"

"We're behind schedule already," the driver says.

"That's not an answer."

"I say we tell them to meet us at the next station."

Sarah lets out an exasperated sigh. She gets back on the radio once she is done. "Is that what Central told you?"

"No, but we're behind schedule."

"If they said to wait, we should wait." She holds the button for a second, keeping the line open. "They can't dock wages over an explicit command."

"Bullshit they can't." The driver's voice rises over the radio. "They've got one minute, and I'm pulling out."

She moves her hand as if she is going to reply, then thinks better of it. "Bet you say the same thing to your wife, asshole," she says to no one. Then, to Ben, "So what's the story? What the fuck is going on?"

She has a can of mace on her belt. Use it.

Ben stiffens at the thought, trying to keep his eyes off her belt. He has to tell her what's going on. The woman who got off could still be alive. It's just possible someone in the station could warn her, get her to safety. There is no play here except for the truth.

"Someone has been sending me messages on my phone," Ben says. "Telling me to find people or else they will be killed." He waits for a reaction, but she just stares at him like she's waiting for the punch line. "I thought it was a joke, like some kind of prank or something, but then the first guy got off and it looked like—"

"Someone told you to stop that guy from getting off the train?"

"Yeah."

"And you didn't say shit to him?"

Ben stares at her. "I thought it was a prank," he says.

"Not even, 'Hey, someone is messing with me, what's the deal?'"

Ben gestures at his face. "You saw what happened when I tried," he says.

Sarah opens her mouth to speak, but Ben can see her brain catching up as she connects the dots. "You were trying to stop that lady from getting off the train?"

"Yes."

"They said she was going to get shot, too?"

"They said she would die," Ben says.

His phone buzzes, three times in quick succession. It feels angry, insistent. He doesn't want to know what the messages say.

The driver clicks through on the conductor's radio. "That's time," he says.

"Hold one," the conductor says into the mic. Then, to Ben, "Show me what they sent you."

While she deals with the driver's outrage at being countermanded,

Ben wrestles his phone out of his pocket, almost fumbling it with slick palms, and unlocks the screen.

> *Get her back on the train, Adam.*

> *Are you paying attention?*

> *Get her back on the train so she can tell everyone who you really are.*

"—he says he's involved in this, and there's something I need to check," the conductor is saying. She holds her hand out to Ben. "Give me your phone," she says.

That same feeling of vertigo he felt when the hand landed on his shoulder hits him again as a decade and a half of fear catches up with him. *Get her back on the train, Adam.* There is only one person that would ever call him that, but they are long gone. There's no way they could be here. Ben looks at the woman's outstretched palm and knows he cannot let that name back out in the world again.

"I can't," he says.

"We don't have time for this," she says. "I promise I won't look at anything else. I just want to confirm—"

There's a shudder as the train's engine engages, straining against the brake. Sarah stops talking to Ben and gets back on the radio. "Look, can you wait just one fucking minute?"

"What the fuck did you say to me?" The driver's voice is a yell in reply.

The brakes disengage, and the train starts moving off with a jolt, the driver's rage translated into a sudden burst of speed that throws Ben into the conductor and both of them against the console. She grabs a hold of Ben's phone as they clash together, and as he regains his balance she shoves him, hooking the back of his foot with her boot so that he slips and falls hard against the door. As the train picks up speed along the platform, she straightens up and inspects the phone, the light from the screen giving her face a bluish cast.

"This text calls you Adam," she says. "I thought you said your name was Ben?"

Ben says nothing. There's nothing to say. The woman that got off of the train is going to die, and it is his fault. He couldn't stop her.

The conductor works her thumb, scrolling backward up through the messages.

"Holy shit," she says.

Before the platform disappears entirely, there is a flash of light and a hard bang, like a bolt of lightning striking the end of the platform. The shock makes the cab shudder like a toy being picked up and shook, and as the emergency brake engages, Ben slides on the floor, his body scything the conductor's legs from under her. The lights flicker off, and Ben is amazed at the silence that follows until he realizes that it's not really silence—the bang has made him temporarily deaf. He can hear muffled bangs and whistling that might or might not be real, and he works his finger in his ear, trying to clear it as the lights slowly come back on. The conductor is lying face down on top of him, her belly over his hips, and when he puts his hand down to try and move out from under her there are tiny fragments of glass—safety glass, because all of them are cube-shaped—all over the floor.

Ben sweeps as many of them to the side as he can and eases his legs out so that he can get to his feet. When he stands, he can see the damage that has been done.

The platform they just left is almost completely out of sight. Ben could have sworn they were still aligned with it when the bang happened, but they must have run on some distance before the emergency brake was pulled and then farther still as the train stopped. He can see the lights of the subway platform bleeding down the tunnel walls, a diffuse yellow-white glow that seems to flicker with movement, as though the light itself is panicking.

The glass of the rear windows has been shattered, cracks like hundreds of spiderwebs all radiating outward and clashing with each other to form a chaotic pattern that fills the frame. It's a wonder that the glass hasn't collapsed completely, and as Ben looks closer he can see that each of the spiderwebs is centered on a tiny, perfectly round hole in the glass, each one no wider than a fingertip.

When he turns around, he can see a constellation of dark spots studding the back wall of the cab. On closer inspection, he can see what each one is: a nail.

The conductor hasn't moved once since he got out from under her. *Fuck.*

If he says it out loud, he can't hear it. Ben grabs hold of her arm and turns her over. There isn't enough room to lie her flat on the floor of the cab, not with the chair in the way, so he gets behind her, one hand under each armpit, and pulls her up into a rough approximation of a sitting position.

She doesn't respond to him moving her. She doesn't flinch from his touch. When he crouches down in front of her, he holds a finger up near her nose and is relieved to feel the slight shift of air that says she is still breathing.

"Sarah." Ben says her name and watches for any flicker of recognition. Her eyes are open—one wider than the other, her left eyelid drooping—but her gaze is fixed on a point somewhere far beyond the walls of the train cab. "Sarah. It's Ben. Can you speak?"

Ben waits. He can sense a shift in the woman, sees the slow gathering of strength as though whatever reserves Sarah has left are being dragged up from some deep well inside of her.

"Buh . . . bub. Bub." When Sarah's lips move, a trickle of blood spills from her left nostril, spattering on her uniform jacket. "Bub." She makes a hissing noise—a brief, forceful exhalation—then is silent.

Ben watches the drops of blood rolling down the cloth of her jacket. It's treated with the same thing his shirt is, the same water repellent chemical that keeps spills at bay. A great selling point if you've only got one and can't afford to wash it. The blood doesn't stick, and each droplet gathers into a sphere as they land, picking up speed as they race in search of level ground.

Ben stands again, his knees complaining at the abuse, and ducks his head a little, trying to match the conductor's height from memory. When he looks out of the window, the holes where the nails came through are in line with where Sarah's head would have been.

Although he saw nothing the first time he looked her over, Ben tries again, shaking his phone so that the flashlight turns on, the blue-white spotlight chasing away the shadow Ben casts over her as he bends down. He moves the light back and forth across the woman's face and head, working upward, looking for any sign of a wound.

Up near her hairline, there is a tiny circle of metal that looks as though it has been glued in place. It is the head of a nail, sitting almost completely flush with the skin on her forehead. The rest of it is buried inside Sarah's head.

No wonder she's not saying much.

He wonders how deep it has gone. Three inches, maybe. Even six, at a push. Deep enough to turn her into a vegetable, that's for certain.

A tremor passes through Sarah while he is considering it, and while she isn't able to make any kind of coherent noise, Ben can feel the distress coming off her in waves. He shuts off the flashlight so that it's not shining right into her eyes. Her skin looks waxy, and Ben can't tell if it has been getting worse, or if discovering the nail has made him more aware of it. He feels lost at the sight of her, like there isn't a thing he can do. There's a first aid kit in the cab, with helpful pictures of bandages being wrapped around bloodless arms and an eager eye accepting a blast of sterile wash. Ben doesn't think there's going to be a cartoon guide for *Nail stuck in brain* on the inside of the case.

Leave the bitch. The door is right there.

The voice in his head is right. He could pop the door and get off the train right now, and maybe the confusion of the blast would be enough to cover his exit.

Don't get off the train. That was the instruction.

If he gets off now, then more people will die, starting with the woman right in front of him.

Ben stretches out a hand to reach for the radio mic that Sarah dropped when she fell. He doesn't want to use it. The last thing he wants is for more people to get dragged into this. To risk more people knowing the name Adam. But he is out of options.

Ben needs to call for help.

CHAPTER ELEVEN

FRANKLIN ST.

Kelly is in the cab when the bomb goes off. She doesn't hear or feel the explosion, but she still knows that something bad has gone down. It's the people on the sidewalk that give it away. They feel the tremor through the soles of their feet and every single one of them stops and looks south, like the worst day of their lives is happening all over again. Her cabdriver senses it, too, putting his foot on the brake and almost getting rear-ended for his trouble, and Kelly knows not to even bother arguing or trying to use the badge as leverage. She pushes cash forward through the grille and he lets her out without bothering to check it first.

She left Rogers to deal with the aftermath of the shooting, the local precinct putting up a cordon too late to be of any use other than to keep anyone from sneaking down and filming the body. There are procedures for everything, and with the MTA having their own procedures to follow, Kelly could see the two of them clashing and potentially creating a gap the shooter might be able to slip through. If she could catch up with the train, or even find a way to get ahead of it, there might be an opportunity to close that gap. The killing feels like it could be a random act, and though it's unlikely she'll catch the shooter, or even be able to identify them, just having a police presence might be the tipping point that keeps them from doing it again.

There are no concerns about presence now. Black and whites converge on the station faster than Kelly can on foot, appearing from every angle with their sirens blaring, the normally obstinate New York traffic melting away to let them pass.

There are people streaming out of the subway station entrance, not orderly like at Cortlandt where the business of a man bleeding out was someone else's problem, but chaotic because an explosion in the close confines of an underground tunnel is by design and intention everybody's problem.

There's a stab of despair in Kelly's gut—that even though she was trying her best to get ahead of the train, and that there's no way she could have got here to stop it, she still feels like she has failed. She picks up the pace, flashing her badge at a uniform who dodges into her path to try and stop her from getting into the station. As she reaches the pack of people pouring out, a guy in a business suit stumbles sideways toward her, holding his phone like he can't understand why the call isn't connecting. From the blood coming out of his ear and down the side of his face, Kelly can tell that he's not having an issue with the signal.

She doesn't know what is waiting for her down on the platform. She wishes she had bummed a radio off of Rogers before heading out. It would have been the correct play—the whole point of having radios was that you don't have to waste your time chasing someone; you throw up a net ahead of them—but instinct had won out over good sense and Kelly was in the cab before her brain caught up to the fact. Still, the uniformed cops are getting the grunt work done, emptying the station and creating space for the people who are too injured to get out themselves. Inside, the number of people who are bleeding or wounded jumps significantly. Some are trying to walk out, but are too dazed to make it to daylight. Others have given up trying, and are sitting in place, hands holding wadded clothing and tissues against their bodies, waiting for the cavalry.

This isn't the worst of it, she knows.

Kelly threads her way through them, letting the uniforms take the lead with triage. With a gun and a badge, the best she'd be able to offer is her jacket to add to the rest of the makeshift dressings, and she's pretty sure if she tried an EMT would show up and tell her she'd been applying pressure to the wrong leg the whole time. From the sound of the sirens outside, there's an army of first responders about to swoop in and do their jobs.

Kelly's job is the shooter.

All of the injuries look alike. That sparks something in her memory. She remembers the FBI doing a lecture to the entire department about how you can tell who is close to an explosion and what kind of casing the bomb has based on the size and distribution of shrapnel wounds. They didn't expect the NYPD to be out there reconstructing bombs for them, but they wanted to be sure that whoever was first on the scene would take plenty of pictures. The wounds here look different to what they showed her: instead of missing limbs, fingers, or heavy trauma to the torso or legs, the victims are all nursing numerous small puncture wounds, like someone opened up on the crowd with a widespread blast from a shotgun. It's only when she steps on a nail and it rolls under the ball of her foot, almost sending her sprawling, that she can see what it really was—a nail bomb.

Escalation is not an uncommon thing for the cops to deal with. An argument becomes a fight, someone grabs a knife and the fight turns into something far more serious, but this is a rapid climb even by the hardened standards of a NYPD detective. Shooting a guy at one end of the line and then dropping a nail bomb on the platform is beyond anything Kelly has ever seen. It could be a suicide bomber, and the shooting was them having to improvise when someone almost made them. They are close enough to the One World Trade Center for the act to feel significant. This could be the end of it, but Kelly knows that's the sort of shit a person can one hundred percent hope for but should never, ever assume.

There is a lot of smoke down on the platform. Without the trains moving to circulate the air, it hangs like a shroud over the scene. Combined with the heat, it makes the air feel thick, like it doesn't want Kelly to go any farther.

There is dead silence, and the air has an acrid bite to it that makes Kelly feel like she's about to sneeze. She has a strong urge to draw her weapon.

At the end of the platform, the smoke is thick enough that she can feel it settling on her face and hair, a thin film that makes her skin prickle. A chunk of the platform is missing, like a giant hand has raked a finger down through the edge of the concrete and broken off a section. There's a shoe next to the hole in the platform with something tan stuck in the top of it, and it takes a moment for Kelly to see that it's a shoe, with part of a foot still inside of it.

Kelly shakes off the shudder of revulsion that is her first reaction. Some people don't get it—the coroner will probably be down here chewing bubble gum and making wisecracks about loving a jigsaw—but for her it's something she's never been able to get rid of, no matter how many dead bodies the job has put in front of her.

The rest of the foot's owner, or at least their lower half, is sitting about three feet to her right, a broken torso and thighs laid out on the platform like a shop mannequin waiting for the rest of its limbs to be fitted. The victim was a woman. Her neck and most of the lower jaw is still on there, but the rest of her head is gone, cleaved off at an angle by the blast. Kelly looks around for more, but she suspects that what hasn't been pasted into the ceiling and the far wall is now part of the same mist that she is standing in, and the metallic edge to the air she's breathing is not just from the smoke.

There are footsteps behind her. It's not a good time to throw up. Not in front of the backup. There are four uniforms coming, all with guns drawn like they are expecting a shootout. Kelly holds up her badge just in case none of them gets the message, and leans out over the railing to see if she can see the train in the tunnel ahead. There are no passengers making their way back to the platform, and there's no sound, but she is sure there's some kind of light down the track, just where it curves out of sight.

"Holy Jesus. Oh fuck." The first uniform to catch up with Kelly is less prepared for what he finds her standing over, and barely makes it to the edge of the platform before he throws up. The others slow their approach, eyes almost popping out of their heads, and the nearest one reaches for his radio to relay the scene.

Kelly chops the air with her hand, miming for him to *cut transmission*. She can see the panic in his face, a mirror to the scrambling sensation that's trying to climb its way up out of her chest. It might well be the most fucked-up scene that any of them have seen, but the last thing they need is someone broadcasting that thought on the police band.

"Multiple casualties," she says. "Ask for an EMT. No details." He stares at her like she's just beamed down from a different planet. "Every scanner in the city will be listening," she says. "Whatever you say on there is going to be live on the news in five minutes."

He nods, suddenly tongue-tied, but one of the others shakes his head.

"That's not going to be a problem," he says.

"No?"

"Someone on the train is on the radio." He gestures toward the tunnel. "Everyone can hear them. A team from Homeland is on the way to lock this place down."

Kelly looks back down the track, toward the dim glow of the rear lights, the train itself just out of sight. "What are they saying?"

"Listen for yourself," he says, offering her a radio. "They want to negotiate."

CHAPTER TWELVE

FRANKLIN ST.

It takes Ben a long time to get on the radio. It isn't from a lack of familiarity. The radio mic is the kind of thing a kid could work out: one button and a grid of holes you speak into. Press the button and talk. That's all he has to do.

And yet getting his thumb to press down and open the channel is a hard fucking ask. He can feel the driver on the other end of the radio, the controllers listening above him—*Central*, the conductor had called them—and beyond that he can already sense the cops. Every cop in the city will be able to hear him. Every federal agent, every news agency earwigging onto the broadcast. A thousand ears to hear him speak.

To hear the one thing he can't bring himself to say.

Get her back on the train so she can tell them who you really are.

That's what they sent him. That's what this is about.

Get her back on the train, Adam.

The radio is slick in Ben's hands. He can't say that name. He can't let it be said. It can't be let back out into the world again.

Ben wants to bang his head off of the counter. If he could do it hard enough, he would not be here for the rest of this. He would wake up and someone else would have dealt with all of it. Or the person on the other end of the phone would kill him and he wouldn't have to worry about it at all.

The conductor, laid at his feet, the weight of her pressing against the backs of his ankles, makes a noise. It isn't anything conscious. A hiss of breath, the flow of air briefly muddied by some fluid bubbling in her nose or throat.

She is dying. Right here in the cab with Ben. She's dying, and he's doing nothing about it. Just like the others.

Ben keys the mic.

"Hello? Is anyone there? I'm in the back car of the train at Franklin Street. The conductor has been severely injured. She needs medical assistance."

"Who is this? Identify yourself." It's the driver. He has the same tiny voice that Ben heard talking to the conductor before, the one she called a dipshit.

"Are you the driver?"

"It's *operator*, asshole. Who are you?"

"My name is Ben. I'm a passenger."

The operator takes a second before coming back to him. "You're the guy she picked up, aren't you?"

"Look, there was an explosion on the platform. She's got a nail or something stuck in her head. She's barely conscious. I need to get her some help."

"Yeah, Oswald I hear you," the operator says. "Sit tight and get the fuck off my radio. Cops will be here to evacuate us in two minutes. Keep her from bleeding all over the floor if you can. That shit is hard to clean."

Ben's phone vibrates with an incoming message, and its arrival is like a stone landing deep in his gut.

No one gets on or off the train.

He puts down the radio mic to type a reply.

> *Are you paying attention? No one gets on or off the*
> *train, Adam.*

Ben's hand reaches for the radio to relay the message, but he stops short of actually picking it up. There's no voice in the back of his head this time telling him to do something. He just knows that he has to.

> *Let the conductor go. I'll tell them whatever you want.*

He types it fast, his hands slick with sweat, the adrenaline spike of defiance making the phone tremble in his grip.

They don't answer as quickly as before. Ben can't tell if that is good or bad.

> *You want to save her?*

Ben takes a long breath in through his nose. They didn't say no. But they didn't say yes, either. They're waiting. This is their test.

> *I don't want her to die on this train.*

> *You think any of those girls wanted to die, Adam?*

Ben flinches at the reply, but he bites down hard on the fear. They played their hand when they used that name. They have no more surprises left.

He needs something. An angle. Something that will convince them to let the conductor go.

Adam.

He doesn't need to reach for it. It's all about that name. The woman who got off the train knew him. She knew who he was. He would bet any money the other two men who died would have recognized him as well. In the back of his head, he wonders how they all ended up here. The same city, the same train, the same time. He acknowledges it and pushes it to one side. Right now, he has to help the conductor.

The cell phone is like a hot, slick stone in Ben's palm as he types the message out. You chose the others because of me, but you didn't choose her. She has nothing to do with this.

They don't respond right away, and he wonders if he has pushed too far.

Not far enough, Ben's inner voice chips in. *Tell them to go fuck themselves.*

For the first time, he gives the voice its due.

Let her go, or I walk, he types.

He looks at the door at the back of the train, tries to imagine himself getting down onto the tracks and pulling the conductor down after him. He might physically be able to hoist her over his shoulders and walk with her back toward the platform, but there is no certainty that the effort wouldn't kill her. He imagines stumbling and the nail scrambling her brain.

They send him a message while he is thinking about all of the ways trying to run could go wrong, and he starts when the phone jumps in his hand.

Only the conductor gets off, it reads. No one else. Here are your instructions.

Ben reads off of the screen as he lifts the radio mic.

"This is the passenger at the rear of the one train," he says. "I want to speak to Central."

The operator jumps onto the transmission faster than anyone else can key their mic. "You stay off this line, dipshit. The police are on their way to evacuate us."

Ben takes a deep breath.

"If any attempt is made to evacuate the train, more bombs will be detonated. Their blood will be on your hands." The phone buzzes. A new message. Ben reads straight from the screen. "If the operator decides that he needs to speak again, then one of the bombs currently on board the train will be detonated to remind him that he should be silent."

The operator doesn't call their bluff. There is a single *click*, the sort of thing you'd get if someone had thought better of pressing the button halfway through making a connection, but otherwise the radio stays silent for a full minute.

It's long enough that Ben wonders if there is a technical issue. Radios don't always play along, especially when the kit is probably older than most of the people that are using it. He can't imagine a nearby explosion is good for it, either.

Ben keys the mic again. "I want to speak to Central," he says. "I have information that is vital to the survival of people on this train."

There's a brief silence, and someone else activates their radio to broadcast. They sound distant, like their signal is a lot weaker.

"This is Agent Hoyt with Homeland Security," a man's voice says. He sounds bored and pissed, like someone's dad who has to get up out of his chair to go deal with some kids banging on the screen door. He's said barely seven words and Ben hates him already. "Who is this?"

Ben hesitates over the name. The killer will want him to say it, but he can't. Not yet. Better to keep things simple until the conductor is clear. "My name is Ben Cross," he says. "I'm on the two-fifteen out of South Ferry, stopped just north of Franklin Street. I need you to put me through to Central. The conductor on this train needs immediate medical attention."

Hoyt comes back straightaway. "Are there any more injured people on board?"

"I don't know," Ben says. "Probably not. No one else was facing the blast." He glances back through the cab window into the rear car. The lights are flickering, and the door at the far end is hanging open. It looks as though the handful of people that were in there have evacuated forward. The light is bad, but he can't see any blood. "I can't see anyone else that's hurt."

"That's good."

Ben grits his teeth. "None of this is good," he says. "Can you please put Central on?"

There's a long pause again, like Hoyt is weighing up the worth of the conductor's life on some kind of balance to see if it comes up to his advantage.

"I'm afraid I can't put you through to Central," Hoyt says. "The subway line and the car you are on are now part of an active investigation. I'm the person you'll be talking to today."

"Great, fine, okay. Send some paramedics and a stretcher."

"'If any attempt is made to evacuate the train, more bombs will be detonated,'" Hoyt says. "That's what you said, right?"

"I did," Ben says. "I did say that."

"Then you understand why I can't risk sending anyone down the tracks to that train."

Ben wipes his face with his sleeve, trying to think what he can say that will get them to do something. "As . . . uh . . . as a show of good faith—"

Ben falters, and Hoyt picks up on the break to cut him off. "Why don't you just sit tight and we'll speak more when you know what you want to say to me," he says.

Ben yells down the mic, "Goddamn it, I have a woman here with a fucking nail through her skull!"

There's a pause on the other end before Hoyt speaks. "Then I guess you'd best do something to keep her blood off your hands," he says.

Ben retains just enough self-control to not push the button when he yells in reply, unable to find a curse word that will fit the shape of his anger. He drops the mic onto the counter and closes his eyes.

Looks like you're on your own. The voice doesn't startle him. It's been lurking there, in the back of his head this whole time. Ben has just been refusing to acknowledge it. He looks down at the conductor on the floor. She's still breathing, but her breaths are getting more shallow, like what little life is left inside of her is retreating. *You could simplify your situation with a well-placed kick.*

Ben ignores the suggestion that bubbles up unwelcome in his head. He takes a deep breath and lets it out slow, counting to ten as his lungs empty. It doesn't feel like his fear diminishes any, but on the surface he feels calm, and that brief moment is enough for him to know what he has to do. It's him, or no one.

Ben reaches for the first aid kit.

CHAPTER THIRTEEN

FRANKLIN ST.

The Department of Homeland Security has one single mission: to secure the United States against all threats, whether foreign or domestic. For Agent Paul McDiarmid, the operative word is *secure*. The department wasn't created to hunt down the culprit, like some kind of glorified cop. He sure as shit didn't step up to sift through the rubble after everything goes down. They are meant to secure, and that means stop attacks before they ever get a chance to happen.

For a bombing to slip through on his watch—and in New York City of all fucking places—it doesn't just look bad. It's a Goddamn humiliation. He hasn't taken any calls that aren't mission-critical since the explosion, but he can feel the storm brewing nonetheless. If he doesn't get this under control and fast, then it won't be a sober handshake and early retirement. They'll crucify him. Forget after-dinner speaking engagements, or private security consulting gigs. By the time they're done, he'll be lucky to get a job guarding the door at a Walmart.

"What have we got?"

McDiarmid can tell from the damage what kind of explosive hit the platform. A pipe bomb. Not the biggest bomb in the world, but in the confines of a subway tunnel, still capable of doing some damage. There is some shrapnel damage to the nearby tiles, and a small arc-shaped patch of discoloration on the concrete that is more likely chemical residue than heat damage. Nails packed around the pipe bomb have caused some mayhem, but then the bulk of them were soaked up by the woman who had the bomb in her bag. They pulled the footage of her within minutes—fast for the MTA, maybe, but slow enough that he spent the wait chewing out everyone in earshot over the delay—and it showed her marching along with a duffel bag so big that if you flipped it upside down it could double as a storm shelter.

He has no opinion on the woman herself. Anyone could be a terrorist, given the right kind of motivation. But the bag is eating at him. If she had wanted to, she could have fit a much larger device in there. And if she had detonated it on the train, the destruction would have been much, much worse. As it was, the blast was small enough and so close to her body that she was the only person killed outright. The nails she'd packed it with had injured a handful more and the smoke had caused a handful of respiratory attacks that would no doubt be beefed up on the compensation forms, but besides all of that they had been lucky. The most damaging thing she had done was to bring the entire New York transit system to a brief and extremely costly halt.

It feels less like an attack than a warning.

If this were Latin America, and the victim anyone of even the most marginal importance, he would have called it an *assassination*.

McDiarmid snaps his fingers. "Hoyt."

Hoyt is as big as an oak and a terrifying sight to the uninitiated. McDiarmid knows Hoyt has aspirations to his office, but that knowledge doesn't worry him in the slightest. Anyone who plays their cards so openly will always end up hanging on to the bottom rungs of the ladder. The only thing that stirs in McDiarmid's mind when he considers Hoyt's massive frame is curiosity: they say that concussion damage is cumulative, but there must have been one moment, maybe during a training exercise or even way back in college on the football field, where that spark of knowledge, that critical faculty that might have made him good instead of just useful, was knocked clean out of his head.

"Been talking to the passenger in the rear cab," Hoyt says. He almost adds a *sir* onto the end, but holds it in with an effort. McDiarmid finds the formality grating. *You know who your boss is*, he'd say. *Just give me the facts.* "He says the conductor is injured. Has a nail in her head. That he wants her taken off the train."

"Can the operator confirm it?"

"No. He's still at the front of the train. The second the passenger radioed the bomb threat, he locked himself in his cab. Says that it's to keep anyone from hijacking the train."

The MTA cut the power to that section of rail the instant they knew there was an attack. Even if anyone got in and got their hand on the dead man's switch, the train wouldn't be going anywhere. McDiarmid would curse the man for a coward, but it's a waste of time. Where else would a coward end up if not stuck going in circles under the dirt?

"What did you tell him?"

"I told him we can't risk sending anyone," Hoyt says.

McDiarmid nods. No one in, no one out. Not yet, at least. "Get a medic on the radio. Walk him through keeping the conductor alive," he says. "They'll have some medical supplies."

"You think he's serious about the threat?"

"I think it'll help us find out what's actually going on. If he refuses the help, he's just trying to draw us in," McDiarmid says. "If the conductor really is hurt . . ." He stops and looks at the damage to the platform again. It feels too tight, somehow. Too focused. He would have expected something much bigger, and with more casualties. He needs to find out who the fuck this victim is as soon as possible. "Why is the guy calling in a bomb threat trying to help her?"

"Operator seemed sure that he's bad news. Said the conductor picked him up in connection to the shooting."

McDiarmid gives Hoyt a look. "Operator sounds like a rag you wouldn't wipe your ass with," he says. "We trust the things we can confirm, or have confirmed." He cocks his head. "Any update on the video from Cortlandt?"

Hoyt pales a little at the question. McDiarmid already asked him to do it, and he has either forgotten or it has fallen to the bottom of the pile. "I'll get someone down there right away."

The word *assassination* echoes in the back of McDiarmid's head. Using a bomb is a crude way to do it, but it's not unheard of. "Send a bomb crew," he says.

"Sir?"

"The Cortlandt shooting might not have been a shooting," McDiarmid says. "Tell them to check for shrapnel, any evidence of an antipersonnel device."

"On it."

"We need to find out who this passenger on the radio is," McDiarmid says, pointing a finger at Hoyt to let him know that this is his personal responsibility. "Independent of what he's telling us. Get on the footage from South Ferry, anything you can get from street level. I want to know where he came from, which route he took, if he met anyone on the way." Hoyt looks too relaxed, so he throws a question on the end of it. "What's our first priority?"

"Find out if he's holding a bag," Hoyt says.

McDiarmid nods his approval of the answer—Hoyt is sharp today, which is good—and takes a deep breath, steeling himself for the next batch of unpleasantness. The air is still thick with the smell of accelerant, and the feel of it in his sinuses and the back of his throat reminds him of the gun range. An unobstructed target and a clean shot would be a Godsend right about now.

"Let's go talk to the cop," he says.

The noise on the platform, the chatter of too many people trying to look busy and important all at once, dies down as Hoyt and McDiarmid start walking. Homeland is holding the ball on this one, and McDiarmid can feel the pressure of the clock ticking on a clean resolution. Everyone is waiting to see what he will do, and whether or not it will get people killed.

Most cops exist in a place far below McDiarmid's pay grade. Uniforms are like worker bees, a whole swarm of them working to fetch and carry or reroute traffic, and while that is a useful thing to have, they might as well be cardboard cutouts as far as he is concerned. Detectives are higher up the ladder in terms of his regard, but not by much. They exist to deal with crimes that have already happened, not prevention, and so even though their methods sometimes throw useful intel into Homeland's lap—bleeding-heart concerns about invasion of privacy going right out of the window when someone in an apartment building gets stabbed—they fit inside a box in McDiarmid's mind marked *Lacks Ambition*.

Detective Hendricks looks as though she lacks ambition. She's dressed in a suit that might meet departmental dress standards but the ready-made quality doesn't match the level of authority that her role demands. She is sweaty and exasperated, her forehead and cheeks shining with perspiration, and even though there is nothing for her to do but wait, she is pacing back and forth in obvious frustration.

"What's with Serpico?" Hoyt asks.

"The demands of the situation are beyond her capacity," McDiarmid says. "Anyone would be testy when faced with that truth."

McDiarmid already has the four-line summary of her file that tells him everything he needs to know about her. A stalled career killed stone-dead when she decided to assault someone in a position to crush her over it. He can see the downward trajectory toward her resignation, even if she can't. If she had played a longer, smarter game, then it would have been the first step on a long climb to the highest ranks a police officer can aspire to. But, as he already knew from long experience of detectives, this will never be the case. The drive just isn't there.

"Detective . . . Hendricks?" McDiarmid extends a hand. A soft opening. As though he wasn't prepped on exactly who is on scene the moment he stepped out of his car. "I'm Paul McDiarmid."

"Homeland?"

"The very same." She shakes his hand, and McDiarmid makes a mental note to find some hand sanitizer or a towel before anything else. If she touches him again, there's probably a legal statute somewhere that says Hoyt can shoot her.

"Are there any updates?" she asks.

"We're trying to confirm as much information as we can before we make any significant moves," McDiarmid says.

"So you're doing nothing." Hendricks glares at him as though that barb is meant to be devastating. She has a temper and runs hot. The best counter is coldness.

"We have been attacked, Officer Hendricks." McDiarmid gestures toward the damage on the platform. "My job is to contain it, find out who attacked us, and—if necessary—prevent them from acting any further."

"And doing nothing to save that conductor helps how, exactly?"

She has been listening. McDiarmid wonders who gave her a radio and if he can get them fired for it.

"We have an EMT ready to walk the passenger through stabilizing her. Now, as far as I know, you were the last person, scheduled updates aside, to make contact with the train," McDiarmid says. "You spoke with the operator, and your last instruction was for the conductor to walk the length of the train to look for anything unusual. Is that about right?"

Hendricks frowns. "I told them to be careful, but to report anything out of the ordinary. We had a shooting on the platform, and I had a hunch the shooter might have gotten back on the train."

"You have video evidence of that happening?" McDiarmid asks. "Or a witness?"

"I just told you it was a hunch."

"So, to go over that one more time, you asked an unarmed woman with no training to sweep a confined space with multiple civilians for a potentially armed threat."

"I didn't—"

"That wasn't a question, Officer." McDiarmid doesn't look at her as he says it. He makes a point of looking around the platform while the cop simmers in the heat of his interruption. A fresh coat of paint aside, the subway is *old*. Technology should be smooth and effortless, and anything less than that is a failure in his eyes. The greatest city in the Goddamn world, and it is nickel-and-diming itself everywhere he looks. He wonders what would have happened if the bomb went off on the train. He can imagine all too easily a two-decade-old pneumatic feed line getting cut by shrapnel, and the sound of fists beating on a door that just won't open.

McDiarmid turns his attention back to Hendricks. To give the detective her due, she's buried whatever anger was bubbling up deep, and is standing at what—among most cops—passes for attention. She is apparently smart enough to know when the shit is hitting the fan. "A few minutes after you spoke to the train, the operator updated Central on the situation to say that they had detained one passenger," he says. "Shortly after that report, an explosive device detonated on the subway platform as the train was leaving."

He can almost hear the gears working in Hendricks's head. The rust that must be getting ground off them with the effort. "You think the passenger is the one who detonated the bomb?"

"We can't confirm it," McDiarmid says. "But we know he was close enough to the victim to plant it, and his sudden concern for the conductor is . . . suspicious."

Hendricks looks from McDiarmid to Hoyt and back again. "You kept me waiting down here because there's a possibility I was communicating with the train," she says.

"You're correct," McDiarmid says. "If you weren't a person of interest, I'd say you have a bright future ahead of you."

"If I'm a suspect, you seem pretty relaxed about it."

McDiarmid has to stop himself from smiling. He's been told that he doesn't have a natural smile. That it looks more like he's about to bite someone. "Officer Hendricks, if I considered you a threat, then the team we had waiting on the stairs after the civilians were evacuated would have put three in your chest for me."

She takes it better than expected. No fidgeting, no shifting her weight like she wants to run or fight. Just stiffens up a little, her mouth tightening into a thin, angry line. "So what do you want from me?"

"I want all my eggs in one basket," McDiarmid says. "If you're not part of it, then you're an asset." She opens her mouth to say something but McDiarmid speaks over her. "Our negotiator listened to the recording of you talking to Central and the operator. They think you're innocent."

"At least somebody is on my side."

"Officer Hendricks." McDiarmid barks it at her. He runs a course for up-and-comers on how to handle anyone who isn't one of their own. *Keep them off-balance. Let them know exactly how powerless, how fucked they are.* "Right now, my team is turning your life inside out. Every phone call, text message, every social media post you've ever made, every red cent you've ever earned. All of it is being pulled apart and if they find a single atom of suspicion anywhere in there, I will personally march you to a windowless cell and leave your paperwork to rot on my desk. Do you understand me?"

There isn't the tiniest amount of panic in the detective's expression. McDiarmid tries not to feel too disappointed. Usually mentioning their social media gets a reaction, but not this time. She's angry, and people forget to sweat about the details when they're angry.

Hendricks clears her throat. "I understand. And when I come up clean?"

For a fraction of a second, McDiarmid warms to her. It's been a long time since someone dared speak back to him. "Then welcome aboard," he says.

The warm feeling fades as he looks over her crumpled suit and the lumpen shape of the vest she's wearing under it. McDiarmid cannot fathom how she would ever expect to survive a serious tactical engagement. He was assured that the NYPD maintained standards across all precincts for urgent response, but clearly that isn't the case here.

"While we're waiting, get rid of that polyester jacket and see our outfitter for something more . . . breathable." He jerks his head toward the platform exit, up to where the temporary headquarters is setting up. "I feel like if I look at you a second longer I'm going to start sweating by association."

Hendricks plucks at her jacket like taking it off will be a relief, then stops when she reaches the vest buried under it. "Even my vest?" she asks.

McDiarmid considers it. The ones they have upstairs are resistant to most forms of penetration, and have a ballistic insert designed to divert the pressure wave from impact sideways, reducing potential blunt trauma to negligible levels. A bullet strike that could break the ribs of anyone wearing an NYPD-issue vest would simply not register as anything but a dull thud on a Homeland one. Still, they are expensive.

"Keep the vest," McDiarmid says.

CHAPTER FOURTEEN

FRANKLIN ST.

The first aid kit offers up no answers to Ben when he cracks it open. Whoever was responsible for it was obviously of the opinion that the presence of the box was enough to fulfill health and safety guidelines, and that actually equipping it was a waste of funds. What it does contain is mostly bulk: saline eyewash, gauze and dressings, simple plasters, a pair of cheap scissors still in their cardboard box. There's a laminated card with CPR instructions on one side, the recovery position on the other, and a suggested script for communicating with emergency services in a font so small that Ben can barely read it. All that's lacking is a copy of the Lord's Prayer, because for anything worse than a skinned knee, putting your hands together and hoping is all you've got.

It makes a weird kind of sense. If they put anything good or useful in the boxes, it would get stolen in a heartbeat, and even if it didn't they would have to give everyone first aid training, and that would cost money. The bean counters at the MTA have built their budget on the assumption that none of their conductors would ever end up with a nail embedded in their skull, and spent accordingly.

On the floor, Sarah's convulsions have subsided to the point where it's just her hands that are moving, fingers jerking inward like she's gathering an invisible thread into her lap. Ben can't tell if he should be relieved, or if it's a sign that things are getting worse.

He can feel the panic in the back of his head like tinnitus: a constant, high-pitched wail that ramps up exponentially if he acknowledges it for even a second. All he has to do is get a dressing on the wound, keep her warm, and try not to panic. That's all. He told them what had happened to her. Not only that, he broadcast it to anyone with the ability to listen in. If their conscience doesn't move them to action, public pressure will. All he has to do is hold tight until that happens.

He doesn't look at the phone. It doesn't buzz, either, and Ben wonders if they can somehow see him or hear him. He can't see any cameras in the cabin, but he wonders if they have hijacked his phone, or bugged him somehow. Struck by the idea, he peels his suit jacket off and wraps it around the phone, folding the cloth over and over until it forms a football-shaped lump with his phone at the center. Looking at it, he feels like an idiot.

You're not paranoid if they're already out to get you.

The thought is so clear that it sounds to Ben like someone speaking aloud, and he is glad the conductor isn't conscious, because it means that no one witnesses him almost jumping out of his skin.

"South Ferry two-one-five, come in."

This time Ben jumps so hard he almost falls over the conductor. Hoyt repeats the request, and Ben scrambles for the radio to respond. The operator has taken his earlier warning to heart, and for the moment Ben and Hoyt are the only two voices on the radio. He feels a flood of relief knowing that they have relented. That the cavalry is coming.

"This is Ben Cross," Ben says. "I mean, South Ferry. It's me." In his panic to get hold of the radio, he can't be sure Hoyt didn't say something else. "Say again, please?"

"This is Hoyt."

"Are you coming for the conductor?"

"I told you, we can't send anyone," Hoyt says. "I have a medic here. She's going to talk you through what you need to do."

The wailing in the back of Ben's head is a flat-out scream. "I don't have anything here to help her with. You need to send someone. Do you understand me?"

"I understand you're in a tough spot, Ben, but this is the best we can do." Hoyt's voice is flat on the line, like he's reading off of a script. "I'm going to put her on now. Whether you talk to her or not, that's up to you. Doc?"

"—a doctor, but thanks." The mic cuts out briefly during the handover, but Ben is heartened by how pissed the woman that comes on the line sounds. It takes a special kind of rage to make the word *thanks* land like a slap. "Hi. Can you hear me? Is this Ben?"

"I can hear you," Ben says.

"My name is Chris, I'm an EMT. I understand you've got someone injured there," she says. "Can you run me through what's happening?"

Ben can feel the words bubbling up out of him, a confessional rush that almost starts the instant the woman stops transmitting, but he forces himself to take a deep breath and hold it. He needs to be brief, to let her ask questions, and give her room to decide what's relevant. "The train's conductor has a nail stuck in her head."

"A little way in, or all the way in?" Ben expects a pause, but there is none. There was more than one nail packed in with the bomb on the platform: this will not be the first the EMT has had to deal with today.

"It's all the way in."

"Is she still conscious?"

Ben has tried not to look too closely, but the conductor is still gathering with her hands. One of her eyelids has opened, but her eye is unresponsive, looking up at nothing. "No. She could speak a little when I found her, but she's not responding now. Her hands keep twitching."

"Convulsions?"

"Yes." During the worst of them, Ben was forced to lean on her with his whole weight to stop her from hurting herself. It felt strange, like he was holding on to a body with no one inside it.

"Is there any bleeding? From the wound site, or her nose or ears?"

"Her nose was bleeding when we got here."

"A little blood, or a lot?"

Any blood at all seems like a bad thing, but Ben figures that with a nail in your head, the tiny amount that dribbled out was the best they could hope for. "A little."

"Hrm." The EMT makes a noise like she wants to speak before letting the mic go silent, and Ben feels suddenly guilty, like he somehow got the answer wrong. The radio is dead for what feels like too long, and she can imagine the discussion the EMT must be having with the brick wall that is Homeland Security.

The line pops—a press of the mic button and released again—and Ben starts to wonder if she is ever coming back. Maybe she argued with Hoyt, telling him that they need to get to the train right now, and Hoyt has pulled her radio privileges.

"Are you still there?" Ben asks.

The EMT comes straight back. "Yeah, I'm here." There's a pause—just long enough for someone to take a breath and steel themselves—and she speaks again. "You're going to have to take the nail out."

"I'm going to have to what?"

"I had a hunch, and I had to make a call to check, but that's what needs to happen. Your friend there, they should be talking, or at least conscious. Hell, I think the world record for having nails stuck in your head is something like ten, and that guy drove himself to the hospital."

"So what's happening to her?"

"It's very likely she's bleeding into her skull, and the blood is putting pressure on the rest of her brain," the EMT says. "If it keeps building up, it will either kill her or leave her brain damaged for the rest of her life."

"So you need me to pull the nail out."

"I'm afraid so."

Ben looks down at the nailhead where it sits flush with the woman's forehead, a perfect seal. "What about infection?"

"Not your problem," the EMT says. "You think that nail was clean when it went in? Get the nail out, tip her head to let gravity help things along, and get some gauze on there. We'll worry about the rest later."

"Okay," Ben says. He doesn't know what else to say. There's no time, no space to back out of it. There isn't even space left for his fear. He just has to do it, and that's all there is. "Walk me through it."

"Here's the deal," the EMT says. "You're going to need focus, and quiet, and both your hands free, which means I'm going to go off the air. Don't wiggle the nail when you pull it. Don't pull it out superfast. Have as many dressings as you can ready to catch the blood. There might be a lot of it. Don't drop anything into the wound, if you can help it."

Ben feels like he is choking, his vision tightening down onto the nail, the surface of it in perfect focus.

"Have you got all that?" the EMT asks.

He can see the slightly oval shape of the nailhead, the tiny imperfections and scratches in a surface that is still mostly shiny, like it came straight out of the box.

"I've got it," Ben says.

"I'm going to stay by the radio. Let me know when it's done."

Let her know when you've finished giving this bitch a lobotomy.

The voice in his head is smug, like it knows failure is a foregone conclusion. Ben closes his eyes and waits for it to go away before he answers. He can do this. He has to.

"I'll get it done," he says, and sets down the mic.

CHAPTER FIFTEEN

FRANKLIN ST.

The hand sanitizer is the first thing. Ben squirts as much of the bottle as he can wring out in a single squeeze into his palm, and starts working it into his skin, scrubbing it in deep as if he just pushes hard enough that will fix everything.

This isn't right. He doesn't know what the fuck he is doing. All he has is a general instruction to get the nail out, and nothing on how he's meant to do it.

Ben scrubs harder, the last traces of the sanitizer evaporating about as fast as his hopes that the conductor will survive this. He can feel it in his gut. Something bad is going to happen.

He wants to look at the phone, even though all it brings is bad news. At the very least it is something else, something that isn't the task at hand. If there's a message, then that would be more pressing. It would mean not having to do this. The people who died weren't with him when they died. He didn't kill them.

The conductor is right here, and Ben feels like no matter what he does, somehow she is going to end up dead.

Ben leaves the phone alone. He bargained for the conductor's life, and somewhere on the train, the killer is waiting to see if he lives up to it.

He has to do this.

Why did they blow that woman up? She recognized him, for one thing, and even that feels as though it was by design. Like there's something more than just the killings, something more than just taunting him with the deaths. The other guy they killed on the platform, quick and discreet, and the train rolled out of the station without anyone so much as blinking. Before that, they killed a dude right at his front door, leaving enough space for the door to swing shut once they'd taken their trophy photo.

Trophies. They commemorated that one kill. Maybe that was their first, and they'd done it quietly, in private. Maybe they had made a little ceremony of it. The two that followed were different. They got him involved when they sent him a picture of the second man, and the third was them going public with a literal bang. They are escalating the situation, and it almost feels like that is what they want. That this panic is all part of their plan.

The conductor is a bonus. They agreed to let her go, because they could tell the cops weren't going to send help. They want Ben to watch her die.

He has to do this. Even if it goes bad, he has to try. If it offers the slightest chance of wriggling loose of the killer's grip, he has to take it.

Ben opens a packet of bandages, leaning over the conductor and putting them on top of the plastic they came wrapped in, trying to keep them off of the floor and touching them as little as possible. As he straightens up, the conductor's hands convulse, working the air like a tide-pool crab gathering invisible morsels.

He does his best to ignore the movement and carefully lifts her head and shoulders, shuffling his knees forward and pulling until she has her head settled in his lap. Her weight pins him in place, his knees twisted awkwardly under her, but the discomfort feels like something to hold on to. It overrides the sensation of how close to death she is, like she's falling away from him, and lets him focus on the one thing he needs to: the nail in the woman's head.

Ben sucks in a tight breath and tries to get a hold of the nail, working his fingers into the unresisting skin of the conductor's forehead, digging to get some purchase so that he can start pulling.

His first attempt fails, and he swears under his breath as a bead of blood wells up around the metal rim of the nailhead before running down the conductor's face. Ben grabs for a dressing and mops at the blood to try and stop the flow, but the effort is useless. He gives it another shot, just with the edge of his fingernails this time, and even though it feels like he catches itand has a good hold, the instant he starts pulling his grip gives way, making him jerk his hand back like her skull is electrified.

On inspecting the damage, he finds his fingernail is bent but not torn: a wipe with the bandage reveals a straight white line where it has folded under the strain. The nail is stuck much harder than he expected, and it will take more than just a quick pull to move it. He dreads the thought, but it might need a twist to get it moving.

Good idea. Scramble those brains like a fucking egg.

Ben ignores the voice. The third time is always the charm. He switches hands and digs into the skin around the nail, using three fingers and a thumb to maximize contact, not worrying how much skin she loses in the process, and gets a good purchase under the nailhead.

He takes a deep breath and twists. Not too much—just a quarter turn clockwise—and now when he pulls the nail starts to come out. Ben holds his breath and pulls, keeping his hand steady by holding his wrist with the other, drawing the nail up and out one slow sixteenth at a time.

He gets about half an inch clear before seeing something flex in the conductor's skull, an unnatural curve lifting next to the wound, the skin of her forehead tightening over it like a bat's wing.

Ben lets go of the nail and the fracture in the conductor's skull sinks back into place, vanishing so completely it feels like a warning not to touch her again. His throat feels as though it is closing up at the sight. He was so close. He thought he had it.

"Fuck!"

It comes out a lot louder than he meant it to, and he follows it up with a full-throated roar at the ceiling. He casts about for something, anything, but there are no answers anywhere. Just the walls of the cabin, folded around him like a cage, and the darkness of the tunnel beyond.

Just slit her throat with those scissors. It'd be a mercy.

Ben stares at the scissors in the first aid kit, out of their box but still wrapped in sterile plastic. For a moment, he considers it. Call it an accident, a mistake. He just slipped. Anything other than this feeling of being dangled over the edge of an abyss.

They aren't really scissors, as such. More like shears, flat-bladed and precise, with the dull sheen of surgical steel. Unlike the rest of the medical supplies, they seem fit to purpose. Ben can almost hear the sound the blades must make when they open and close, the whispering rasp of an impossibly close tolerance, the flat faces barely moving as they cut through cloth and flesh alike.

He can use the scissors.

Not to cut her, although that idea lingers long enough for him to consider its pros and cons. It would be easy to cut away at her skin, but the problem lies deeper. Giving the fractured portion of her skull even more freedom to move seems counterproductive.

The image in Ben's head is to mimic the back end of a claw hammer, the two flattened tines on the back side biting into the nail and drawing it free. If he uses the blades of the scissors to catch the sides of the nail and puts his hand under it, he can lever the nail up and out while bracing the broken section of skull in place.

That is, as long as the rest of her skull isn't fractured just as badly, ready to give way under the weight of his hand like a foot landing on too-thin ice.

The scissors look very clean when Ben unwraps them, but he squeezes the last of the hand sanitizer along the length of each blade anyway, opening them and closing them until the liquid has mostly vanished. He tries not to touch anything below the handle while he moves the dressings closer. It's the best he can do.

Ben moves his free hand down toward the woman's head, his palm and fingers already matching the curve of her forehead, and freezes just short of touching her.

He can do this.

Ben takes a deep breath and opens the scissors so that he can get the blades on either side of the nailhead. While he was getting ready, it pulled back until it was flush again with her head, drawn down into place by the negative pressure he created trying to get it out. He presses the blades down flat into the skin on her forehead, trying to get in under the metal edge, and fresh blood wells up at the contact, running down the blade and dripping onto his fingers. It feels hot on his skin, hotter than it should, and he can feel a pressure building in his sinuses, a sympathetic pain like someone is slowly pushing a spike in through his frontal lobe, and he frowns hard, screwing his face up tight to try and stay focused on the job in front of him.

The scissors don't catch at first, and Ben has to press them in again and again, pushing far harder than he ever expected to, feeling like he's going to push the scissors clean into her head, before the blades slip under the edge of the nailhead and he closes them, feeling them bite on either side.

He changes his grip so that he's holding the tips of the blades together, giving them no chance to slip, and at the first tentative tug he sees the bone under her forehead flex with the same threatening certainty of failure as before.

Ben shifts his other hand, walking his fingertips spiderlike across the woman's forehead, feeling for any hint of the fracture and spreading the span of his hand wide to try and cover as much area as he possibly can. When he feels like there's no more that he can do to create a stable base to lever off of, Ben adjusts the position of the blades against his knuckles and pulls up on the scissors.

He imagined the nail coming smoothly out in a single, clean motion, maybe coated red from where it has been, but no more than that. Instead, it comes out slowly, a stop-start struggle against the vacuum that is forming every time he pulls with nothing inside to take its place. The sides of the nail grind against her skull, and Ben feels every gritty shift and vibration of it magnified through his fingers and up along the length of his forearms. There's a little blood, but most of what comes out is a thin, transparent liquid, and tiny chunks of gray-white matter that can't be anything but brain. Ben can't help but wonder what each piece once was—the memory of a good friend, or maybe a complicated word she once knew. He feels his stomach lurch just thinking about it, and he tries to put it to one side. *If she lives, she can learn it all again.*

When he reaches the very tip of the nail, a burr in the metal catches on the woman's skull and Ben gives it a sharp twist—one final turn can't do anything worse than what's been done already—and the nail jumps free. Once it is out, the blood follows: rising slowly as it fills the hole the nail has left—it's only after it fills that Ben understands that he was looking into a hole that went all the way down into her brain—and then much faster as it breaks surface tension and rolls freely down the conductor's face. Ben reels back from it, cursing and fumbling for a dressing, forgetting to put the scissors down in his rush to cover the wound.

Ben watches the conductor's face for any kind of change. A rush of color or a gasp of breath. There is nothing.

The dressing under Ben's palm is dark with blood, and even though he is exhausted, even though he doesn't want to acknowledge a single second more of this futile effort, he pulls a fresh wad of gauze from the pile. The bloody dressing comes away like the rind of a fruit, a ripping wetness as it parts reluctantly with flesh, and he tosses the dark wad into the empty first aid box while putting the new one in place. His hands, when they are not doing anything, are shaking.

Ben feels the dressing changing under his palm. Becoming more substantial. Like it is feeding off of the very last of her.

He closes his eyes and tries not to think of how badly he hoped that this would work. That for a moment, he had actually dared to think she might survive.

The conductor stirs under his palm, her neck and shoulders tensing up.

"Who the fuck," she says, her voice so thin it is almost inaudible, "has got their hand on me?"

Ben doesn't have the energy to jump. When he looks down, he can see that, for the first time, she has closed her eyes completely, and some of her color has returned. If it wasn't for all the blood, she could be sleeping.

"You're okay," he says. "Help is coming."

The conductor makes a noise that could be an acknowledgment or agreement, and relaxes. She isn't unconscious. Ben can see her lips moving, and after a moment he works out what she is saying.

She's praying.

Ben remembers prayers. Sundays with his father, on the road to church, and spending the day together after.

All the lessons his father taught him.

Ben wishes that she wasn't praying, but he doesn't dare try to stop her.

He should radio the EMT and let them know that she's conscious, that she didn't die. That he hasn't killed her. Maybe that'll get them to send help. As he is reaching for the mic, his phone vibrates, the motion so sudden and hard enough that the plastic shell dances on the anti-slip metal plate that's riveted into the floor.

For a moment there, Ben had forgotten where he was. He'd forgotten about the train, the killer, and the messages on his phone. About everything that had led to this. Now that he remembers why he is here, all he feels is hollow.

Ben picks up the phone.

Tell them to move the train, Adam.

The name is like a spike being driven into him. Nobody is meant to know it. Nobody is meant to use it. And yet, here it is, dug up from the hole Ben buried it in all those years ago.

Ben knows why the person on the other end of the phone is doing this. He knows why they chose him.

It's because of his dad. Because of where those prayers—those lessons—ended up leading him to.

He looks down at the conductor, at the mic in his hand, and he knows that there's no way he can explain this. There's no way that any of them will understand.

They will blame him for all of this.

Maybe that's why they chose you.

Ben keys the mic. "We have to move the train," he says. He doesn't identify himself, because he's afraid of what he might say when he does. The name doesn't come up easily, but Ben can feel it sitting in his throat waiting to be said out loud. He swallows hard on the taste of it.

"Say again?" A voice on the other end. Hoyt, maybe. Ben isn't listening. "Who is this?"

Ben flinches at the question. He doesn't have to tell them everything. Not yet. They'll find out anyway, he's sure of it, but for the moment he doesn't have to say it. "We have to move the train," he says, "or more people will die."

CHAPTER SIXTEEN

FIFTEEN YEARS EARLIER

The mug on Doctor Hardy's desk is the same taupe color as the walls in the waiting room. It isn't an accidental choice. The one that says WORLD'S NUMBER #1 MOM is tucked away in the bottom drawer of her desk, safely out of sight. For some of the people she helps here, it's better this way. There is nothing on her desk or about her office that isn't deliberately neutral. Not a single thing to suggest that, while the door is closed, the rest of the world exists outside of it.

Some of the people she helps don't need any reminding that it exists.

Adam Crane is eleven years old, but he looks eight. He's not underfed, or at least there's nothing in his medical notes that suggests the level of malnutrition that would stunt his growth, but still he is a lot smaller than she expected him to be. He is very thin, and the pale stretch of wrist and ankle showing past the limits of his clothing suggest that whoever dressed him thought he was much, much younger as well. She resists the urge to write anything, but makes a mental note to suggest he get new clothes as soon as possible. His awkward, scarecrow appearance makes him stick out, and sticking out is the last thing he needs right now.

There's a pervasive myth that children who experience trauma are aged by it. That they have seen too much to still be considered children, and rather than accept that a child still exists in there, it is easier on the conscience to conclude that there must be some instinctive response that makes them old before their time.

Adam Crane has not been aged beyond his years. This is the first time that they have met, but his caretaker's notes suggest that he has regressed. His speech is slow, they say. He can barely write. He can eat, with some help, but they have to be careful. He is very sensitive about being touched, and shows a strong tendency toward claustrophobia.

Adam is staring straight at her, his eyes wide and unblinking, and she can tell from his body language that it's not a curious stare. He's watching her because he's afraid of her. Afraid that if he looks away or blinks, something bad will happen.

This isn't going to be easy, and Doctor Hardy's heart sinks a little as she thinks about how many times he's going to have to come to this office, and when he is done or gets old enough to say he has had enough, it might just be that none of it was any help to him at all. Even with that in mind, even though just getting him to trust her at the most basic level will probably take up most of the clinical hours she spends with him, she knows that she still has to try.

A thought occurs to her.

"Do you like my cup?" she asks. Of all the possible questions, all the things he might have been thinking would happen when he came in here, there isn't a chance on God's green Earth that he would have anticipated this question.

He blinks, confused, and Doctor Hardy tries her best not to let the triumph show on her face when he tilts his head and takes a long considering look at the cup on her desk. "No," he says.

"Me neither." Doctor Hardy pulls open the lower desk drawer without looking and fishes her own cup out, and sets it up beside its beige colleague. "This is my real cup." She catches the look on his face. "It's not much better, is it?"

"No." Then, with his brows creased together, "Why do you have two cups?"

"A woman must have her secrets," she says, with mock seriousness. She lifts the beige one. "This is for guests, and the other is for me."

"That's too many cups," he says. He seems extremely set on the issue.

Doctor Hardy takes her beige mug off the desk and puts it into the drawer, taking care not to spill the contents as she sets it upright. "Better?"

Adam nods.

"My name is Tasmin Hardy," she says. He flinches when she says her name, just the barest flicker of fear crossing his face, and if she hadn't got him to drop his guard for a moment, then she guesses she wouldn't have seen it at all. "I'm one of the doctors here."

"Am I sick?"

"I'm not that kind of doctor," she says. "I help people who have had bad things happen to them."

"You make them forget?"

Doctor Hardy takes a deep breath. "I help them move on. Now, with that in mind, I want you to take a minute and think. What name would you like me to call you by?" He gets the same look on his face as he did when she showed him the two cups. "One name on paper, another name for us." She holds up her file by way of an explanation, and makes a show of pulling open a desk drawer and shutting the file in it. "It can be anything you like," she says.

He sits in an imitation of thinking, but Doctor Hardy can tell that whatever bucket he just sent down hit the bottom of an empty well. He looks up and points at her cup. "Who gave you that?"

"This? My son did."

"What's his name?" The question is as heartbreaking as it is inevitable. For all her cleverness, she didn't anticipate it. Doctor Hardy knows that if she stops to think, that if she hesitates and lies, then he will see it and she will lose her chance with him completely.

"Ben," she says. There aren't many times she's cried in front of a patient at work, and it takes a real effort to keep from adding today to the list.

"Ben." He says it once, to get the feel of it, and nods his approval. "You can call me Ben," he says.

CHAPTER SEVENTEEN

FRANKLIN ST.

The good thing about having an assistant like Hoyt is that he is not a subtle man. For one thing, there's no need to say or do anything that could be held against you as a threatening behavior when you have him looming at your back. For another, McDiarmid always knows when he is on his way. Besides the thunder of his footsteps, Hoyt's presence is almost as tangible as the man himself. He takes up so much room that you can't help but know when he's standing at your elbow.

"What have you got for me?" McDiarmid asks it without turning around and before Hoyt can speak. He feels a surge of pleasure at the EMT doing a double take next to him.

"A lot of the passengers have started putting videos up online from inside the train."

"How many?"

"Hard to count." Hoyt spreads his hands. "People are already reposting videos from other people, trying to ride piggyback on the news cycle."

McDiarmid's first instinct is to shut it all down, but that is easier said than done, and considering the situation it might even be counter-productive. "How does the situation look?"

"Like a lot of pissed-off New Yorkers."

A pressure cooker, in other words. "We've got eyes on everything that's getting posted on the internet?"

"Yes, sir."

"Get as much as you can out of it. Names, faces, any chatter that might tell us what's going on in there. How much they know, what the rumors are," McDiarmid says. "I want to know who is sitting in which seat in every single car, or as close as we can get."

"Sir."

McDiarmid knows exactly how much manpower that is going to take. Even a single video feed needs a lot of eyes and ears to keep from missing anything. Analytics is good—they are the sort of hard data nerds that can pull a half-million stack of digital credit card receipts and tell you the name and address of every single person who bought a pair of black leather gloves on a Thursday in April—but there aren't enough of them to cover all the material coming out in real time. In a subway car full of smartphones, there's just too much, and a lot of potential for something to slip past. "Get the crazies working it as well."

"Sir?"

"Get hold of Thompson in Analytics. Tell him to get on social media, start seeding the conversation with stuff like 'clues,' or 'escape room,' or 'conspiracy.'" McDiarmid clicks his fingers. "'False flag' is a good one."

A few years back, McDiarmid read a piece in *Newsweek* about a company that solved how proteins folded by turning it into a puzzle game. Thousands of eyes on the problem, brains working full-time, and at almost zero cost. It didn't take a big leap of the imagination to apply the same concept to filtering the flow of conversation online. There is way too much information on social media for Homeland to reasonably flag up every potential threat and assess the likelihood of it ever happening, but there are also more than enough people sitting looking at their phones, gripped by a heightened state of paranoia, every one of them thinking they had found the next great danger to the United States of America.

"I'll let him know," Hoyt says.

The hippies watch the nazis, the nazis watch the hippies, and the febrile atmosphere that is the baseline for social media discourse means that everyone is on high alert, all of the time. Every so often Thompson would check how well things were working by making a few fake accounts to push some extreme position. Normally, none of them lasted past a day before they got flagged to the authorities by one of their opponents.

"Anything on the male victim at Cortlandt?" McDiarmid asks.

"Bomb squad pulled some plastic and a couple of metal shards out of the platform," Hoyt says. "The bulk of it is still inside his chest but they rushed an X-ray to try and find out what caliber of bullet was used."

"Let me guess, it looked less like a bullet and more like someone folded a flat piece of copper in half?"

Hoyt doesn't even need to nod to confirm it. "They're running an analysis on the explosive used to confirm, but—"

"It wasn't a shooting," McDiarmid says. "The victim was carrying a bomb on his person the whole time."

"Not much of a bomb, sir."

"Enough to put a hole in his chest you could put your hand through," McDiarmid says. He lifts a hand to his chest, about the right height for the blast wound, and finds himself touching the lapel of his suit jacket. "It was made up to look like a package," he says. "Something they knew the target would have slipped into a coat pocket."

"How can we be sure he was targeted?" Hoyt asks.

"Look at the second victim," McDiarmid says. "The woman at Franklin."

"The bomb was in her bag," Hoyt says.

McDiarmid nods. "A bigger bomb. But why?"

Hoyt considers it. "The first victim put it in his pocket," he says. "She had hers in a bag. If they used the same size charge for both, it might not have guaranteed a kill."

"That's a reasonable conclusion," McDiarmid says, "but I don't feel like it's the whole story. Whoever did this wanted to kill her, sure, but they also wanted to escalate the response. It's almost like they want us down here looking for them."

Hoyt shifts the folder full of papers he's holding from one hand to the other, like he's keen to hand them off. The edges of the paper look uniform, like they've just rolled off the printer.

"Are those the background checks?"

"The first pass on everyone you wanted me to run."

"Good." McDiarmid had asked for the bare minimum. Rap sheets, known associates, red flags. Quick and easy. They could dig a lot deeper, but the problem with having all that data at your fingertips is one of time. The boys back in Analytics could spend a month turning a person's life inside out and still ask for a week's extension compiling their report. "Let's start at the bottom of the pile: the operator."

"Nothing special," Hoyt says. "Had a DUI that got struck off his record in exchange for a recovery course, says here he turned up to all the sessions. Got some debt run up, looks like he switched booze for ponies, but otherwise he's clean."

"Nothing on his internet usage?"

"Nothing." Hoyt pauses. "He watches a lot of porn."

McDiarmid, who has seen the stats on what Homeland would consider baseline consumption of pornographic material, is taken aback. Hoyt never adds commentary. "Define 'a lot.'"

"Like other people watch TV, sir."

"Jesus." He has only spoken to the driver on the radio, but he can still imagine the guy perfectly in his head. "The conductor?"

"Clean."

"Too clean?"

"Ordinary clean, sir. Active in her church, got a second mortgage she probably shouldn't have taken out."

McDiarmid clicks his tongue. "That figures." There's a tendency among bombers, willingly or not, to end up on the list of the injured or dead. It would have made things a lot easier if this had been one of those times. "What about our Good Samaritans?"

Hoyt checks his notes before he answers. "The NCO at Cortlandt has a few question marks hanging over him. No arrests, no stops that anyone bothered to write down. Good grades, good school, doesn't even get a year into the course before he throws in the towel and joins the NYPD. We're chasing down a contact at the university to see if there's some incident they've covered up."

"Check for deceased parents," McDiarmid says. "Or hospital bills." He's seen the pattern before. Kids that could have been something, except they never cut the cord. "Could be involved somehow, some kind of payoff in it for him. Turn the family over, just in case."

"Sir."

McDiarmid waits for the last one, but Hoyt is silent, his presence suddenly absent in the sphere of his boss's awareness. That either means he has something, or he has fucked up. "Tell me about the passenger," he says.

"Ben Cross," Hoyt says, then clears his throat. "He graduated this year from the University of Texas at Austin—"

"Don't pad it out," McDiarmid says, cutting him off. "What's the bad news?"

"Ben Cross appears to be an alias, sir."

"Appears to be?"

"Everything about him before the age of eleven is sealed."

"Juvenile record?"

"We don't know, sir."

McDiarmid thinks. "Did he file to have the records expunged when he was eighteen?" He turns to watch Hoyt flick through the pages, knowing already what the answer will be. If he had filed, the system would have flagged it when they called up the information. Whoever coded it had built it to be paranoid, which meant it fit in well with Homeland's directives.

"No, sir."

"You said he went to university in Texas. Were the records sealed there?"

Hoyt double-checks it. "It all happened here. State of New York."

"Crap." If it had been Texas, a single phone call to a sympathetic judge would probably have solved all their problems. Even if they lean heavily on the terrorism angle, it's going to be a tough sell getting a New York judge to unseal a preteen kid's court records. Still, there's more than one way to get the information they need. "Okay. Get someone working on having them unsealed, let them beat their head against that particular wall for us. You said he was eleven? How long ago was that?"

Hoyt frowns as he does the math. "Fourteen years, sir. No, wait. Fifteen."

"Right." McDiarmid knows that there's no such thing as serendipity. Breaks come from working the problem from every angle you can find. "Fifteen years ago, the state of New York, every major news story or court case you can find. Cross-check sentencing and closure dates against the date of that seal getting dropped on our boy Benjamin. Cross-check for any mention of any kids. If they drag their heels breaking that seal, we might get lucky if it was a big news story at the time."

Hoyt should be moving already, but he lingers instead.

"So Ben Cross was the bad news," McDiarmid says. "What's the worse news?"

"The mayor wants an update on when we are getting the passengers out of there."

"Did the mayor ask you himself?"

"No, sir. One of his assistants rang. They said they tried to reach you directly."

McDiarmid knows they did. He switched his cell phone off when it started buzzing every ten seconds with a new call. There's going to be hell to pay when he finds out exactly who passed on his number. "One of his assistants . . ." The arrogant prick.

"What did you tell them?"

"I told them that they should make any and all inquiries through official channels and that I was not at liberty to make any comment."

"I bet they liked that."

"It could have been anyone, sir." Hoyt keeps his face blank when he says it. McDiarmid makes a mental note to give him a pay bump in his next review. He was dimly aware that the EMT had picked up their radio while he was speaking to Hoyt, but the frantic wave of her hand draws his attention. "What is it?"

"It's the train," she says. "They say they have a message from the bomber."

McDiarmid feels the skin prickling on the back of his neck, like it was some kind of fate that this would be the exact moment they make contact. He shakes it off. Superstition is a dangerous habit to get into. "What do they want?"

"They want the train to start moving."

Hoyt makes a dismissive noise and McDiarmid glares at him. The train is currently right underneath an expensive part of the city, and even though there is a stack of barriers between him and news from the outside world, he knows that aboveground is currently in chaos because of the bombing. Moving the train somewhere they can control is a gift. "To where?"

"They don't say, but—"

"Tell them we need time," McDiarmid says. "We need to get the conductor stable, and make sure that we can get her off the train and to a hospital."

He ignores the blank look the EMT gives him. She had protested as strongly as anyone had ever dared to about letting a passenger carry out amateur-hour brain surgery rather than let her within fifty yards of the train, and the sudden turn has thrown her. He doesn't care about her opinion or approval. What he cares about is finding out who planted the bomb, and whether or not they remain a threat.

"We're going to take her off the train?"

"Yes."

"I'll prep a team." Hoyt stands tall and ready as he says it. Useful as he is, he still has one terrible weakness. Four years at a desk and little field action has left him desperate to prove himself. Eventually he will learn that there's nothing to prove, and that macho shit is for crayon eaters. Still, McDiarmid can't just slap him down. You play the person, not the position.

"No team," McDiarmid says. "If our boy in the cabin with her is playing us, we want to get the drop on him. Going straight for the train with an assault team, he might detonate another device."

"So we go in looking like an ambulance crew. Secure the conductor, neutralize the passenger?"

McDiarmid nods. "If it's not him pulling the strings on this, then at least we have simplified the equation."

Hoyt mulls it over. "I'm not sure I can pass for an EMT, sir."

"Hmm." Hoyt has him there. He is the wrong fit for the job: too big, too intimidating, too driven. If McDiarmid were a mad bomber, he'd press the detonator the instant he saw him coming. They need someone harmless looking. Someone who, if it comes down to it, is expendable.

McDiarmid looks around as the solution comes to him. "Where did we stash Hendricks?"

"The detective?"

"Get her mic'd up and down here as fast as you can," McDiarmid says.

"Should we brief her?"

"Oh, no." McDiarmid almost smiles at the thought of what the cop's face will look like when he tells her where she's going. "I'll brief her myself."

CHAPTER EIGHTEEN

FRANKLIN ST.

Ben holds the phone like he is scared of it getting away from him. Every time it buzzes with new instructions or fresh mockery, he jumps a little bit, and every time he thinks it is going to drop clean out of his hands. All he can think about is how a shard of the conductor's skull had almost lifted free when he was pulling the nail out, and now even though her forehead looks undisturbed, it is still there, still loose. A single, solid blow—like a smartphone being dropped on her—could drive it straight into her brain.

Ben keys the mic on the radio. He doesn't try to get up to check the controls: his legs are cramping from holding the conductor's head and shoulders up, and he can't be certain of getting out from under her without causing her any more trauma. Besides, Homeland and the MTA knows what channel he is on. Knowing how fast bad news travels, half the city is probably tuned in.

"This is, uh, South Ferry two-one-five," Ben says.

He feels sick. He needs to get off this train, get rid of his phone, and now is the time to do it. The cops are right there, less than the length of a football field away, and even if they throw him in a cell, then at least he'd be free of this nightmare. The conductor isn't stable, though, not close to it, and Ben can't leave her. The dressing could come loose, or she could regain enough conscious control to try moving and hurt herself even more.

"This is South Ferry two-one-five," he repeats the call.

The EMT who spoke to him earlier responds, "How's our patient?"

"She's alive," Ben says. "She can speak."

"Is she awake? Looking around?"

"She's got her eyes closed but I think she can hear me." Ben looks down at the conductor and sees that she is very slowly trying to give him the finger. "She's giving me a thumbs-up, but should probably try and stay still."

"Good," the EMT says. "How is her wound? Is it one hole or is there more trauma? Like bits of her—"

"The people who set the bomb made contact," Ben says. "They have been sending me instructions. Do you understand?"

"I, uh." The EMT keeps the mic open and while Ben misses what she says next, it sounds like she is scrambling for a pen. She gets back on the mic and her voice comes through clear again. "I hear you," she says. "I understand."

"They are also responsible for the shooting earlier today. They have killed a third man. They killed him on his doorstep this morning, somewhere in the city."

"The shooting earlier," she says. "Okay."

"They want the train to start moving."

"Moving, uh-huh." She keeps the mic open again, and after a second's pause she takes a deep breath and speaks as though every word she is saying weighs a ton. "Look, Ben, this is above my pay grade. I'm going to have to get someone else you can speak to."

Ben's gut feeling is an instant surge of dread. The messages didn't give him a deadline, but somehow it feels as though he is running out of time.

They're playing you. Buying time so they can put a bullet through your forehead the minute you look out that window.

"Is that okay, Ben?" the EMT asks.

Ben ignores the voice in his head. "Please be quick," he says.

The radio goes silent, and Ben is left holding the mic up like an idiot, waiting for a call that is probably going to be a long time in coming. The conductor shifts in his lap, and he shifts his weight in response to keep her from sliding off of his knees.

"Why?" the conductor's voice breaks the silence, her voice a paper-thin rasp.

"Why is this happening?" Ben asks.

She nods, a tiny tilt of the head that registers more in the way her neck muscles tense against him than any visible movement.

With a hole in her head, Ben feels like she has earned some honesty. "Something bad happened when I was a kid," he says. "And now this is happening." He feels like he is a kid again, sitting in a chair trying to get words out and finding that they just won't come. "I think this is my punishment."

The conductor is completely still, long enough that Ben almost starts to panic about whether she is breathing or not. Before he can work out how he is meant to check, she speaks again. "You kill someone?"

Ben tries to answer, but the words catch in his throat. Sometimes, when Ben tries to sleep, all he can see when he closes his eyes are flames. A fire in the dark. He looks up at the ceiling, gulping at the air like he's trying not to drown. "I—"

"This is Hoyt." The Homeland agent's voice fills the cabin like a shout, and Ben jumps at the sound, suddenly aware of the tears that are running a trail down each cheek. The conductor, stuck in a place far beyond the point where anything can surprise her, doesn't even so much as breathe harder. "We received your demand. Where do you want the train moved to?"

Ben says nothing. They didn't say in any of the messages. Just to get the train moving, and that there would be consequences if he didn't. He wonders if asking them will get an answer, or someone else killed.

He lifts the mic to speak into it. "I don't know. They want the train moving—"

Ben's cell vibrates in his hand, the buzz loud in the cramped space. It just reads 181st. He should have known they would be listening.

"They want the train moved to 181st Street," he says.

Ben knows it. Washington Heights, right up next to the Hudson. It's a deep station, something like a 140 feet down. He heard about it once, that it was meant to be one of the places people could shelter if the city was about to get hit by a nuclear bomb. It'd be a cold comfort to anyone stuck south of the George Washington Bridge when the four-minute warning hit, but apparently *could* was higher up the list than *would* in that particular thought experiment.

It doesn't seem like the kind of place to take hostages if you are planning on escaping, and that thought chills Ben to the bone.

Down in the dark, about as deep as the subway goes.

"It's going to take us some time to make that happen," Hoyt says. "And since whoever is sending you messages can hear me, I'm going to ask directly that they let the passengers off before it goes anywhere."

"Everyone stays on," Ben says. "They said the conductor could go free if I helped her."

"And they're willing to let us come get her?"

Ben can feel the plastic grow slick under his palm. This is his chance. He needs to push for every advantage he can get. "They've kept their word on everything else so far," he says, and braces himself for the message telling him they've changed their mind.

No one past the rear car, the message says. She gets off. No one else.

Ben relays the instructions, and Hoyt acknowledges.

The phone vibrates again.

Aren't you going to tell them, Adam?

Ben stays silent.

That's why they want to go to 181st St. They want to take him as deep as they can. Back down to where it all happened. They want to show the world who he is, and what he has done.

Ben knows that Homeland will discover who he is, that he should try to take some control of the situation, but he can't find the strength to say it out loud. Every time they use that name in a message, it's like a stone being laid on his back. Eventually the weight of it is going to crush him.

The phone buzzes in his hand.

It doesn't matter, the message reads. Keep squirming. They have five minutes to get the train moving, whether she's on it or not.

Ben thumbs the mic. "You've got five minutes," he says.

CHAPTER NINETEEN

FRANKLIN ST.

The instant Kelly says yes to McDiarmid's request, two Homeland agents descend and pull her suit jacket off with terrifying speed. She's briefly concerned that her blouse is going to go the same way—and that the next time she turns up for confession she might have to bring the priest some popcorn to go with the tale—but they slap a ballistic vest on her and hold up an EMT's starched blue shirt for her to put on, each of them holding out a sleeve like an impatient parent who needs her out of the house right this very minute.

She bristles at the sight of her jacket—her semi-nice one, not quite interview quality but enough to make a good first impression—tossed to one side onto a pile of debris from the platform. To add insult to injury, one of the agents made sure to crumple it into a ball before throwing it.

"You going to pay to have that dry-cleaned?" she asks.

"The city will cover it," McDiarmid says, then glances at the spot where it fell. "We also offer incineration. You sure you can do this?"

Kelly lifts her arms into the sleeves, and the agents pull it tight over the vest before buttoning it up. The vest feels lighter than the ones she is used to wearing—the stiff armored plates biting into her rib cage feeling more like plastic than the usual slabs of metal—but she is willing to bet that in a head-to-head test this one will stop more bullets.

"I'm sure," she says. Even if the clock weren't ticking, she wouldn't have to think about it. The instant you say no, you are voluntarily taking yourself out of the loop. She saw how the guy on the platform at Cortlandt ended up; she was one of the first on the scene here. They aren't the kind of things you see and put to one side.

She can feel the pressure building, like watching a thunderhead form on the horizon, knowing that it is on its way. This situation is already beyond almost any incident she's ever had to deal with, and it still feels like it is warming up. If she can get into the center of it—the eye of the storm—then maybe she has a chance of stopping whatever endgame they have in mind.

This is her collar. She knows it deep in her bones, knew it the instant the crowd back at Cortlandt started shifting in response to the shooting. Kelly knew she got reassigned in order to eat some humble pie, but she had made her peace with that. The minute she stepped onto the subway, it became her patch. Shit-ass coffee or not, she had a job to do and this fucking piece of shit bomber had come along to fuck it up for her. Never mind her penance, or getting things squared away so she can watch Hernandez on his climb to captain. This is personal. Homeland can strike as many important poses and come up with as many dumbass schemes as they like: she is going to catch this motherfucker herself.

"Hendricks," McDiarmid says. "Let's walk."

The Homeland agent starts moving, and the looming tower of Hoyt—likewise stripped of his suit jacket and sporting an extra large version of the same uniform Kelly is wearing—falls into step behind him. Kelly hustles after them, not wanting to get left in their wake like some kind of hanger-on, and she can hear the two agents that dressed her scrambling to pick up their gear so that they can follow. "Hoyt will go with you to the train. He'll take point at the front end of the stretcher, you take the back. The EMT, what was her name?"

"Chris Janson," Hoyt says.

"Right. Janson will be with you to make sure the conductor is stable." One of the agents catches up and jams an earpiece in Kelly's right ear, and she jerks her head to one side, lifting a warning hand to let him know that if he tries anything like that again she will push his nose clean through his head. A rushing, hollow sound fills the right-hand side of her head, followed by a short electronic beep. The agent waves his hand at her—*Is it working?*—and she reluctantly turns her raised fist into a thumbs-up. It's working, and now she has Homeland dug into one ear like a tick. "We're going to cut it as close as we can," McDiarmid says. "You get on board, get the conductor on the stretcher. As soon as she's secure, we'll start the train moving and you're going to slide her out of the back door."

It sounds like half a plan. "What about the passenger?"

"He stays on," McDiarmid says, after the kind of pause that makes Kelly wonder how he got so high up in Homeland without every learning how to tell a fucking lie.

"What if he tries to get off the train?" Kelly asks. "People panic. Things happen."

"We can't risk the train," McDiarmid says. He's more confident on this point, like he's warming up to the task. "That's why we are leaving it to the last second." He nods to one of the assisting agents. "Give her a gun," he says.

Kelly didn't like handing over her own weapon when they took over the blast site. She insisted on a receipt, and they had had to go find some paper before they could give her one. That they're giving her one now makes her feel even more suspicious.

"Have you ever fired a Springfield?" one of the agents asks.

"No."

"How about a Shield?"

"The Smith and Wesson?" She knows it. "You're not packing Glocks these days?"

"We got a discount," the other agent says, and lifts the back of her shirt to slide the weapon into place under the ballistic vest. The gun is a hard lump against the small of her back, but if she stands up straight it will stay hidden. "You're a righty, correct?"

"That's right."

"Velcro patch is the best we can do. Don't jump around too much and it won't fall out. Safety's on the left-hand side, you've got seven in the mag and one in the pipe. Laser sight turns on ahead of the trigger guard, right side."

"What color?"

"Green. All our teams are on green."

Hoyt holds out a radio in one hand and a cell phone in the other. Kelly takes both of them.

"They're listening to the radio," McDiarmid says. "We're keeping most communication running on one channel to keep them thinking they're ahead. We have to assume they can hear you in the tunnel. If you suspect they are in the open and we have a chance to isolate them from the train, hit send on the phone to let the snipers know. Keep it hidden otherwise."

Kelly nods and tucks the phone into the left-hand pocket of her pants. Almost every cop she knows keeps their phone in an impact-resistant case and the toughest screen protector they can buy. Her reason for doing it is to protect the phone, but the honest reason for most cops is because the brand uses words like *tactical* and *military grade* in their advertising. The one Hoyt has handed over is slim almost to the point that it doesn't feel like a phone at all, the kind of thing you'd have to refinance your house to afford. Kelly is willing to bet you could drop it from orbit and still get a signal afterward.

"You good to go?" McDiarmid says, looking at his watch like she's the one holding everything up.

At the end of the platform, a Homeland agent in full tactical gear is kneeling against the wall, shoulder and head out over the rails just enough to aim the rifle they're holding. From here, it looks as though they are just aiming into darkness. When she steps down between the rails, they will be aiming past her head.

Across all police shooting reports in the last five years, only 20 percent of shots landed on target. Kelly wonders what kind of scores Homeland got on their last statistics report. From the shine on those rifles, she wonders if the number of shots they have fired—firing range skills test included—is even close to double figures.

Hoyt claps her on the shoulder. "Better be. We're out of time."

His hand lands hard enough to let Kelly know that it's not law enforcement camaraderie. It's intended to get her moving. Hoyt hustles down a short steel ladder Homeland has put down to connect the platform to the rails and Kelly follows suit. The second her boots hit the gravel, an orange stretcher swings into her face in expectation of being caught.

"Watch the third rail," Hoyt says. "The train will be moving out, so it's live." They both put the stretcher on their right-hand side, holding it like a shield to ward the electrified rail away, and start moving. As Hoyt flicks on a flashlight to light their way, Kelly hears the EMT descending, and her footsteps picking up the pace to close the distance.

The train is closer than she thought. She can see the cabin at the back of the train almost as soon as they leave the platform behind, the windows lit by the same unnatural blue-white that is ubiquitous to the subway. There's a shadow there, someone's head, some shoulder visible as well, and she wonders if whoever it is can feel the sniper's crosshairs trained on them, like that feeling when you just know someone is staring at the back of your head.

No one past the rear of the train. That was the message the passenger relayed. Kelly wonders how the suspects could possibly watch and know without giving themselves away. It feels like a massive bluff, and yet with a chunk of platform missing and the possibility of another explosion still close at hand, the smart play is to take it seriously and collect as much information as they can before making a move.

As Hoyt reaches the bottom step of the rear cabin and pulls himself up to the door, Kelly reaches back to where the pistol is strapped to the small of her back. Hoyt, the human-shaped extension of his boss's fist, doesn't hesitate to take point, even though it puts him directly in the line of fire. If things go south, a big step over the third rail will put Kelly in darkness and give the sniper on the platform a straight shot into the door. The EMT has instructions to hit the deck, offer as small a target as she can, and be ready for when the shooting stops.

Hoyt slams the flat of his gloved hand on the door, like he is trying to free up a rusted lock by hitting it as hard as he can, then works the handle to open the door. Kelly can't see much at first—just the open space inside and someone trying to shuffle out of the way—but then Hoyt steps down and out of the way to wave her inside.

"Get the board in there," he says. "We need Chris up here."

The conductor is sitting on the floor of the cabin like a puppet with cut strings: shoulders slumped, feet splayed in front of her, and her head cocked over to one side. A wad of dressing has been clumsily bandaged over the right side of her forehead and eye, the cloth covered in dark red swipe marks where they have tried to apply the dressing with bloody hands. Her eyes are open, but one of them is dark from what looks like the worst eight-ball hemorrhage Kelly has ever seen. If she lives, she probably won't keep that eye.

The passenger is holding the conductor up. He has the top half of her torso hoisted up into his lap, his arms around her like they are posing for the planet's most fucked-up prom photo and as Kelly climbs up into the cab she decides not to bother asking what the fuck his problem is.

The conductor is having some kind of seizure—her arms jerking upward like she is trying to hit herself in the face—and the passenger's hold on her is the only thing keeping her from putting a hand to the dressing on her forehead and tearing it away. He isn't shushing or trying to calm her. He's just holding on, mouth set tight, like he has been stuck in this position for a long time and doesn't have a lot left in the tank for courtesies. He meets Kelly's gaze but there's no real recognition in it. She has met a lot of survivors in her time, and the expression on his face—like someone has wrung his soul out like a wet rag—is deeply familiar.

"Hey." Kelly tries to maneuver around the conductor's legs and not hit her with the board. The passenger, Ben, leans away from her to try and help but there is no real space for him to give up for her. He smells sour—the whole cab does—like his sweat is somehow rotting the shirt off of his back. Hoyt gives the stretcher a push and the front edge catches Kelly in the back of her calves, almost folding her legs up under her, and the jolt brings her attention sharply back to the task at hand.

"Two minutes," Hoyt says, and the train comes to life like it has heard him, lights all around the conductor's cabin flickering on as the electrical systems boot back up.

The EMT climbs up to the door and stops short of joining Kelly in the cab. "There's not enough space to take her out on her back," she says. "Turn her this way, then slide the board under her legs. You'll have to support her head while we pull her out."

"Are you sure?" The conductor's hair is flat and stiff with blood. She looks as though she's barely hanging on, like a good shake would be enough to flatline her. McDiarmid had said that the conductor was injured, but she didn't think it would be this bad.

"Get her on the fucking board." Whatever patience the EMT might have had evaporates as something fires up inside the train, making a deep vibration pass down its entire length.

Kelly jams the stretcher under the woman's thigh like she's shoveling snow, the thick plastic edge catching on the thick polyester pants of her uniform.

"Ninety seconds."

The EMT reaches in and yanks the conductor's leg up, and the passenger grunts as he has to work to keep her upright. Kelly gets the board under one leg, and they rock her to one side then the other, lifting her hips while the EMT pushes the board hard to get it completely under her. In her half-upright position, the end of the stretcher sticks out of the open door where Hoyt is waiting to catch it.

The train vibrates again, and the PA system comes to life with the faint sound of the operator's voice.

"Ladies and gentlemen, because of the incident on the line the NYPD have asked us—"

"One minute."

Kelly slides her arm behind the conductor's back and brings her other hand over to support her head. She looks straight at the passenger as she takes the woman's weight. "Get your legs out of the way."

As the passenger stands up, the EMT grabs a fistful of the conductor's pant leg and pulls, moving her down the stretcher. Everything moves a lot faster than Kelly was expecting, and as the conductor moves she loses her balance, letting go so that she doesn't fall on her. The drop is only a couple of inches, but the solid smack of the back of the woman's head against the hard plastic makes Kelly's blood run cold.

"Jesus fuck," the EMT says.

"—won't be any stops between here and there but this is for your own safety—"

"Get her off the train." Hoyt starts pulling the stretcher from the bottom, and Kelly fumbles one of the straps across the conductor's chest, closing the Velcro fastener in the vain hope of it holding if someone's grip fails. As she lifts the top end of the stretcher, the passenger darts forward and squeezes the conductor's hand. *Good luck.* If the conductor squeezes back, she doesn't see it.

She crab-walks the short span of distance between the back of the cab and the door, turning so she gets behind the stretcher, handles held underhand, arms straight to take the weight without turning it into a slide. As more of the stretcher leaves the train, the more Hoyt and the EMT can take the weight, but even so Kelly can feel her knuckles burn as the stop-start traverse takes the skin off of them one by one.

"Thirty seconds!" Hoyt doesn't have the freedom to look at his watch, but as sure as shit there is someone yelling it in his ear. He lets go of the stretcher, letting the EMT take the strain with a grunt, and draws his weapon so fast it looks like a magic trick. "Keep your hands where I can see them, and step down from the train!" He shouts it at the passenger, who puts his hands up, but doesn't move an inch.

Instead, he looks at Kelly.

"Better get off the train," she says.

"I can't."

"Lace your fingers behind your head and step down from the train now! I will shoot you if you do not comply!"

Every so often, the department will spring for a lecture from a psychologist or an expert from the FBI or wherever, and it will always be some bullshit about how to read body language, how to spot a liar, or how your intuition is always guiding you. Kelly has never bought into any of it, because if it was really true, then it would be a core part of Academy training instead of an excuse for a half day on full pay.

Even so, Kelly can tell that the passenger is not their killer. He's caught up in all of this, sure, and he must have a hell of a reason for not wanting to get off this train, but everything about him screams, *Victim*.

By her count, there are about ten seconds left before the train leaves. It shudders into life around her, and she can feel the floor shift as it strains against the brakes, ready to move off.

Kelly steps into the line of fire and braces her foot against the top edge of the stretcher. "Get her out of here," she says, and starts pushing.

"Get the fuck out of the way!" Hoyt yells it, but he's already moving, the gun dropping as he lunges to catch the stretcher as it falls. It was a gamble, but Hoyt is more of a field agent than his boss is, and he is hardwired to save lives first. McDiarmid would have let the conductor fall and taken the shot.

With the screech of metal on metal, the train starts rolling, almost sending Kelly flying out of the door with the first lurch forward. She grabs hold of the door, every single muscle down her left-hand side screaming at the jolt, and while the train car barely seems to be moving at first, Hoyt's flashlight and the orange slab of the stretcher shrink so fast they look like they are falling.

Kelly steadies herself and pulls the cab door shut, trying to slam it but some kind of hydraulics built into the mechanism makes it fight her all the way. While it might be over for the conductor—outside of however long she'll need in the operating theater, and then the multiyear lawsuit for the compensation to pay the bill for it—there is still a long way to go for everyone else stuck on the train. She straightens up and ignores the spike of pain that flashes the length of her rib cage. *Maybe you can book a massage while the paperwork clears on your suspension,* she thinks. She'll be lucky if it's just a suspension. Knowing her luck, Homeland will commission a rocket to have her fired into the Sun.

Kelly looks at the passenger. Out from under the weight of the conductor, he is in bad shape. His hands look like he's dipped them up to the wrist in a bucket of blood, and he is shaking so hard he can barely stand.

"Hey," she says. "It's Ben, right? My name is Kelly. I'm a detective with the NYPD."

He doesn't say anything, but she catches the look he gives the uniform she's wearing.

"We weren't sure who was watching the train, so I put on a disguise." She points to the conductor's chair. "You want to sit down?"

Ben looks at the chair like it is electrified, then back to her. "Are you here to arrest me?"

"I'm here because I was on the scene when a guy got killed," she says. "At Cortlandt Street. You know about that?"

Ben nods once. "Did he die?"

"Yes, he did," Kelly says. "I'm here because I want to know what happened, and I think you are the one person here who can give me some answers."

The passenger's eyes are saucer wide, a real deer-in-the-headlights look, and he swallows hard before speaking.

"They killed him because of who I really am," he says. "Because my name isn't Ben."

"What is it?" Kelly asks.

It takes a long time for him to get the words out, and for most of it Kelly finds herself backing up, because he looks like he's about to vomit.

"My name is Adam Crane," he says.

CHAPTER TWENTY

FIFTEEN YEARS EARLIER

There isn't much call for subtlety when you work with children. Not normally. In Tasmin's experience, it tends to be a necessary strategy for dealing with adults. Grown-up clients arrive with their defenses complete, and it can be a struggle to overcome them. You have to work to strip away the years—sometimes decades—of repression, distortion, and denial in an attempt to reveal whatever truth remains.

For children, the trauma is usually a great deal more immediate, and there isn't much need to dance around the truth when they have a tendency to just tell it straightaway.

For Ben, though, it's different.

She's never seen a child so consumed by fear. He wears his terror like a second skin, an aura that expands outward and infects the world around him. People go quiet in their offices when he walks down the hall. The admin staff, normally a boon with their constant need to fuss around the children that come in and shower them with stickers and all manner of sweets, get tongue-tied and shy, like a lifetime of knowing exactly how to flatter a kid with attention just evaporates in his presence.

And yet there doesn't seem to be any root cause to it. She asks him about how things were before the *incident*, and he talks about his daily life with his mom and dad like it was some kind of idyll. That would be cause for suspicion in and of itself, but he speaks so readily and so consistently that Tamsin can't help but be convinced by it. Everyone tells lies, even when they are trying to tell you the truth, but Ben isn't old enough to build something this elegant. Lies for boys his age go places they don't mean them to, get bigger with every retelling.

He has to be lying. If Ben is telling her the truth, or thinks that he is, then there's only one conclusion she can draw: this fantasy of a perfect childhood that he has built is a defense mechanism. A way to keep this colossal fear haunting him at bay.

He's created a whole new childhood to protect himself from the one he actually lived through, and now Tasmin has to try and pry it open without breaking him apart in the process.

"I'd like to talk about your eleventh birthday, Ben."

According to the police John Crane's final victim went missing on the same day his son turned eleven. *Alleged victim*, she thinks. They never found her body.

Ben doesn't look up at her, but that's not a deviation for him. "I'll be twelve soon," he says. Diversion is in his tool kit, though.

"Happy birthday in advance, Ben," Tamsin says. He likes it when she uses his new name. "Have you thought about what you'd like as a gift?"

"Who's going to get me anything?"

Tamsin leans back in her seat like she's considering it. "I'm sure I've got a spare mug somewhere I can gift wrap," she says.

It doesn't earn her so much as a smile, which she takes as a warning sign.

"So, let's go back to your last birthday," she says.

"Why?" She can see him tensing up, which is a change from their previous sessions. He usually sits with his palms flat on his thighs, fingers turned inward, but now she can see that he is pressing down on them. Hard.

"It's important that we find out what happened, Ben," she says. "So that we know how to help you. I know it's not comfortable, but I wouldn't be asking if it wasn't important." In Tamsin's opinion, asking someone to relive trauma is like sending a deep-sea diver down into the black. You don't let them drop without a tether to help pull them back up. "Let me know if you need a break."

"Mom put up balloons," he says. "With my—with the name up there."

"It's okay, Ben." His name is still a serious trigger. It is early in his treatment, but already she doubts that he will ever feel safe acknowledging it again.

"She put a table out back for breakfast," he says. "Borrowed it from Mr. Johnson across the street." He pauses, and a tremor passes through him like there's a draft in the room. "Mom said I had to have some real food before I had any cake. Dad said that the flies would get it if we didn't eat it first."

Tamsin is tempted to end it right here. Everything he says is so matter-of-fact, and yet his body language is undeniable. Something is upsetting him. On the other hand, this is the first time he has mentioned his father directly in any of their sessions without hesitation, evasion, or trying to change the subject.

Tamsin makes a note for the police to check with the neighbor about them using the table.

"Was it going to be a party? Were there any guests coming?"

"No." Ben shakes his head. "I didn't . . . Mom said we couldn't afford a party this year."

The police interviewed the teachers and principal of the local school. Ben had already been marked out by the other children—and, as a result, by the staff—as a loner. No incidents of bullying, or at least none that were recorded. It's hard to keep from thinking that they knew to avoid him.

"Cake for breakfast sounds like a good time, though," Tasmin says. "What about after?"

Ben rocks in his seat, making an involuntary noise at the back of his throat. She wonders if he is afraid of his dad, that somehow he can still reach him.

"We went camping."

"All three of you?"

Ben shakes his head. "Just me and Dad."

"Do you remember where?"

"Upstate." It comes out tight and hard, and Tasmin is certain that while he might not be lying, he isn't sharing everything with her. He rocks a little harder in the seat, like he wants to get up, and she doesn't press him any further. She makes another note, for the cops to check for maps or any gas station stops that they might have made.

"Did you like going camping?" Tasmin asks.

"I . . . I liked it." He sounds lost.

"Tell me something you liked about it."

It takes a long time for Ben to settle down and answer. Like he needs time to think about what to say.

"He taught me about the outdoors," he says. "He let me put up the tent."

Tasmin remembers her own dad trying to teach her brother, and her brother's total lack of enthusiasm. The sound of flint striking in wet kindling, and the only heat that resulted was a simmering resentment between the two of them. "Did he ever teach you how to start a fire?"

It is the wrong thing to say, apparently. Ben is sitting bolt upright in his chair, staring straight at her like a deer caught in the headlights. He doesn't answer, but he doesn't try to evade the question, either.

This is new.

Tasmin feels a shiver of excitement at the thought that maybe she is close to a breakthrough with him. She tries, and fails, to keep the interest from her voice. "What else did he teach you, Ben?"

There was something else in the police notes, back from before they ever knew that there were more bodies. They had found some pieces of rope linked with a knot, suggesting that the killer was familiar with hunting.

"Did he ever teach you how to tie knots?" she asks.

Ben nods in answer, and it feels like they are on safe terrain. She feels like she is the one stalking prey, circling back around toward the question she has to ask him.

"And how to make tea, every camper needs to know how to make tea."

Ben still looks wary, but he answers. "We made coffee," he says.

Tamsin is so close. He is so close. Every part of her training, her whole conscience says that she should stop, that she should end the session now. That they have all the time in the world to see this through. And yet she can't help but push. *They never found her body.* "Did he teach you how to hunt, Ben?"

Ben doesn't answer. Instead, he punches himself. Hard. It's so sudden that Tamsin jumps, almost as though he went for her instead, and she is horrified when he does it again, his fist moving through a six-inch arc that crunches into the side of his mouth with a dull, wet sound.

"Ben!" She shouts his name but he is gone, and all she can do is stumble to her desk and hit the alarm, summoning the nurses to come and help her restrain and sedate him.

When they finally get the needle in and put him under, she has to hold his head up so that he doesn't inhale the blood pouring from his mouth. She can see teeth where the flesh of his lip has given way, and the impact against them has split open the first two knuckles of his right hand.

Once the mess is cleaned up and Tamsin can look at her notes, she puts a neat, black line through the word *hunter*. His name isn't the only trigger, it seems.

The police will want to hear about the camping trip, though. She picks up the phone and tries to dial, but her hands are shaking too much for her to hit the numbers right.

Tamsin puts her hands flat on her desk and curses herself for pushing him. He is a victim, and it is unprofessional for her to think of him as anything else, but when she looks him in the eyes all she can see is John Crane staring back.

CHAPTER TWENTY-ONE

CANAL ST.

The phone vibrates twice, the case almost jumping with the force of each one like the tiny motor inside the case has been knocked loose. Ben almost lunges for it, but he knows that the attempt would just make things even worse. The cop doesn't even blink, just swipes away the notifications and keeps scrolling.

"I need to answer that," he says.

"They're just trying to rattle you." The cop's face is stone-hard, giving nothing away. Ben can feel the panic coming on, each breath getting more and more difficult like his diaphragm is rising up into his chest. He's trapped. Trapped in this metal fucking box and he can't get to the phone and they're going to kill someone else if he doesn't. He's sure of it.

The cop glances up at him, like she's just remembered that he's there. "Run through this Adam-Ben thing for me again," she says. When he doesn't answer, she sighs and holds the phone up for him to see the latest message.

Hope you're holding on tight, Adam.

They aren't going to kill someone. Not yet. The knot of panic in his chest sinks back a little, but doesn't disappear entirely. "My dad is John Crane. He was . . . is . . . a serial killer."

"John Crane."

Ben nods. The way she says it, it's like she's still testing it out, trying to place it. "The papers gave him a name . . . they called him the Tuxedo Park Killer."

"Because that's where he picked up victims?"

The way she says it all so easily is unsettling. Everyone who ever knew Ben as Adam knew exactly who his father was, what he did. It made them act weird around him. It was all they ever wanted to talk about. Even when they made the effort to talk about something else— his feelings, what he wanted for dinner, baseball—he could feel them waiting for the right moment to ask about his dad.

This cop has never heard of him.

The bitch is lying. She's read your file twice.

"S-some of them," Ben says. He tries to shake off the voice in his mind, jerking his head to one side so fast that his neck cracks, and he wonders if she thinks he is losing it.

You are losing it.

The cop clicks her tongue. "See, I hate that," she says, and Ben wonders if he just said that out loud. "Giving serial killers a catchy name. To do what? Sell more newspapers? Land a fucking TV show about it?"

Ben lifts his chin. "I t-think it was the police that used it first," he says.

"Touché." She doesn't even lift an eyebrow. "So your dad killed a bunch of people, got caught, and is now doing time for it."

"He's in an institution."

"An insanity defense?" She sniffs. "I'm sure the victim's families loved hearing that."

Fucking cops. Fucking smug bitch.

The voice is like a fingernail scratching the inside of Ben's skull. Even though he's so afraid that he could easily be convinced that fear is all he has left, there's something else buried inside his head. He can't place it, but it's there all the same. A dry little voice, brimming with rage.

The cops, the politicians, the bean counters, the street sweepers. All cogs in the same machine. All of them against you.

When Ben hears the voice, it isn't defiance or disgust it's selling. It's hatred.

"So what do they want from you?" the cop asks.

"I don't know." Saying it makes him feel sick. The voice doesn't say anything, but he can feel its silent laughter in the back of his mind.

"Did you even ask?"

The answer is slow in coming. The question is like a tick digging in under his skin. He knows what they want from him. He just can't bring himself to acknowledge it. "Yes," he says.

"But it's definitely about your dad."

"It's the only way they could know that name," Ben says. He closes his eyes, like if he can't see her, then all of this goes away.

Bitch didn't get on this train to do you any favors.

The voice cuts through all of the confusion, all of the noise in Ben's head, and gives him some semblance of clarity. This is what the killer wanted to happen. This is why they picked him out, why they are using him as a buffer instead of contacting the police with their own demands. They want him to take the fall for all of this. Make it sound like something he has cooked all by himself. The big EMT—the other cop—wouldn't have thought twice about pulling the trigger if he'd known the name Adam Crane.

Suicide by cop.

When they get to 181st St., there will be an army of cops waiting to finish the job, and in the aftermath no one will want to mess with what will look like an open-and-shut case.

They'll probably decide he's as crazy as his old man, and that he sent the messages to himself.

The cop waits until he opens his eyes again, and when she speaks he can tell she's making an effort to sound reasonable. "Look. You're saying that this whole train and everyone in it is under threat of being blown up because your dad was a serial killer, and all I am trying to do is find out how that's supposed to work."

"I don't know how it's supposed to work."

"They see you on the platform this morning and think, 'Hot damn, I'm glad I brought my spare bombs with me?'"

Ben looks up at the ceiling. He knows she's right—that there's more to this, that they have all been brought here as part of some bigger plan—but right now all he wants is for her to stop talking. "I don't know. Can we please just—"

"How did they even know what train you'd be on? You think they've been following you?"

"I'm not supposed to be on this train!" Ben yells it at her. "I was supposed to be at work but I got canned and now I am stuck in this fucking tube waiting to find out who dies next. Now can you shut the fuck up for one minute?"

The cop stares him down, her expression blank. "Well, there's the psycho daddy gene kicking in," she says.

Ben lunges at her in a surge of rage that feels cathartic and terrifying at the same time. As he gets a hold of her shirtfront, he's not even certain what the hell he is trying to do, but whatever concerns he has are solved when she takes a quick step forward and punches him hard in the gut. Before he can even register the shock of that, she has his arm halfway up his back and his face in intimate contact with a steel panel.

The cop didn't look like much at first glance—short and frazzled-looking, like someone coming to the midpoint of a twenty-year hangover—but the hold she has on Ben's arm is very much the real deal. On the spectrum of uncomfortable, it feels closer to the end that threatens irreparable harm rather than something you could twist out of. It feels like she could, if she wanted to, wring Ben's arm like a wet rag.

"Let's just try to stay calm," the cop says. The way she says it sounds

like something straight out of cop school, the leaden inflection imply-
ing that not calming down is going to be the incorrect choice. "You said
you got canned?"

"I got fired today," Ben says. There's a clarity of thought that can
only be accessed through a faceful of cold steel, and the knowledge that
you won't be rid of it unless you answer some questions. "That's how
I got here."

"You notice anyone following you?"

"No."

"No one called you before you got on the train, maybe an unknown
number?"

"No."

"Someone was following you," she says. "Or knew exactly where
you were going to be. You always take this train?"

Ben nods. "Not usually at this time of day, though."

"You always walk the same route to get here? Don't stop for a coffee
or anything?"

"Can't afford a coffee," Ben says.

The cop huffs at that, like she isn't satisfied with the answer, but at
the very least she doesn't break his arm. "You didn't wonder about any
of this yourself?"

Ben remembers talking to the conductor, half distracted by the feeling that he was on the edge of a breakthrough. "I got distracted by a
nail bomb," he says.

The cop considers it. "That's fair," she says. "I'm going to let you up
now. Are you going to behave if I do?"

"Yes, ma'am."

"Officer Hendricks is fine." The cop lets him go and as Ben straightens up the rush of sensation back into his arm is a revelation at how
tight her grip was. His forearm and the last two fingers on his right
hand tingle with pins and needles.

"I'm sorry," Ben says. "I just . . . when people talk about it, it's too
much for me." It feels hard to breathe, like there's a fist-sized lump

inside his chest that is keeping him from taking a full breath. "I changed my name so nobody would ever know."

"Sorry for the cheap shot about your dad," the cop says, and even though every word of it is still burning in his head, Ben waves it away like it is forgotten. "Can I be straight with you?"

"Sure," Ben says.

"I took a big risk getting in Homeland's way back there," she says. "If everything had gone to plan for them, you'd be face down in cuffs right now."

Not a cop, then. Homeland Security. He wondered why she got in the way. "So why did you?"

"Because every instinct I have says that you are innocent," she says. "But now I'm here, I'm going to need your help proving it." She spreads her hands apologetically. "I'm not good at dancing around all this stuff about your past, and it looks like it's hitting you hard but . . . I need more."

It's only when she finishes that Ben figures out what she is getting at. "You want me to talk to them."

"It's the only way," she says. "Find out everything you can about them, maybe we can work out who they are."

The sound of bitter laughter echoes in Ben's head. *They want you to be a fucking hero now.* He can see his reflection, caught in the glass screen of his phone. The blood on his face looks black, like part of him is missing. "How am I meant to do that?"

"Push them," the cop says. "You say you know it's about your dad, so use that angle. Rattle their cage and see what happens."

"What if they set off another bomb?"

The cop gives him a look, like she was trying not to think of that herself. "I said rattle the cage, not kick it down the stairs," she says. "But I'm pretty sure they won't blow up the train."

"How do you know?"

"They want to go to 181st Street," she says. "Not uptown or the end of the line. Perps who improvise are always vague with the details when they don't know how things are going to end." She points at Ben. "They got you on this train—this specific one—for a reason. They have some kind of plan, and no amount of shit talk from you is going to stop them from following it."

Ben stares at her for a moment. "Was that pep talk to convince me, or you?" he asks.

"A bit of both." She shrugs. "Anyway, it's not like you have the tough job out of the two of us."

Ben bristles at that, his damp clothes suddenly cold and heavy on him as he straightens his back. "Babysitting me, you mean?"

"No, I'm leaving you to it," she says.

"What are you going to do?"

"I'm a detective," the cop says. "And when you're a detective, sometimes the only way to get to the truth is to go and get a bunch of people who really don't want to talk to you, to talk to you." She reaches into her back pocket and retrieves a phone. Ben doesn't recognize the brand, but it has the sleek, liquid look of a high-end model, and he wonders where she got it from. "Sometimes you even get close to the truth."

"You're going to talk to the passengers?" Ben asks.

"Yeah." She doesn't look too happy about it.

Suddenly all of Ben's problems seem small in comparison. He jerks his head toward the back of the train.

"There's still time to throw ourselves out of the back door instead," he says. It earns him a bitter laugh as she unlocks the phone and starts typing. "They are going to be so pissed. What are you going to say to them?"

"I'm going to offer them something that everybody wants," she says. "And nobody ever gets." The cop makes it sound like a riddle.

"What's that?"

"I'm going to offer them compensation," she says.

CHAPTER TWENTY-TWO

FRANKLIN ST.

When Hoyt and the EMT come out of the tunnel with that stretcher, McDiarmid wishes he had the foresight to have a photographer down in the subway to take a picture. It would have needed a bit of pixelation, given all the blood, but the sight of them coming out of the darkness and into the light, Homeland and the emergency services working together to save a civilian . . . it would have been one hell of a bitter pill for those bleeding hearts at *Time* magazine to have to put that on their cover.

When Hoyt updates him on the stunt the cop pulled, he's glad there isn't anyone with a camera nearby. It isn't often that he loses his temper, and photographic evidence of how one of the tech laptops got kicked clean across the tracks and bounced off of the far wall would do him no favors whatsoever.

Still, the conductor looks as though she's going to pull through, and that at least will be something. Part of being the lead means having to consider every scenario, including the worst-case ones. If every single person on that train dies today, there will be a reckoning, and while Mc-Diarmid has his own backup plans for the day he leaves the service—the private sector not being a place where civilian deaths counted as demerits, as long as you know the right people—minimizing any negative publicity is the smart play. More simply: if you're going out on your ass anyway, at least make sure you have a soft landing. Having Hoyt play the hero foot soldier, putting himself in the line of fire to pull an injured woman from a moving train and single-handedly carry her to safety, is just the kind of ace in the hole McDiarmid needs to play against that outcome, but it would have been worthless if the woman died.

The EMT and Hoyt are standing watching him like they are waiting to see if he's going to fire them or call the mayor to book their ticker tape parade.

"Has Hendricks checked in yet?" McDiarmid asks. "What's her status?"

Hoyt doesn't startle easily, but the question almost gets him. His eyes widen a little, and he shifts his weight from one foot to another like just thinking about it makes him uncomfortable. The EMT doesn't catch any of it, doesn't even look at him for most of it, but McDiarmid sees. Hoyt is still thinking of her as a nuisance, that she got in his way, but that's something for them to deal with later. Better to pivot and think of her as an asset, because she has eyes and ears on the train and—more crucially—a weapon.

"I almost put a bullet in her," Hoyt says. He doesn't sound pleased about his show of restraint. McDiarmid can sympathize—he sent him there to simplify the situation, but it turned into a clusterfuck.

"I'm glad you didn't. Imagine the paperwork you'd have to fill out for ventilating a NYPD detective," McDiarmid says. "Even a disgraced one."

Hoyt nods. "I'm not sure how much use she'll be," he says.

There is a tendency—by design—among the younger agents to treat anyone not under the Homeland umbrella as a liability at best and, at worst, a threat. "Well, we know she can take the initiative," McDiarmid says. "And having her there to question the passenger is better than hanging on the radio."

Hoyt grunts. It's as close to agreement as McDiarmid can hope for. "What about the passenger?"

"A limp dick's got more uses." Hoyt glances at McDiarmid. "Sir."

"That bad?"

"A buck seventy soaking wet, fear paralysis, looked like he was having a panic attack the whole time."

"He pulled a nail out of this woman's head," the EMT says. McDiarmid almost forgot she's there. "Saving her life has to count for something."

Hoyt considers it in silence. "He didn't fuck that up," he says, eventually. It's a big day for Hoyt to be so nice, and McDiarmid takes it as a good sign.

"Get in touch with Hendricks," McDiarmid says. "I gave her one of our phones. See what information she's managed to gather. If she doesn't answer, get onto our techs to fire up the LoJack on it."

The EMT clears her throat. "I should really be going," she says. "To see if I'm needed." She has been waiting for McDiarmid to dismiss her. He tries not to make a face: anything he needed, he would have gotten from Hoyt. There was no need for her to stand on ceremony.

"How was her performance, Hoyt?" He asks it over his shoulder, not taking his eyes off of the EMT.

"Brisk, sir. Strong for her size," Hoyt says. "I'd say adequate."

The EMT flushes a little bit on her cheeks and neck, but otherwise she keeps a lid on her reaction. McDiarmid smiles blandly at her and offers her a hand. "You've done the city a great service here today," he says. "On behalf of the city and the DHS, I'd like to thank you."

A look crosses her face like she's about to protest, but instead she just takes the compliment as it is offered. "Thank you, sir."

"You were able to keep up with Hoyt," he says, fishing in the inside pocket of his suit jacket. "Which I would say is far beyond what any normal man would call adequate." There's a slim metal case in his pocket, which he pulls out and opens to reveal a stack of business cards. They have his name on them, but the number attached goes to a recruitment officer. "If you ever get tired of cleaning up after, then maybe you'd like to help us stop these kinds of things from ever happening at all."

He's been told off for this in the past—in general for poaching recruits from other services and specifically him lowering himself to shilling for the DHS—but McDiarmid has strong opinions about the personal touch. Stick to recruitment through ads, and you're going to spend 90 percent of your time sifting through the trash to find someone that is going to be an asset as an agent. Targeted recruitment of promising individuals by senior field agents might not make up all the numbers, but the kind of people McDiarmid is aiming for are the ones whose experience and drive will make up the weight. And he isn't lowering himself to do it. Authority gives the request real heft. If he left the job to Hoyt, she would never take it seriously.

She takes the card and looks at it for a moment. "I have a question, sir."

"Go on."

"You think you can get all those passengers off of that train alive?"

One of the techs pauses as they go past in what McDiarmid reckons to be the greatest moment of serendipity he has ever experienced. It gives him a reason to break eye contact without looking like a liar. "Cameras and sound are coming online now, sir."

McDiarmid nods to acknowledge the man before looking straight into the EMT's eyes. "I guarantee it," he says. "When the doors open and they come off of that train, there won't be any threat left to stop them."

He says it with such conviction that she doesn't even pause to think through what that might entail. "Thank you, sir."

She turns and starts off up the stairs, taking the steps two at a time. There isn't a shred of fatigue in her. *Brisk*, McDiarmid thinks, *was an understatement.*

"You think you can get all those passengers off alive?" Hoyt watches until the EMT is gone before echoing her question.

McDiarmid gestures back at the damage on the platform. "Low explosive power, probably another pipe bomb," he says. "Maybe a couple of them daisy-chained together. If they detonate when we take the train, then we are looking at a car full of broken eardrums and a couple of corpses."

"And if they have something bigger?"

There are an endless number of technical details when it comes to explosives, but the one thing that has stuck in McDiarmid's head is detonation velocity. The nail bomb that killed the woman on the platform at Franklin was likely using some kind of black powder mix. They don't explode as much as burn superfast, reaching two to three thousand feet per second. Stuck in her bag, just the incendiary alone would have burned her badly, but not killed her outright. It needed the closed pipe and the nails to not only give it some killing power, but show Homeland that they mean business.

A high explosive, like dynamite, really does explode. Depending on the composition, it has a detonation velocity of ten to fifteen thousand feet per second. Some of the more specialist mixtures—dynamites with nitroglycerine bound in cellulose gel—can break twenty thousand. A stick of that going off anywhere inside the confined space of a subway car wouldn't need nails or a casing. The shock wave alone would cause a massive spike in the intracranial pressure of anyone trapped in the box with it. The lucky ones would lose consciousness before they died, while the rest would get to observe their cerebrospinal fluid and the occasional chunk of brain draining out through their sinuses before they succumbed.

"It would be catastrophic," McDiarmid says. Best to keep it simple. "But it's a bomb, and bombers have habits. This one wants the circus, but they've kept the body count low. I think the risk of a larger device is low."

"Low, but not zero."

McDiarmid nods. "We let the train run. They think they're getting what they want, we get time to collect intel without them escalating on us. By the time they get uptown, we should have a positive ID for the assault team."

McDiarmid glances at his watch. They have a car waiting upstairs, and there will be a clear route to it, but the traffic will be gridlock. Even with sirens and a full escort bulldozing the road for them, getting ahead of the train will take some doing. As he mounts the steps, his phone buzzes in his pocket. He fishes it out, still walking, and sees the notification is coming from Records and Administration. *Records*. He can't think of a single time that Records have had something urgent or relevant enough that it couldn't sit for a week on his desk in whatever dust-caked folder they fished it up in. They really should give him someone to field this shit for him, so that he can keep his mind focused on the task at hand. Still, he opens the alert to see what the hell they have decided is worth bothering him with.

And stops so abruptly that Hoyt almost takes him clean out.

Records have dug into the two dead bodies and came up with a link between them. Both victims worked in the same court a little over fifteen years ago. One was a cop on loan to bolster security for a high-profile murder trial, and the other was a clerk who had been recording in court at the same time. They cross-referenced everyone that was working that same trial, and in doing so found a link to a third dead body found halfway across the city this morning: some lawyer who got his throat carved up during a possible home invasion. The fact that all three had died in close proximity was a big enough deal that someone high up the chain authorized Records to access Ben Cross's sealed file and confirm that this wasn't a coincidence.

He isn't some nobody after all.

A buck seventy soaking wet he may well be, but Ben Cross's real name is Adam Crane, and his father, John Crane, is the Tuxedo Park Killer.

CHAPTER TWENTY-THREE

FIFTEEN YEARS EARLIER

It takes the janitor some time to find a table and chair that will work for Adam to give testimony. They've taken care of everything else—the camera and tripod, the microphones, the screen with a view of the judge's bench—but somehow they seem to have forgotten that Adam isn't an adult. When he sits down on the seat they've put out for him, almost half of his head disappears, the camera's view blocked by the table.

Roy Lopez makes a note on his legal pad to bring it up with the judge. The district attorney has fought tooth and nail to have John Crane's son on the witness stand in open court, and while Crane's defense team have opposed them, it has had the air of being oppositional for the sheer sake of it rather than out of any genuine concern for the boy's welfare and recovery.

The court has seen plenty of turmoil over the past few weeks: every morning a crowd gathers on the courtroom steps like a storm cloud, and they don't leave until the prison transport pulls away, its police escort being pelted from every side with food, paint, and the occasional rock. The judge herself intervened and brought Roy on board as a para-legal to make sure the risk of trauma to Adam Crane during his witness testimony is limited as much as possible while still having him testify. She had sold it to him as being a good chance to get up close on a high-profile case, but not so close that he'd be tarred and feathered by association. That said, with neither the prosecution or the defense on his side and no real authority without the judge standing at his elbow, it has not been an easy ride.

The video equipment is a loaner from the state court, ostensibly made available for all courts to use on an as-needed basis, but it means filing a request that came back twice before they granted it. Never mind that the second set of revisions were reversions of the changes he'd made on the advice of the first one, but in the end he had got it done. Finding a room in the courthouse was almost as bad, with administra-tion staff playing out some kind of passive-aggressive grudge by batting him back and forth between them with reassurances that the other person would solve the issue for him. And now the table and chair are wrong, but Roy forces himself to remember that the custodial staff probably just weren't informed, and took the closest furniture to hand so they'd save themselves a backache.

There's a change in the janitor when he comes back with the new table and chair. He barely nods in answer to Roy's thanks, and when he sets them out—plastic and steel outdoor furniture that clicks into place when you unfold it, the uneven frames rocking gently in expectation of grass or sand to hide their flaws—he does it so quickly and quietly that it almost seems like reverence. Before he leaves, he fishes a pack of cigarettes out of his back pocket, dumps the contents into his shirt pocket, and then carefully folds the box a few times to make a wedge he can slide under one leg of the chair to ensure it sits steady. Roy realizes the man isn't doing it for his sake.

He's doing it because Adam is outside.

As the janitor leaves, Roy finds himself double-checking the video camera in an anxious surge of activity. You can tick every box on your to-do list and still feel unprepared. They had agreed to limit Adam's exposure to the courthouse—one visit to get him prepped, one to testify—and so this will be the first time Roy has met him. He flattens his hands on his pant legs, the sweat prickling at his palms, and curses himself for not bringing a pack of tissues or something to take care of it. He crosses the room and opens the door as wide as it will go.

Adam Crane is small for an eleven-year-old. Small enough that the clothes they have given him hang off of him at odd angles, dead spaces puffed out with air or collapsing from a lack of structure underneath. He looks like someone has come to court with a miniature scarecrow. A uniformed cop is at Adam's left shoulder, stiff-backed and pissed, his salt-and-pepper buzz cut standing out against the redbrick color of his face.

"Roy Lopez?" the cop asks.

"That's me."

"Delivery for you." The cop bumps Adam in the back as he says it, not hard enough to call it an outright push but the intent is clear.

"Where is his escort?" The protocol they agreed with the judge is that Adam is meant to have at least two escorts at all times, and one of them should be a representative from child services. "And there's no need to push him around, Officer . . . ?" Roy leaves the question hanging.

"Look, smart-ass, you can take him or I can leave him downstairs," the cop says. "Maybe a reporter will recognize him? Who knows what could happen?"

Roy looks for the man's badge number, but it is covered with a strip of black electrical tape. He doesn't imagine for a second that it's accidental. "You can go inside, Adam," he says. "Thank you for your assistance, Officer."

The cop snorts, like he was expecting more pushback. "Yeah, don't mention it."

As the cop leaves, Adam hesitates on the threshold. He isn't looking at Roy—hasn't even acknowledged him—but instead is staring into the room like it's some kind of death trap.

Child services haven't done a formal assessment of Adam yet, but the notes they sent ahead are enough that Roy knows he has a problem with enclosed spaces. Doesn't like closed doors, and people standing in the way of the exit, even if he has no intention of leaving. Knowing it is one thing, but dealing with it is entirely another. Roy has a whole toolbox stuffed with strategies for handling adult clients—shy ones, scared ones, angry ones—but an eleven-year-old might as well be an alien from another planet as far as Roy's skill set goes. *Where the hell is the kid's handler?*

Roy settles for letting Adam decide for himself. "Hey," he says. "My name's Roy Lopez. I'm a paralegal working on behalf of the court for the next few weeks."

Adam looks up at him like he's just noticed that Roy is there. "On my dad's case, you mean?"

"Yeah, that's the one."

"Which side are you on?"

Roy gets what he's asking. *Prosecution or defense.* "I'm on your side," Roy says. "Judge asked me to come in and make sure we did the right thing by you."

Adam looks back at the door. "Like he is meant to be on my side?"

"Yeah, I'm going to find out who that guy was and the judge is going to make sure he doesn't get back in here," Roy says. "Look, I'm not sure where your escort went, but if you want to come in and have a seat, I'll give them a call and let them know you're safe."

Roy heads back into the room, and he offers silent thanks to the Gods of Faking It Till You Make It that Adam follows him inside and takes a seat. Roy gets his work phone out and checks the signal before flicking through the folder to find the number of the contact at child services. No way they should have left him at all, let alone in the care of a walking misconduct suit.

"Is that camera filming me?"

Roy glances up from what he's doing to the camera set up across the table.

"No," he says, and points. "No red light on the front? It's not recording."

"But that one is." On the screen next to the camera, they can see the empty bench and the judge's microphone.

"I wanted to show you what you'll be able to see while you testify," Roy says. "That's where the judge will be sitting."

"What about everyone else?"

"You won't see them."

"I just talk to the judge?"

"That's the rules. She'll ask you some questions, and all you have to do is answer them the best you can."

"About my dad, right?"

The notes say that Adam doesn't like talking about what happened. There is nothing in there about what to do or say if he brings it up. Roy takes a deep breath.

"Yeah, Adam. She's going to ask about your dad," Roy says. "It's going to be tough, but just do your best."

"What if I don't know the answer? Will I go to jail?"

Roy almost laughs, but checks himself. It's the sort of thing a kid's imagination would conjure up. "No, you won't go to jail. If you don't know, you say you don't know. If you can't remember, you can't remember. Nobody is going to be mad at you. You're not in any kind of trouble."

"What if I say the wrong thing?"

Roy stops. This feels like a question for social services, but it sets off something in the lawyer part of his soul that he can't let slide. He wonders if the cop said anything to him on the way up. "What do you mean by that?"

"This is about putting my dad in jail, right?" Adam asks, but Roy can tell that it's rhetorical and gives him space. One of the best pieces of advice he ever got was about not jumping in on someone talking. You give them silence, and they will try to fill it. "It's just . . . what if my testimony means that they have to let him go?"

If it were an adult, Roy's gut would be doing somersaults. But Adam is an eleven-year-old kid, an eleven-year-old kid who ended up with a bullet in him because his dad knew the police were closing in.

"Would I have to go back to live with him?" Adam asks.

Roy has seen enough of the case materials to know that there is no way that the kid's testimony is going to change a damn thing about the outcome of this case. John Crane is going to rot in a cell until the sun winks out in the sky.

Roy takes a deep breath. "That won't happen," he says. "And you don't have to worry about saying anything wrong. All you have to do is tell the truth."

Adam blinks, his eyelids fluttering like the answer has taken him by surprise. Roy tells himself that he's just a kid, that there's nothing to read into it, but he can't shake the feeling that the words *the truth* have just shaken Adam to his core.

"Is the judge nice?" Adam asks, and Roy has to think for a second to follow the change of topic, reminding himself that kids aren't mature enough to manipulate a conversation. What feels like subtlety to a grown-up is probably more like free association as thoughts bounce around inside the kid's skull.

"She's nice," Roy says. "For a judge. She's got an important job to do, so she can come across a little serious, but she's a good person."

Roy can feel the sweat patch building in the small of his back just thinking about how deep the shit will be if Adam freaks out, but the kid seems to be taking it all in stride. He just nods, like the answer is what he expected to hear.

Roy finds the numbers from child services at the back of his file. There's one that looks like a generic switchboard line, and a second that is marked with the name *Dr. Hardy*. The personal call is always better. "I'll just call this number for your escort and we'll see where the hell they—"

"What's going to happen to me?"

Roy pauses mid-dial. "What do you mean?"

"If my dad goes to jail," Adam says. "Where am I going to go?"

"Well, you'll stay with child services for a little bit, and I guess they'll try and find somewhere for you to stay." Roy shrugs to cover the fact he's dancing around having to mention the foster system. "I really don't know that much about it."

"Do you think they'll let me stay with my mom?"

Adam's mom is on life support in a hospital on the other side of the city. When Crane saw the police coming, he pulled a knife and stabbed her four times in the back before heading out to give himself up. Each stab wound was a foot apart, like he was marking out the corners of a square, and from the tearing on each wound they reckon he did all four in less than two seconds. He didn't say a word about it, except to apologize to his arresting officer for getting blood on their handcuffs.

Roy resists the urge to put a hand on the boy's shoulder. He doesn't like to be touched, and the instruction is repeated in the notes with regards to men.

"I don't know," Roy says. "She could pull through, but even if she does, it might take some time before she feels well enough to look after you."

Adam is on the verge of tears. Hell, just thinking about it has Roy feeling the same way. He squats down, so that they are on the same eye level. "Look. I can't promise anything, but if it was my mom she'd try her hardest to be there for me, okay?"

Adam swallows. "Okay."

"That's just what moms do, right?"

Adam blinks, and a tear rolls down his face, but it doesn't feel like a bad thing to see it. Considering the circumstances, it'd be worse if he showed no emotion at all.

Roy straightens up to see that there's a woman standing in the doorway. Gray suit, blouse, low heels, and the face of someone who's sprinted the whole way to get here. It looks like he won't need to call child services after all.

"Hey! Doctor Hardy, right?" Roy puts his hand out. "My name's Roy Lopez. I'm a paralegal working with Judge Williams—"

As Roy comes around the far side of the table—trying not to stack bodies between Adam and the doorway, just like they asked—he realizes that he has made a terrible mistake. The woman doesn't acknowledge him at all, and instead charges at Adam, her face twisting in rage as she grabs hold of his arms and hauls him bodily out of his chair.

"Where is she? Where is my daughter?"

Adam doesn't even react as she bears him along with her, and Roy scrambles to get back around the table, knocking against the tripod as he passes, his hands fumbling to catch the camera and keep it from falling. He sets it upright, hitting the Record button on the way. Better than her word against his, if this goes bad.

"Tell me where she is!" She pushes Adam against the far wall, hard enough that his head hits it with a loud, hollow smack, and she would be falling under the sudden weight of him sagging in her arms if Roy wasn't there to grab Adam by the shirtfront and, with his other arm, sweep her away.

"You can't be in here, lady!" He yells it at her, loud enough that he hopes someone in the hallway outside will hear, because there's no panic button in this room, and even if his phone wasn't over on the table, he now has both hands occupied trying to keep Adam's limp body upright.

"He knows where she is! They were all in on it together! You get him to tell me where she is!"

She's the mom of one of the victims. She's still screaming, her face blank with panic, and Roy can see that she hasn't planned for any of this. She's looking at the half-conscious kid he's holding, then at him, and even though she's still yelling she is starting to back away, like somewhere below all that rage and pain, there's a part of her that knows this is a bad idea.

"Don't do this, ma'am," Roy says. "This isn't the right way." *He's just a kid*, he wants to say, but he doesn't need to. She moves to say something, but Adam is heavier than he looks, and when his weight shifts Roy has to jump to catch him, and the sight of the boy hanging limp in his arms scares her.

"I didn't mean to hurt him." Her voice is small when she finally speaks.

"I know," Roy says. "You were upset. You weren't thinking." He lowers Adam down to the floor, then starts taking off his jacket, balling it up to make a cushion to put under the kid's head.

"Am I under arrest?"

Roy looks down at Adam. He can't remember if there's a recovery position that's just for kids, or if he is not meant to move him at all. They did first aid training back when he first started, but all Roy can remember of it is that the coffee was real bad.

That's just what moms do, right?

"Look," he says. "You go back the way you came, and you don't come near this kid again, and I'll talk to the judge. We'll call it bad luck. That you walked in the wrong door, and you were caught off guard."

She has to know that she's in the wrong, and yet something in her still bristles at the offer. "I need an answer," she says. "I'm not leaving until I get one."

Roy lifts his arm and points at the camera, where the red light shows that it is bearing witness. "You leave now, or I go find the cop who tipped you off," he says. "I see you within a hundred feet of this kid again, this tape and his name both go to the defense team and they will drop all the insanity bullshit they're teeing up and push straight to mistrial. Do you understand me?"

She nods once, her expression just like the one the cop had. Hatred, locked up tight behind a face like stone. "I understand."

CHAPTER TWENTY-FOUR

CHRISTOPHER ST.-STONEWALL.

The rear car of the train is empty. One of the windows down at the back end of the train has been shattered, a spiderweb constellation of cracks caused by a glancing blow from some fragment of shrapnel, and that seems to have been enough to drive everyone forward into the next car. That none of them tried to jump down to the tracks and run for freedom doesn't surprise her in the slightest: everyone might be thinking about it, but nobody wants to be the first one to take the leap.

Being out of the cramped rear cab is a relief. Getting away from Ben, or Adam, or whomever he is, is a relief. They offer de-escalation training for mental health interventions on the force, but from what she has seen of him, he is far past the point of being talked down from whatever is going on in his head. Half the time she was with him, he looked like he was off on his own planet. More than once she caught him desperately trying not to vocalize whatever conversation was happening inside his head.

Kelly has never heard of the Tuxedo Park Killer, but she is certain of one thing: he did a fucking number on his own son.

Maybe she shouldn't have told him to push the suspects, but then it could well be that showing them a bit of backbone is exactly what he needs to get centered.

In any case, to answer for the sin of suggesting it, Kelly has to deal with the passengers.

Walking the length of the empty car, Kelly can understand what a deep-sea diver must feel like on the way down into an abyss. All your training, all your experience is there to prepare you for this moment, and yet when you turn your lights on down in the crushing darkness, it means coming face-to-face with something alien, a world different to everything you've ever known. Opening that door on the first car full of tired, too-hot, and—worst of all—late New Yorkers, she doesn't even try to brace herself. Whatever is about to hit her will hit her full force, and there isn't a damn thing she can do about it.

What is waiting for her is nothing. Every passenger with a phone is held thrall by their screen, scrolling through social media or reading the news. Everyone who isn't holding a phone is either watching someone else's in their peripheral vision or simply staring off into the middle distance like there isn't a single fucking thing left in the Universe that could surprise them.

Still, Kelly has a job to do. Hoyt responded quicker than she expected, and without a single mention of her obstructing his shot or how her ass is going to end up in a sling over it.

She guesses that he is leaving that as a special treat for if she gets out of this alive.

Homeland approves of her canvassing the passengers, but warns her against answering any questions, especially about the explosion at Franklin St. In Hoyt's words, the more information she gives, the greater the potential for a worst possible outcome. Kelly gets the feeling that the real sticking point for him isn't the outcome itself, but the timing. They would rather have a bad thing happen and be in control of everything around it than have it simply happen, and for once Kelly doesn't disagree with him. If shit is going to go down, you want it where the ambulances are waiting.

It takes only a few minutes for Homeland's tech guys to hook themselves into the MTA's refund system and send her a link she can share with the passengers.

A full refund, dependent on the person's willingness to share enough personal information that Homeland can find out everything about them: it's either going to work like a charm, or Kelly is unwittingly adding *incitement to riot* onto the list of charges she will be coming out of this with.

She takes a deep breath and straightens up, getting ready to speak loud enough that the whole car hears it.

"Everyone, if I can have your attention please—"

"Pipe down, we heard it already." A guy sitting by the door on Kelly's left says it. He's sitting with his legs spread wide, elbows on knees, his forehead pressed into the palms of his hands like he's trying to hold his eyeballs in.

"Excuse me?"

He lifts his head and glares at her. The word *hungover* doesn't do his appearance justice. He looks like a statue carved out of cigarette ash, like a ghost taking the 1 train on its way to a new job haunting the inside of a grandfather clock.

"Driver announced it. We gotta go all the way up to 181st before we can get off. The police have closed off all the other stations."

"Homeland, you mean."

"Whatever," he says. "You got any water or a Coke or something?"

"Do I look like a concession stand?"

"You ain't the conductor, I saw her already."

Kelly almost looks down to check for any blood on her outfit. She was sure none got on her, but in the chaos of the transfer she could have missed something. The passenger says nothing else, so she plows on. "I was going to tell everyone that the mayor's office has authorized the release of funds for compensation," she says. "But if you don't want to hear it . . ."

"Compensation? That'd be a Goddamn first."

Kelly shrugs. "Homeland shut down half the city," she says. She has no idea if this is true or not. "Guess they've put his ass in a sling and he's aiming for reelection."

"How much are we talking about?"

"Full fare plus something for the time wasted." She brandishes the phone that McDiarmid gave her, the screen already active and showing the MTA site with a QR code on it. "All I know is you fill in your details here—where you got on, where you were going—and they'll work out how much you're owed."

"There it is," he says. "Government form to fill out first. Probably get twenty bucks and my name on a watchlist for the rest of my natural life." Kelly says nothing, and after a moment's indecision he gets his phone out to take a picture of the QR code. His hands are shaking so badly that it takes him three tries to get it. "You know how much the cops get from this city?"

"No clue," Kelly says.

"Ten thousand dollars a minute," he says. "Five point five billion a year."

"Is that right?"

"You think they'd do something to earn it," he says.

Kelly keeps her expression neutral. "You want to know how much I get for being stuck on here?"

"How much?"

"Not a Goddamn thing."

"Then you should talk to your union rep." He doesn't look up from his phone screen when he says it, indicating that his interest in their conversation has expired.

The people sitting farther up haven't spoken or glanced in Kelly's direction a single time, and yet as she moves forward they are all getting their phones ready to scan the code she's bringing with her. In her head she has been practicing her spiel over and over, anticipating having to say it again and again, explaining to half the passengers how a QR code works, trying to get past all their questions about *when will we get there?* Or *what the fuck is going on?* Instead, all she has to do is walk down the car with the phone screen facing outward, like an offering, and everyone waits quiet and patient to take their turns in accepting it. The only chatter is the occasional whispered argument about the details they are putting into the form—*You said we'd get off at Times Square, not Penn. Faster? The hell it is*—but otherwise the car is silent.

It's only near the end of the car Kelly recognizes her mistake. The passengers aren't enraged, or outraged, or inclined to any other kind of outburst, because they are still in the thick of it. She remembers footage from some kind of bomb shelter, a windowless basement room packed from one wall to the other with terrified kids and the occasional surviving parent. Every single one of them was silent. None of them so much as looked at the camera. Nobody asked when it would end, or if they were going to eat, or why this was happening to them. While the camera was running, a missile or a bomb struck close by, and the frame juddered with the shock wave, a violence notable by the complete lack of reaction from the people crowded in the shot.

If they weren't on the train, if they were safe, they would be full of questions. Instead they are stuck here, and every one of them has personally experienced the explosion from the platform. They are stranded way further up shit creek than they ever thought they would be and all they can do is hunker down, and hope that they get through this.

Kelly lets the last few scan their codes, gives the car one last look for weirdness, and moves on to the next.

The offer of compensation has not been authorized by the mayor at all. The website might belong to the MTA, but the information it is gathering is all going to the Department of Homeland Security.

Just get them to fill in the form. That's all the message says. And if they don't want to do it, try and remember what they look like, where they are sitting, if they have anything with them. Kelly has her own personal checklist—if they make a fuss about the form, obvious creeps, lugging a massive bag—and she is doing her best to take it all in: who is coping well, who is on the verge of breaking, who is trying to hide something.

The next car goes by much the same as the first one—everyone that can scan the code getting started on the form as soon as they can get it to load. It doesn't take long before Homeland starts getting bandwidth issues on their end, and Kelly is apologizing for how long the page is taking to load; assuring people that if they keep trying, they'll get through; yes, they will get their money.

Weird how the whole question of survival goes clean out of the window when there's a risk that everyone else but you could be in line for a cash payout.

A hand waving Kelly on brings her attention back to the passengers. The guy waving her on is big: from the way he can't quite sit comfortably without getting his legs in someone else's business, he's probably pushing six-three or six-four standing up. Broad-shouldered, too, but soft around the edges, like a college linebacker who didn't quite make the cut for pro and has let things slide since. His expression seems friendly, but Kelly has met enough of the public to know when someone is pissed and trying to put a good face on it.

"Don't stress it," he says. He doesn't sound American. "Don't think they'll bother wiring money to us, we're meant to be flying back tomorrow."

Kelly doesn't have time to answer before the woman next to him cuts in.

"Oh my God, Lawrence, just fill it out."

The man's expression doesn't change, but he draws in a deep, exasperated breath in through his nose. "So we're just giving my name out to everyone, are we?"

"Nobody is listening to us!"

"Yeah, but here I am trying to politely get out of giving up every one of my details to yet another database, and here's you just throwing my name around."

The woman groans and clutches at the air with her palm upward, her gaze lifted to the roof as though imploring an unseen Heaven beyond, a gesture instantly recognizable to any woman who has ever had to deal with a man. She is a lot smaller than her partner, with the last tint of what was once an electric blue dye job fading from her blond hair. Kelly dreads to think of the state of every pillow her head has touched, and is impressed that secondhand contact hasn't left her with the complexion of a Smurf.

"I don't get it," she says. Kelly thinks that maybe they are British. Out of state accents sound foreign to her, and even though tourists swarm the city, she hasn't met that many people from outside the continental US. They mostly stay clear of murder scenes. His accent sounds more like what she's heard on TV, and while the woman's is more distinct, it doesn't sound like she's speaking a second language. "Anyway, even if they don't give us any compensation, we can use it to show we were here and claim on the travel insurance."

"Claim what, though?"

"I don't know? Stress, emotional trauma, losing out on a day of our trip? Maybe we just say we got whiplash or something when the train stopped."

"They'd want to see a doctor's note for that. If you want, I could kick you in the face so you'd have something for the ER."

"I could kick you in the balls."

"So romantic."

"Learned it all from you, didn't I?"

Kelly stands with the phone held out to them, waiting for the bickering to stop and for one of them to just scan it. She bristles at the way he dropped a threat so casually, but the woman doesn't seem even slightly alarmed. It's more like she is relishing the opportunity to return it with interest.

The man, Lawrence, breaks off and leans toward Kelly, speaking in a much lower, faster tone. "But seriously, what is going on?"

"We're moving all of the trains out of the city."

"Yeah, I got that bit already from the announcement," he says. "I'm asking what's really going on."

"I . . . don't know what you mean," Kelly says.

"Oh, here we go," the woman says. "Don't blame me now you've got him started."

Lawrence ignores the jab. "So. There was an explosion, back at the other station, yeah? But not a big one because if it had been a big one this train would have been kicked off the rails or they'd be trying to dig us out." He waits for some kind of confirmation, but Kelly has her best *no comment* expression ready. It doesn't put him off in the slightest.

"I'll take the silent treatment as a yes," he says. "Now, for a five-pound explosive device, the preferred evacuation distance is twelve hundred feet. For a fifty-pound explosive, it's eighteen hundred and fifty feet. All we had to do was move half a kilometer down the tunnel, maybe even as far as the next station, and we would have been considered in the safe zone."

"Maybe they're worried it's bigger," the woman says.

"Fifty pounds is about a suitcase worth," he says. "Any bigger and you'll stick out a mile, not just because it's massive but also because you'd be sweating like a racehorse just trying to carry it."

As much as she was worried about holding every weirdo and crank in her short-term memory, she doesn't think she'll forget this one in a hurry. "What is it you do for a living, exactly?"

He grins, like he can't help it. "That's classified."

"Thanks for that," the woman says. "He loves telling people his job is classified."

"It is, though." He glances at his partner and the grin vanishes. "Look, the only other explanation is that you don't need to do an evacuation if you get rid of the problem." He leans closer. "Which would mean the problem is on the train."

Kelly can feel her eyes creeping downward, looking for a suitcase that could hold, all told, about fifty pounds in weight.

"You don't have to say anything," he says. "We'll scan your code and fill the form in. Just give me some sort of sign so I know that, if it comes to it, I need to be ready to get her out of here."

There is no case at their feet. While he gets his phone ready, Kelly weighs up the risk of telling him what's really going on versus the likelihood that he's going to kick off a panic. He doesn't seem tense or twitchy. Doesn't give any sign that he's worked out exactly where the threat lies, or that he's looking to try anything. He looks honest and, after years of door knocking and interviews, for Kelly to actually feel like someone is being honest with her is a special occasion.

"You folks bring an umbrella?" she asks.

"Nope," the woman answers. "It's been so hot."

"Thought you Brits took one everywhere." Kelly meets the man's eyes. "Never know when a storm's gonna hit."

Before he can acknowledge her, she's already moving on to the next passenger, her phone held out screen-first.

CHAPTER TWENTY-FIVE

CHRISTOPHER ST.–STONEWALL.

The first thing that Ben tries to think of when the cop leaves is what excuse he can give her when she comes back. He doesn't want to send a message. He doesn't want to acknowledge the killer at all. Being on his own—being Ben—has kept him safe for a long time. It has kept him steady. Being Ben makes him feel like he's a normal person, and that he isn't faking it.

Messaging them means giving that up. It means accepting that for all the time that has passed, he is still Adam, and that nothing has ever been or will ever be normal for him again.

It means accepting what he did.

If he had to make a call, or use some kind of video link, it would be easy to lie to the cop. He could say that the signal kept dropping, or that he wanted to save what battery he has left. Messages go through easily, and even if they don't, then it still shows that you tried. All she has to do is look at the screen, and the story will fall apart.

He could break the phone. Just smash the fucking thing, and be done with it. He should have done that right at the start of this, at the very first picture of a body. He should have gotten off of the train and tossed his phone and disappeared.

He should have known.

He let himself get too comfortable, thinking that no one would ever connect him back to his dad again.

Nothing stays buried.

Something about the thought fills Ben with a powerful sense of dread. He can't quite place why, but it's like carrying a bad tooth: he can feel himself working around whatever it is because every time he comes close to recognizing it, he breaks out in a cold sweat.

Anyway, he can't smash his phone. Not now. Things have gone too far for him to just leave the killer on the other end of the message chain in the dark. How many people would they kill trying to get his attention? Or, if he frustrated their plans, would they just detonate whatever bomb they have left, long before reaching their destination?

"Find out everything you can." That was what the cop asked for. Ben doesn't even know where to start, and even if he did, he isn't certain that he is ready to go there. They know who he is, and who his father is. The thought of how much more they could know terrifies him. It's like he is standing back at the entrance of the subway station, staring down into the dark, except this time it isn't a fear of the unknown that scares him.

It's that he knows with absolute certainty what's down there.

The phone is shaking in his grip. He can't just sit here and do nothing. Doing nothing at all means that the killer's plan—whatever it is—will play out exactly how they want it to. They want to keep him under control, and they are using his fear as a leash. That's why they are taunting him with the name: because they know he doesn't want to say it. They know that he's scared.

Ben remembers the way the cop reacted to the name Adam Crane. It felt like insanity to say it out loud, to admit who he is—who he was—and for her to not even blink. Like hearing it was the very least of her problems.

Maybe the killer hasn't taken that into account. Fifteen years might have sharpened the razor-thin edge of their grudge against him, but for everyone else those crimes have disappeared, washed away by a constant flow of fresh atrocities fed from all over the world, straight to people's phones. Maybe the one thing they have in common with Ben is that they are the only ones for whom Adam Crane has any meaning at all.

Ben unlocks the phone. The battery icon is about half empty now—lower than half if he is honest about it—and opens the message app. They have not tried to get in touch since the train started moving.

He needs to get their attention.

Ben doesn't send them a message. Instead, he picks up the radio mic.

"This is South Ferry two-one-five," he says.

"Go ahead, South Ferry," Hoyt answers right away, like he has been waiting for the transmission.

"I was . . . wondering how the conductor is." The mic is shaking in Ben's hands. He can't say the name. Giving it up to the cop is one thing, but on the radio it might as well be the whole world he's saying it to.

"She'll pull through," Hoyt says. "She took a bump getting off the train, though."

There are things that Hoyt can't say on an open line, either. Ben can almost feel the pressure from the silent radio, willing him to keep his mouth shut about Detective Hendricks, to buy as much time as possible before the killer works out that someone got on the train.

"I'm being set up," Ben says.

There is a bigger pause before Hoyt answers. When he does, he sounds every word out carefully. "Tell me about that, Ben."

Hearing Hoyt say *Ben* is like having a bucket of cold water dumped over him. Hoyt knows. Ben isn't sure how, but Homeland has found out about his past. About who he is. He feels as though it should be terrifying, but instead it feels like a weight being lifted.

"I wasn't born Ben Cross," Ben says. He takes a deep breath. "My real name is Adam Crane. My dad is John Crane. Fifteen years ago, he . . . he killed twelve girls in upstate New York. I was given a new name to protect me after they put him in a padded room for the rest of his natural life."

"You say you're being set up." Hoyt's voice is flat on the radio, and Ben can't tell if it's a limit of the technology or that Hoyt just doesn't believe him.

"They know about my dad," Ben says. "The people doing this. They keep calling me Adam in all the messages they send. I think . . . I think they did it so I would try and hide it from you."

"Why would they do that, Adam?"

The sound of Hoyt's voice saying it down the line makes Ben feel like he is being folded in half. He has to put the mic down and press his hands together, knuckles white with the effort of keeping them there, until he calms down enough that he can speak again. "Please call me Ben," he says.

"Okay, Ben," Hoyt says. "Whatever you want."

"Whatever they plan on doing, they want me to take the blame for it."

"How does that work?"

"I . . . I've been in and out of care my whole life," Ben says. "On top of that, my dad is a serial killer." He can picture what would have happened if the detective hadn't been there to stop him from getting shot. He can almost feel where the bullet would hit him: a single round high on his chest—an attempted head shot spoiled by a quirk of geometry— the wound spiraling outward toward his back, the hollow point opening like a flower in bloom. "I'm a walking red flag. All they had to do was point at me and I'm your prime suspect.

"They want you looking at me," he says. Ben's phone buzzes. They might be biting, but there is no point in him looking or responding until the hook has caught. "Because they know once I'm dead or in cuffs then no one will ever look any further."

His phone vibrates again. It jumps in Ben's hand, and he imagines that it is somehow angry that he hasn't answered the first message.

He has them, but he has to make sure.

"That's why they chose me," he says. He's almost forgotten how easy it is to lie when you need to. "Because if I take the fall, then they get to walk away."

Ben misses whatever Hoyt is saying in reply—a question, maybe—as he turns the phone to face him, sweat prickling across his brow and the damp cloth of his shirt suddenly cold where it clings to his sides.

The first message is still there on the lock screen, waiting to be acknowledged: Stop telling lies, Adam.

The second, below it: Do I need to make you stop?

Ben unlocks the phone and types out his reply.

I haven't lied. Push them, that's what the cop said. Rattle their cage. They have chosen him for a reason, but maybe if he makes it seem small and petty, they will lose their temper and let something slip.

He just hopes that the thing they let slip isn't a detonator.

I'm telling Homeland what they need to know, he types. Somehow you found out who I was and you saw your chance to make me a patsy.

They answer fast.

Are you trying to get a rise out of me?

Ben blinks at the screen. A nonanswer. He knows enough from spending his entire adolescence being bounced from one therapist to the next about what it means when you avoid the question.

You killed three people. Ben shivers as he types it out. It was very close to being four. Seems like you're mad enough already. So what am I lying about?

> You think it was chance that led me to you? Just finding you took me a long time. I've been dreaming of this moment even longer.

> You've been dreaming of killing innocent people? If this is about me, why do any of this? You could have just turned up at my door with a gun.

> No one innocent has died today. But you can change that if you keep pissing me off.

A chill passes through Ben at that, but he has momentum now. He types fast, letting the screen be the mask that keeps them from seeing how scared he is.

> I don't believe you. You were going to kill those people anyway. You're just like every other person who knows I'm Adam Crane: all you want is to use my dad's name. Most people would want to sell a book, but you need an alibi.

All of the replies so far have come in hot, like the killer can't type them fast enough. Now, the screen stays dark. Ben feels the train judder and shift as it rolls on, like it finds the silence uncomfortable. He knows a reply is coming, though. He can feel the tension between him and the killer, the pressure he has built up by taunting them straining to be released. Ben imagines them typing it out, stabbing the letters one at a time, pressing the screen hard enough that they would put a finger clean through it if they could.

After what feels like an age, a new message arrives.

> You are on this train because I want you on it. The cop I killed. The clerk with the bag. They were not here

> *by chance. I brought them here so that you could see them one more time before they died. You are going to die too, Adam, but before you do I want you to admit what you really are. I put you on this train so that the whole world can witness your punishment.*

Ben stares at the message, the words *you are going to die too* searing themselves into his consciousness like burning letters etched across the inside surface of his skull. Up until this exact moment, he has been able to fool himself about his chances. That no matter how many taunting messages they send or how many other passengers die, he will be able to walk away. A simple statement of fact is enough to tear away that conceit, and Ben can feel his heart racing as panic takes its place.

The clerk with the bag. The woman at Franklin St. She recognized him. She knew who he was, and was afraid of him. That fear got her killed, and Ben wonders if that was part of it. If they knew she would run from him.

His phone buzzes again.

Don't think I don't know about your friend walking up and down the train, the message says. Push me again and I'll make sure she regrets it.

Reading the message, Ben feels like he's been caught wrist-deep in a cookie jar. He tries not to imagine the cop walking down the train with a target on her back. That she has been made, and she doesn't even know it. Won't even know it, until there's a click and any other thoughts in her head go through the same kind of acceleration that every other victim's does.

Ben doesn't send any message in return. He can't.

He can't type because his hands are shaking too much for him to type. He can't tell if it is fear or excitement, but Ben has had a revelation.

He knows who the dead man is. The first one. The one in the photo. The one killed on his front doorstep. He couldn't place him before now, but with the words *the cop* and *the clerk* something clicked in

Ben's memory and he can put his finger on the exact place and time he first saw him.

A clerk of the court.

He was some kind of lawyer assigned to watch Ben during his dad's trial. Roy something. Ben remembers him because he was someone his eleven-year-old self trusted, and the number of people in that particular corner of his mind is very limited.

The woman on the train knew who Ben was because she had been there, too. He never spoke to the guy who got shot, but he doesn't doubt there would have been a flicker of recognition if he had.

You are on this train because I want you on it.

Ben told Homeland that he was being set up to take the fall for the bombing, but the fact that all of these people have died—two of them on the same train that he is on—test that theory past its breaking point.

It's all about Ben. About the trial.

About why even if they locked his dad up forever, he could never tell them the truth.

CHAPTER TWENTY-SIX

FIFTEEN YEARS EARLIER

District attorney is a powerful position to hold, and given the ease with which the role could be abused, Roy Lopez has always understood there are certain expectations for the public face that the DA presents. Sober. Measured. Responsible. He never considered it until this moment, but it stands to reason that those expectations would evaporate once the public is removed from the equation.

From how their meeting has gone so far, DA Ross Armstrong has failed to be measured or responsible. While he would never consent, and no one present could compel a blood alcohol sample, between the smell of him and the indigo-to-violet color chart that is his complexion, Roy would put hard money that he'd be incapable of checking off sober on that list at any point in the next four to six hours.

"I want that kid back in the courtroom." Armstrong stabs his forefinger into the desk like he's trying to hammer his point in like a nail. Roy wonders if being angry makes you numb, because there's no way that isn't going to hurt like a bitch in the morning. "Not on a video screen. Not in another room. I want him in the courtroom."

Doctor Hardy, for her part, has barely moved or spoken since Roy and the DA came into her office. Roy got the tip that Armstrong was on the warpath after Adam's—*Ben's*—testimony and got there a slim thirty seconds ahead of the other man's BMW, taking the turn into the parking lot at roughly twice the acceptable speed and losing most of its tires' rubber in the process. The receptionist called security as Armstrong stalked past her desk, and Roy followed in their wake in the vain hope that he'd get to see the DA take a waist-high tackle from two ex-linebackers in white polo shirts. Doctor Hardy stayed put behind her desk as Armstrong went into her office. He tried to slam the door open for maximum dramatic effect, but hadn't reckoned on the fact her room was hardened against that exact type of outburst. Softened by springs or some kind of hydraulic damper, the door sprung open six inches and stopped, before slowly giving way in a smooth, even manner. She waved off her security team, but not before one of them put a heavy hand on the DA's shoulder and brought his indignant charge into the room to a clean halt six feet short of her desk.

Doctor Hardy steeples her fingers, then apparently thinks better of it and places her hands palms-down in front of her, as though bracing herself.

"That will not be possible," she says.

"Bullshit. I want him back in there. Tomorrow."

"And you've okayed that with the judge?" A look at Roy as she asks it. He offers up a just-perceptible shake of his head by way of an answer. Roy isn't sure how good Armstrong's peripheral vision is. "I'll take your simmering silence as a 'no.'"

"That kid sat there and straight up lied," Armstrong says. "And it doesn't matter what you feel, or what the judge will say when this fuck-ing asslicker"—he gestures, blindly, in Roy's direction—"tells her. He lied to her face. I know it, you know it, and everyone in that courtroom knows it."

Doctor Hardy's expression doesn't falter, but she cocks her head at the last part. "To what part of my professional duty are you seeking to appeal to, Mister Armstrong? Because you have no legal grounds on which to compel me."

"Don't tell me what the law says I can and cannot compel you to do."

"I hardly need to when you come barging into my office, reeking of whatever bottle it is you keep in the bottom drawer for times of stress," she says. "I imagine if there was some law-based conduit by which you could achieve your aims, I would have received a phone call or a hand-delivered letter from one of your underlings." She lifts her right hand from where it has been resting on the table in front of her to pick up a pen, and Roy can just make out the sheen her nerves have left on the wood. She makes a brief note on the pad to her right. Roy, long used to watching what people write upside down, can see the date and time alongside Armstrong's name. She adds Roy's name alongside three more, which he assumes are the names of her colleagues and the security team. "Did you drive here today, Mister Armstrong?"

"That kid sat in court today and described, on tape and on the record, an event that did not happen," Armstrong says. "Where did he conjure this birthday party of his up from, exactly? Perhaps we should subpoena your office to see what kind of coaching you have been giving him."

"Adam Crane told you the truth as he understands it," Doctor Hardy says. "He is a victim of severe psychological and possibly physical trauma. You cannot simply yell at him and expect anything better than you have seen to date. That he was able to testify at all is close to a miracle."

"Testify, and completely destroy the hopes of that family!" Armstrong snatches the pad she has been writing on and throws it, spinning, to crash against the wall. Roy jumps at the violence, but Doctor Hardy answers it by becoming, impossibly, even more still.

Roy clears his throat. "I must insist that you take a seat, sir."

The district attorney rounds on him. "Find your balls, did you?"

Roy tries to take some courage from the doctor's complete refusal to react to his tantrum, and holds Armstrong's gaze. "With respect, risking the outcome of this trial over witness intimidation and an assault charge will not help that family find their daughter."

Armstrong's nostrils flare so wide that Roy imagines with the right angle and a powerful flashlight he would be able to see the underside of the man's brain, every neuron pulsing with suppressed rage. After a moment's consideration, the DA sits down.

"Adam Crane testified today that a birthday party took place at his family home on the sixteenth of April last year." Armstrong's anger is gone, completely. He lays out the facts of Adam's testimony like he's reading off of a rap sheet in court. "That cake was served. That he went camping with his dad, which got canceled because of rain, and later that night he got in trouble for wearing shoes in the house."

"He did."

"We know for a fact that they never had cake in their yard. We have spoken to the neighbor. The Crane family didn't borrow a table from him. They were rarely seen by him, let alone on speaking terms."

"I am aware of the discrepancies," Doctor Hardy says.

Armstrong ignores her and presses on. "He did not have camping gear in the house. The weather report from that day says that less than a millimeter of rain fell across upstate New York."

"I know that as well."

"Here's something you don't know," Armstrong says. "We went over every inch of Adam Crane's bedroom. Fiber, prints, DNA." He leans forward. "No child has set foot in that room in a year or more."

"I understand that the evidence contradicts—"

"You're not hearing me, Doctor. No child—not even Adam Crane—has ever been in that room."

That shakes her. She controls it well, but Roy sees the shock pass across her face before she can smother it.

"So," Armstrong says. "Our hope was that young Adam could shed some light on where his father went the day that girl disappeared. Instead, he gave his dad an alibi."

"I don't understand," Doctor Hardy says.

Armstrong shifts in his seat, sensing some kind of triumph. "We put that kid on the stand, and we pick this fantasy of his apart in front of him, and maybe he'll tell us—"

"No," she interrupts him. "That's not going to happen. What I'm asking is, if Ben wasn't in his room, then where was he sleeping all this time?"

A vein on the side of Armstrong's head looks like it is about to break through the skin, but he restrains himself from smashing anything. "Beats me, Doctor. Why don't you ask your patient?"

CHAPTER TWENTY-SEVEN

23RD ST.

Even with the police convoy driving a wedge through traffic for them, McDiarmid can sense that they are falling behind the train. It shouldn't matter—the response team are at 181st and have set up a perimeter already—but there is a psychological disadvantage to not being there as it happens. Doubly so to be crammed into the back of a bulletproof car whose forward progress is being mocked by the number of people casually walking past on the sidewalk. If he wasn't certain that someone would get fired for doing it, McDiarmid could almost swear that they are slowly rolling backward.

The team is working against the clock in more ways than one. Homeland got the lead on the explosion by two routes: the Transport Security Administration being firmly under their umbrella gives them ultimate authority over security on the MTA, and the obvious terrorist implication of an explosion on the subway meant that everyone else was too busy playing hot potato with the potential of a catastrophe to actually step up to the plate. The revelation that the suspect and all of the victims are linked to a convicted serial killer muddies the water somewhat. With the endgame looking less like a career killer—limited yield explosives, deep enough and far enough away from Manhattan that nobody important is going to be inconvenienced by a blast—the Justice Department and the FBI have both developed an interest in getting a slice. Some very connected people have been leaning on McDiarmid's superiors for progress and, if there is none, collaboration. In response, his superiors have started leaning on him.

McDiarmid is trying to make the best of it. Cooperation is a two-way street, so he has run requests for every case file and interview they can lay their hands on about both the Tuxedo Park Killer and the circus that was his trial. Information on the son is scant, but he's asked for everything from his dental history to his school transcripts to make sure all the bases are covered and that everyone has their hands full. Keep them all scrambling, and he might be able to resolve the situation without ever having to give anyone but Homeland a single ounce of credit.

"How are the surveys looking?"

Hoyt angles the tablet he's holding toward McDiarmid so that they can both look at it together. The primary goal was to build a quick passenger list and start running background checks for potential suspects or—on the outside chance—assets on board the train. It's too much to hope that the hijackers will identify themselves, either by accident or design, but it never hurts to give them the opportunity. The boys in the tech department have outdone themselves, however, and built a tactical map based on the login data. Using the timestamps to create a timeline and estimating Detective Hendricks's likely rate of progress, they have taken a computer-generated model of the train and populated it with everyone that followed the link to the survey site. It doesn't matter if they filled it in or not: every single browser that connects to the site is being logged and tracked.

For every passenger that has filled in the survey, they have added age, sex, and estimated height and weight based on what information they've managed to find on them so far. The whole thing is being updated in real time, and it's almost like a magic trick as the model refines itself before their eyes: adding data, resolving inaccuracies, and flagging up every felony, misdemeanor, or ill-spirited social media post on every single passenger. McDiarmid almost regrets not authorizing the addition of a malware program to the link that would have given them access to every phone that used it, but the risk of it being discovered seemed too great in the thirty seconds or so he had to consider it. He wonders if they have time to contact the NSA. They will one hundred percent want a piece of this, and he can only imagine what kind of information they will be able to pull out of it given that this kind of shit is their specialist subject.

McDiarmid points at the bottom right of the screen. "What's that icon?" he asks, but hardly needs to. It is bright yellow with a cartoon bomb, the fuse fizzing, pictured in mid-flight.

"They are adding explosion simulations and damage estimates."

"Based on what we know, what's the most likely scenario?"

"Highest passenger density toward the front and middle of the train," Hoyt says, selecting the bomb icon and adjusting some settings. "An explosion in one of these cars would be devastating to anyone in the immediate vicinity." He taps the icon again and the model flickers, the second-to-last car—the most densely occupied—deforms as though bursting from the inside outward. The passenger icons change from their variegated shades of blue to red, the brightest centered on the explosion's central point.

"Would the car really burst like that?"

Hoyt taps the screen a few more times, then shakes his head. "It looks like the model doesn't take into account the structural density of the car. It's all set to one value, so this probably wouldn't happen."

"Damage to the tunnel?"

"Minimal. Probably cosmetic at worst."

"What about the other cars? How many casualties?"

More taps. "If the train isn't moving, zero."

McDiarmid allows himself a rare smile. The official statement almost writes itself. *Thanks to the efforts of our ground team, we were able to minimize casualties and reduce collateral damage such that no one else was put at risk.* If the FBI drag their heels as he suspects they will, it could be implied that deaths could have been avoided had certain other agencies consented to sharing information instead of playing politics over jurisdiction. "Double-time those background checks. See how many people we can rule out. I want to know what car that bomb is in."

A shadow moves up to the window and taps twice on the glass. Surprised, McDiarmid turns and finds himself staring at one of the Homeland techs who has just walked through the immobile traffic and straight up to their car. McDiarmid wonders how she knows it is his car, but belatedly realizes that she probably just went straight for the one with reflective tint on all of the side windows. He lowers the window to an unpleasant jump in street noise. Everyone who isn't yelling at the cars on either side and in front of them is leaning on their horn to make up for it. Unbelievably, a police officer's whistle cuts through it all as someone up ahead somewhere tries to direct this shit show.

"What is it?"

"There's new information on the—"

She is cut off as a gap appears in front of them, and McDiarmid's driver takes the initiative by driving into it as fast as he can release the parking brake to do so. "Motherfucker!" McDiarmid slaps his palm off of the armrest, and as the tech runs to catch up with the car, he unclips his seat belt.

"Hoyt, move over." He opens the door, sliding over toward the center of the car as the tech catches up. "You, get in."

Technically, Hoyt is already in the far-side seat, but he is a big guy and sitting at ease in the back he takes up more space than he has any right to. He shuffles up as much as he can but even so McDiarmid finds himself getting uncomfortably acquainted with an upper arm and shoulder that seem more like granite than flesh. Hoyt senses the discomfort and tries to angle himself against the door, but it has little effect beyond making him loom even bigger in the cramped space.

The tech climbs in and pulls the door closed behind her.

"What's your name?"

"Cheryl, sir."

"Don't bother with a belt, Cheryl," McDiarmid says, before she can reach for hers. "Closest we'll get to dying in here is of old age. What is it?"

"There's some new information on Adam Crane," she says. "You know how we were trying to get around the court seal by looking for gaps in the records?"

McDiarmid nods. "Go on."

"Well, the system flagged some other kids who ended up on the system around the same time as the Ben Cross file was sealed," she says. "All boys, and all of them were about the same age as our target."

Her use of the past tense doesn't bode well. "What was the flag, exactly?"

"All of them are active murder cases, sir."

He doesn't need the file in front of him to picture the lawyer they found across town. "Let me guess: All of them got their throats pulled open?"

Cheryl makes a humming noise as she shuffles through her papers, like she wants to hold her place in the conversation until she finds the detail she's looking for. "Garroted," she says, "Although the coroner in one of them says it was with a surgical saw?"

"They mean a wire saw," McDiarmid explains, miming the action of cutting through something by pulling alternately on two handles. "Used for amputations." He thinks back to the mess of the lawyer's neck and wonders why their coroner didn't pick up on it. Using one to rip out someone's throat is probably so far off the map for a doctor's experience that it would take one hell of a leap for them to connect the dots. He doesn't put his hand out for the files. Just the fact that the murders have happened tells him all he needs to know. "So we aren't the only people who have been looking for Ben Cross," he says. "What's the latest on Crane Senior? Any chance all of this is his doing?"

Cheryl makes a face. "He knows something is going on," she says. "We're not sure how he knew, but he's looking to lawyer up."

"Smart for someone who's meant to be insane," McDiarmid says. "Someone must have bragged about it, thought they were getting one up on him."

"Should we find out who it was?"

He waves it away. "Don't bother. Since the cat is out of the bag, get them to toss Crane's room, see if there's any communication or keepsakes tucked away in the padding." McDiarmid thinks about it for a second. "Give him his lawyer. It will keep him quiet and if he comes close to making a case for mistreatment we can push to have him cleared as sane and have a judge put him away in real prison."

Cheryl makes a note. "Sir."

"Is there anything else?"

"Sir, just one thing. We were going through the files for the Crane trial. There's still a lot left to go over, but you said to let you know if anything—"

"I know what I said," McDiarmid cuts her off. "What is it?"

"Well, the Tuxedo Park Killer is listed as having twelve victims," she says. "But he was originally suspected in the disappearance of thirteen girls."

McDiarmid nods, but he wonders if she is padding her report so her department looks busier than they are. It might not be common knowledge that there were thirteen suspected victims, but a cursory flip through the case file is enough to fill McDiarmid in. Between Crane's refusal to give up any information that might help investigators find them and the increasing sophistication of his disposal methods over the duration of his "active" period, they only found remains from twelve of his victims. Still, the DA was confident enough in their case that they added a thirteenth name—Emily Walker—to their list in the hope that he would give up where he buried her to try and cut some kind of deal regarding his sentencing.

"I'm aware of that," McDiarmid says. "There was no evidence for the last victim ever being one of his."

"But that's the thing," Cheryl says. "Emily Walker wasn't ruled out because of a lack of evidence. She was ruled out based on the testimony of John Crane's son."

McDiarmid sits up, almost headbutting Hoyt's shoulder in the process. None of that was in the case summary, and whoever left it out is going to be in deep shit if he ever finds them. "What was his testimony?"

"The judge asked him to recall the events surrounding his birthday from the previous year." The tech adjusts her glasses as she is speaking. Even with the air-conditioning on full blast, the air in the car is almost as hot as out on the street, and her face is damp with sweat. "Emily disappeared that same day. The DA assumed that he would confirm that his dad was absent, at least for enough time for him to go and snatch Emily off of the street."

"He did the opposite?"

"The complete opposite. Testified that his dad spent the entire day with him, that they had a birthday party, the whole nine yards."

"So he was covering for him?"

She shakes her head. "Judge's notes suggest otherwise. Apparently he was undergoing psychological assessment and hadn't been cleared by the psychologist to take the stand. Everything he said was contradicted by witness statements and physical evidence from the house."

"So why wasn't it struck from the record?"

"It looks like a lot of it got hushed up but there was a real snafu around them putting this kid on the stand. Apparently the victim's parents got involved? There's some references to one of the bailiffs being dismissed and some kind of closed-door meeting between the DA, the judge, and the defense counsel before the trial could proceed."

McDiarmid thinks it over. If one or both of the parents tampered with a witness, then that would have been damning to the DA's case. "It sounds a lot like someone fucked up."

"Enough that the DA agreed to drop Emily Walker from the rap sheet."

"And the parents?"

"Issued with a restraining order. Neither one of them was allowed within five hundred feet of John Crane or his son, Adam."

"A restraining order against parents of a victim?" Hoyt asks. He lets out a low whistle, loud in the confines of the car.

"They got to the kid," McDiarmid says. "No access to Crane, he would be under guard the whole time, but his son? You have a riot every day at the courthouse, three or four different agencies with competing responsibilities for looking after him." He nods. "They got to the kid, and it fucked any hope they had of getting his testimony struck."

McDiarmid wants to see the notes for himself, but already he can feel the certainty of it building in his gut. Revenge is a powerful motivator, and not only were they cheated out of justice by John Crane's son, but also by the very people that were meant to deliver it. "Please tell me you have a current address for Mr. and Mrs. Walker," he says.

"We pulled everything," she says. "Addresses, work history, medical: a full workup. Turns out Mrs. Walker died shortly after the Crane trial ended."

McDiarmid can spot a leading statement from a mile out. "I take it she wasn't ill?"

"Suicide," she says.

"What about the dad?"

"As far as we know, he still lives at the same address."

"Did he remarry? Get into drink? I need details."

"We're looking into it, but he doesn't seem to have much of a digital footprint," she says. "It's almost like when his wife died, he started trying his best to disappear off the face of the Earth."

"We should see if we can reach him." McDiarmid says. "Get some uniforms out there, as soon as we can."

"There's no need, sir." Cheryl pushes her glasses back up into place with a firmness that has nothing to do with them slipping down her face. "I made the call myself. They're already on their way."

CHAPTER TWENTY-EIGHT

FIFTEEN YEARS EARLIER

There is no such thing as an easy choice when it comes to therapy. Tamsin Hardy knows this as well as any of her peers. In every session you walk a fine line with regards to the outcome of treatment. Every time you push, you risk regression; every time you hold back, you risk a lack of progress. In all cases, a therapist has to think about the harm they could potentially cause, and the ethical responsibility that stems from their care. There are no easy choices, and yet Tamsin could always take a measure of comfort in knowing that her judgment was good enough to avoid making bad ones.

Until now, that is.

She had expected the trial to be traumatic, even before the terrible situation with the Walker family had unraveled, and had prepared herself to have to start over from scratch with Ben. Instead, it almost seemed like closure for him. With his father gone—safely and truly gone, with no chance of parole, no means of reaching him—Ben seemed to shed layers of trauma like he was taking off a coat. He spoke more often, and for longer. He was open about his experiences, and while there were some areas he shied away from, he had even started to wonder aloud if some of the happier things he remembered were true, or if they were things he had dreamed once and wished they were true. He was eating properly, and sleeping through the night, and the effect it had had physically was noticeable whenever he came for his appointments. He could even sit in the waiting room with the door closed now, and sitting upright in the chair across from her, he seemed like an entirely different boy. Someone that maybe, one day, could be discharged from care and return fully functional to society.

Which is why she hates herself for what she is about to do to him.

Emily Walker and her parents have been on Tamsin's mind ever since the trial. She keeps thinking about the girl's face, the way she was caught mid-laugh in the photo her parents carried everywhere. She keeps thinking about the way John Crane laughed like a dog barking—a rude, ugly sound—when the judge told the court that, following Adam Crane's testimony and on the balance of evidence, Emily Walker would be removed from the list of victims.

What the Walkers did in court—to Ben—was out of line, but that doesn't mean they don't deserve justice. Some closure. And if she can maybe get that for them, it is worth setting Ben back. He has a chance to recover. A chance that Emily will never have.

"I want to try something a little different today, Ben," Tamsin says.

"Okay, Doctor Hardy." He is straight-backed and keen, like a puppy. Eager to please. The stack of pictures under her left hand feels hot, like it is pressing up against her fingertips, hardly restrained. Ready to be set loose, just as eager as he is. She doesn't like the association, but can't help making it.

"I'm going to show you some pictures," she says. "I'd like you to tell me your reaction to them, and maybe we can have a chat about each one?"

"Like an inkblot test?"

Tamsin has never done a Rorschach test. The last time she even picked up a set of cards for it was in med school. "Not quite. The inkblot test, as you call it, uses a set of images that could have many meanings, and tests how a person reacts to them."

He stares at her like maybe half of the words she said made sense to him.

"Let's just start, shall we?"

She lifts the first picture off of the pile and holds it up for Ben to see. She doesn't need to ask if he knows what it is. All of the color drains out of his face, and his jaw goes slack, like his brain can't process the shock fast enough.

"Do you know who this is?"

"I—I—"

"Her name is Neve," Tamsin says. She's afraid her voice will break when she says the girl's name, but it holds firm. "Do you know what happened to her?"

"M-my dad killed her."

"She was thirteen years old when she died. Do you know where they found her?"

Ben is looking everywhere but at the picture. "I don't—"

Tamsin leans forward in her seat, so the picture looms in his vision. He has to answer. She has to make him answer. "Where did they find what was left of her, Ben?"

"There was a tunnel. Dad dug a tunnel under the garage. He—he put her at the end of it."

"Her skull and pelvis," Tamsin says. She slaps the photo down on the table. "The rest he smashed after burning them." Ben is trembling as she picks up the next picture. He knows what is coming. He can see how many pictures there are. "Do you know who is next?" she asks.

"I don't know." He shakes his head, eyes wide and fixed on Tamsin's hands. It strikes her how young he is, and how much smaller he is than kids his own age. How his head looks too big for his body. That this is three years of progress and they haven't even come close to undoing the damage that his father wrought on him. It takes all of her will to hold the picture up and keep going.

He will heal. Time will heal him.

"Isabella Garcia," she says. "Do you recognize her?"

Ben doesn't say anything, but he nods, his lips pressed together so tightly that his mouth is a thin line. Tamsin shifts herself up in her seat to see where his hands are, and he is gripping the sides of the chair so hard that his fingers are stark white.

"Did your father kill her?"

He twitches when she says *father*, but answers promptly, "Yes."

It's not therapy. More like an interrogation. The opposite end of the spectrum from hypnosis, where no matter what the patient sees or experiences, they always know that they are safe. Tamsin has plunged Ben headfirst into something worse than a nightmare, and he is starting to realize that there is only one way out.

He has to answer her questions.

"Do you know where Isabella was found?"

"T-They found some of them upstate," he says. "Dad bought some land, said he was building a bunker so we'd have somewhere away from the population centers when the government went down."

What he's saying is true, but it isn't where they found Isabella Garcia. "She wasn't there, Ben. Where was she found?"

"Oh, no," he says. "No." He squirms in his seat, like he is trying to dig his way out through the back of his chair using only his shoulder blades.

"Where did they find her?"

"She was in—" He stops to gulp in a breath. "She was in the house. Under the water tank."

"What was left of her was," Tamsin says. "A partial skull. Four ribs. Her left ulna and radius, along with three partially destroyed metacarpals." She indicates the bones on her own arm and hand as she talks, like she is running a tutorial on anatomy.

"Why are you making me do this?"

Tamsin doesn't answer him. Seeing him recoil from her, she doubts that she could answer him, even if she wanted to. Instead, she lifts the third picture and shows it to Ben. "Do you recognize this girl?"

He nods.

"Say her name for me, please."

"I know who she is."

"Then you know her name, and you can say it."

Another nod. Tamsin takes a breath to speak, to force it out of him, but he beats her to it.

"Emily." He mumbles it, but he says it all the same.

"Do you know where she is?"

Ben doesn't answer. He's staring at the picture of Emily Walker. He doesn't try to avoid looking at her picture, doesn't try to escape. The effect is unsettling, like stumbling onto the perfect stillness of a deer caught out in the open on a woodland path.

"Do you know where she is, Ben?"

What really disturbs her is that he doesn't cry. He has cried before: easily, when he felt that he was safe to do so. Now that she has taken that trust and crushed it, the walls that they spent so long patiently dismantling are starting to go back up. She is pushing him to his absolute limit, beyond any kind of ethical boundary her profession would expect of her, and he hasn't shed a single tear.

"What happened to Emily, Ben?"

"Don't." His breathing changes pace, quickening to the point that he sounds like a dog panting. Hyperventilation.

"Where is she, Ben? What happened to Emily?"

"*I won't!*" He yells it, his voice breaking as he jumps to his feet and turns to grab hold of his chair. "*I won't do it!*"

Tamsin presses the Alarm button on the underside of her desk and pushes herself back from it two-handed as Ben lifts his chair with surprising strength and swings it around and up in an arc, throwing it at her. She goes sideways out of her own seat and the only thing that saves her is that the chair hits the desk before it goes rattling over, the impact sending her notes and the stack of pictures flying, before smashing into where she was sitting. If it had flown freely, it would have hit her.

The door opens and two orderlies are in the room before the chair reaches the floor, and by the time Tamsin gets her head up to see what's happening, they are each holding on to one of Ben's arms.

"*Fuck you!*" He screams it and fights against their grip, squirming one way and then the other. It seems chaotic, until he gets enough slack from one of the men to duck his head down and bite the man's forearm. If he was expecting to be let go, he is mistaken: the orderly forces his arm hard into Ben's mouth, pressing him back against the wall of his partner, and after a few moments Ben starts to choke. He stops biting, releasing the man in a shower of spittle, and they quickly switch tactics. One of them snakes a thick arm around Ben's neck to keep his chin up while the other cranks his elbow and wrist into an uncomfortable position, making it painful for him to struggle.

"Fuck you!" It comes out as a gurgle with the arm around his neck, but Ben is still fighting as they drag him, kicking and spitting, toward the door.

As Tamsin gets to her feet, she sees that Roy Lopez is standing in her office. She didn't think he was going to stick around waiting for Ben's session to finish. He must have come in from the waiting room when the orderlies ran past.

"Are you okay?" he asks.

"I'm fine," Tamsin says. She is not fine. She hadn't expected Ben to escalate so rapidly, or that he had the capacity for such violence. She doesn't know exactly what she has done to him, but she knows that now she will never get the chance to fix it.

She broke every rule of her profession, and didn't even get an answer out of it.

Roy is looking at the ruin of her desk, and she can see the change in his face as he sees that, scattered among the fallen papers, there are pictures of John Crane's victims. He looks up at her.

"What the hell did you just do?"

CHAPTER TWENTY-NINE

59TH ST.–COLUMBUS CIRCLE

Walking back along the full length of the train earns Kelly a few questions and a lot of commentary. *Why are we going so slow? What's the holdup? Lady, I need to take a wicked piss, how long is this going to take?* Homeland might be getting some good data out of their survey, but getting the passengers to engage with it has broken the surface tension bubble of dread that has been keeping a lid on the aggressive self-entitlement that is the natural condition of every commuter on the New York subway system. Now that everyone feels like a confirmation email from the MTA means that they are definitely getting out of this alive and unharmed, all they want to know is exactly when that will be and how big their payout is.

Kelly hustles past the majority without acknowledging them, and those that she can't avoid she gives them an NYPD standard-issue noncommittal grunt as she passes, both of which just serve to piss everyone off even more. The last car, with its shattered windows and scattered belongings, should be a sobering reminder of how serious their situation is, but all Kelly feels when she slams the door on the voices still calling out in her wake and finds herself surrounded by near silence is relief.

Hoyt told her in the tunnel to gather as much intel as possible from the train. She noted how proud he sounded when he said that Homeland can take any observation, no matter how small, and make good use of it. She has some thoughts on that assurance—mostly that it is some hard PR bullshit—and wonders if Hoyt was trying to sell her on it, or if he really believes it himself.

She doubts that his boss would say it with as much conviction.

Her head is spinning from trying to keep everything she saw and heard close to coherence—like trying to build a jigsaw puzzle while holding all the pieces a foot clear of the table—but the more she struggles with it, the more convinced she is that there is something very off about the whole thing.

They tell fresh recruits at the Academy that there is no such thing as a hunch. That evidence is the foundation of their work, and that they should get it straight in their Goddamn heads before they get themselves into serious trouble by thinking their feelings mean anything.

Any cop after their first year free of probation knows that the Academy instructors are full of shit.

They have to lie—God knows what would happen if an undercover journalist went through the Academy and heard the phrase *vibe check* being used in all seriousness—but humans are hardwired to know when trouble is coming. Knowing when someone is watching you; feeling the hairs rise on the back of your neck; having your heart start beating double time from a sudden burst of nervous adrenaline: all of these happen because your body knows that it is time to hightail it long before your brain figures it out. The longer a cop spends in the field, the more stress they experience, the sharper that sense gets.

Walking the train and talking to almost every single person on board at least once, Kelly has the distinct feeling that their bomber isn't among them. Sure, some of them are trouble, and plenty are trying to hide something, but she's willing to bet that most of the people on that list are holding a bag of weed or a quarter-gram of baby laxative masquerading as coke. What she doesn't get is the impression that any of them are itching to kill.

Kelly pauses halfway down the car and holds on to a railing so that she can stretch out her back. Something grinds and pops up near her left shoulder blade, and she is shocked by the sudden flush of exhaustion that follows it. Everything aches. All of her limbs are heavy. Her feet feel swollen inside her shoes, and she wonders if she's going to get blisters. Even her hands feel weird: the strip of flesh from the heel of her right hand to the tip of her little finger has gone numb, as though the nerves have been deadened.

The physical response to stress is almost always negative. A bottle of water and some carbs would go a long way to helping, but Homeland didn't think to hook her up with either when they were getting her ready. Bullets, yes; something to stop her hands from shaking, no. Kelly fakes out the yawn that was building and turns it into a deep, hard intake of breath, her teeth snapping shut on the back end of it so there isn't a single ounce of oxygen lost. She's had bad days before. This might be the worst by a country mile, but she will be damned if she lets it be the one that breaks her.

When Kelly pops the door on the rear cab of the train, all the unease she failed to pick up on when walking the train hits her in one fell sweep.

Ben Cross has the look of a man with a guilty conscience. He's still standing up, which is one good sign at least, but aside from that he's a wreck. While the sweat isn't pouring off of him, he's produced enough that his shirt is stuck to him like it was pasted on. Everywhere the cloth touches skin has turned translucent, and that contact has him shivering in spite of the heat. Whether it's to fend off the shivers or to hide them, he has picked up his briefcase and is clutching it across his chest, both arms wrapped solidly around it. As she comes in, he won't even look up at her, and he flinches when the door clicks shut in her wake. Even scared out of his wits, he shouldn't be this cagey. So, fear aside, all that's left is guilt.

Moving past the stations without stopping means that the nine miles between here and 181st St. are going to vanish quick. Kelly wants to see his cell phone—see what he said to the killers, if he said anything at all—but she knows that if she pushes him too hard, she's going to lose him. There isn't time for a truly soft approach, but maybe if she comes at him sideways, then he will be too busy thinking to still have his defenses up.

"I've been thinking about how they found you on this train," Kelly says. "You said you got fired today, right?"

Ben starts at the question, literally jumping out of the trance he'd managed to get himself stuck in. "Y-yes."

"Okay." She's got him looking at her and talking. All she needs now is to keep him rolling, keep the questions coming. Keep him on her side. "Where did you work?"

"DataDyne Solutions."

"Never heard of them." She knows the type, though. *Solutions* sounds like shorthand for moving shit around, running fetch and carry for bigger companies who don't want to do it themselves. The corporate analog of the guy who knows a guy. A single floor of a Manhattan office building acting as the main attraction, a head office based out of Delaware for tax reasons, and a Teflon-coated acronym that doesn't stick in the memory long enough for you to ask what it stands for. "What are they, logistics?"

"Used to be," Ben says. "They do environmental assessments, ordnance and compliance. Between private clients and what gets farmed out from the government, the logistics side got carved off as a separate entity."

Kelly nods. Everyone wants to avoid getting fined when the EPA assessors come around; nobody wants to be the one to have to read the whole rule book and get it done. Basing your business on making sure everyone is up to code sounds like lucrative work, even if it sounds boring as shit. "Are they a big deal?"

"Turnover was almost a billion last year," Ben says. "They hit that in the first four months of this year."

"Lots of staff."

"I was one of ten new hires. This week."

"You work there long?"

Ben shifts his feet. "Today was the first day after orientation."

"Right. So how long was orientation?"

"One week."

A week would be long enough for someone to lock down his routines if they were surveilling him. A young guy with a new job, no local friends, and just enough cash in his pocket to cover the commute, it probably wouldn't have taken the full week. Whoever wanted to know wouldn't even have had to follow him: Kelly can think of half a dozen guys off the force retired for the private sector who would do it for a hundred bucks an hour, fifty if they have a discount code.

"So, you're at work for a week, you get settled in, you learn the name of the girl at reception," Kelly says. The look of panic on Ben's face suggests he wouldn't be able to pick the receptionist out of a lineup, let alone name her. "And then you get fired on your first full day. They tell you why?"

"Incompatible with the company's aims and culture," Ben says.

"That means they found out who your dad is," Kelly says. "The question is, who told them? How many people know about your alias?"

"Nobody."

"Someone always knows." Kelly ticks the list off on her fingers. "Your mom, she's still alive, right?"

Ben pauses. "She's alive," he says.

"She's out there, and she knows you're around."

"My mom . . ." Ben trails off, and Kelly wonders if she has accidentally opened a wound with that one. "She would never tell."

"Never said she would, but this is the list, right?" Riding it out is the best option. Kelly waits for him to nod, and she moves on. "Now, what about court records? That change has to be listed somewhere."

"Court records are sealed."

"Sure, they got sealed, but that needs a judge, a clerk, probably a couple more people in the know, even if they don't think anything of it." She adds two fingers to the count, and Ben doesn't argue either of them. "You got a lawyer?"

Ben nods.

"You pay for him?"

"Them. There's a fund that was set up after sentencing."

"So there's a law firm that knows who you are." Two more fingers— the whole hand—and Kelly starts counting on the other hand. "And whoever manages that fund, either with the state or your mom's insurance company." Three more, for good measure. "You got a therapist?"

"I've had several," Ben says. "One right now."

Kelly adds another to the count. "Bet you a dollar all their admin staff know, too."

Ben doesn't say anything, but Kelly knows what the answer is.

"You get any fan mail?" she asks.

"What?"

"Weird letters. Requests for interviews. Books people want you to read so they can put your dad's name on the cover."

"Nothing like that," Ben says. "I keep waiting for it, bu—"

"How about prank calls? People putting stuff on your doorstep. Sliding into your DMs."

Ben shakes his head. "I don't have any social media." Kelly watches him flex his hands, making them into fists and stretching the fingers out alternately. Like a coping mechanism they teach kids to calm down, doing stretches and counting under their breath. "My therapist thinks I should try it, just to try and engage more, but I don't think it would be good for me."

"You afraid someone would find you out?"

Ben's face goes tight, his mouth turned into a sharp, angry line. "I know he is allowed to use the internet," he says. "He's not allowed a . . . presence, but I can't help but think that if I was on there as myself, he would find me."

Kelly hasn't considered that. She has never heard of John Crane before, but she imagines he's just like every other serial killer. Probably keeps a list of how many times he was mentioned online, and jacks off to the fantasy of getting his own movie one day. She puts that thought aside. Just the mention of him is putting Ben on his back foot.

"Look, we've gone from nobody to at least ten people who know exactly who you are," she says. "And while it's not common enough knowledge that you're getting pawed at by murder groupies, you have to accept that it's out there." Kelly nods as she talks, and she's pleased to see Ben mirror the motion.

"I want to message Homeland and tell them about this DataDyne Solutions place," Kelly says. "Find out who passed on your name to them."

Ben looks distraught, and Kelly has all her tactics lined up and ready to go—appealing to his conscience, the common good, they burned that bridge already—but he surprises her. "You think that will help?"

"I think whoever got you turned out of that building wanted you on this train," she says. "And somehow they got at least two bombs on here alongside you. That takes planning, and organization, which means that no matter how smart they think they are, they will have left a trail for us to follow. So do I have your permission to talk to them about it?"

Kelly couldn't give a shit about his permission, but it feels like she has found her moment. When he nods in agreement, she makes her move. "You know why they picked you, don't you, Ben?"

He doesn't jump, doesn't flip out, or start screaming. Doesn't tense up or start looking around for an escape route. His whole body slumps like he just dropped a weight at his feet.

"I'm on this train because of Emily Walker," Ben says.

The name means nothing to Kelly, but she can guess. "Was she . . . one of your dad's victims?"

"It was my fault," Ben says, and something in his voice makes Kelly suddenly very aware of the weapon she has strapped underneath her ballistic vest, and how far away her hand is from it. He doesn't look up. "I killed her."

CHAPTER THIRTY

FIFTEEN YEARS EARLIER

Down here, in the second layer, the walls are wet to the touch. The damp seeping down through the earth, worming its way through miniscule cracks and breaches; condensation from Adam's breath in the air, mingling with the girl's, settling like dew on the cold concrete.

Dad would never accept these conditions upstairs, in the first layer. In the bunker where they were going to survive when the end-times come around.

Up the bunker there is no noise except for the smooth hum of the extractor fans pulling air down from the surface—filtered on the way and monitored for quality—and the dehumidifiers working to keep the humidity in check. Every wall up there was scrubbed clean, even behind the pipes and shelves, or at least as far as Adam's hands allowed him to reach.

He doesn't try to talk to the girl. He's been warned already not to try, by his dad when he brought Adam down here, telling him all the way that *it's time* and *he's ready* and never really saying what he thinks Adam is ready for.

Being ready is a big thing to Adam. It's all he's ever thought about, ever since he was little and his dad told him all about the bombs that could blow up a whole city, kill everyone, and leave the good Earth poisoned for a lifetime. He knew it was real, because Dad had shown him videos of them going off in the sea, pictures of Japan after they dropped them there. He told him about Chernobyl, and how the Russians had tested a weapon on their own people and covered it up. Told everyone it was an accident.

He took him out of school not long after, when Adam started telling everyone in class about the bombs and how the "radio waves" coming off the ground after would make your skin fall off at the slightest touch.

He took Adam out of the house when his mom started talking about how his dad shouldn't rush him into it, that he should *let the boy have a childhood.*

That was when they moved to the first of his dad's shelters, and they started talking about getting ready to live off the grid.

He taught Adam himself: taught him about survival. About the different plots of land he'd invested in and dug bunkers beneath. He'd made them places to live in at first, but then each time he started a new one he converted the last into a cache, to store nonperishable food, seeds, and ammunition against the day that the whole family would need them.

He taught Adam about hunting. How to track an animal, how to trap it and tie it, how to lift a carcass that was longer than he was tall and, finally, how to kill it.

He showed him all the ways you could tell an animal was contaminated, poisoned from the inside out. How you could tell just from the way it walked and moved that it was no good, and that it had to be destroyed.

He showed him how the best way to rid the world of a contaminated animal was to burn it hard, and bury the ashes deep.

And now, he brought Adam down to the space he'd made beneath the bunker, the place where his true work lay hidden, to give Adam his final lesson.

His rite of passage.

The girl is looking at him now. Adam doesn't like it when she looks at him, doesn't like that his dad has left him down here with her. Even with the bars of the cage dividing them, Adam feels like he's in danger. She is bigger than he is, older for sure, like one of the teens he used to see on rare trips to the mall or clustered together near the steps of the local high school. They were an unknown quantity, one of the few types of people who wouldn't step out of the way or show any kind of deference to his dad. Just that fact alone—that there were some things in the world beyond even his dad's control—made the sight of them feel exciting, like every time he walked past a teenager, he was taking a risk.

The girl in the cage doesn't make him feel excited at all. He feels sick, sicker than he has ever felt. He'd feel better if she wasn't staring at him, but he knows that if he tells her not to she's not going to listen. If anything, it will make her stare harder.

The girl has been down here a while. There's a trash bag in the corner, stuffed with paper plates and compostable cardboard cutlery. There's no toilet, but there is a large plastic bucket with a lid and a roll of rapid-dissolving toilet paper on top. There are splatter marks on the wall near the door where she has thrown her shit, probably trying to get Adam's dad on the pass. She looks like she has been fed, but that is the best of it. Dad hasn't washed her, or let her wash. Her skin is filthy, caked black with soot. What were once her clothes—jean shorts and a T-shirt—are now ragged from where the stitches have been torn loose, or the cloth has simply given way. Her hair is matted, where there is hair left. She has pulled some of it out, the clumps left sitting where she has thrown them, and his dad—Adam guesses—has cut the rest short to keep her from finishing the job. The wounds in her scalp are ugly, the scabs thick and ragged where she has worked at them with her hands. She can't stand up in the cage. It is barely big enough for her to sit upright, and there are no signs that his dad has let her out to exercise any. She barely moves except to try and shift her weight. When she does move, Adam can see the sores that have formed from where she has been stuck in one position for too long.

Adam shifts uneasily on the chair Dad brought down for him. The scars of his own sores—a mirror to hers, a reminder of what will happen to him if he is bad or doesn't do as he is told—itch under the cloth of his pants.

The girl's head comes up, looks off past Adam to the door, and he realizes that she is tuned in to the sounds his dad makes when he descends. He watches as the light in her eyes—focused, alert, a feral edge to them—fades away and her posture changes. By the time Dad comes through the door, she is a different person entirely: she looks numb, like it would take every one of the bombs dropping and the end of the world to rouse her.

Adam knows that she is faking it, but even as he tries to find the words to tell his dad, say something that will win his approval and maybe stop this from happening, the words get stuck in his throat.

Dad hates weakness. Any sign of it is a sign of contamination, of the chemicals they put in the water and in all the food to keep people from knowing who they truly are. The girl is caged, and has been for some time. He knows how Dad will react if he tells him. *Of course she's faking it*, he'll say. *She knows her place.*

His dad bounds into the room with as much energy as the low ceiling and the gravel floor will allow him to. He's grinning like the room doesn't smell of damp and ashes, like he's having the time of his life.

"How are you two young kids getting along?" he asks. "She say anything to you?"

Adam doesn't answer the first question. He knows his dad well enough to know which questions need no answers. "No, sir," he says.

"Not a word? From this little firecracker?" His dad comes closer, and Adam clenches his thigh muscles to keep from leaning away. If he stays still, then Dad won't see the weakness in him. Won't put him back in the dark place that his dad says all liars deserve. "Not even a whisper?"

Adam can almost feel the lid of the box closing on him, forcing him down so he can't stand right, and there isn't enough space to sit down. The last time his dad put him in, he pissed himself straightaway. Even though he scrubbed himself hard in the shower, he can still feel the stink of it on his skin.

Show him what he wants to see, unless you want to go back there.

Adam looks his dad straight in the eye. "No, sir."

Closer still. His breath smells of nothing, not coffee or toothpaste or tobacco. He doesn't use them, not out here at least. He says that animals can smell them, that the scent will drive good hunting away.

He claps his hands together, hard, right in front of Adam's nose. Adam is expecting it. It's one of his favorites, at least when they don't have company—strangers to the family might not understand that it's all in Adam's best interests when his dad lets a hand fly—and so when it happens Adam barely flinches.

"Excellent," his dad says. "Let's get started."

Adam knows that his dad isn't a big man. He isn't someone that people take notice of. People don't talk to them in the street, don't stop by to see how things are. His dad likes to say that he could disappear if he wanted to, just by looking dumb and walking the same direction as the flock. *A wolf in sheep's clothing.*

In the weak light of the fluorescent strips overhead, his dad grins and shows Adam every one of his teeth.

"Here," he says. "Take this."

In his hand is a sheathed knife. Adam knows which one it is without even taking it. The blade is a little less than three inches long, a drop point for detail work but still plenty of belly in the blade as it curves back to the handle. His dad bought it for him, complete with custom notches in the back of the blade to help him control the blade while carving or skinning.

Jimping, that's what it is called. Adam finds a rare moment of plea-sure in saying the word to himself, of enjoying the sound of it.

Adam takes the knife. He can see his dad's hands trembling as he lets go of the sheath. It's not from the cold, even though it is cold enough down here that you could store meat. His dad is excited. Like it's Christ-mas morning, and he can't wait for Adam to see what's under the tree.

Jimping: notches carved into the back of a blade to keep your hands from slipping when opening your presents.

"You know what I want you to do, Adam."

Adam looks from the girl, to the knife, and back again. He has been here before. A rabbit caught in a snare. A deer lamed by an arrow, bucking and kicking as it tries to get away. The knife in his hand, and his dad watching him close.

"I know what you want me to do," Adam says.

His dad draws in a long breath and hunkers down, his hand on Ad-am's shoulder. "I know you're nervous," he says. "Believe me, I know how nerve-racking it is. But this is it. This is the Good Work. This is what you were born to do. I . . . I just found the truth of things as I stumbled along through life, but for you, son . . . this is your destiny." He comes closer, his empty breath warm on Adam's face. "This is just the beginning. You have bigger things than this to look forward to. But for now"—he taps the sheath with a finger—"just enjoy the moment." His hand moves up to the back of Adam's neck and he whispers to him, "And bring me her heart."

CHAPTER THIRTY-ONE

79TH ST.

The cop is watching Ben closely. He's not looking at her, doesn't even know if he can look at her with the weight of all that shame on him, but he can still feel the pressure of her gaze. Ben can't tell if she's watching him like she'd watch a snake—given his confession, he would not be surprised—or if she is, in fact, the snake.

He expected her to have him in cuffs by now. Instead, all she's doing is watching him.

Her gun is in an awkward place. If she goes for it, you could get her eyes.

The thought comes on like a convulsion, so clear in his head he almost feels like he has said it out loud. Ben stiffens, trying not to react to that fear, and feels the burn of acid rising in the back of his throat. He coughs twice, trying to clear it, and when he recovers he can see the cop has reached behind her back with one hand.

Here it comes, coward.

The cop digs into a pocket and brings out a paper tissue. She offers it to Ben, extending her arm slowly like she's not sure if she'll get his fingers back, and Ben nods his thanks before coughing again and spitting the resulting mass into the tissue.

Maybe I am the snake here, Ben thinks.

The urge to violence is a natural one. That's what every therapist has told him in the past fifteen years. That people driving cars will sometimes wonder, *What if I jerked the wheel and drove into oncoming traffic?*, or if confronted with a high vantage point will imagine throwing themselves off; there's a part of the subconscious mind that constantly conjures up the unspeakable, if only to satisfy itself by rejecting it. It's perfectly normal. Everyone feels this way sometimes.

Every single therapist has said it to him, and then watched him like the cop is watching him now. Like giving the side of a water tank a kick and then waiting at the surface to see if they managed to shake something loose.

He can't stop thinking about the cop's gun. The fact of its existence is scratching at the inside of his skull like a persistent finger. *This is your escape route. Getting it is your way out and the longer you leave it, the harder it will be.*

"What happened, Ben?" she asks.

"I killed a girl," he says. "They thought she was his last victim." Ben can feel tears coming, and with them the fear of what will happen to him if he cries. "But it was me."

"Emily Walker." She repeats the name like she's memorizing it. "And they thought your dad killed her?"

Ben nods. When he closes his eyes, he can still see the girl in the cage.

"So that would be fifteen years ago?"

He can feel tears track down his face when he tries to nod a second time, so Ben forces himself to bring his head up and opens his eyes.

Show no weakness.

"If you don't mind me asking, Ben, how old were you when this happened?"

Ben takes a big gulp of breath before he can answer. His mouth feels thick, and he has to wipe away spit with the wadded tissue so he can speak. "I was eleven," he says.

"Jesus fucking Christ," the cop says. "Okay."

"I'm not like him," Ben says. "I didn't want to—"

"Ben," the cop cuts him off. "This isn't the time for it. Please." She gets out her phone, and starts typing a message on it, her thumb working fast while half keeping an eye on him. "I'm going to tell Homeland. You understand why."

"I understand." Ben nods. There is no catharsis in the confession. He has been carrying the lie for so long that the space inside of him has scarred over.

"I'm also telling them about your employer. They'll get people over there, get them working on it."

"Do you think they'll find anything?"

The cop gives him a look. "It's going to take some time," she says. *More time than you have, idiot. Get the gun.*

If hearing the voice shows at all on his face, she doesn't react to it.

"You say you killed this girl," she says. Her voice is calm and even, like she's taking her time and choosing every word carefully. "And that is something we will deal with, okay? I can't promise there won't be any consequences, especially considering you kept it a secret all this time."

"I know that," Ben says.

"Just think," she says, and there is a hard edge in her voice, "if you'd told the truth fifteen years ago, then maybe we wouldn't be stuck on a train with a bomb right now. Wouldn't that have been a thing?"

Ben knows the question is rhetorical and keeps his mouth shut. He suspects any attempt to apologize would be met with a punch.

"Well, at least we know why they picked you," she says. "Did you talk to the bomber?"

Ben nods. He wants to say yes, but his throat feels like it has closed up shop.

She holds her hand out for the phone. "Would you mind if I looked at the conversation you had?"

Even though he knows that he needs to hand it over, Ben still hesitates. It feels like a violation, like she is demanding something private from him.

He picks up the phone off of the console, and in the brief moment of turning back imagines grabbing her outstretched arm and jerking her toward him. He imagines using that momentum to reach up under the back of her vest and getting a hand on the bulky shape that is her gun.

He can imagine the feel of the gun as it settles into the V-shaped wedge between his forefinger and thumb. The bite of the cross-hatching on the grip against his skin. Ben once read an article on small-town preachers in the Appalachian Mountains who handle snakes as proof of their faith in God. When their hands touch, he flinches back from the contact, and Ben can't tell if it is for fear of biting, or getting bit.

All he knows is that Detective Hendricks is putting a substantial amount of faith in him right now, and instead of giving her answers all he can think of is how to hurt her.

The urge to do unspeakable things is inevitable. You let them play in your head so you have the satisfaction of rejecting them in the end. Ben lets that thought chime like a bell, not clearing out the fear but pushing it to one side for a spell. Maybe everyone has a voice in their head urging them toward evil, and nobody ever talks about it.

Ben takes a deep breath. He pulled a nail clean—or almost clean—out of a woman's skull to save her life. He can do this.

Ben tries to speak, but instead of saying anything he doubles over like he is about to throw up. There's a high-pitched ringing in his head, a note that feels like it never stops climbing. The voice is in there alongside it, sunk into his brain like a shard of ice. It is talking to him, calling him every kind of cunt idiot under the sun, telling him that he's weak for giving himself up.

"Are you okay, Ben?"

He almost says that he's fine, a reflex action, and that thought—that he would try and dismiss the question in this situation—forces out something that is almost a laugh. "No," he says. "I can't . . . I'm not—"

You chose this, you stupid fuck. You chose to be meat.

All Ben can think of is chill air and the smell of blood. The knife with its notches along the back and a furnace waiting. The memory of them piercing him like a missile launched in a fifteen-year arc, its flight following him down through the years until finally finding its target. The walls of the cab feel tight, like his claustrophobia has magnified itself a hundredfold, and Ben struggles to draw a breath past the panic.

You don't have to tell her the rest. The voice is calm now. It sounds almost as though it is trying to reason with him. It feels like a trap.

The cop is talking to him.

"It's okay, Ben." She is talking to him softly, repeating it over and over. "Just catch your breath. It's all right."

Ben nods, agreeing with both of them. He doesn't have to tell her the rest.

Ben swallows over and over, swallowing air, his throat burning. The images—the smell—are gone, and he's back in the train again. Still trapped. He nods, and the effort makes him dizzy. His head feels too heavy, and the noise of the train is muffled, like he's hearing it through a layer of padding. The cop steps back, like she's expecting a stream of vomit to hit the ground at her feet.

"The people they killed," Ben says. "I know who they are. I didn't see it at first, but then I remembered. The first guy, the one they killed on his doorstep, his name was Roy. Roy something."

"Lopez," the cop finishes it for him. Homeland must have sent her the details. It feels strange knowing that she has all this at her fingertips, that in less than an hour they have pulled out names that Ben has spent half his life trying to forget.

"That was it," he says. There are only a handful of people who have deliberately gone out of their way to help him in his life, and Roy was one of them. Ben feels bad that he didn't recognize him right away. "He was some kind of lawyer, or a lawyer's assistant. He was there to look after me in court."

Talking about it makes it easier to remember the man. Trying to do a good job, trying to keep a scared kid calm. Squatting down so they'd be the same height, always asking if he wanted a soda or a snack. Wiping his hands on his trouser legs, over and over, to keep them from sweating. Fifteen years later, he was rewarded for his efforts by having his throat pulled out.

"I remember the others, too," Ben says. "The woman they killed with the bomb. The one I tried to stop." He remembers the way her face changed, the way she almost ran for the door when she recognized Ben. "She was a clerk in the court. She came to collect the tapes they made of me testifying."

The cop nods. "Go on," she says.

"The guy that got killed at Cortlandt—" Ben chokes on the words. He didn't even try to stop him from getting off of the train. Back when he thought it was some kind of joke. "He was a guard, or a cop, or something. He was meant to escort me up to the interview room." The man doesn't live in his memory as a real person. More like the distillation of every shove or curse word that came his way from the day he left the hospital and went into care. A dark shape at his shoulder. "He . . ."

"You have any idea how they ended up on the same train as you?"

Ben stares at her. He has nothing. He never saw them get on, never even knew they were alive or in the same city as him up until the moment the killer put them in his path.

The thought comes to Ben that he might not know how they got here, but that he came very close to not being on the train at all.

"There was a man," Ben says. "When I was getting on the subway, I had a— I mean, I almost didn't get on." He can't think of how to frame his claustrophobia as something that makes sense—a feeling, a premonition, a warning—so instead he stutters over it. The cop doesn't call him out on it. "He was so calm about it. He kept me moving, made sure I got on."

"You think you'd recognize him if you saw him again?"

"I only saw him as he passed me," Ben says. "Tall, white hair, checked shirt." He leans forward, toward the cop. "But I think I know who he is."

"Who do you think he is, Ben?"

She is keeping her cool, but Ben feels a rush of adrenaline at having put it together. It has to be them.

"Emily—"

Ben's voice catches on the name, and all of that adrenaline turns to rot in the pit of his gut. "Her parents made a big scene during the trial. That guard, the man that died, he brought her mom up to the room where I was meant to testify, and . . ."

"They interfered with a witness," the cop says.

"It all got covered up," Ben says. "I knew something bad happened because they never asked me about her again. If they had, then maybe I would have—"

"You think it's the mom and dad?" the cop asks. She is watching him again, her head cocked like she is waiting to see which way he is going to fall on this. Ben takes a breath and gets it out as steadily as he can.

"It's her mom and dad," he says. "They would be older now. As old as the guy that got me on the train."

"They want to know what happened to their daughter," the cop says. "And punish all the people that kept them from finding out."

"I think so," Ben says. The hand on his shoulder felt so familiar. Like an old friend guiding him on. He should have known not to trust it. "It has to be them."

The cop sighs out loud. "It never occurred to them to just turn up on your doorstep with a set of jumper cables and give the rest of us a break?"

Ben shakes his head. "They want more than that," he says. Just like everyone else, they have bigger ambitions than Ben himself. "They want my dad to know that they got me."

"An eye for an eye, is that it?"

Ben drops his head and looks down at the floor, like he's offering his neck for the executioner's blade. "Something like that," he says.

THE SURVIVOR

CHAPTER THIRTY-TWO

96TH ST.

The whole convoy is moving uptown quickly, now the worst of the traffic has been cleared. There are still plenty of cars on the road, but there's enough room for them to move out of the way, and the black and whites in the vanguard are like a snowplow clearing the route for Homeland to get to 181st before the train gets there.

The inside of the car is busy, with Hoyt fielding three or four calls simultaneously, playing triage for McDiarmid, and Cheryl has been co-opted to field everything else, frantically jumping back and forth between every radio frequency and conference call that Hoyt can't be on just in case something vital needs to be passed up the chain.

McDiarmid, being the most senior Homeland agent in the car, has his attention split between two things: one, making sure the assault team is prepped and in position; and two, finding out everything he can about how the victims ended up on the same train as Adam Crane, and in possession of the bombs that—ultimately—killed them.

If Homeland can work that out, then maybe they can work out where the bomb is on the train, and who is holding the detonator.

Finding the bomb isn't the only reason, though.

Somewhere down the line, no matter how this turns out, people are going to want answers. *How could this have happened? How do we keep it from happening again?* And McDiarmid is not the kind of person who goes into those conversations without something up his sleeve.

We're looking into it, might be good enough for the press, but it cuts no ice with the director.

They lucked out at finding the Franklin victim's phone intact, or at least intact enough that the tech team could do something with it. On the other hand, the Cortlandt victim's phone was reduced to something close to powder by a close-proximity detonation. McDiarmid wonders if the phone itself could have been the device, but the mass of explosive and the copper plate alone would have made it almost twice the weight. It wasn't the phone, but it was likely in the same pocket, and the victim would have placed it there himself.

They didn't have his phone, but that didn't mean they couldn't find anything out. McDiarmid tried to brute force the phone company by calling himself, but the attempt was met with significant resistance. If someone had told him that a corporate entity existed that could outdo Homeland for creating an obfuscating cloud of red tape when confronted by a hostile demand for information, he would have maybe guessed the IRS. He did not account for the labyrinthine defenses that the Pacific Trident Telephone Company had prepared against the possibility of ever being found liable for anything.

After getting bounced back and forth from the local switchboard, to their state office, and finally to their headquarters, he invoked Homeland and the potential risks of impeding their investigation. Putting a squeeze on the operator seemed like a good idea at the time, but McDiarmid didn't consider that Homeland has exactly zero pull with a corporation that barely answers to anyone, and his threat produced the opposite result. After a short burst of sarcastic groveling, his call was routed to a barely operational pay phone at the back of an Alabama chop shop where it rang for two minutes solid before being answered by a pissed-off guy named Dale asking where the fuck his drugs were.

McDiarmid leaves Cheryl to clean up the mess and fix it for him while he deals with a softer target: John Crane's psychiatric team, who are doing the legwork on sifting through Crane's fan mail. He gives up one whole minute of his time to okay the use of flash-bangs in the enclosed space underground with the tactical team—and suggests they think of how best to deal with getting several hundred half-blind and almost-completely-deaf survivors upstairs—before Hoyt holds out a new phone to him.

Doctor Robinson is the lead on the psychiatric team. McDiarmid lets him talk a little about their work, even though the seconds are ticking away. Getting burned by the Pacific Trident operator still smarts, and a touch of professional interest is a small price to pay to make sure it doesn't happen again.

"Has anything shown up in the letters?" McDiarmid asks.

"Yes and no." The signal on the line isn't great, and Doctor Robinson's voice sounds as though he is making calls from the bottom of a lead-lined well. McDiarmid cracks his neck before jamming the phone hard against one ear and putting his hand over the other so he can hear the man. "—if we could contact some of the journalists who've written to him and cross-reference our notes?"

"Absolutely not, don't contact any of them," McDiarmid says. "Did any of the journalists focus on the trial or undiscovered victims?"

"Okay." There's a pause on Robinson's end. "Uh, if you wait five, I can go check through the summary list the team is putting together—"

"If you could do that after our call, Doctor, there have been some developments in the investigation and it might be key."

"Oh, well, then certainly. We'll make that a focus," Robinson says. "There is one thing that really stood out to us, though. Couldn't make head or tail of it, so we put it in a pile of its own next to the proposals pile."

"What is it?"

"Birthday card. Not the only one he gets, but this one is different. No message, no return address, postmarks move around from state to state."

McDiarmid sighs. Locked in a room with nothing but Crane's mail, they are probably seeing a killer in every other letter. "That still sounds like something for the crank pile," he says.

"The thing is, it never comes on his birthday."

McDiarmid never considered himself a sloucher, and yet there's still a little flex in his spine that he can straighten up out of. "Did they all come on the Sixteenth of April?"

Another pause from Robinson. "Yes, or as close as the mail lets it. How did you know?"

McDiarmid punches the air, making Cheryl flinch as he almost hits her in the process. "It's his son's birthday," he says. *And the day Emily Walker was taken.* Emily Walker's father has just climbed a notch higher on the suspect list. He could have been trying to get under Crane's skin this whole time, letting him know that the world has moved on but he hasn't forgotten.

"That is interesting. Do you think that it's his son sending them? John Crane has a real fascination with how Adam is getting on, even though we don't indulge it—"

"We have a lead," McDiarmid says. "That's all I can say right now. You understand the need for discretion, especially with regards to the risk of information leaking to John himself."

"I understand completely," Robinson says. His voice sounds flat on the line, even through the distortion, and McDiarmid makes a mental note to drop the full weight of Homeland's displeasure on the man should a single mention of this conversation make it into the media.

"The cards were blank, you said?" McDiarmid asks.

"As far as we can see."

"Check again for me please. Starting with the most recent. And please check if Crane has access to a UV light source, or heat."

"I don't think he has either of those."

"Access to the right type of light bulb would be enough," McDiarmid says. "Check again."

A long pause from Robinson. "We'll check," he says.

"And gloves for everything." McDiarmid resists the urge to chew him out over their obviously sloppy protocols. "We'll print everyone who has handled them, just in case, to rule out any accidental contact." He doesn't say *contamination*. He needs Robinson on his side.

"There is one other thing," Robinson says.

Across in the facing seat, Cheryl looks up sharply from her phone and waves frantically at him. McDiarmid ignores her. "What is it?"

"Would you like to speak to him? Crane, I mean."

McDiarmid considers it for a moment, and discards the thought just as fast. Serial killers are often subject to the kind of law enforcement mythologizing that sets his teeth on edge. Yes, they can be clever, for a narrow definition of intelligence. They can be manipulative. But what never gets mentioned is how desperate they are for attention. John Crane will be bursting at the seams wanting the world to look at him, and that level of narcissism, elevated way off of the baseline, means that any attempt to interrogate him is doomed from the beginning. If he knows anything at all, which he might not, they could put him on prime-time television and he still wouldn't give it away.

McDiarmid hangs up without answering and feels his grip tighten on the phone, the creak of the plastic case the only outward sign of his frustration. Even if the birthday cards have some secrets left to reveal, it will take too long to get hold of them. Robinson's team aren't sharp, and the offer to put him on a line with Crane speaks to a lack of sound judgment on the man's part. He feels like swearing, but Hoyt is still on a call and the sound of him throwing a tantrum in the background isn't going to do anyone any favors.

"Sir," Cheryl says.

"What is it?"

"Analytics have got access to both victims' email accounts," she says. "We know why they were on the train."

McDiarmid holds his hand out for her phone. "Tell me."

"Both of them were hired as couriers," she says. Looking at the messages from Analytics, McDiarmid can see that it is some kind of hub for gig work, but he doesn't recognize the name.

"Is this company legit?" he asks.

"They are. We're leaning on them now to get access to who placed their contracts."

Whoever set them up put some real effort into making sure they would be there. Analytics has turned over the victims' accounts and both of them were first contacted several weeks' prior, to carry documents across the city.

Practice runs.

"Why were they both working as couriers?"

"Both of them were retired, sir," Cheryl says. "Maybe they needed the money?"

"They were struggling? We know that?"

She stares at him. "Everybody's struggling, sir."

McDiarmid chooses to ignore that and goes back to the summary from Analytics. The work offer they received has details of the size of each package, how much it would weigh. The "client" even offered a bag to the second victim to make it easier to carry. They were both given itineraries, right down to the number and time of the train they were meant to take. A few minutes before he died, the first victim submitted a photograph of himself sitting in the train car via a portal on the website, so the client knew he was on the way.

"I want this motherfucker's details," McDiarmid says.

"We're working on it, sir."

"I want them. Right now. Get onto this freelancer site and tell them we want details on every package picked up in the Manhattan area this morning, and how many of them are still in transit. If they give you a single fucking atom of resistance over it, tell them they will be on the news tonight and in court tomorrow morning for aiding and abetting a terrorist."

They are so close that McDiarmid can almost taste it. Whatever mayhem Patrick Walker had planned must have taken him years to put together, and an insane amount of luck to pull off. The lawyer he killed across town must have been a loose end, the one person he couldn't put on the train to complete the set.

McDiarmid makes a mental note to get the list of everyone involved in the trial and follow up on all of them, just in case there are more bodies out there waiting to be found.

Hoyt puts his hand over his phone and nods to get McDiarmid's attention. "Local PD upstate reached the Walker household," he says.

"Nobody home?" If there were someone there, the phrase would have been *made contact*. Shorthand for the express delivery of three nine-millimeter rounds to the chest, or one to the head.

"Patrick Walker was found dead on the property."

McDiarmid closes his eyes and takes a deep, steadying breath. "Please tell me he died peacefully in his sleep, and this is not related," he says.

"Door was closed but not secured," he says. "Our team saw a blood swipe and entered the property. Blood trail down to the cellar suggests he was tackled on the doorstep and dragged there after. They found most of him."

McDiarmid presses his palms together and bows his head, trying to center the chaotic whirl of thoughts that are churning in his head.

"Most of him?"

"He was cut into pieces. Forensics are on the way but the team leader thinks his limbs probably went into the furnace."

"He still has his head on?"

"Just." Hoyt's voice is deadpan, but his complexion is considerably paler than it was a few minutes ago. He is very carefully keeping his phone screen from hitting any kind of angle where the analyst can see it. "Whoever it was, they made sure he suffered."

Finding out about the Walkers felt like a breakthrough in the case, an anchor point that turned a potentially career-killing snafu into something with direction and purpose. Finding the Walker family patriarch was a clear goal that everyone—regardless of agency—could unite behind. With him dead, all of McDiarmid's efforts have been cast adrift.

He can picture the subway train in his mind's eye without having to look at the computer model. All of the people they had filtered out as not matching the approximate age and ethnicity of the Walkers will all have to be relabeled as potential targets. There are too many for even Homeland to work through before the train reaches 181st St.

But then they don't have to. Only one person on the train knows what happened to Emily Walker. Only one of them knows John Crane, and the kind of games he would play with his victims. Only one of them would have had cause to make a trip upstate to carve pieces off of Patrick Walker.

The man who has been playing them all this time. Ben Cross, or as McDiarmid thinks of him now: Adam Crane.

CHAPTER THIRTY-THREE

CATHEDRAL PARKWAY

When the cop reads a message from her phone and tells him that the Walker family is dead, the dull headache that has been ever-present in the back of Ben's head builds so fast that he can't even find the words to tell her what's happening. It's a weakening presence, pressure like a spike pressing outward through the back of his sinuses, trying to turn his face inside out. Every jolt or shudder that passes through the train amplifies the pain, and if he did not know better Ben would almost swear that the train is accelerating. With his hands pressed hard on either side of his head, he can barely hear the cop as she tries to coax him into sitting down on the floor.

You fucked it up. That's why you're here.

Ben straightens up, taking his hands away from his face and lowering them. The steam-kettle whistle of the headache isn't gone. It doesn't fade, not really. It's just that it moves somewhere else in his mind, pressed out of the way by something much stronger. More primal. Something Ben recognizes like an old friend.

Fear.

"You said they found him dead," Ben says.

The cop nods, carefully, like she's trying not to make any big movements. Like he's something dangerous. "That's what they said."

He's been so sure that the guy on the steps had a part in this, but he was just some random guy trying to help. Trying to do him a favor.

Hell of a Goddamn favor.

"Did they tell you where they found him?"

"They didn't say."

Ben closes his eyes. He can almost see it. The darkness below the bunker. The wet brick walls, the gravel floor, and the tunnel down to the furnace. "If he had a cellar, that's where they found him."

You fucked it up. If you had just done what you were supposed to do, we wouldn't be here.

"How do you know that?"

He can't see both of her hands. She has one behind her back, like she is reaching for a weapon. Ben doesn't blame her.

"If he had a furnace, that's where he'd be."

You fucked up. The fire didn't do the job for us.

The voice in his head is clearer now. Louder.

You know what happens when you don't do as I say.

Ben knows whose voice it is. He has always known who it is, who it would be. The psychiatrists and the therapists and all those care workers were meant to help him move on, help free him from his past, but in the end all they ever wanted to do was bring him back to his dad.

Why did he do it? How did he choose them? What did he say to you?

Did he try to teach you, Ben?

None of it was ever meant to help him. They all wanted to know what he did to Ben, what he made of his son.

All Ben could do was bottle it up in response, tell them nothing, and push every single memory down inside as deep as he could make them go. Take pills to sleep, pills to ignore the whispers that came echoing up out of that space inside of him.

It's always worse in the dark. Worse in cramped, tight spaces. Worse when he knows that he can't get out, that there's no escape. Here on the train, it's not a whisper anymore. His dad's voice is like having another person right there, stuck inside his head with him.

"You figured something out." The cop's phone is buzzing, but she isn't answering it. She's talking to him like it's just the two of them in here. "What is it?"

If only the cop knew. Ben doesn't try to shy away from the voice. It sounds just as terrified as he is. *She would know to be scared.*

"There is no bomb on this train," Ben says.

Whatever the cop is expecting him to say, this takes her by surprise. She straightens up and looks at him like the top of his head flipped straight open to reveal his dad at the controls. She opens and closes her mouth a couple of times before she finds the words to ask a question. "How do you know?" she asks.

"They want to kill me," Ben says.

"That doesn't mean there isn't a bomb."

Ben takes a breath. It's straightforward in his head, but difficult to say. "One Hundred and Eighty-First is one of the deepest stations," he says. "That's why they wanted the train there." He's never been there, but he can imagine it. Brick walls that are wet to the touch. Gravel in the space between the rails.

"What is it, Ben?" the cop asks. "Why is that important?"

"They want me underground." Ben can feel his voice thicken, and he tries his best to keep from crying. He knows what happens if he cries. "My dad . . . the girls he killed. He killed them underground. He burned them."

The cop nods along, like this is not news to her.

She knew all along, you sniveling fuck.

Ben flinches from the sound of the voice, and the cop crouches down next to him, her voice softening. "It's not enough that they got you on the train, is it?" she asks. "They need to get you to 181st Street."

"They want to kill me like he killed them," Ben says.

"Then that's where the bomb will be," she says. They are at Parkway now. Even with the operator slow-playing the journey, they are less than ten minutes out. "I need to call Homeland. We're driving the train onto it."

CHAPTER THIRTY-FOUR

HENRY HUDSON PARKWAY

With the Hudson on their left and the George Washington Bridge growing ever larger in the tinted bulletproof glass that separates the back seats from the driver, it's hard to deny the feeling of victory that's starting to push its way forward and demand ever more of McDiarmid's extremely divided attention.

He's already okayed the team to activate body cameras for when they haul Adam Crane onto the platform—he can see it now, Crane's body sagging at both ends like a downturned mouth, the team carrying him with so little effort that he might as well be a gear bag—and Hoyt is on standby to leak the footage the instant it uploads to the central server. A heroic action by Homeland agents to secure a dangerous terrorist: that's what people will see, and what they will remember. There'll be a flood of interest in the Tuxedo Park Killer once Crane's identity goes public, naturally, and all the usual cranks will do their turn on the talk show circuit, but by then the ink will be dry on McDiarmid's promotion and he will not care in the slightest.

Hoyt will be an issue, though. He is ambitious, deep down inside, and he won't be so much gunning for McDiarmid's old post as turning up to that meeting with a howitzer. The problem is that he isn't made for it. He came up from Tactical, benched from a promising career of kicking in doors and shooting people with a range of high-caliber weapons by a patch of wet floor and the torn meniscus that resulted from it. While that means he is loyal and can think on his feet, it also means that he's burdened with the same no-man-left-behind code of honor that Tactical infects all of their recruits with. Running field ops means having a certain degree of moral flexibility regarding decisions about what's necessary to achieve your aims, and as much as Hoyt is experienced in every other regard, he just doesn't have the stones to send a man to his death.

McDiarmid could feel Hoyt's disapproval when the EMT brought up the likelihood of casualties should a detonation occur. If Hoyt truly was a successor, he would have understood that a detonation of the kind he described—small-yield explosive in a closed compartment, causing multiple deaths and injury—is not just an acceptable outcome: it is a favorable one.

Shutting Manhattan down for the sake of one guy catching a bullet and a single, small explosion will, in retrospect, not be viewed as a success. Once the bean counters start picking the operation apart—if they are not doing it already—then there will be a reckoning over the balance sheet. Millions of dollars in lost business, every single cop putting in their overtime, every fender bender insurance claim—all of it will be put in the debit column and McDiarmid, as Homeland's point man, will be held liable for the credit.

The only way to make it all balance up is if people understand how bad it was. Nobody will be inspired to tell him he did a good job if all he has to show for it at the end of play is an undetonated bomb, and a small one at that. It won't be an impressive sight. No ticking countdown, no red and blue wires to snip. It'll just be an overnight bag or a backpack, and when bomb disposal get done firing shotgun shells into it, it won't even be that. There isn't a computer simulation or demonstration in the world that will convince anyone that the shredded remains of a gym bag and ten pounds of ANFO were worth even close to this much effort.

Bodies, however, will.

Even at half capacity, there are approximately two hundred people on board that subway train. A detonation will kill between two and ten passengers, depending on where they are and how tightly packed the group is, and severely injure at least ten more. A 5 to 10 percent casualty rate falls right in the center of the window McDiarmid considers a success. One or two murders is a hard sell when you're trying to justify the major incident you just presided over. A dozen, though, is a massacre, and beyond that threshold people stop asking questions. Instead, they start to think about how much worse it could have been.

It has nothing to do with morality. Letting things develop far enough that people get to find out how bad things can get is the correct play. The vast majority of the passengers will live. They'll climb up out of the dark, choking from the smoke, half-deaf and disoriented, and they'll be embraced by a grateful world.

The rest are the cost of doing business.

Hoyt jogs McDiarmid's elbow and hands him a phone.

"Hendricks." Hoyt says the detective's name with the level of disdain other people reserve for the dog shit they've just stepped in.

"About fucking time." McDiarmid doesn't cover the mic. He wants Hendricks to hear him. He puts the phone to his ear. "Were you too busy to take our call, Officer Hendricks?" Hoyt has been trying to get ahold of her in the belief that she might be able to neutralize Crane before they ever reach their destination. McDiarmid wants her to stick with him, because nothing breaks hearts quite like a hero cop caught in the blast.

"I understand you are busy, but I have an update from the train."

For a moment McDiarmid is afraid that Crane has given himself away, and that she has subdued him herself. It can't have happened, though. A high-profile arrest like this would save her career from its current downward trajectory. If she already had Adam Crane in cuffs, Detective Hendricks would have called it in on the radio for everyone to hear.

"Go ahead," McDiarmid says.

"There's no bomb on the train," she says. "I think they set it up at 181st Street. We're driving the train onto it."

McDiarmid doesn't have the energy to waste on a sigh. This operation has to go smoothly, and while she might have been a useful tool for filling their computer model of the train, Hendricks is starting to feel like a bump in the track. "Remind me again of the extensive counter terrorism training you've had that arms you to make that decision."

There's a noise, like the phone is being muffled in a sleeve while someone swears out loud.

"With all due respect," Hendricks says, "I have walked the entire length of this train and have seen no evidence of an explosive device on board."

Distortion clips the edges of her words, the call on the verge of disconnection, and McDiarmid wonders if that is what is making her sound so pathetic or if it is just her default state. "I ask again, can you tell me expressly what experience you have had of explosives to make that call with confidence?" he asks. "Remember, Detective, I have read your file."

"Why the fuck are we going to 181st Street, then?" she snaps down the line at him. "Do you think they just really like a historic fucking lighthouse?"

McDiarmid pulls the phone from his ear and mutes the microphone with the flesh of his palm. He can hear Hendricks's voice, tiny in the speaker, calling him a prick. "We've swept the platform at 181st, right?"

Hoyt meets his gaze and nods a single time. He's probably pissed that McDiarmid feels it necessary to ask.

McDiarmid gets back on the phone. "Negative on a device at the station," he says. "Our team has swept ahead of your arrival, and they are—unlike you—trained for this exact possibility."

"Ben said that his dad used to take his victims underground to kill them," she says. "That they are mimicking what his dad used to do. If we could check with the MTA, see if there's something we've missed—"

"You shouldn't give too much weight to his opinions," McDiarmid says. He wants to shut her down, but he doesn't want to give the game away and risk her tackling Crane herself. "Regardless of your feelings about his victimhood, he is too close to the bomber and is emotionally compromised. We cannot take anything he says at face value."

The cop is silent on the other end of the line. McDiarmid can almost hear the cogs turning in her head as she tries to work out another angle of attack. Now is the right time for a pep talk, to derail her thinking and soften her up for her role as bystander and, possibly, victim.

"I don't want you to think this is personal, Detective," he says. "I place an extremely high value on the intel you've given us, and the insight you've provided. But until we are one hundred percent sure, we have to assume that there is still a device on board the train."

"If there's nothing at 181st Street, then . . ." She trails off. It's the first time she hasn't sounded absolutely certain of herself, and McDiarmid leaps on it.

"You did the right thing to call it in," he says. "I'll even get our team on the ground to liaise with the MTA maintenance crews, see if there's anything they could have missed." He moves to hand the call back to Hoyt but Hendricks is already talking and he pulls the phone back. McDiarmid is certain that Hoyt would not give her the time of day but nevertheless he is determined not to let communication with her happen outside of his direct control.

"Do we have any suspects at all? I can work the passenger list from here if your tech guys can share it with me."

"I have a whole team of analysts working that list," McDiarmid says. "Your primary concern right now is to do nothing that might provoke a detonation. We want zero casualties on this, and I don't want you to risk anyone of their lives over a feeling in your gut. Is that understood?"

"Yes."

The informality of her reply is not lost on him. "I have full operational jurisdiction on this, Hendricks," he says. "Do you understand?"

"Yes, sir."

"Good. Sit tight, Detective. You're almost home."

McDiarmid corrects his earlier mistake and hangs up the phone before handing it back to Hoyt.

"Isn't Crane with her in that cab?" Hoyt asks.

McDiarmid is ready for the question. "You want to know why I didn't tell her that Crane is our primary suspect."

"She's an NYPD detective," Hoyt says. "Maybe not up to our standards, but she is trained and armed."

"There are too many factors that I don't control," McDiarmid says. "And that makes me nervous. Crane could potentially have been able to hear my side of the conversation. Hendricks could let it slip by accident, or think that she's able to talk him down."

"You think he'd detonate."

"As professionally indifferent as I am to the NYPD," McDiarmid says, "I would very much not like to get one of their detectives killed because I fed her intel at a vulnerable moment." He takes a deep breath and holds it a second before he speaks, as though steeling himself to impart wisdom. "That's part of running an operation like this. You'll find that out yourself, when you're in my shoes."

Hoyt doesn't even twitch at the mention of a promotion, and McDiarmid is surprised by the degree of self-control he is demonstrating. Maybe it's the stress of having to carry this entire operation himself creating a sense of doubt, but McDiarmid is struck by the feeling that he has underestimated the man.

"Leaving Detective Hendricks in the dark doesn't sit right, to tell you the truth, but it's the right call. We get that train into the station, and we will have a full tactical unit to back her up. Crane wants us there to talk. To negotiate. To show off." McDiarmid holds his left hand out, palm up, and hits it dead center with a chopping motion from his right. "We're not going to give him the chance."

It isn't his best performance, not by a long shot. The interrogation team would chew him out for saying "to tell you the truth," like it isn't the verbal equivalent of hanging a giant neon sign that says I AM LYING TO YOU around his neck.

Still, you can never be too careful.

"Can I count on you to be my eyes on the ground?" he asks.

"Sir?" Hoyt asks.

"I want you down there," he says. "Alongside tactical. Connect with Hendricks, and make sure she gets out."

Hoyt's expression changes, something unreadable behind the stoic facade. He is skeptical—McDiarmid can see that, as clear as day—but he knows better than to protest. He's hitched himself to McDiarmid's wagon, for better or for worse.

"I'll call ahead to Tactical," Hoyt says. "They'll have a spare set of gear."

McDiarmid feigns interest in the updates on his tablet to keep him from having to make eye contact. He feels awkward, exposed, but there is relief in knowing that feeling won't be hanging around for much longer. Any suspicions Hoyt might have about McDiarmid's motives are going to become secondary to the more immediate problem of having his eardrums driven six inches into his head when that bomb goes off.

He taps Cheryl on the knee with the corner of his tablet, making her jump.

"Call the mayor's office," he says.

"What am I going to tell them?"

Success is so close now, that McDiarmid feels like he could just reach out and grab hold of it. Like plucking fruit off of a vine. "Tell them to schedule a press conference," he says.

CHAPTER THIRTY-FIVE

125TH ST.

The hardest thing to justify is a hunch. You either feel it in your gut or you have absolute proof, and there tends to be very little travel distance between those two points. Having walked the length of the train and back, Kelly feels like there should be some kind of middle ground where there isn't anything definitive, but every other scrap of circumstantial evidence points toward the same conclusion.

She can't prove it, but Kelly is convinced that not only is there not a bomb on the train, but they aren't even bound for 181st St.

Working her way up the train, she felt wired the entire time, every one of her nerves stretched to breaking point trying to spot the bomber, thinking about what would happen if they saw her and jumped the gun on a detonation.

Every step of the way back, she felt relaxed. Still watching, still thinking, but not jumping every time someone spoke to her or lifted their phone to get a better angle for a selfie.

Kelly remembers the English couple who worked out her explanation was bullshit, just by using their common sense. When it comes, it's like one of those optical illusions that, once you see the trick, you can't make it go back to how it looked before.

The reason she relaxed on the way back is because she couldn't spot anyone who could be the bomber. Long before Ben put the idea of the bomb not being on the train in her head, her instincts were telling her that the threat was bullshit. Long before McDiarmid shot down the idea of 181st St. being rigged to blow, she knew that they would never get that far up the line.

If there is a bomb—which there isn't—then everything the bomber has done up until now has been counterproductive. They have no demands, beyond moving the train to 181st St.; they have given up the bargaining power of being under one of the highest-value sections of the city for a place that no one at city hall gives a single shit about; and any escape route they might have had in mind is out of contention considering that their destination is a station so deep underground that it might as well be a tomb.

The word *tomb* resonates badly in Kelly's head. She has a hunch—a proper one this time, a deep gut feeling—that whatever the bomber is planning, it doesn't include getting out of this alive.

McDiarmid was cold on the radio, like he has his endgame locked in already. They are waiting at 181st St. for the train to pull in, and if she follows her instincts to the most probable outcome, their plan is to shoot Ben and call that a clean win. If she's going to change that plan any, then Kelly needs more than just her own instincts to back it up.

Evidence would be a good start. She looks at Ben, who is watching her like he's caught her stalking him through long grass: eyes fixed on her, completely still but tense like he is ready to run at the slightest movement.

He isn't a big guy, but Kelly knows not to take that for granted. The one time he flipped, he moved a lot faster than she expected, and she is willing to bet that he's stronger than he looks. She has met addicts who were little more than skeletons with a thin layer of skin knock down guys in full assault gear. You never base your estimate of how much trouble a perp will be on how big they are. At the Academy, they remind every recruit that a four-foot-tall chimpanzee could easily over-power and kill a man if given the opportunity.

She would offer an olive branch, some bond of mutual trust, but Kelly gets the feeling that it wouldn't stick. He was raised by a serial killer and has probably spent the past decade and a half lying flat on a therapist's couch: Ben can probably count the times a conversation with a grown adult not circling around the subject of his dad on one hand. The only time he has let his guard down so far has been when Kelly admitted she didn't have a clue who the Tuxedo Park Killer was.

So make it about him. Get him working the problem with you. If he offers anything about his dad, no matter how leading, deadpan it.

Fuck it.

"I want you to look at the passenger list," Kelly says.

Ben starts when she speaks, and swipes one hand across his face like he's just woken up. He's pale, and visibly shaking, but he holds it together enough to answer her. "I can look," he says. "What am I looking for?"

"Someone has been following you," she says. "You might not have noticed them, but there's no way they could have known which train you'd get on without knowing your movements inside and out."

Ben blinks twice. "You think I might have seen them?"

"It's a long shot, but who knows? Maybe you won't see it until you know you're looking." She unlocks the phone Homeland gave her. "I'll get us the list."

It takes a long time for them to pick up, but in the end Hoyt answers.

"What is it?" he asks. There's a lot of background chatter. They sounded like they were in a car before, so they must be at 181st St. already.

"I need access to the passenger list," Kelly says. "With pictures."

"McDiarmid already told you that we have people working the list." He grunts and Kelly listens to him pulling a zipper shut and the crackle of Velcro. She suspects that both sounds are deliberately loud and made so for her benefit: that he is gearing up and doesn't want to say it on a party line. "And you don't have the authorization."

"I collected that data for you."

"And you have the thanks of a grateful nation." He's trying to keep it light, but she can hear the tension in his voice. Hoyt is being put on the spot, and while he had the linebacker look of a guy who spends a lot of time wearing body armor, she guessed from the fact he's a step behind McDiarmid at all times meant that he's moving up in the world.

Apparently not.

Even though they will never be on one another's Christmas card lists, it sits badly with her to think of the guy who caught that stretcher as it fell from the back of the train getting burned by bad intel.

"Since we're double-checking everything, did you contact the MTA about 181st Street?"

"You mean other than about them being down to one elevator?"

"Those things are a pain in the ass, but I'm guessing that's not the only thing that's pissing you off," Kelly says.

Hoyt makes a noise, a deep, throaty *hmmmm* to show he takes her point. "They've got a water problem down here. It's rubber boots all around."

Kelly once read that on a dry day the MTA pumps a little north of fourteen million gallons of water out of the subway system. Considering the Hudson is almost on top of them, she can believe it. "Right."

"They're trialing powder-based extinguishers because of it. All the sprinklers got pulled out and replaced. If something goes south down here, there's going to be more fake snow than Christmas at Dollywood."

"Like the ones over on Second Avenue?" They passed the training video around the precinct. The powder is meant to suppress fire instantly without suffocating everyone in the vicinity; what it looks like is a zero-visibility clusterfuck, with bonus punishment for anyone who forgets to pack their inhaler.

"Those are the ones," Hoyt says.

A decade and change of casework—of looking at a whole bunch of facts and trying to see the thread that links it all together—means that the question is on its way while her brain is still lining up the pieces. "You think maybe they want those to go off when the train pulls in?"

Hoyt is quiet on the line.

"It would be chaos," Kelly says. "It wouldn't take much for them to set it off."

"That's a good point," Hoyt says. "I'll talk to the maintenance crew off the radio, get them to pull the breakers just in case."

"You watch yourself, Hoyt," Kelly says. McDiarmid won't call off the assault team, not on her word. The best she can do is make sure that Hoyt knows she is on his side. "I'll try and work the problem from this end."

"Thank you, Detective," Hoyt says. "I'll get you that list, if I can."

"Thanks."

"Don't hold your breath, though." Hoyt hangs up.

"What is it?" Ben asks.

"No dice on the list," Kelly says. "Homeland aren't in a sharing mood."

"So what do we do now?"

"Tell me about your job," she says. The thing with the sprinklers has got her thinking. There's no such thing as coincidence. Not in her experience. "How did you get hired?"

"They recruited me," Ben says. "I met the guy at a job fair, filled out a form. A week later they called me about an interview."

"You got an interview off the back of a job fair? What did you say to him?"

Ben's blink rate doubles, like he's trying his best to remember something that his brain never stored in long-term memory in the first place. Kelly worked a job fair once, right back when she was out of the Academy and looking to be a team player. She almost fell asleep standing on her feet. "Nothing special," he says.

"So you meet a guy at a job fair and he offers you a job a heartbeat later, and you never stop to think why they picked you?"

Ben shrugs. "I thought it was because I was cheap," he says. "All the guys with ten years on their résumé would run them seven figures plus."

Kelly stares at him. "Seven?"

"Ninety-nine percent of your working hours are spent building spreadsheets or looking at other spreadsheets," Ben says. "People don't stick around because they like their job."

Kelly gets it. It must have fit him perfectly. The salary was almost meaningless: what he was looking for was a drone-level office job, to be one of a few hundred anonymous number crunchers all wearing the same suit with the same haircut. No one would ever bother to look at him twice, let alone see exactly who he had once been.

The offer of a fresh start was the ideal bait, and he took it without a single doubt in his mind.

Hoyt can't give her the passenger list; McDiarmid won't give her the passenger list. Homeland has their eye on the endgame of 181st St., but she has to try anyway. She sends a message to Hoyt asking him to check out the company Ben got fired from. Maybe the bomber works there, or they found a way to get him in the door.

Ben makes a sound that, if circumstances were any different, would sound like a laugh.

"What?" she asks.

"You said whoever got me on this train must have been following me," Ben says. "But it's dumb luck that I made it. First, that guy on the steps, and then the train didn't move for like thirty seconds." He puts his head back. "I was sure I'd missed it."

Kelly feels dizzy when it hits her. Of course the bomber isn't among the passengers. There's no way they could send all of those messages and risk being seen. They would need to be certain that nobody would be able to interfere or distract them, and most important of all they would need to know for sure that Ben was on the train.

There's only one place where that could happen, where they could stay in complete control of the journey. The one place where Kelly didn't go, because the operator had locked the door and refused to let her in.

"I know where the bomber is," Kelly says. The back of the train jumps as the train rattles through 137th St., and she watches as the platform goes past faster than any of the others have so far. She didn't register it until now, but the train has slowly been picking up speed.

There are three stops left until 181st St.

She pushes Ben aside and pics up the mic, keying the button that will patch her straight through to the operator's cab.

"This is Detective Kelly Hendricks," she says.

"Hello, Detective." It isn't the operator's voice. It is a woman. She can see Ben watching in her peripheral vision, and she sees the color drain from his face.

"Who is this?" Kelly asks.

"Adam knows who I am."

Ben is shaking, his eyes wide. "It's Emily Walker," he says. "She's alive."

CHAPTER THIRTY-SIX

FIFTEEN YEARS EARLIER

There hasn't been a single moment since she woke up in the cage that Emily hasn't thought about escape. Thought about it, and known down to the very core of her bones that her dream of escaping is a doomed one.

Until now.

She didn't know that John has a kid. She knows that he's married, or pretends to be, from the wedding ring he wears, but right up until the moment he marched the boy through the door and into the dungeon he's been holding her in, she never once considered that he might have a kid. Monsters don't have kids, or that's what she thought. Like they weren't capable of it.

She should have known not to underestimate what John is capable of.

Emily has been in the cage for almost three weeks now. She doesn't need to keep a calendar to remember. John makes sure she knows it. Every time he comes down to feed her and switch over the bucket she shits in, he tells her the date and how many days it has been since he kidnapped her. It's one of the few things he says, and she knows he only says it to taunt her. On her first day in the cage, she tried to rattle him by saying that her parents knew where she was, that they followed her everywhere, and that the police would be on their way right now.

At the time, she almost believed it herself. Mom always knew where she was, no matter how many times she changed plans, or how quietly she snuck out of the house. It bordered on the supernatural how quickly her mom could find her and dispatch Dad in his fucking Volvo that he was so proud of to embarrass her into coming home.

Almost three weeks and she has realized that it isn't any kind of supernatural power. Everyone's mom knows everyone else's, and some of them feel like it's their duty to track everyone else's kids at all times. She'd call them snitches, or worse, but considering her current situation Emily is willing to grudgingly admit that maybe they have the right idea.

Emily can tell the boy is his kid. First off, he looks just like him. He's thinner in the face, and his darker hair looks like it will probably stick around longer than his father's did, but the family resemblance is still there.

The other reason that she knows the boy must be his son is because John hasn't killed him yet.

When he brought the first girl in, three days after taking her, Emily thought he was going to put her in the cage as well. She felt a thrill at that, and the heartbeat's span of time their eyes got to meet before he dragged the girl off down a passageway, she imagined that they would team up somehow and overpower him.

Then she heard him grunting, working the saw as the girl tried to fight him off, the muffled screaming, and finally the roar of the burners as he switched the furnace on and burned her alive.

Emily remembers the sounds the girl made as she burned. She doesn't want to remember them, but they are impossible to forget.

The second girl, she pleaded for. He took her five days later, and when he dragged her down through the door, Emily was already talking, begging him to let her go, shouting at him, threatening every kind of hell and punishment she could think of, telling him that whatever this was, whatever he was doing, he didn't have to do it.

In reply, he hauled her cage—the whole thing—down the tunnel to the furnace, every weld shrieking in protest as he pulled, the gravel rolling and scraping as she scrambled and fought to keep her hands and feet from getting caught under a bar as it moved.

He made Emily watch it all: the way the girl kicked the steel walls until they rang as he tried to feed her feet-first into the furnace chamber; how he held her down with one knee to saw off the leg that offended him, the rasp of the wire as it cut through the bone.

How even with her leg cut off, she still fought him. He had to peel her fingers free where she caught hold of an edge on the way in and held on it so tight that she bled. Emily hid her face when he pressed the button, the girl saying *no, no, no* through the cloth over her mouth and at the very end *mommy* before the flames caught and she was screaming and the smoke that was once her boiled out into the room and covered Emily from head to toe, smothering her in her cage.

When he brought the third girl in, over a week later, Emily didn't speak. She didn't even look up, even though John made a point of kicking her cage as he dragged the girl past. He took her gag off at the end, let her scream her lungs out as he pushed her in, so that Emily wouldn't miss a second of it.

It was almost a relief when the burners went on, and the fire cut her off.

All she could think was that she was glad it wasn't her.

But it left a question hanging: If he wasn't going to burn her, then what had he put her in the cage for?

Turning up with his son answers the question.

It's difficult to see what is going on—she knows not to let John see her watching, because he'll make her regret it—but from between her forearms she can see him talking to the boy. There's no mistaking the knife blade when it appears: a bright, clean shape in the middle of all this darkness. This is what he wants her for, why he's been cutting her food and keeping her awake the past few days.

He wants to bond with his son.

Emily watches the boy as he approaches. She keeps her head down. Pretends she doesn't see the knife he's holding, or that she knows what John wants him to do. She has to keep all her anger, all of her strength hidden until the last possible second. She's fucked if he slashes at her through the bars, but she knows that won't be what John wants to see.

She has been ignoring the things men say to her and about her since she was seven years old. He wants to see his boy climb in here with her, to become a man, make him proud. That he wants him to use a knife to do it doesn't really change things.

He's at the padlock now, and Emily can see the knife dangling while he fumbles around, trying to shake the rust out of the mechanism by jiggling the key back and forth. She almost gives in to temptation, almost goes to snatch it, but a knife will be next to useless if that padlock isn't open and the bolt drawn back so she can get out.

He works the bolt, fixes it in place, and grunts with effort as he pulls the door open. Whenever John left her alone in the darkness, she kicked and bucked to try and sink the cage down as far as she could into the gravel, just so he would have to work to get into it. As the door opens, the boy has to lean his weight on it, plowing a path through the stones and dirt, and Emily hopes that it will take as much effort to bring it back the other way.

The boy is crouched at the door of the cage, but he doesn't come any closer. She's ready for him. She knows exactly what she will do when he comes into the cage. She'll roll onto her back and kick him upward, use the strength in her legs and the hard steel bars to knock him senseless, and once he goes down she will get her hands on that knife and show John exactly what will happen to his son if he doesn't let her go.

The only problem is, the boy isn't moving. Emily lifts her head, just enough to see straight ahead, and instantly knows what the delay is.

He's afraid. Whatever resemblance he has to his father is gone, and all Emily can see are the same terrified eyes she saw in the girls as they went to the furnace, the same ones they probably saw when they looked at her.

She would feel sorry for him, but that luxury is long gone. If John gets his way, she'll be going into that furnace without her arms or legs to help her, and no amount of pity is going to stop that.

Emily straightens up and glares at the boy, straining to make her eyes big and startling. When he doesn't move in response, she starts inching forward, making her way toward the cage door.

He has the knife in his right hand, but he is holding his arms out too wide. The span of his arms is just wider than the cage door, and if he swings now, then all he will do is hit the bars. The realization gives her courage enough to fake a lunge, just one quick jerk of her head, to see how he reacts.

When she moves, he jumps back from her, far enough that there is room for Emily to take hold of the bars—a sudden flood of strength filling her as her arms stretch out and her blood pumps freely through them—and pull herself out of the cage.

Emily is hungry. It has been too long since she last ate, and her gut spasms as she stands, tight with the need for food. Every one of her joints aches, a fine, crystalline pain that flares when she straightens her legs and stretches out her arms. Her mouth is so dry that her tongue has swollen in her mouth, and when she grins—to scare the boy even more than he is already—her top lip splits and floods her front teeth with blood.

The boy brings the knife to bear, but keeps his distance. He looks as though he will start growing roots before he ever makes a move.

Emily needs the knife and the boy. She needs them both to get past John.

She turns, just enough to reach out and pull the padlock from the latch. It feels heavy in her hand, a solid weight, and the loop of the shackle hangs out over her knuckles, the notched end of it putting her in mind of a fishing hook. She imagines plunging it overhand into the flesh behind John's collarbone and heaving down hard on the lock to set it deep.

She wants to see John bleed, but his son will do in a pinch. "Come on," she says. Her voice is a rasp, but she wants him to hear it. To know that she is ready to fight him. Ready to kill him, and his fucked-up dad along with it. *"Come on!"*

Emily gets tired of waiting, of watching him just stand there, and she swings at him. It's clumsy with the weight of the padlock and the pain in her arm combining to throw off her aim but somehow she still manages to connect. It's not a clean hit, but it just catches him in the jaw. There is such a thrill to the impact that she almost forgets the knife, and it is only out of sheer luck that the point goes past her arm when he flails back at her. When she pulls away, the edge touches her arm, only for a moment, and yet that is enough to open her up, the cut going right down to the muscle.

Somewhere, in the back, John laughs.

This is a game to him. He'll let his kid piss himself with fear and cut her to pieces, just for the sheer sport of it.

Emily is stronger, and would be faster if moving didn't hurt so much. Two of the fingers on her right hand have gone numb from the cut. She can feel the hot trickle of blood dripping down the outside of her forearm, hear the sound it makes as drops of it hit the floor.

She is bigger and stronger but neither of those things matter. The knife is so sharp that all he needs is one good cut and she will be finished.

Emily needs something else. Something to catch him off guard with.

"Hey," Emily says. "I wanna tell you something." She barely has a voice, but the blood in her mouth helps get her tongue moving. "I'm not the only girl he's brought down here."

The boy's eyes are wide in the dark. He glances at his dad, unsure of what to do. John's voice rings out, hard with authority.

"We don't talk to our meat, son," he says.

"He burned the others," Emily says, ignoring his voice. "Funny thing is, before he killed them, he dressed them up like little boys." She grins at him. "Shirt and pants just like the ones you have on now."

John's voice rings out. "Don't you listen to her!"

Emily ignores him. "He called them 'son' before he did it," she says.

The lie hits the mark before she's finished saying it. It's like the boy forgets she's right there in front of him, his knife hand dropping to his side as he turns to look at his dad, to see if she is telling the truth.

Emily doesn't wait for them to discuss it. She charges at him, reaching for the knife even as she lowers her head and powers straight through, taking him clean off of his feet. The knife comes out of his hand as he flies, and she tries not to grab it by the blade, more luck than skill, and once she has a good grip she rounds on John to show him how sharp the edge is.

The sound of him pulling the hammer back on the pistol he's holding brings her to a dead stop.

"That was a good fight," he says, eventually. "I underestimated you."

Emily says nothing. She forgot to hold on to the boy. Just barged him clear and went for the blade, and left herself completely exposed.

Her one bargaining chip lost, and now she's going to end up in the furnace, just like the others. It's not any kind of comfort to know he's going to have to put a bullet in her before she'll ever let him. She spits at him, the wad of blood falling far short of the mark, but her intention is crystal clear.

"What a spirit," John says. "What a shame to waste it." He takes aim and pulls the trigger.

Emily didn't grow up around guns, but she has heard enough about them to know that sometimes a bullet will go straight through a person. In one side and straight out the other. Whatever John loads his gun with, they aren't that kind of bullet. In the split second it takes him to pull the trigger, his son finishes flailing his limbs around trying to pick himself up off of the floor, and he straightens up right into the space between Emily and the barrel of his father's gun. The bullet that goes into the boy's chest doesn't come out the other side, doesn't do anything but make him jump as if the bang just scared him.

Emily doesn't stick around to watch him fall. She runs, not toward John and the door and the certainty of another bullet, but down the passageway toward the furnace. She doubles over as she runs, trying to make herself a smaller target, the knife still gripped tight in her hand.

CHAPTER THIRTY-SEVEN

145TH ST.

The voice that comes over the radio is warm and calm. It's the kind of voice they hire to record flood and storm warnings. A voice that says that you are in good hands. Emily Walker has the voice of someone who doesn't have a single worry in her life, because everything in it is going exactly how she wants it.

"I've been thinking about your part in this for the past thirty minutes, Detective," she says. "Has Adam told you about me?"

"He told me what happened," Kelly says. "He said you died."

"I came close to it," she says. "You shouldn't interfere in this."

"Yeah, that's a no can do," Kelly says. She looks at Ben to see how he is doing, but the fact that he is curled up into a ball by her knees confirms that he is very profoundly not okay. "There's this whole thing about killing people, it turns out that it's against the law."

"The NYPD kills people all the time."

God, give me a fucking break. Kelly stares up at the ceiling. You know public trust is at an all-time low when even the psychos are getting on your case about it. She keys the mic. "Then what better way to expose our hypocrisy than by taking the high road and giving yourself up before anyone else gets hurt?"

Emily tries to laugh, but it turns into a coughing fit that only cuts off when she stops transmitting.

Kelly leaps into the gap. "You don't need to do this," she says. "This isn't revenge."

Emily keys the mic, but doesn't speak. Kelly can hear her ragged breathing, like recovering from the coughing fit took some effort. "This isn't about revenge," she says. "It's not. If I wanted justice—if there was such a thing as justice—I would have gotten it a long time ago."

"What do you want, then?"

"It's not about wanting anything. I made myself a promise." She pauses to correct herself. "I made *them* a promise. Now all I need to do is see it through to the end."

The train rattles through 145th St. It is really rolling now, all pretense of slow progress gone out of the window. One more stop until they reach Homeland, and however many bullets they decide will be enough to end this.

All she can do is keep her talking in the hope that she makes some kind of breakthrough.

"Must have taken you a long time to set this up," Kelly says.

"You wouldn't believe me if I told you."

"You knew about the trial, what happened with your parents."

"I found out," Emily says. "I knew something happened, but it took years before I got hold of the details."

"You never tried to contact your mom and dad?"

Nothing from the other end of the train, for long enough that Kelly thinks that she has lost her.

"I called home, once," Emily says. "Dad answered. I didn't know my mom was dead, then." All of the confidence has gone out of her voice, and Kelly lets it hang for a second before pushing again. Maybe this is the angle.

"What happened?"

"I told him I wanted to come home," she says. "He told me to fuck off, to never call him again."

"You killed him because he thought you were a prank caller?"

"He didn't even give me a chance." She enunciates every single word, driving each one home like she's beating them into the mic with a hammer. "You know, when I finally—finally—went to see him, it was because I wanted to say goodbye. I thought that, even though we might have hated each other, he deserved to know the truth." Emily falls silent, but Kelly can hear her breathing on the mic. Building up to it. "He wasn't even happy to see me. He blamed me for it—for all of it. Said that if I hadn't been such a disappointment, then I never would have got myself in trouble. That Mom never would have killed herself. Like I had had some fucking choice in the matter."

"So you killed him."

"He deserved it." Emily coughs once, a violent, hacking sound, and even just hearing it is painful.

She's losing her. Whatever crack in the door the story about her dad has opened, Kelly can sense it rapidly closing. "That's tough," she says. "But killing isn't the answer."

"It's the only one I've found that works," Emily says. She sniffs, and there's a muffled sound like the mic moving on cloth. Wiping her face with a sleeve, Kelly guesses. "Is he there? Tell me. Does he look scared?"

Kelly glances at Ben. He doesn't look up, doesn't react at all. "He's here," she says. "To tell you the truth, I don't think he's ever looked anything but scared."

"I remember him," Emily says. "I remember his face coming at me in the dark, and knowing that even though he was scared of me, his dad scared him even more." Her voice is low on the speaker. "He would have cut out my heart, if I had let him."

Kelly takes the mic away from her mouth and presses her knuckles against her own mouth to keep herself from reacting. She pushes hard, the pressure not unwelcome as it distracts her from thinking about a kid with a hunting knife reaching out in the dark.

"Don't do this," she says, at last. "Just let the train roll into 181st and give yourself up. Hell, just walk away. Get in among the passengers and walk. Talk to someone. Get help."

"Find someone to listen to all my problems?" Emily asks. "Imagine how that would work out, the instant they found out what happened to me. Telling me it's okay, that they understand, while in the back of their head they are already writing their book."

"I mean, that sounds like a problem you could fix with a lawyer."

"You don't understand," Emily spits out the words. "I made a promise."

The train reaches 168th St. They go past the platform far faster than MTA regulations would ever allow them to, and the pressure of the wind batters the sides of the train with a deep, hollow boom that makes Kelly feel like screaming.

"I'll tell you what," Emily says. "You put a bullet in Adam for me and I'll let all of these people go."

Kelly stares at the mic in her hand like she can't believe what she just heard. It's not like she didn't expect the other woman to make an offer that there is no way she can accept, but something about it just feels wrong.

It's in the way she says it and the timing of it that sets Kelly's instincts alight. It's as though Washington Heights coming and going was a surprise, and that surprise has forced her hand. Kelly has never been a gambler, but she knows that Emily is bluffing.

Kelly keys the mic. "There's no bomb on this train," she says. "Is there, Emily?"

A pause before she answers.

"I just want Adam," Emily says. "You need to walk away."

The defeat in the woman's voice brings everything into line in Kelly's head. She might not have every scrap of evidence to hand, but she has enough. There's no way that she wanted this to end with a standoff, or by putting Ben in Homeland's crosshairs. She has something else planned.

A chill passes through her at the thought of a derailment, of what would happen if the train jumped the rails.

"There's no bomb at 181st Street, either," Kelly says.

She knows that the MTA can hear them. That Homeland can hear them. Even with the train going too fast, there are fail-safes on the line that will prevent it from crashing if it reaches the station at speed. If they're quick, they might even be able to cut the power now.

"You're right." Emily's voice is distant, like she's not the one holding the mic. "But we're not going to 181st Street. We never were."

Before Kelly can reply, a red light goes on in the cabin and the emergency brakes activate. There's no delay between the light changing and the sudden deceleration: Kelly has no chance to brace against it, and inertia flings her forward, bouncing her hard off of the door of the cab, her left shoulder and rib cage taking the brunt of the impact. Ben, still hunched over the moment the brakes hit, rolls through her legs like a bowling ball hitting a strike, and she falls, landing on top of him hard enough that it knocks the wind out of her.

The train travels on for a hundred feet or so, and the floor of the cab vibrates like a saw blade as the wheels lock under them, the screech of metal not just deafening but making every bone in Kelly's body feel like they are being ground to powder. To give credit to the engineers that designed it, the train doesn't come apart or derail. Nothing major detaches or fails, and with a final, bone-juddering shunt, the two-one-five out of South Ferry comes to a complete stop.

CHAPTER THIRTY-EIGHT

FIFTEEN YEARS EARLIER

No gunshots follow Emily's flight down the corridor to the furnace, but she moves as though expecting one. Her feet slip in the gravel as she lurches first one way and then the other, and every time her hands find the concrete walls she leans heavily against it, trying to give some relief to her legs. When she was in the cage, she tried to keep herself from sitting too long in one position, but not being able to stretch her limbs out for so long means that her body is shocked to discover that standing upright is not just a memory. Her calves are trembling with the effort of running, and with every step each muscle feels as though it is set to spring up her leg in protest and wrap itself in an obstinate, useless ball at the back of her knee.

There isn't any pain, not really, but Emily knows that it is coming. She can feel it hanging dangerous inside of her, like the taste of thunder in the air on a clear day, and she knows that her body has pushed it all to the side, telling it to wait for later. That she will give the pain its due, if she lives.

A hollow bang echoes down the corridor, and Emily cries out like she has been shot as it overtakes her, but it is just the sound of the steel door closing.

She takes no comfort in hearing it. It could be a trick. She can still feel the heat of John's attention on her back, see in her head the swinging loop of his aim as he tries to find her in the darkness.

Moving blindly forward, staring into black so deep her eyes conjure shapes to defy it, Emily still knows when she is close to the furnace. The slaughterhouse smell of old blood and burned meat rises up like a wall in front of her, and her steps falter as she sinks face-first into it.

There is no back door to the bunker. No other staircase or secret ladder. There is only the door that John brought her in through, and to take that is to accept that a bullet will meet her on her way up.

She could wait. Could hunker down in the hope that John's son is so severely wounded that he won't have the time to come back down and finish her off, but Emily knows in her heart that it would be a mistake to depend on John to do something human. If she waits, he will come back for her, and even armed with the knife and the chance to surprise him, she knows that he will kill her.

There's only one option left: to get inside the furnace and climb the chimney at the back of it.

Emily cuts a strip from her shirt in the dark by feel and wraps it around her forearm where John's son cut her. It doesn't seem to be bleeding so much with her holding her arm against her ribs, but getting up the chimney will be a different matter. She has to use her teeth to tie it, and the wave of pain that comes with pulling it tight makes her gag on the cloth.

The handle on the furnace door is a thick metal bar that lifts up to reveal the broad, horizontal mouth of the furnace itself. Emily heaves, expecting it to be heavy, but instead it lifts easily, the weight of the door canceled out by the dull clank of a counterweight moving inside the furnace walls.

Whatever care John took with the door is missing when she climbs inside.

He hasn't cleaned it out at all. The first thing she puts her hand on is a thin curve under her palm, and in the second it takes to register that she is leaning on a bone it snaps under her weight. Emily can feel herself bleed where the bone has cut her, and she forces herself to pick as many of the brittle shards out of her hand as she can before she moves on.

Sweeping the ash and debris to the sides, she can't tell if all three girls are in here with her, or if it's just the remains of John's last victim. Every time she presses forward, she dreads the thought of putting her hand out and finding a skull waiting to fit into the palm. Waiting to remind her that her life is still hanging by a thread.

At the back of the furnace, two racks of spiked metal rings—the burners—hang down at a shallow angle. They rattle loose in the rail that they hang from and are easy to push past, but once she is past them an accidental kick with her feet tells Emily that they only give way in one direction, and that she is now trapped in the furnace.

The panic that she has been able to keep ahold of until now springs loose at the thought, and she lashes out, kicking at the burners and letting out a scream that sets the ash of the other victims swirling inside the close metal walls, their last act to cut her scream off dead and send her into a fit of coughing that makes her forget the panic that caused it.

All she has to do is get to the chimney. That's all she can do now.

The cuts in her hand from where the bone shattered are starting to ache. The makeshift bandage she put around her arm feels too tight and everything from that point down to her little finger feels numb, but she can't stop now. She has to get out of here. She couldn't do anything about the others dying, couldn't stop him from killing them, but she can make sure that they aren't forgotten.

I promise I'll get out of here. Emily squeezes her hand into a fist, feels blood warm in her palm, binding her to it. *I promise I won't waste this.*

At the back of the furnace, there is a ninety-degree bend that turns upward into what feels like empty space. Emily shifts over onto her left side, and then her back, shuffling all the way until her head meets the back wall, roughly aligned with the center of the furnace. Using the back of her head and her hands to brace her weight, she starts pushing herself up until the sharp metal edge of the corner stops her and she has to shuffle herself, a fraction of an inch at a time, slowly up into a sitting position.

The effort is exhausting. By the time she is sitting upright and her weight is no longer held by her arms, Emily can feel the first taint of defeat creeping into her thoughts. That she is going to die here, that none of this matters, and all she has done is just put herself in a coffin.

Something touches Emily's face, and she flinches before she understands that it is fresh air, and there is a draft coming down from the surface. It feels cold, cold enough to make her whole body shiver, and that motion alone is what gets her moving, gets her knees through the complicated combination of angles and tension to pull her legs into the space with her and then up, feeling with her hands for the opening of the chimney.

The chimney mouth is a flattened cone, the back of the furnace tightening down to a circular hole that Emily reaches up inside and finds the lip of a metal tube giving way to what feels like brick. When she stands, she finds that it is just big enough to fit inside and no more, and that to climb it she will have to make the decision now to have her hands either above her head, or down by her waist. With no space to pull even if she could find a grip, Emily opts for the latter: with her arms pinned from shoulder to elbow, she kicks and jerks until her foot catches on the metal rim, the rubber toe of her sneakers giving way like the rind of an orange as she pushes off of it and steps up and out of the furnace into hell itself.

Emily has no sense of how long she has been in the chimney. There's no light and no sound to speak of, no smell beyond the acrid touch of soot that makes every breath burn on the way in and out. She doesn't even have the bones of the other girls to keep her company anymore.

All she has is the knowledge that if she breathes in as deep as she can and presses her elbows out hard, then she can lift her feet something like six inches, and on the exhale push herself a fraction farther up the chimney. A fraction closer to the surface.

Everything that was once Emily is now gone. Every dream, every crush, every secret hope. All she is now is that same six inches of motion that exists between one deep breath and the next, repeated over and over, and the pull of the cool air that is waiting above. The rest of her can wait.

A smell rises from underneath her. It is faint, but in the darkness with nothing for her mind to focus on, even that tiny hint is enough to send her senses into overdrive.

It's gas.

There's no roar from the furnace, no smoke rising to meet her. John isn't down there with his hand on the button, waiting to see what happens.

He has loosened a valve somewhere, and is filling the bunker with gas. He said that fire is the only true purge, that anything else is a lesser effort.

He has failed, and now he is trying to purge that failure.

It doesn't make her feel panicked. Or afraid. Emily as she was would have been afraid, but here and now all she can feel is a cold sense of resolution. An absolute certainty of what she needs to do. She needs to climb, and to get out of this chimney, and then she needs to show John exactly how much he has taught her about the cleansing power of fire.

Emily stares upward in the darkness and tries not to imagine how far she has to go. Instead, she thinks about how much of her body is blocking the chimney, and that if the fresh air from above can't get past her to meet the gas below, then there is a chance that maybe there won't be enough oxygen for it to ignite.

It is a slim hope, but there is nothing else for it.

Somewhere off to her left there is a faint tremor, like a distant explosion. Emily clenches her jaw hard and tries to put it out of her mind.

A wave of heat roils up from below, and she feels her bladder releasing in blind terror at the thought of how much worse it will be before she ever reaches the surface.

Emily thinks about what she is going to do to John to pay him back for this, and his son alongside him. She takes a deep breath, pushes her elbows hard against the brick wall of the chimney, and climbs.

CHAPTER THIRTY-NINE

168TH ST.—181ST ST.

As Kelly's hearing comes back to her, she can make out shouts from farther up the train, screams of alarm and pain. She tries not to imagine the number and severity of injuries Emily Walker has just caused. She hopes that everyone else on the train was, at the very least, sitting down.

She uses the chair to help climb back to her feet, her hands and fingers grasping numbly like she has been drugged, and as she gets her feet under her Kelly can see that Ben has got himself out from under her and is already upright. He's saying something to himself, over and over, but the ringing in her ears means it takes three repetitions for her to catch it.

She's alive.

"You told me that you killed her, Ben." Kelly says. "What happened?" She tries to control the volume of her voice, but it is hard when she can barely hear herself speaking, so she keeps the question firm and deliberate.

Ben is on his knees, straight-backed, fists hovering in the air just above his thighs. It's as though a weight has been laid across his forearms, and he is straining to hold it. He takes a shuddering breath before answering,

"I thought she died," Ben says. "My dad, he . . . he built a way to destroy the bunker in case the government ever came for him. He said the only way to truly clean something was with fire. There was a valve, hidden behind a locked panel, that he could use to vent all the propane into the bunker. When we got there, he told me . . ." He trails off, unable to keep himself from sobbing.

"You thought the fire killed her?"

"I thought—" Ben nods, but he can't seem to say it. Not right now, at least. "My dad, he put me in the bed of his truck and he told me . . . he told me it was finished. That I had made my choice. He told me that I was the one who would carry on his work, once he was gone."

"And then what?"

Ben lifts his head and looks straight at her. "I ended up in a hospital bed. He drove me there, rattling in the bed of the truck like a sack of tools he'd forgotten to strap down, dragged me out onto the steps and took off home. Someone at the hospital called the police and they got down there as fast as they could. By the time they arrived, he stabbed my mom four times and made himself a pot of coffee to drink while he waited for her to die."

"Jesus." Kelly breathes the word, trying not to let him hear it. She wonders about the way Ben pauses before saying he woke up in the hospital. How much of that story is true, and how much has he forced himself to let go. The brain forgets trauma, not for a lack of space to hold it, but as a defense mechanism. Even just that little distance—*I blacked out, I don't remember*—might have been enough to keep him from breaking entirely.

"She survived, but . . . she wasn't the same. She went into a coma, and part of her never came back." Ben looks down at his hands. "Didn't want to come back."

"And Emily Walker never gave you any sign that she was alive?"

Ben doesn't answer.

If she ever tried to contact him down through the years, then he doesn't know it. Kelly can imagine how many calls his psychologist must have screened, how many cranks they must have had to fend off. No wonder they gave him a new name and shipped him out of state.

The ringing in Kelly's ears has faded enough now that she feels confident that she can get to her feet and not throw up or fall over. She pulls the weapon that Homeland gave her and checks that it is loaded. There is a bullet in the chamber, and the safety is on. She thumbs the laser sight, and a green beam lights up, scattering off of the dust that has been hanging, unnoticed, in the air. "What did she look like?"

"What?"

"Emily Walker. What did she look like?"

Ben tries his best to describe the girl that Emily Walker once was, but it is useless. *Blond hair, round face, pretty* are words that could describe one in every twenty women in the city. The way he talks about her, it's like he's describing a photograph, all of his emphasis on her expression and posture and very little on what she actually looks like. As he says it, Kelly feels like she can imagine the shot, her brain filling in the blank of the girl's face with one that she has probably seen on a poster. Trying to get back to the mental image of the train, all she can see is that same poster face, superimposed on every person in the car.

She changes tack. "You might have met her," Kelly says. "At Data-Dyne today, or before you started. She would be a lot older than you remember her, somewhere in her late twenties. She could have changed her hair, or have glasses."

Ben tries, or at least it looks like he tries. He shakes his head when he is done thinking. "They all seemed so normal," he says. "I feel like I would know . . . I mean, even if I thought she was still dead I feel like I would still have known." He thinks about it for a moment. "How long has she been watching me?"

Kelly is too distracted to even try and answer the question. It feels like her brain is being pulled apart by the possibility that almost every single woman that she saw on her way to the front of the train could be Emily Walker.

Or that she could be none of them.

There is a pneumatic hiss that echoes down the length of the train, and all of the doors in the next car open. From the sound of it, all of the doors have been opened. It feels like a diversion. Creating chaos so that she will miss something. Kelly wonders how long it will take Homeland's assault team to start moving down the track once the MTA tells them that the train has stopped.

"Get everyone off of the train," Kelly says to Ben. "Take them back along the rails to 168th Street."

He blinks at her, like he was expecting her to say something else. "You want me to just . . . leave?"

Kelly sighs. "This isn't your fault, Ben. And it sure as shit isn't your problem."

She takes a step toward him, and Ben starts back from her like he is expecting some kind of violence. Instead, she pulls off her body armor, the sound of Velcro loud as it rips loose, and lifts it over her head to offer to him.

"Wear it," she says. "If she gets past Homeland, and gets past me, she might still find you in the tunnel. She's got some kind of surgical saw, like a garrote, but don't assume she won't put a bullet in you to try and end this."

Outside the train, the first passengers are already stumbling along the track, their footsteps illuminated by the light of a hundred cell phone flashlights, all of them trying to move fast but not so fast that they fall and cause a pileup. Kelly can hear at least one person talking about compensation already.

She puts a hand on Ben's forearm as he lifts the body armor over his head. "Don't put your head out until I get past the first car," she says. "Emily is trying something, but we can use the chaos to our advantage. Get lost in it, and get yourself to safety."

Ben meets her eye, and for a second he almost looks defiant.

"Homeland will probably arrest you," she says, "but jail is better than dead, okay?"

"Okay." Whatever she saw in his face before, it's gone now. Ben closes the straps on the ballistic vest, twisting to check to see if it fits. It's far too short for his height, and she doesn't have the heart to tell him that it looks like he's wearing a tactical crop top. "And I'm sorry," he says.

"What for?"

"All of it." He gestures at the train, the track, the oncoming crowd. He takes a breath and hesitates.

"What is it, Ben?"

"I should have told the truth," he says. "At my dad's trial. I should have told them what happened. I was afraid . . . I was afraid they'd put me away along with him."

Kelly tries not to think about the clock ticking on Emily Walker, and how she should be moving right now to try and intercept her. There are a lot of tunnels down here to get lost in, and the longer a head start Kelly gives her, the greater the risk that their bomber will slip the net.

"Don't worry about it," Kelly says. "You're a victim, not a killer." She steps to the door and works the handle. "None of this is your fault."

Kelly steps down from the train and turns on the flashlight on her own phone, collaring the first passengers to arrive so that she can direct them back to 168th Street, and safety.

When she takes a look back up into the conductor's cab, Ben is gone.

CHAPTER FORTY

FIFTEEN YEARS EARLIER

Even though he can't see anything, Adam knows that his dad has carried him up to the first level. He is lying on concrete, not gravel, and all he can hear is the sound of the ventilation system humming as it pulls air through the bunker. He has moved him, but they are still underground.

"So you're awake, then?"

Adam doesn't think that he moved or made a noise, but then his dad has always known things like that. Like he can tell Adam is getting tired from how sloppy his work is, or that Adam is hungry because his aim goes to shit. Or that he can tell when Adam is lying, even when Adam feels like he is telling the truth.

"Took you long enough."

His dad sounds mad, and that makes Adam afraid. He can't feel his chest. It's like everything between his collarbone and waist has gone missing, has been cut right out of him. Adam knows he should be afraid of that, but what really scares him is knowing that he has made his dad angry.

There are always consequences when he makes Dad angry.

Adam tries to apologize, but there is cloth over his mouth that makes it hard to speak. That's why he can't see. His dad has put the bag on him. Beneath the cloth, the floor is hard against his nose and lips. He doesn't think that he was lying face down, but it is hard to argue with concrete. When did Dad turn him over?

"Calm yourself, now."

Adam can't tell if he is breathing hard or not at all, and he wonders if he is really awake, or if this is a bad dream. When he was little, he used to scream to try and break out of bad dreams. Adam knows better than to try and scream his way out of this one.

"Hold still."

Above him, the sound of plastic tearing, and something being poured out. Dry, like grains of something.

"This will hurt."

His dad puts his palm flat against Adam's back, and the void where his chest had been fills up with fire, like his dad has taken a blowtorch and lit it inside of him. Adam tries to scream, but he can't because the pain in his chest is too much for him to even breathe, let alone make a noise.

The pain drops off, but doesn't disappear entirely. It feels like he has been branded, a circle of skin on his back burning a permanent awareness of itself into his consciousness, and as Adam takes a ragged breath he can taste iron. He knows what his dad has done to him. There are bags of WoundSeal all over the bunker, packed away with dressings and gauze and bottles of isopropyl alcohol, all ready for the day when the world falls and you can't just go to a local pharmacist. His dad told him that if you ever needed to use it, it would burn like hell but that the pain would be worth it if it kept you alive.

Adam remembers what happened. He got in front of the gun, hoping his dad wouldn't pull the trigger if he got in the way. If he didn't shoot her, then maybe the girl would get away.

Instead, his dad shot him in the back.

There is another burst of pain, and Adam isn't there for all of it, but when it is over he is sat up against a wall, and the bag is being pulled free of his head.

They are in the bunker, just like Adam thought. He can't move his neck to look around, but he knows that they are in the airlock, the double-door seal that Dad built to keep the outside world at bay should the need ever arise. His dad has opened a hatch set into the wall i.e. right now, almost level with Adam's head. He can just see inside, where his dad has put the key into the keyhole and turned it all the way to the right so that the key lines up perfectly with a label marked PURGE. The label is peeling free on one side, and as Adam looks at it, his dad lets out a grunt of dissatisfaction and reaches out to smooth it back down with his thumb.

Below the key in its keyhole, there is a round, red button, the surface matte from where his dad has sanded off the words EMERGENCY STOP.

Adam's dad doesn't need to ask him if he knows what it is. He made a point of making his last resort the first thing he explained to Adam when the bunker was ready. If he presses the button, the gas bottles he uses for fuel will vent into the bunker, mix with the air, and ignite. Every load bearing structure in the bunker has been designed to collapse in the heat of that fire. Anything that doesn't burn will be crushed when eight hundred tons of topsoil and concrete compacts down onto it.

His dad is looking at him. He doesn't look mad, but then Adam knows that his dad doesn't ever *look* mad. Every time he puts Adam in the dark, he looks just like he found something that needed fixing, and that before he can do anything else he needs to get it done.

"I blame myself for this," his dad says. "I thought that you were ready. That you would be up to the task." He shrugs. "Obviously, I was wrong. I got ahead of myself."

All Adam can do is wait. Breathing feels hard, like every breath has to be worked for, and even if he thought that he could speak, he knows that there's nothing he could say that wouldn't be a disappointment.

"You lost a lot of blood on the way up here," his dad says. "Bet you're feeling pretty sleepy right now. I can see you checking in and out." He reaches out a hand, like he's going to hold it to Adam's cheek, and gives him a single, sharp slap. The pain of the slap is nothing compared to the jolt that travels down through his neck and into the wound on his back. He jerks upright, and all of his senses feel pin sharp, like he can see every line and scar across the knuckles of his dad's right hand.

"I need you awake for this, son," he says. "You see, with the Wound-Seal, I reckon you're probably not going to bleed out anytime soon. What's going to get you is infection, and you know that when it comes to infection, time is a factor."

Adam remembers his lessons. About the bugs that try to get inside you, how they can give you a fever. How they can kill you. Adam knows how to wash a wound and how to look after it, because when there are no hospitals and no doctors to help you, there won't be any antibiotics. He knows that even if he finds some antibiotics that they might not work because the bugs are smart enough to defend themselves.

"Son, I know that sometimes people make bad choices because they don't know better." His dad watches Adam to see if he is listening, and Adam makes an effort to try and nod, to move his head enough so that he won't get slapped again. "You can spend a lifetime training yourself to meet the most important moments of your life with a clear head, and still let impulse fuck things up for you."

His dad picks up his pistol and holds it where Adam can see it.

"When you jumped into my shot, you fucked things up for both of us," he says. "And I want to give you the chance to think about that. You wouldn't jump in front of my rifle if I had a ten-pointer in my sights, would you?"

Adam watches his dad's hands work the safety on the pistol while he talks, the red dot next to the slide winking at him as it vanishes and reappears over and over.

"The girl and the buck are one and the same, Adam. There's no difference between the two of them. You understand that, don't you?"

Adam tries to breathe, but something catches in his throat and he panics, almost falling sideways as he tries to cough it up. His dad waits for him to clear it, then sets him upright.

"You understand, don't you, Adam?"

Adam doesn't want his dad to be angry, or disappointed. He doesn't want him to hit him again.

He doesn't want to die.

Adam tries to blink, feels his eyelids move like they are on a delay: first one closes, and then the other rushing to catch up. It's enough for his dad to take it as a yes.

"So I am going to wait outside this door," his dad says. "And when you are ready, I want you to press that button. When you do, I'll come get you before the fire gets this far up." His dad cocks his head to one side, and Adam can see that he isn't looking at him anymore. He's looking at the gun. "If you don't press it, well, I already wasted one bullet on you. Don't feel like there will be much reason for me to open that outside door again, if you and I can't agree."

The safety goes back on, and the gun goes back in its holster as his dad stands up. He stretches, arms up over his head and then out to the sides, puffing his chest out like he's limbering up. Adam feels a pulse of heat from the wound in his back and imagines the tiny bugs burrowing deep, making themselves at home in there. He tries to move his arm, but only his fingers move in response. His dad sees it and leans down to look.

"You can move that arm if you really want to," he says, and puts two fingers on Adam's shoulder. The touch is gentle, like a blessing, and Adam can feel the tears building hot under each eye, getting ready to fall. His dad leans closer.

"Be a good son," he says, "and kill the bitch."

CHAPTER FORTY-ONE

168TH ST.–181ST ST.

You fucked it up, son.

The pain in Ben's head is like something alive. A bloated, heavy presence at the base of his skull that shifts and pulses with the cadence of his dad's voice.

The fire didn't kill her. You didn't kill her.

The words are so loud in his head that Ben talks back. "It can't be her," he says. The cab feels too small, like the walls are about to crush him. He plucks at the bulletproof vest, the Velcro straps ripping as he pulls them loose. The panic builds so fast that he can't stop it, can't do anything to stop it. "It can't be."

Ben pushes the cab door open and surges blindly forward into the rear car of the train. There's more space here. The air is cooler. It isn't much, but it's still just enough to tamp down the fear that is starting to overcome him.

All Ben can think of is Emily Walker's face. The one picture they all used—her parents, the press, the lawyers, the psychiatrists—of her caught laughing while out on a winter walk, knit cap pushed back on her forehead, cheeks flushed from the cold, her eyes looking at some-one just off to the photographer's right-hand side. They showed it to him, over and over, pressed him with it, and over the years he almost came to accept it as what she looked like.

Not like the last time he saw her face, every curve flattened into a mask by streaks of blood and soot, a single glance backward before she ran headlong toward her fate.

"She's alive," Ben says. There is no one here to hear it. Ben doesn't care.

You didn't kill her.

"I didn't kill her." Hearing it in his own voice feels different. Like he isn't a disappointment. When Ben finally pressed the button to purge the bunker—fought to press it, screaming every inch of the way, just desperate to survive—he thought he killed her. When he closed his eyes, he saw her die, and in his heart it was just the same as if he had used the knife. Knowing that she got out changes everything. He isn't the thing his dad wanted to turn him into. He isn't a killer. "She's alive," he says.

Emily Walker is alive, and she wants to kill him.

She has been dead in his mind for fifteen years. All the time, she must have known that he survived, that he was still alive. She has been actively hunting him. She could have walked up to him in the street and put a bullet through the back of his head. He would never have seen it coming. She could have burned his house down while he slept, or hit him with a car. At any time, at any distance, she could have killed him.

But she didn't. Emily Walker wants him down here, in the dark, trapped in this metal cage she has made for him. She wants him to witness his own death, and to know that she is the one that made it happen. That it was always going to be her.

A memory of the notches along the back of a freshly sharpened blade surfaces in his memory. The weight and feel of it in his hand. How easily she took it off of him.

Emily Walker doesn't want to end this with a bullet.

She wants to kill him with a knife.

Ben wonders if it will be the same one she took off of him.

He should have known when the train started moving. He should have seen the damp walls and felt the weight of all that earth above him.

He never truly left that bunker. Fifteen years of therapy, and all he ever learned was how to lie to himself about it. Fifteen years, and he can still see the shock on her face when his dad pulled the trigger, the way she jumps and how he thought that she had taken the bullet anyway.

That he didn't make it in time.

Ben can feel the smooth outer coat of the ballistic vest under his fingers. Some things he can't remember, but he has never been able to forget the feeling of the bullet inside of him. A cold, dead spot, heavier than the rest of him, hanging high in his chest, right next to his heart.

Fifteen years, and he can still hear his dad telling him that it is his choice: to kill her or die himself.

Ben's phone rings in his hand.

He looks up along the length of the car, expecting to see her at the far end. The car is completely empty. The seats and the floor are a mess of food wrappers and bottles, plastic bags and books: all discarded when the train stopped dead halfway between stations. There's something unsettling about the emptiness. Even though Ben is certain no one is in the car with him, he can still feel a presence, like someone is expecting him.

He waits: takes a breath and holds it, listening for any movement, any sound at all, like the ringing phone is a trick to distract him.

There is nothing.

Ben looks at the screen. The number on there is one that he never expected to see, one that he memorized a long time ago so that if he ever saw it, he would know not to answer. His first instinct is to drop-kick the phone, to smash it beyond repair. He wants to find the cop and have her put a bullet through it. He wants to run and never look back, and let Emily Walker find her own way out, no matter who she ends up killing on the way.

Ben lets those thoughts run their course without doing any of them. There is no need to avoid it. Not now. He sits down to answer the call.

"Hi, Dad," Ben says.

"Hello, Adam," John Crane says. "Or should I say Ben?" His dad's voice is unchanged by incarceration or age. It is exactly how Ben remembers it, and he can hear how pleased his Dad is. The way the words bounce like he's standing over a stripped engine holding the nut that worked loose, or like he's just keyholed his last shot at the shooting range. "I wrote to you, but they told me it was unlikely you'd ever receive them. Did you ever get my letters, Ben?"

Ben knows that his dad wrote to him. Not one of them ever reached the outer wall of his dad's psychiatric unit, let alone the postal service. He asked that they be destroyed, and had to have his lawyer contact the unit administrator to confirm that they had complied with his request. They had wanted to keep them. *"For posterity,"* they had said, but what they really meant was for their own gratification.

As always, all they had cared about was John Crane.

"What do you want?" Ben asks.

"I told them I needed to speak to my lawyer," he says. "And . . . I know it's difficult for you to process what's happening, but I'm glad we got to speak. The time we spent together was one of the happiest times of my life."

Ben checks that the door he came in hasn't opened while his dad has been talking. He can feel himself getting angry. All those years, all that distance, and his dad has stripped it from him with a single phone call. "I didn't hear an answer," he says.

"What I want," John Crane says. "I want you to know that I have done a lot of thinking about what happened. I know you've given it a lot of thought as well."

"I've tried not to." It comes out faster and higher than Ben intended, almost manic. He can't believe that this is what it has come to. His dad—a killer—talking like he's some kind of reformed alcoholic wanting to go over old regrets.

"And in the course of my introspection, I wondered if it was something I had done," he says. "Something in the way I raised you or trained you. That maybe I pushed you too hard. Rushed you into things before you were ready."

"I was eleven years old, you fuck." The phone shakes in Ben's hand. His eyes are smarting, and he desperately wants to wipe them but he can't make himself do it. He heard once that when you get electrocuted, every muscle in your body seizes up. That you can't let go of the thing that's killing you, even if you try your hardest.

"Then I came upon a revelation." His dad waits on the line for a question that isn't coming, then answers it anyway. "It realized that it was you, son. You never liked the hunting, or the killing. It made you feel squeamish. I thought it was just childishness, but really I should have recognized the truth: that you just didn't have it in you."

"Yeah, well, I'm sorry to disappoint you," Ben says. "Sorry I didn't want to follow in your grand tradition of killing girls so you could get your dick hard."

"I'm not disappointed, of course." His dad is talking like he always did. Like only half of the conversation—his half—matters. "It was a relief, really, to know that my only mistake was letting my hopes get the better of my judgment."

Ben feels like screaming into the phone, but he can't find the strength to. Fifteen years of therapy and all Ben can do is sit in mute, angry silence while his dad leaves him hanging, like a day hasn't passed since they put him away.

"You know, when you jumped up in front of my gun like that, you set in motion a series of events that even I could not have foreseen. When the first birthday card arrived, I thought it was from you. A faint, paternal hope, which was another mistake by me. It was only when she started sending letters, pretending that she was some kind of journalist trying to find out more about me, that it struck me that that girl was still alive."

"You knew?" Ben forces the words out.

"It wasn't a shock," his dad says. "I left you to finish the job, after all."

"What did she want?"

"She wants you, Ben." He says *Ben* like it's a joke, a secret nickname they share between them. "Me too, of course, but then she knew she'd never be able to get me, not while I was in here."

"But you didn't know where I was."

Ben is forced to listen to his father put the handset down because he is laughing too hard to hold it. It's the same mocking bark that he has always had ready, for every missed shot, every letter or number turned backward.

For every time Ben cried in front of him.

"Son, I knew exactly where you were," his dad says. "From the day you changed your name, from the moment they moved you out of state."

"So you told her?"

"And have her end it right off the bat? I think not." There is a creak of movement, rubber chair legs on a vinyl floor, and Ben can almost see his dad leaning back and putting his feet up to savor the moment. "I gave her a few breadcrumbs, enough to keep her hungry. Suggested a few ideas on how she might go about finding you." He laughs. "She was so keen to get started. Those poor boys. She knew as soon as she found them that none of them were you, but she killed them anyway . . ."

His dad trails off, and Ben wonders if he is proud, or jealous.

"You manipulated her," Ben says. "Made her do this."

"Oh, no. All I did was give her a little help. A push in the right direction." There's a thud as he sits back up again, putting his feet down flat on the floor. His serious voice. "You can't begin to understand the path she has been on. Ever since she climbed up out of the flames and the dark. She has so much courage. Patience. Tenacity. Everything I told myself I saw in your timid little face, I see now in her."

Ben starts at that. "You can't be serious."

"I am, son. You see, she went dark after I suggested she take a closer look at the trial, and I knew then that she had found you, and that she didn't need my help or advice to take the final step." He's breathing hard into the line, unable to hide how excited he is. "And I'm so proud. Of both of you. Because if you hadn't taken that bullet, I would have ended up killing the one person worthy of being my successor," he says. "The daughter I never had."

Ben has got it all wrong. He isn't down here to be punished for his part in this. He's here to be replaced. "But you only have enough love for one of us, right?"

Again, that rush of breath, the pleasure in his voice. "You were always a clever one, I'll give you that," he says. "I didn't know she would make such a spectacle of it, to be honest. I thought I might get a finger in the mail. But . . . here we all are. It's a shame there isn't enough room in the world for both of you."

Ben takes a deep breath and tries to compose himself. It doesn't do much good. He feels angry and ashamed all at the same time and he can't get free of the knowledge that his dad has been able to reach out from the padded cell they kept him in, past every lock and wall that stands between them, and take up the same strings Ben thought had been severed fifteen years ago. All this time he thought his life was his own, and here he is playing the role that has been set for him, except this time his is the sacrifice, and the woman that was once meant to be his victim is now the executioner.

"She's waiting for you," his dad says. "In the tunnels."

Ben wants to say something smart, something that will cut his dad to the quick, something that will force the knowledge into his brain that no matter what happens, he was, is, and always will be just some piece of shit who thinks killing people made him important.

He doesn't even try, because he knows that none of it will even stick. His dad is insane, a walking shell of violent impulse where a human once existed. Ben's mom just might come back one day, but there is nothing he can do or say that will ever reach his dad.

"Bye, Dad," Ben says. "Whatever it was that broke you inside, I'm sorry it didn't kill you before you got your hands on anyone else."

His dad makes a noise into the line, the same unpleasant, tuneless humming he would do if he saw Ben not making a knot just so, or if he lost a fish from the hook.

"Good luck, son," he says. "I hope she doesn't kill you too quickly."

Before his dad can hang up the phone, Ben drops it and steps on the screen, feeling it crack and grind under his weight, hearing the sound of the phone—and his father's voice—dying.

CHAPTER FORTY-TWO

168TH ST.–181ST ST.

As the passengers work their way down the length of the train, all heading for 168th St. and the promise of safety, Kelly waves them past with as little interaction as she can. A couple ask about the third rail and how likely the risk of electrocution is, but Kelly grunts and moves them on. She hopes that someone at the MTA has put two and two together and cut the power after seeing the emergency stop go off.

If they haven't, well, it's probably for the best that she doesn't mention it. Tell a bunch of New Yorkers not to put their hand on something and there's going to be a race to see who can be the first to touch it and show the world that nobody tells them what to do.

Not all of the passengers acknowledge her as they pass, and Kelly can see that they are badly shaken. Plenty of them are limping, probably from losing their footing at the sudden stop, and nobody is pushing to get ahead. At the speed they are going, she guesses it will be five to ten minutes of walking before they reach the platform at 168th, and anyone who doesn't have a phone to light the way—or enough battery life left to make that happen—is going to have a hard time keeping their feet.

Part of her wants to lead the way. To set a good pace and get every single person—herself included—out of this tunnel as soon as humanly possible. It would be the pragmatic choice, and not just the one that would put her aboveground at the same time.

Kelly stays put. Counting heads as they pass, looking at faces, trying to keep track of all the people she saw when she walked the train.

Looking to see if Ben is somehow among them.

Her gut says that he has gone after Emily Walker, but she still has to check. One Hundred and Eighty-First Street is a long walk from here. It's more likely he's still close to the train.

Kelly doesn't have much of a wait before the operator shows his face. She's sure there are still people from the last cars to come, but he shows up before they do, skipping past the slower-moving passengers like he is trying to beat them to the Black Friday sales. In the weak back cast of the flashlight he's holding, he looks like a human-sized rodent: between the pale skin and the slicked-back hair, his head darting nervously from one side to the other as he moves forward in little fits and starts of rapid motion, all he needs is a set of whiskers and a tail, and the illusion will be complete. He dodges around one last woman who has already reached Kelly, almost pushing her over in the process. As he tries to press past, Kelly gets ahold of his shirtfront and hauls him back before he can go any farther.

Grabbing him is a mistake.

As soon as she gets a grip on him, before she can even pull, he lets out a scream that is so loud and so high-pitched that the woman whom he just overtook jumps and screams herself. Looking down the train, Kelly can see the lights from the remaining passengers jerk to a stop, and all of them point in her direction.

"Get the fuck off of me!" The driver recovers quickly, his fear channeling straight into anger, and he backpedals hard, trying to jerk himself free.

Kelly turns the fistful of his shirt she's holding through a half circle, tightening her grip and pulling her back toward him. The woman he shoved edges carefully past them, and he leers at her as she passes. Kelly has never disliked a person so intensely at first sight as she does this guy. She feels like she will need to wash her hands after touching him, and that even soap and steel wool might not be enough. She makes a mental note that, once she gets out of this fucking tunnel, to get the guys in Cyber Crime to take a look through his internet history, even if it means they have to burn the servers after they get done.

"Is everyone off the train?" Kelly asks. He ignores the question and turns to head down the tunnel, but she grabs him again and pulls him back. When he looks at her, his face is wild with fear.

"Don't fucking touch me, bitch," he says.

Kelly is tempted to punch him, but she isn't about to give him the satisfaction of an assault charge. "Answer the question," she says. "Is everyone off the train? If you don't know, we can walk back and check."

Kelly straightens her arm and shoves him, pushing him toward the way he came. That gets his attention, and the defiance in his face vanishes by the time she has taken ten steps down the track.

"Train's fucking empty," he says. He leans over her arm and spits onto the track in disgust. "Everyone but your boy."

"My boy?"

"Saw him walking back that way to go sacrifice himself," he says. "Better him than me. If I was in his shoes, I would have run." He lifts his chin as he's talking, and as the shadow lifts off of his neck Kelly can see for the first time the ragged red line all the way down from underneath one ear and across his throat. It looks raw, and his collar is stained with blood where whatever was wrapped around his throat has broken the skin.

Kelly lets go of his shirtfront. He might be a piece of work, but she can remember the sound he made into the mic when Emily Walker strangled him. A surgical saw: a loop of serrated wire that can cut through skin and muscle and bone like being drawn through butter. Nobody deserves that.

"What was she like?" Kelly asks.

"She's fucking crazy," he says. "Stone cold. I don't know what your plan was but that guy? He's a dead man." He sniffs. "Thought she was going to kill me but she hopped off the train and started walking."

"Walking? Where to?"

"How the fuck should I know?" The operator spits the words at Kelly, then shows her his back. "She went across the tracks, probably looking for one of the old tunnels," he says. He tucks his head down, more vulture than rat with it almost at the level of his shoulders, puts his hands in his pockets, and starts walking. "I wondered why she stopped the train when she did," he says.

"You think this will be on TV?" The woman who jumped in shock has been standing next to Kelly the whole time, probably waiting for the operator to walk on rather than risk getting shoved or groped by him in the dark.

"What?" Kelly asks.

"I asked if you think this will make the news," she says. "I, uh, took a day off work today. Told them I was sick. If they see me out here, then . . ."

Kelly's head is full of the thought of Emily dropping down into the dark, and the question of what she is planning to do with Ben, but the part of her that used to walk a beat doesn't miss a single step in answering. "Get someone to put a blanket over your head," she says. "Ambulance crews will have dozens. Maybe even a foil one. Camera guys won't want their lights reflecting off it."

"I never thought of that," the woman says. Her face lights up, like all of her problems have been solved. "Hey, thanks!"

She doesn't go anywhere, though, and Kelly wonders if she is waiting for someone else to catch up before she moves on. They stand like that for a good half minute, the woman hopping from one foot to the other like she's got ants in her pants.

"So are we going, or what's happening?" she asks.

Kelly didn't even register that the woman is waiting for her. She was thinking about the emergency brake, and how Emily pulling it wasn't done in panic. It wasn't a mistake.

They were never going to go all the way to 181st St. She stopped the train here so that there would be a panic; forced the operator to speed up so that there would be more injuries, more chaos. Emily did all of it so she could have Ben to herself.

Kelly saw the state of the operator's neck, bruised and cut all the way around, the scream he let out when she touched him. She did that to him, just because he happened to be in the way.

She can't imagine what Emily has planned for Ben.

"I have to go the other way," Kelly says. Ben could be getting skinned alive while she hesitates. It will take too long for Homeland to organize at 181st and start moving down the tunnel to back her up. She needs to move.

Kelly reaches behind her and touches the gun strapped to her back. She doesn't pull it—better leave it until the woman moves on, keep her from panicking—but the solid weight of it against her fingertips is like touching a good-luck talisman. "You'd better get moving. Just follow the lights."

Kelly leaves the woman standing there as she picks up the pace and starts jogging down toward the front end of the train. Between the running lights and the shooting gallery formed by the train and the subway wall, she regrets giving Ben her ballistic vest. A rescue won't count for much if she gets herself shot for the effort. Seeing more cover and surer footing back on board the train, she hops in through the nearest open door and starts running.

CHAPTER FORTY-THREE
168TH ST.–181ST ST.

They don't brick up old tunnels in the subway. Disconnect the junction, and for the train and all the passengers on board it might as well not exist. Turn off the power to the lights and, in the heartbeat span of a train passing, nobody will ever see it.

"She's waiting for you in the tunnels."

That is what his dad said. Ben knows that he should run, that he should get to 168th St. and into some kind of protective custody. He can see in his mind's eye the picture she sent him of the lawyer she killed, his throat sawn almost all the way through.

He should run.

Instead, Ben is going to find her.

He didn't kill her. Ben has carried the guilt of her death for a long time. The knowledge that he was a *good son*, and that no matter how he tried to deny it he would always be the killer his father made him. Knowing that he didn't kill her is not a relief. No weight has been lifted. He doesn't feel any different.

Ben didn't kill Emily, but he didn't save her, either.

What happened to her in the bunker broke her, just like it broke Ben. But while Ben has had therapists, and care, and time to try and heal, she has been on her own. What hope her parents might have had was crushed when Ben testified in court, and that is not his dad's fault.

It's Ben's.

Ben won't run, because he knows that neither of them left that bunker. Not really. Ben doesn't expect forgiveness from her—or any kind of mercy—for what he did to her. The least he can do is try and offer her a way up out of the darkness.

He knows that she will try to kill him. That if she has planned all of this, all the way up to stopping the train at this very point, she will most likely succeed.

Emily Walker has become the killer his dad wanted, and Ben knows that he is, in part, to blame. Not because he hit the button and tried to incinerate her, but because he was too scared to tell the truth in the aftermath.

Ben will answer, because the thought of walking away—of failing her one more time—is too much for him to bear.

He finds the tunnel mouth on the far side of the track, his instincts making him cut across at a right angle to the train when he hopped down from the driver's cab. Emily won't be headed back with the passengers, and with the train dead in the tunnel by her design. The only way left to go is across the tracks and into one of the hidden tunnels on the far wall.

The darkness makes his head swim. Ben can feel his dad in there alongside him, his voice demanding to be heard. Speaking to him has made it stronger, more insistent, and now it is telling him over and over that killing her is the only way out of this.

She's hunting you. Waiting for you to blunder into her trap.

The tunnel mouth is a circle of darkness cut out of the main route. Rail tracks, severed at the nearest point, run off at an angle to the tunnel Ben is in and are swallowed by the black. The mouth of the tunnel looks like it is moving, eternally shrinking inward while the perimeter stays unchanged, and Ben can feel it pulling at him, drawing him forward even though he knows what is waiting for him in there.

The best place to attack you was when you were getting off the train.

Ben doesn't want to agree with the voice on anything, but it is right. A snare set between cars, or just outside the train ready to snag an ankle as he stepped down, would have been the perfect opportunity to disable him. Even if he was armed, there would be enough pain and confusion that a good hunter would be able to close the distance quick enough to make it irrelevant. His dad taught him that.

Ben wonders what she has learned about hunting in the past fifteen years.

She could be right there in the dark, just out of sight, waiting for him to silhouette himself against the opening.

Ben waits, listening for something—a breath, a footstep, any sign of impatience—but there is nothing. He took a flashlight from the driver's cab at the front of the train; an aluminum tube almost the length of his forearm, heavy with batteries, and he turns it on now, playing the beam around the edge of the tunnel, looking for any sign of Emily.

She isn't waiting for him. Not here.

Ben turns off the flashlight, wary that she will have seen the beam and now knows exactly where he is, and lets the draw of the old tunnel pull him in, slipping past the event horizon and into darkness.

He reaches out, fingertips searching for the wall, and finds it farther away than he expected. Working in the dark shortens your steps, and you have to adjust accordingly. His dad would have hit every outstretched finger with a switch as punishment for groping blindly.

Ben's hand brushes concrete, presses against it to confirm and finds it damp to the touch, and with that point of reference to work from, he starts walking.

Easy. One step at a time. She'll want you nervous. Jumping at the slightest noise. That's what I would want.

It was only in therapy that Ben understood the reason for all of his dad's survival training. What all of their trips out into the wilderness were meant for. He taught him how to track prey, how to drive it into the killing ground. He taught him about how to stalk, and when to strike. He taught him about the dark.

He wanted him to become a killer.

And as much as Ben has tried to deny it, it's all still in there, every scrap and fragment of it etched deep by a son's burning need to be just like his dad.

All Ben has to do to survive this is give in to it.

She thinks she can beat us. Stupid bitch.

Ben puts his hand flat against the concrete wall and presses hard, trying not to make any kind of noise as his gut spasms, a physical need to vomit out the badness that is roiling up inside of him. He wants to scream out loud, to run, to get away. To do anything but let the voice take over. His fingertips cut shallow furrows in the crumbling damp of the wall as his hand closes into a fist. Fifteen years of running rolled back in a single afternoon, everything he tried to make of himself stripped away, and now it feels like all that separates Ben from the Adam his dad tried to build is a single decision: whether or not he tries to kill Emily Walker.

He is so tired of having to choose. So tired of going to sleep every night knowing that he turned the switch that would kill her. That he didn't just do it: that he fought to do it. He's tired of spending every waking moment knowing that there are worse things to lose than your life.

It's why he still hears his dad, why there isn't a therapist or a pill that can get rid of his voice. Because he did what he wanted. Because he made the wrong choice.

Ben waits for the spasm to pass, a long string of saliva stretching down from his open mouth until he jerks upright to try and break it, like letting it connect with the ground will poison him somehow.

He straightens up. Ben knows the choice he is making now. A second chance to try and get it right. He wants to try and save Emily Walker, even if she won't let him.

Even if it costs him his life.

He moves on, and when the floor lifts underfoot Ben tests with his foot until he finds the edge and, a shade higher than waist height, the railing that goes with it. He is on a walkway, and that means there must be a platform up ahead.

The subway is littered with ghost stations. Some are famous ones, grandiose spaces full of century-old architecture and detail that is meticulously cleaned and kept open for the kind of visitors who can afford to throw a party there. Most are just rotting boxes of steel that got sidelined by a planner moving two lines on the city map half an inch to one side. Listening to the insistent drip of water—the Hudson must be close, little wonder that they moved it—and the distinct lack of a cocktail party tells Ben that it was probably the latter.

She'll get you at the corner, where it opens up.

Ben ignores the voice. She didn't get him at any of the other corners. It's just repeating old ideas his dad might have said, a release valve for every paranoid thought that creeps up from his hindbrain.

He finds the corner when the cold air hits his shoulder and neck, a draft of dry air coming down from some unused vent still open, and confirms it by hooking his heel around the edge of the wall. He puts his hand to the wall and feels brick instead of concrete.

She has a surgical saw. If she's going to do anything, it will be to hide in the dark and wait for an opportunity to slip it over his head. Ben holds the flashlight vertically, still keeping it turned off, with the body of it just next to his face.

Of course she could use it as a snare and have it ready to take one of his ankles out from under him, but Ben feels like leaving his neck exposed is the greater risk.

He looks out into the dark, turning through a slow one-eighty from left to right, hoping that there might be some kind of light that his eyes can adjust to. All he gets are purple shapes bursting in his vision from the effort of looking at nothing at all. He can't even see his own hand in front of his face, let alone anything beyond that.

He listens, straining to hear anything beyond the sound of his own pulse, a thick, throbbing noise that, if he focuses on it, tries to fill his head.

A single drop of water lands somewhere off to his right, down where the rails would be, with a fat plop that suggests it is dropping into something a lot deeper than a puddle. Ben is glad he didn't walk down the tracks—the sound of him walking into a pool of standing water would have made him easy prey.

The station smells rotten, like things come here to die. Ben can smell old piss and the stink of alcohol, and wonders if there is another way down here, a secret staircase that the homeless use. It's a hell of a distance down the track for a drinking spot.

There will be pillars in the station. No space this big would keep from collapsing without them. Emily will be waiting for him somewhere close by, waiting for him to make a noise or use a light or something that will give her a target. If he can find the pillars, he can gauge how far it is between them, and that will give him a grid to clear.

She'll be clearing, too. Counterclockwise.

Most people draw their circles counterclockwise. They drift that way, too, if left to their own devices. Ben doesn't want to. Counterclockwise puts his back to the rails, and a three-foot drop onto them if he gets pushed off.

"You should have killed me."

Emily's voice doesn't ring out. It is thick, a rolling, heavy sound that echoes off of the walls like thunder. Ben turns his head trying to get a sense for where the sound came from, but the effort is useless. She spoke quickly so that he wouldn't be able to pick out her real voice among the echoes and tell how far away or how close she really is.

You won't know until she's on you.

"I didn't want to kill you."

"What you did." She pauses mid-sentence, and Ben wonders if she is hurt. "Was worse."

She isn't hurt. She moved during the pause. Stole a few steps to close the distance between them. Ben can hear it.

He slips around the corner and takes a chance. He steps forward.

"I spoke to my dad." Ben says it fast and loud. He takes another step forward while the echoes are still ringing. "He said you got in touch."

As soon as he is finished talking, he takes the same two steps back and to the side, putting his back as close to the wall as he can. He hears a scrape, like she is rushing to get to him, and he starts moving counterclockwise, away from the sound.

There's another sound, a swift, tearing noise, like a wire being whipped out into the darkness and only catching air.

"Did he tell you what he thought of me?" Emily asks.

Ben can hear the disappointment in her voice, but all he has won is a little time. She doesn't even try to hide where she is now, her feet scraping along the platform floor as she tests each step. She knows that she has him running.

Ben backtracks a little, projects his voice to make it feel like he's not made much progress. If she runs at him, then maybe he can knock her out with the flashlight.

"He told me you were my replacement," Ben says. He steps away, feigning a retreat this time. "That you were the daughter he never had."

Emily replies with a hollow laugh. There's another snap of movement in the air, like she is lashing out with her loop of razor wire. Ben hears it bounce off of metal.

"He told me the same thing," Emily says. "What a fucking idiot."

Another snap. Closer. Catching on nothing, he hears the wire whine as it cuts through the air.

"He didn't even need working on," she says. "One letter, and all he could think of was how I could honor his legacy."

Emily isn't running. She's changed her tactics. He knows exactly where she is, because she is whipping the air with her saw, working her way toward him in the dark.

"All of you are alike," she says. "All he could think about was himself."

Ben starts moving, feeling for a pillar to put between them. If she lashes out at him, he wants something to be in the way.

"When I climbed out of that bunker, the burns on my legs were so bad I thought that all the skin had come off." Emily's voice is hard. "There was so much pain, I was sure they were on fire. That I was still burning."

Ben doesn't answer. The saw cuts through the air close enough that he feels it passing, and he waits her out, knowing that when she speaks it will give him enough cover to move.

"A guy from the forest service found me trying to put the fire out with dirt," she says. Ben slips away, getting on the far side of another pillar. He has a good idea where the next one will be. He has no plan, other than to get himself as far away from that saw as he can while he thinks about what to do.

"He put me in the back of his car and drove me out to this cabin he had," Emily says. Ben can hear her footsteps. She's still moving parallel to the wall, while he is heading across the platform. He's making distance, which means he is gaining time. "I remember him telling me it was closer than the hospital. That he'd get me help." She cracks the saw through the air like a whip. "Like I was in a position to argue."

If Ben can get behind her, he can use the flashlight to disarm her. Hit her when she's whipping it out, make her drop it.

"He cleaned me up, washed off my legs, put Saran Wrap over the wounds," she says. "Stuck me in a bed and told me not to move, that if he moved me I might get infected. That the infection would kill me."

She lashes out with the saw, not once but three times, and then another three, and Ben jumps as a tiny chip of cement flies out of the darkness and catches him in the cheek.

"I woke up one day to find him trying to work out how to get my panties all the way off." she says. "He got them down to the wrap, but when he pulled it further my skin started to peel off. Woke me up through the painkillers. Even that didn't stop him from sticking his hand between my legs."

Ben can feel the blood on his face, a warm spot in the cold air. He doesn't dare talk. He suspects that she has slowed her assault to make sure he hears her.

"He didn't know I still had your knife," she says. "And when it was done I knew one thing for certain. That there wasn't another soul alive that I could trust."

Ben stays quiet. He tries to feel the cadence of Emily's breath in what she's saying, tries to match it as close as he can. He doesn't aim for stillness, because his dad taught him that if you try to stay perfectly still, then your body will betray you.

"I stayed in that cabin until the food ran out," she says. "He stockpiled a lot while I was unconscious. I guess he had plans. No one came looking for him. While I was up there, all I could think about was what I would say to my mom and dad. What I would tell them."

She stands silent for a second.

"When I could finally walk out of there," she says. "When I finally got to a phone, my mom was already dead."

She isn't using the saw anymore. Even so, he can still tell roughly where Emily is. She made her way along the wall and took a right turn, and now she is roughly level with where Ben is hiding, maybe twenty feet away.

"When I was climbing, I told myself I would get John for everything he did to those girls," she say. "But the more time has passed, I realized that I wasn't doing it for them anymore."

He wonders if there is a back wall, or if she is walking along the other edge of the platform.

"I'm doing it for me."

If it was the edge of a platform, he could rush her.

Or she could take one step to her left and watch you fall, you fucking idiot.

"There's only a couple of ways to get to John," she says. "I tried to get a job there, but the background checks would have found me out. I always hoped for a heart murmur, so that I would be able to find him cuffed to a table in the local hospital."

Safety is the best option. Finding distance; making time. Ben wants to talk to her, but she is hunting him, and any sound he makes will betray him. Even if he could speak freely, he doubts there is anything he could say that she is interested in hearing. His best option now is to try and disable her somehow. Bait her into moving past where she thinks he is and swing for her head with the flashlight.

"I wrote to him, though," she says. "You would be surprised how easy it is to get hold of a serial killer. You know they pay the guys who mop the floors minimum wage in there? They were slipping him letters from fans already. I was just another customer."

Ben falls back, feeling for the next pillar. He is roughly in the middle of the platform now, so there should be at least two more pillars before he is in danger of falling off of the edge.

"And after a while, I realized that while I might not be able to get to him, then maybe they'd let him come to me," she says. "But for that, I would need to find something he couldn't resist. Some kind of media circus."

Two quick steps and she closes the distance between them like she has known where he was this whole time. The saw comes snapping out, hissing as it uncoils, and carves through the space where Ben was standing a moment ago. It's so close that he feels the air shift as it passes.

"Something like his son's funeral," Emily says. Ben can hear her breathing hard from the effort of swinging the saw at him. "He might not give a shit what happens to you, but he won't be able to resist getting in front of a camera one last time."

The tactics have changed again. It isn't about stealth anymore. It's about survival.

Ben moves as fast as he can, diagonally across the platform, bouncing from one pillar to the next, just trying to get as much space between himself and the saw as he can.

As he reaches the next pillar—almost at the far end of the platform, he can't tell—his foot lands in something liquid and he slips. Unable to control the fall, both of his feet go out from under him and he lands heavily on his left side.

The smell of alcohol rises from the thick fluid that Ben has landed in, and too late he realizes that this is the killing ground, and she has driven him into it.

There is a fizzing noise, and a burst of orange-red light as Emily lights a road flare.

Ben's eyes aren't ready for it, and he holds up a hand to ward off the brightness.

Emily Walker is little more than a silhouette, and yet it feels as though he recognizes her immediately.

You should have killed her.

All Ben can think of is the girl in the cage, her back against the bars. Of how scared he was. That he didn't want her to die.

"I'm sorry," he says.

Ben knows that he should be afraid, but the fear isn't there to claim him. He feels empty, as though there is nothing left to be afraid of.

Emily holds the flare in front of her, and as Ben's eyes adjust he can just make out the look on her face. It isn't rage, or frustration, or even triumph.

She looks as though she is completely at peace.

"Tell God that, when you see him," she says, and tosses the road flare into the pool of ethanol gel that Ben is lying in. The orange-red flame vanishes, and for an instant Ben is left staring at an afterimage and wondering if the fuel hasn't taken.

There is a sudden gust of wind, like the subway station just took a breath, and a bright blue flame races through the dark to swallow Ben whole.

CHAPTER FORTY-FOUR

168TH ST.—181ST ST.

It takes Kelly some time to work out where Ben has gone. She half expected to find him still on the train, and once she cleared the operator's cab, she took her time checking the far side of the track before finding the tunnel he must have gone down.

As she stares into the tunnel mouth, a patch of darkness that angles off of the main track in the direction of the Hudson, every single nerve in her body is singing the same refrain: that she shouldn't have let Ben go alone.

She should have brought a bigger fucking flashlight than her cell phone. It's good for showing her what she's about to step on and maybe for picking out movement at ten or fifteen feet, but otherwise the beam is too spread out to be useful. The dark just eats it.

Kelly checks the sidearm that Homeland equipped her with. She has no complaints at all on that front. It's probably better than her service sidearm, although she wishes they had swapped out the laser dot sight for a flashlight mount, even if strapping it to her back would have ended up putting a couple of her vertebrae out of alignment.

She finds an access ramp leading up to a walkway off to the side of the track, and a couple of scuff marks that could be footprints.

Ben has come this way.

She shouldn't have left him to go after Emily alone.

It felt like exactly the right call when she made it. Even with the train stopped and all the doors open, even with the absolute conviction in her mind that there was no bomb on the train, she still had no concrete proof of it. And without proof, she could not risk endangering the operator or anyone else on board if Emily Walker happened to have a second device on her, just in case.

Leaving Ben in the cab was the right call at the time.

Homeland would call it the same way, she is sure of it. Her captain will probably agree. When they finish the inquiry into this whole incident, she will probably get a commendation for it.

But Kelly, and every other cop that reads the transcripts, will know it was the wrong one.

Maybe if they had just headed back to 168th St. along with the other passengers, Emily Walker would have given herself up. She must have known that the second the train stopped she would lose what little control she still had of the situation. A crowd of people in the dark, all stumbling down the track to 168th St., there would be too much confusion for her to target Ben, and once they got aboveground it would be too late. Maybe if Kelly had found a way to rile her on the radio, she would have missed her mark to stop the train and they would have run right onto the assault team waiting at 181st St.

If she had just done something different, there would have been better options in play than letting Ben throw himself at a Goddamn psycho because he felt guilty about what his fucking dad did to him.

Or maybe it wouldn't have worked out that way at all, and they would be in exactly the same situation they are now, except with more dead bodies added to the pile.

The farther she goes down the tunnel, the more Kelly's doubt drags at her, slowing her down. She remembers her training. It's all about the present moment. About focus.

You started the day wanting to get out of shit duty, she thinks. *Well, here you are getting your wish.*

There is a corner up ahead. Kelly can see the edge where the wall just vanishes, and she guesses that it used to be a platform. She slows up and points her flashlight toward the floor, trying not to telegraph her approach too hard.

One of the SWAT instructors who ran the close-quarters combat training told her once that, when she was ready to go, Kelly should say the astronaut's prayer. She mouths the words into the dark.

Dear Lord, she says. *Please don't let me fuck up.*

A wind picks up around her, pulling at her hair as it passes, and from the platform comes the whoosh of an ignition. The whole of the platform up ahead lights up with an unearthly blue color, and Kelly hears Ben scream.

There's no time to think. Kelly flicks off the safety on her weapon and runs toward the light.

Stealth isn't the answer here. Emily Walker wants Ben dead. She wants him burning in the dark, and the fire is already lit. She won't be waiting to see if he has backup. This is her ideal outcome, not bait for a trap.

Knowing this, Kelly goes straight around the corner and out into the open space, gun up, moving past the pillars that are holding the ceiling up, trying to get a clean shot.

Dead center in the middle of the platform, Kelly finds Ben struggling to fight off Emily Walker.

Caught in the beam of her flashlight, it doesn't look like either of them are on fire. The blue flames surrounding them disappear in the light, weak as it is, but Kelly can still feel the heat from where she is standing.

An ethanol fire. It's not a bomb, but Emily Walker had a plan after all.

Ben is on his knees, his body upright, back arched, and both of his arms up in front of his face as he tries to keep a thick, silver-gray wire from closing around his neck. In one hand he's got a flashlight, a foot-and-a-half-long Maglite, and it is doing the lion's share of work keeping the saw at bay. His other arm is caught, too, though, and the wire has cut deep into his forearm. The blood running down from the cut is bubbling, cooking in the heat from an invisible blaze.

Emily is standing tall behind him, one foot lifted and set in the middle of Ben's back, her hands clutching two handles attached to either side of the wire, gritting her teeth as she hauls on it, as though trying to pull it clean through him. Her clothes have caught fire as well, but she doesn't seem to notice.

The air is thick with the smell of burning: clothing, hair, flesh. Every breath of it reaches for some primal place in Kelly's soul, flooding her body with adrenaline.

Kelly doesn't shout a warning. She doesn't need to. Emily is looking right at her, her face a mask of rage, every one of her teeth showing as she heaves on the wire harder, desperate to finish what she started.

A real shoot is nothing like shooting at the range. The range is for working the fundamentals: make safe, make ready; line up your target and your sights; take your shots and learn to ride the recoil. The range is a place where you drill the basics over and over, letting the memory of shooting center of mass sink into your neurons until they become second nature.

A real shoot is something they can't work into any kind of drill. It's about the choice you are making, the last choice when every other option has been ruled out: that you are ready and willing to use deadly force.

That you're going to kill someone.

The gun comes up into line fast because the gun is lighter than she is used to, but her arm corrects the ascent before it can lift any higher than the intended line of fire.

Even if Emily can't see the gun, she can see how Kelly moves and knows what's coming. She tries to turn her grip and wrestle Ben around to put his body between the two of them.

It doesn't work. She pulls as hard as she can, using every pound of leverage and every ounce of pain to try and move Ben the way she wants him to, but he is fighting her every inch of the way. Both feet planted, his whole body straining against the pull of the saw, he is trying to break free. He doesn't see Kelly. She can't be sure he sees anything. He's fighting her because all he has left is the will to survive.

The gun might be lighter, but its trigger has the same five-pound pull that Kelly has drilled with since the Academy. It doesn't fight her in the slightest. There is no hesitation between Kelly making the final decision to kill Emily Walker where she stands and the gun firing.

Kelly doesn't wait after the first shot. She fires three rounds, both eyes open and looking straight at her target, letting muscle memory do the work. All three rounds are clean hits to Emily Walker's center of mass, as tight a group as Kelly can make it. Shooting Emily—killing her—takes Kelly less than four seconds.

By the time Kelly finishes her third shot, she is already aware that Emily has started to fall. She has been adjusting her aim the entire time, following Emily down after the first shot hit. Kelly lifts her head, finger easing off the trigger, and she sees the surgical saw dropping loose on either side of Ben where he stands. Emily Walker's body collapses, her leg folding underneath her, and she lands, a dead weight, in the pool of her own fire. The flames flare around her, a wave of blue, and vanish again.

By the time Emily Walker has landed, Kelly is already moving forward, running straight into the fire. She drops the gun and her phone as her pants catch fire, the pain a sharp flare that leaps up the whole length of her leg in an instant, and as she grabs Ben and hauls him out of the burning pool he's lying in, she can hear someone screaming.

Kelly doesn't want to think about the fact that the voice is hers.

CHAPTER FORTY-FIVE

181ST ST.

No plan survives contact with the enemy. That was the parting shot that McDiarmid's predecessor had offered him when he took over the man's role. After hearing this nineteenth-century field marshal's maxim for battlefield maneuvers, McDiarmid was sure at the time—and every day since—that the old man had chosen it because it sounded pithy rather than out of any genuine belief in the advice.

That certainty lasted right up to the moment that train two-one-five out of South Ferry came to a complete and unexpected stop in the tunnel somewhere between the stations at 168th St. and 181st St. He'd been patched into the conversation between Adam Crane and the woman claiming to be Emily Walker along with everyone else, but that conversation hadn't come as a shock to him. Crane was trying to muddy the waters before the train could reach the station, looking to sow the same kind of doubt that had kept Hendricks from slapping a pair of cuffs on him the moment she climbed on the train. Crane was trying to control the situation, not aware that by doing it, he was playing right into McDiarmid's hands.

The shock came when the train stopped.

All hell broke loose on the radio: the MTA jumped onto the main channel to ask if they should kill the power to the track immediately; someone else took that as an admission that they had cut the power and the train had stopped because of them. What was a clear line suddenly turned into a shouting match between the different agencies involved, all of them desperate to be the first on record to say that it wasn't their Goddamn fault.

Rather than waste his time trying to shut the argument down, McDiarmid adopted the standard operating procedure that Homeland recommended when presented with hostile inter-agency fighting: walk away and let them use up all their energy fighting each other. Hoyt and the tactical team were on a separate channel and their radio discipline was, by necessity, excellent. It would take a lot more than their personal feelings on the train stopping to break it.

The silence on the radio is more unsettling than the chaos on the other line, so he pushes the button to transmit. "This is McDiarmid," he says. "Status report."

"Holding position." Hoyt's voice is unmistakable, even over the radio.

For maybe the first time since he took Hoyt on, McDiarmid envies the man. Down on the station platform, it will be quiet, and while it won't be calm—the simmering tension of an operation about to commence is anything but—there will be a sense of shared purpose that is sorely lacking here at the street level.

A cascade of blaring horns catches McDiarmid's attention, and he looks up and through the barricade of ambulances and cop cars to see what the hell is going on. Two of the news vans—two of the closest to the action—are trying to turn around and get back onto a street that is already gridlocked. They look like they are in a rush. One of the vans has its doors open, and the crew are throwing in gear even as the driver lurches the vehicle back and forth trying to find space he doesn't have. The camera crew from the other one is already running, trying to get clear of the crowd and away in case their van never gets free.

No plan survives contact with the enemy. McDiarmid has always thought his predecessor was full of shit, but maybe he just hadn't phrased it right. Maybe what he should have said was: if the press know what's happening before you do, you're fucked.

McDiarmid catches sight of Cheryl and waves her over. She has a radio earpiece in one ear and a cell phone held against the other, but she still catches the gesture and makes a beeline for him.

"What the hell is going on?" McDiarmid asks.

"We're getting reports that there are people on the tracks heading back to 168th," Cheryl says. If his ignorance surprises her, she doesn't show it. "It sounds like all the passengers are getting off the train. NYPD are there already waiting to pick them up."

Seeing that there's no follow-up, Cheryl goes back to her phone. McDiarmid is filled with the sudden urge to snatch it out of her hand and put it through the window of the nearest vehicle, but he bites down hard to keep it from manifesting.

That piece-of-shit Crane has lost his nerve, and with it McDiarmid is going to lose his collar. The whole operation is falling apart before it can even get started, and all that will be left afterward will be some extremely pointed questions about how he lacked the foresight to keep it from turning into a three-ring circus.

McDiarmid's grip tightens on the radio. He still has the tactical unit down at the platform. If he can force a confrontation between them and Crane in the subway tunnel, then there might be an opportunity to salvage this. At the very least, they'll get the collar over the NYPD. Or maybe faced with all that firepower, Crane will rediscover his nerve and detonate.

McDiarmid lifts the radio. "This is McDiarmid," he says. "Move immediately into the tunnel and engage the target."

Standing at the midpoint of the platform looking down the mouth of the tunnel, Hoyt doesn't acknowledge the transmission from McDiarmid. The tactical unit has a good position on the platform: there's a lot of light, good cover for every man, and little risk of cross fire. The tunnel will be the opposite. They will be completely exposed, strung out in a line, and their flashlights won't be powerful enough to penetrate the darkness but will give away their position to anyone farther down the tunnel.

One of the guys on the other side of the platform catches his eye as he gestures toward the tunnel with the same lack of enthusiasm that Hoyt feels. Hoyt lifts a hand and signals back. *Wait one.*

There's no reason for them to go in there. The whole unit has been listening to the police band, and to Hoyt's ears the situation sounds like it is about as good an outcome as they could have expected. The NYPD will have the dubious honor of corralling a couple of hundred pissed-off commuters piling out of the station at 168th St., and anyone that decides to come north will walk straight into the sights of the tactical team. Hoyt's priorities are the safety of the public and the safety of his team, and with both of those secure, he couldn't care less whom Crane surrenders to.

Hoyt's radio crackles in his earpiece. "Are you receiving, Hoyt?" McDiarmid sounds pissed. "Get into the tunnel and take that train."

McDiarmid cares, though. There's no other reason for him to give an order like that. He keeps telling Hoyt to step back and think about the big picture, but it looks like that picture is making sure his career is safe. Hoyt isn't going to risk a single man on his team for the sake of that.

"Acknowledged," Hoyt says into the empty air, his throat mic picking up the sound of his voice and transmitting it for him. As he speaks, he signals to the rest of the tactical team. *Hold positions.*

There's only one thing bothering him. The cop, Hendricks. If she has Crane under arrest or somehow managed to talk him down, she would have contacted them by now. Hoyt isn't the kind of guy who spends a lot of time on the hypotheticals, but her silence itches at him.

The second she agreed to take the other end of the stretcher with him, she became one of the team, and Hoyt will be damned if he is going to leave her hanging down there.

He lifts a hand and presses the button on his harness to transmit.

"If you're going to walk someone into a death trap, sir, I'd rather it just be me," Hoyt says, keeping the button pressed down so that McDiarmid has no chance to respond. "Seeing as you're too chickenshit to do it yourself. All units hold position. If there's any detonation, clear to the surface ASAP. No hero shit. If anyone else comes down that tunnel but me, detain them." He reaches down and thumbs the Power button before ending his transmission. It might be a petty breach of protocol that pales next to the insubordination, but if he's going down that tunnel, then Hoyt would rather not have McDiarmid in his ear the whole way.

Hoyt ditches the radio and checks his weapon before starting along the platform at a jog. When he passes Murphy standing on point at the end, he can just make out the tinny, buzzing noise of McDiarmid losing his shit through the other man's earpiece.

As Hoyt climbs down, Murphy grins at him and gives him a thumbs-up.

Even as he heads into the darkness of the tunnel, Hoyt can't help but feel it is all worth it just to piss McDiarmid off.

CHAPTER FORTY-SIX

168TH ST.–181ST ST.

There is a pool of water down on the tracks. Kelly didn't look at it, didn't shine her flashlight in that direction or acknowledge its existence in any way, but she knows it is there just as surely as she knows that if it isn't, then she and Ben are both as good as dead.

There isn't a prayer for this, or any kind of training. Kelly lifts Ben up on her shoulder and feels her hair burning on the left-hand side of her face. She runs for as many steps as her legs will carry her and throws him forward off of the edge of the platform. As she rolls after him, Kelly is just barely aware of the splash Ben makes when he lands, and a wave of relief makes the hard fall a hell of a lot easier to take.

Kelly can't tell what is water and what is concrete when she hits it. All she feels is a shock that transits her entire body, from head to toe, both freezing cold and viciously hard.

Her head goes under and she spasms, legs and arms flailing hard to get herself upright and out of the water. She spits salt water, gasping for breath, and flinches as a burst of blue flames reach out over the edge of the platform, long fingers of it reaching to try and chase her down.

She isn't on fire anymore.

There will be pain to come, Kelly knows, but right now the important thing is that she isn't on fire.

Ben.

She finds him lying in the pool less than an arm's length away. He is face up, and when she reaches to check to see if he is breathing, Kelly finds him shaking as though he is having a seizure.

She finds his right hand, and the flashlight he is still holding on to. She has to pull hard to get it free of his grip. When she turns it on, the light is so bright that it takes her a moment to register what she is seeing.

Ben is lying with his eyes open because he doesn't appear to have any eyelids left. Most of the left side of his face has been burned, and all down the same side his suit is disintegrating in patches. The wire Emily cut him with is still hanging from his forearm, but it doesn't look like it is bleeding.

It is as though the fire has burned the wound shut, sealing the wire in alongside it.

There will be EMTs on the way. There's even a hospital at 181st St.

Kelly knows that he doesn't have time to wait for them. She needs to get him moving.

She needs to get him back on the train.

There is no smoke from the fire—alcohol burns fast, and there's no ash left when it's done—but the air feels changed. It hurts to breathe it, and when Kelly speaks it feels like she is chewing aluminum foil. "Can you hear me, Ben? Are you okay?"

She asks the question even though she knows he is not.

"I want to move you."

He doesn't say anything, but his eyes twitch in her direction. One of his legs moves, like he is trying to walk. He can hear her speaking, and from the way he's kicking his foot out, it looks as though he wants to get moving, too.

It's a damn sight closer to consent than she was expecting from him.

Kelly fumbles with her belt, opening the clasp and threading it out of her pants. Ben might not be bleeding, but when she pulls him upright the wound on his forearm is going to tear, and then it won't matter how close the hospital is. He'll bleed to death long before he ever sees the surface.

She crouches next to him, jamming the flashlight behind one knee so that she can have both hands free. There's just enough light for her to see what she is doing, and not enough that she has to look at the wreck that was once his arm while she does it.

"I'm going to put on a tourniquet," Kelly says. He doesn't even twitch, but she keeps talking anyway. She feels more sure of herself saying it out loud. "We'll head back to the train and radio for help from there."

It isn't just the air that makes speaking painful. Kelly can smell burned hair, and resists the urge to lift her hand and confirm how much of hers is gone after diving through the flames to get Ben.

He groans aloud as Kelly works the belt under his arm, getting it as close to his body as she can before leaning on his arm and pulling the belt as tight as she can. Ben lets out a noise like a kettle boiling itself dry on the stove.

When she sits up, there is enough give in the belt loop that she can get a finger under it. It isn't tight enough. Her heart sinks at the thought of putting him through it twice. She steels herself, and for a moment considers not telling him what is coming.

Better to let him know what he is in for. "Last one," she says, bending close and putting her weight on him. "I promise."

Kelly tightens the belt again, and Ben makes no noise at all, his whole body going rigid from the pain, like she just put fifty thousand volts through him.

With Ben as stable as she can make him, Kelly tries to get her feet under her so that she can stand. By the time she gets up off of the ground, her legs are shaking so much that she feels like they are going to buckle under her. Just walking herself out of here feels like it will take everything she has. She knows without even trying that she will never be able to carry Ben. She's going to have to drag him instead.

Kelly picks his arms up one at a time and crosses them over his chest, the injured one on top, then gets rid of the flashlight. She needs both hands to pull him, and the flashlight is heavy enough that getting rid of it feels like shedding unnecessary weight. Holding a handful of his clothes underneath each armpit, she turns him so that his head and shoulders are pointing toward the main tunnel, then starts pulling him out of the pool, one step at a time, using the edges of the tracks to get as much drive out of her legs as she possibly can.

It's only once they are out of the pool that Kelly realizes how much the cold water was masking her own injuries, and as she starts backward down the tunnel toward the train she can feel the burns on her legs and arms starting to pulse in time with her breathing, every ragged pull of the poison air echoed in her skin.

Step by step, she pulls Ben along, trying her best not to jog him too hard, trying not to focus on how little progress she is making, or how far she has to go. The metallic tang of whatever chemical residue burned alongside the ethanol still hangs in the air, and it is only when it starts to clear—the thin, clinging feel of it on her face and hands pushed away by swirling eddies of hot air from the main tunnel—that Kelly knows she is getting close.

Kelly can see the train when she loses her footing and sits down hard in a scatter of gravel.

She lets go of Ben and gets her legs free so that she can stand up, and it feels as though she no longer knows how to balance herself on her legs, like the memory got jolted out of her in the fall. She leaves Ben lying on the ground for a moment to shake the fatigue out of her arms, and even though she feels marginally better for the effort it isn't a one hundred percent certainty that she will be able to pick him back up.

"We're almost there," Kelly says, more to psych herself up than anything else, and the sound of a voice that isn't her own anymore makes her feel dizzy. It comes out older, more brittle, and she sways on her feet thinking that she sounds like her mom did the last time she saw her. When they took the tube out, so that she could say goodbye.

Kelly can barely walk, and even if she left Ben here to wait for the cavalry, she feels too weak to go on by herself. Her arms and legs are too heavy, and her head is spinning. All she wants to do is sit down and go to sleep.

We're not going to make it.

The doubt is like acid poured straight onto her brain. It makes her angry, angrier than she has ever been, to think about giving up. The train is right fucking there, and she didn't flip a two-hundred-pound asshole through a Goddamn table of cocktails to just die in this shitty tunnel.

The train is right there. The lights are still on. The power is still on.

Between them and the train is the third rail.

They can make it, but she is going to have to pick him up.

You can do this.

Kelly stands down by Ben's feet. She bends, pulls his knees up, and grabs his good wrist in one hand and the hanging end of the tourniquet belt in the other.

You have to.

She draws a tight breath in through her nose and deep into her gut, feeling her whole torso tighten up to stop her back from blowing out on her, and pulls as hard as she can, heaving Ben into a standing position. As he comes up, she is already squatting so when he ragdolls down onto her shoulder, she is driving upward to meet him. Kelly lets go of the belt so that his body is across her shoulders in a fireman's carry, and with a single short step to keep herself from pitching over, she has him.

A shudder passes through Kelly's left thigh, the quadriceps muscle fluttering like it wants to detach itself from her kneecap, so Kelly gets moving before it can make good on the threat. She steps over the third rail without looking down at it or pausing, and staggers around the front of the train before tripping over her own feet and pitching forward, throwing Ben off of her shoulders and down onto the gravel.

Kelly gets ahold of him again, but when she tries to back up the steps and haul him on board the train, he is too heavy to move.

She can't leave him like this, but she doesn't have the strength to move him.

He is going to have to help.

"Sorry about this," Kelly says. She grabs the wire that is stuck in his arm, the metal cutting her palm as she closes her fist around it and pulls hard. Ben screams and jolts back to a state that might not be fully conscious, but whatever it is it gets his legs moving. Kelly lets go of the wire and pulls, letting him kick his way up the steps until she can dump him on the floor of the train.

Kelly heads into the driver's cab and takes a seat at the console. The controls look like a nightmare, but she can see where the radio is. If she can get Central, they can talk her through it.

Kelly pics up the radio mic and thumbs the button.

Nothing happens.

No lights, no transmission, no static. Nothing.

There must be another button. Kelly looks for it, but the labels are swimming in her vision. She ducks her head down to get a closer look.

A bullet smashes through the front window of the train, and Kelly feels it bury itself into the headrest with a sound like someone just hit it with a baseball bat. Shreds of faux leather and foam padding fall past her face, and Kelly moves her whole body two feet to the right before lifting her head up to look out of the window. Out on the track, directly in front of the train, the walking cadaver that was once Emily Walker is pointing Kelly's gun straight at her. Kelly doesn't wait around to see anymore and throws herself to the floor. Two more shots go through the cab window, each one ricocheting off of the back wall with a bang that is louder than the gunshot was, but Kelly is already out of the door, fast-crawling on her hands and knees as she heads back into the train car to look for shelter.

Kelly almost trips over Ben as she runs out: he has somehow found the strength to pull himself along the floor in her wake, and is sprawled in a pool of his own blood just short of the door. She scrambles over him—she doesn't have the time or strength to pull him inside and use the door for cover—and casts about for something, anything to defend herself with.

There is nothing. All she has is herself, and with the train ready to move all of the lights are on. There is nowhere to hide.

Emily limps up to the open door of the train, and Kelly can see that the lower half of her body is soaked with blood. Whatever the fire might have done to seal the gunshot wounds and keep her alive, her pursuit has opened them back up again.

She is badly hurt, and for a moment, Kelly thinks she might ask for help. Instead, Emily lifts the gun, the effort making her arm shake, and tries to take aim. There's no hope that she will miss. Not at this distance.

There is a gunshot, and Emily jerks to the right, the top half of her head disappearing in a red-brown mist as she does so. Kelly watches her fall, not quite able to connect the gunshot and the fall to work out what has just happened.

It's only when Hoyt appears at the door of the train, rifle still pointed toward the dead body on the ground like she might somehow be able to get back up, that Kelly understands that it is over.

Emily Walker is dead.

"You okay?" Hoyt asks.

Kelly tries to nod, but the pain in her face and neck make her think better of it.

"Injured," she says.

"EMTs are on the way," he says. "Adam Crane?"

"Ben is up there," Kelly says, pointing the way. "In a bad way." She doesn't feel like she can say any more than that. The adrenaline that has kept her going up until this point is gone now, and all that is left is the drop.

"Gonna pass out," she says.

Hoyt gives her a long, hard stare, like he's amazed she hasn't passed out already.

"Just get me the fuck out of here," she says, before the darkness pulls her under.

CHAPTER FORTY-SEVEN
NEW YORK-PRESBYTERIAN

Whenever Kelly wakes up, the television bolted to the wall in the top left corner of her room catches her up on everything she has missed. There's a helicopter shot that gets played on repeat of the chaos around 181st St. station. The pilot and the cameraman must have been making their play for some kind of award because they fly in from the south, following the subway line so exactly that some networks have added a graphic overlaid on top of it that shows where the train came to a stop.

The helicopter flies straight for 181st St., then veers off at the last second to fly in a wide circle, taking in the whole circus and spiraling back in to focus on the station at the very end.

She can see Homeland there, at the center of it all, their unmarked cars with black-tinted windows. SWAT and the FBI are on scene as well, along with what looks like every ambulance and firetruck that they could fit on St. Nicholas Avenue.

The police tried their best to put up a perimeter, closing off everything from the junction at 179th up to Bennett Park, but they hadn't anticipated passengers from the train heading up from 168th St. and straight into the wall of waiting media to get their fifteen minutes of fame. What was originally a quiet crowd has turned into a shit show of local and network news trying to work out who the real victims are, and who has just come down from their apartment to see if they can get their face on television.

It's a hell of a shot, and Kelly is glad she was unconscious for most of it.

Her captain has not been to talk to her. There are flowers from the precinct, and Hernandez has filled her in on the grapevine: there's a general air of embarrassment over her involvement in all of this, and none of the brass know what to do about it. Putting her on shit duty was step one in a multipoint plan to flush her career and send it swirling, and now the mayor's office won't stop calling to ask when they are scheduling a medal ceremony.

A knock at the door tells her that Hoyt is back. He always knocks the same way, and Kelly would never have thought someone could make a knock sound formal until she heard it. All of the hospital staff knock like neighbors turning up with an apple pie. Hoyt knocks like he's been summoned for a court-martial.

"Come." Kelly doesn't raise her voice. It still isn't right, and she wonders if it will ever improve, or if she will just get used to it.

Hoyt lets himself in. He's wearing a blue suit that is in dire need of a tailor's help. He looks like a second-string wrestler on the steps of a courthouse waiting to hear what's happening about their DUI.

Kelly doesn't tell him that.

"It's good to see you awake," he says. He has two cups of coffee with him, and he sets one down on the table in front of her. She isn't meant to have coffee, but Hoyt knows his business. People who walk out of a fire on the fried drumsticks that were their legs get to drink whatever the fuck they want. "Have you been walking?"

The way she hears it, he carried her out himself. Walked the whole way to 181st and then ran—*ran*—up one hundred and twenty steps to get her to the Tactical unit medic. There is apparently a picture, although Kelly has managed to avoid seeing it so far.

"I managed to piss without an honor guard this morning," she says. "To be honest, I was starting to get used to having them around."

Hoyt doesn't even crack a smile, but that he lets the comment go almost counts as growth. The first time he came to visit, he inspected her bandages with the bedside manner of a drill sergeant, upbraiding her the entire time for tackling a fire with no protective gear or training.

He gestures at the coffee.

"You going to drink that before it hits room temperature?"

Kelly picks up the cup. She takes a sip and grimaces, then forces down a good-sized mouthful, regretting every second it is in her mouth before she can swallow it. It isn't the worst coffee she has ever had in her life, but it is damn close.

"Thanks," she says. She knows Hoyt could get her better coffee. She figures that he is doing it to force her to get out of bed and start getting it herself. For a guy who acts like he has to take a pill if he ever senses an emotion coming on, he's surprisingly thoughtful. "How is Ben doing?"

"He's alive," Hoyt says. It's amazing how much he can say by not saying it at all. Ben survived being burned and cut, but an infection in the ICU almost killed him. He has a long road ahead of him to get back to normal.

"He able to say anything yet?"

"Apparently he wrote the word 'cop?' On a nurse's palm with his finger," Hoyt says. "They think he was asking about you."

"What did they tell him?"

"That you got him out of there," Hoyt says.

Kelly sits with that for a moment. She wakes up thinking about it. When the hospital is quiet, and her legs itch under the bandages, and there's nothing to do but stare up into the darkness and feel it pull at her, taking her back underground.

She can't imagine what it must be like for Ben.

She hopes that somewhere in there, there's some kind of relief.

Hoyt is watching her, and Kelly shifts uncomfortably under his scrutiny.

"What is it?"

"You've got questions," he says.

"How do you figure that?"

"You wouldn't be a cop if you didn't."

"You got a timeline for Emily Walker yet?"

Hoyt shakes his head. "It's patchy," he says. "We found a bag in the tunnels with a fake ID; the name matched a couple of job requests on the gig firm that ended up putting the first victim on the train."

"They cooperated?"

"Every package they accept was meant to have been checked by a security team," Hoyt says. "They cooperated without a single reservation."

"You said it was patchy."

"Doesn't look like she was using just the one alias," Hoyt says. "Someone tipped off Ben's employer by email, told them they'd be risking their reputation with a killer's son on the payroll, but we're still running that one down. The timeline matches, though."

Kelly sniffs once, not exactly satisfied by the answer but not upset, either. She has had more than enough of Emily Walker to last her the rest of her life, and untangling her movements leading up to the hijack of a subway train is someone else's ball of yarn to untangle.

One thing is for certain, though: it isn't Homeland's, either.

"How is your boss doing?" she asks.

The last time she saw McDiarmid was when they pulled Ben out on a stretcher. McDiarmid tried to have him arrested on his way to the ambulance. An entire squad of big guys in full tactical gear had gotten it into their heads that Ben had been the one who stopped the train, and as far as they were concerned, he had got himself burned to a crisp saving them from walking into an active bombing. They went through McDiarmid like he wasn't even standing there.

"The director put Analytics onto his call logs and everything they recorded from the incident." Something in Hoyt's face twitches, like it is embarrassing to have to say it. "They suspect he was withholding information to intentionally escalate the situation."

Kelly would whistle, if she could do it without it feeling like her gums might start bleeding. "That's real bad," she says.

"He just made the universal shit list of every operational agent in the state," Hoyt says. "I give it two days before he's gone."

"I suppose someone's head has to roll," Kelly says. "Might as well be the guy at the top for once. What about you?"

"They asked me to step up to McDiarmid's role," Hoyt says.

"Congratulations."

"Pending a clear ruling on the shoot, of course." It takes Kelly a second to work out that this is the closest Hoyt gets to having a sense of humor. For the first time ever, he shifts his weight like he's not sure of the ground he's standing on. "I turned it down," he says.

If Kelly still had eyebrows, she'd raise them. "Really? What will you do instead?"

"I've been going over the whole thing with the FBI," he says. "Turns out that Emily killed more people over the years. Men with sealed court records, about Ben's age."

"She was looking for him."

"All of them went unsolved for years until now," Hoyt says. "They had a lot of similarities that fell through the gaps."

Kelly can put the pieces together herself. "You're going to work cold cases for the FBI? That sounds like retirement."

"It won't just be the FBI. NYPD and Homeland want to cover their asses, and have offered cooperation as well."

"You . . ." Kelly leans back against her pillow and tries to imagine why someone would even volunteer for that. Being pulled three ways by different precincts is bad enough. This is high-order shit duty, beyond anything she has ever experienced, and he almost seems eager to get on with it.

She takes a breath, tries to work out what she wants to say.

Congratulating someone for giving themselves high blood pressure doesn't feel right.

"Get your funding signed off ASAP," she says. The PR power of hero magic fades fast, so he won't have long. A week at best, with the current speed they cycle through the news. "Get three years. Five if you can. No strings on it."

"You think it will dry up?"

"Don't want them all thinking the other guys are going to pick up the bill," she says. "And make sure you know who you report to. Who gets the credit on a breakthrough. Who talks to the press."

"You've thought about this," Hoyt says.

"When you find yourself up to your neck in it," Kelly says, "you figure out how to swim real fast."

Kelly wonders if Hoyt is looking for some kind of approval from her. Like coming up here is something his therapist has suggested.

Kelly can still picture the way Emily Walker's head jumped when the bullet went through it, the gray-white spill of her brains, a detail that she tries very hard to forget. Hoyt went through the same thing, and when she passed out it was left to him to pick up all the pieces, her included.

With anyone else, she would have danced around it, but Hoyt is all about straight answers. He can handle the question.

"Why do you keep coming up here, Hoyt?" she asks.

He fixes her with the most intense look she has ever seen in her life, his eyes the color of steel, and for one terrible second Kelly is filled with the dread sensation that she is going to be asked out on a date.

"I want to offer you a job," Hoyt says.

CHAPTER FORTY-EIGHT

SIX MONTHS LATER

Ben does the crossword while he waits in reception. It isn't so much for the crossword itself, but the writing helps keep his fingers active, which is all part of the rehabilitation process. Sometimes, he imagines that he can feel something other than stiffness or pain, but since he also feels things in the two fingers he lost, Ben recognizes it as a phantom of what might happen rather than what is.

A woman comes just as he gives up and starts filling in the boxes with the alphabet instead, and he makes sure to fold the paper up and take it with him. Ben can't be sure that she doesn't recognize his face or his name, or that she won't read something into his spoiled crossword that he didn't intend beyond practicing getting his letters right with half a hand to write with.

She leaves him at the door of the office and walks away without glancing back at him once.

How times have changed.

The voice barely registers. Ben knows it is still there, but he hardly pays it any attention these days. Someone from the police or the feds—they all blurred together, the number of people he's had to talk to about it all—came to tell him about how they'd locked down his dad's access to the outside world. That he'd been able to correspond with Emily Walker and reach out to Ben was an embarrassment to all involved, so there was a ground-up overhaul of how they handled his communications. They were afraid his dad would try to leverage something out of it—another book, interviews, a TV special—so they went to a judge for a gag order, citing the risk to public safety that John Crane represented.

His dad would spend the rest of his life making calls that went no further than his lawyer's office, and sending letters straight to an evidence box at the FBI. Nobody will ever hear from him again, and that knowledge helps keep his dad's voice at bay.

Ben knocks on the door and waits for a call from inside before entering.

Doctor Hardy isn't waiting for him behind her desk. Instead, she's standing in the middle of the room, a pace forward from the chair where a patient would usually sit, her back straight, her hands clasped together. "Hello, Ben," she says.

"Doctor." She doesn't look as though she has aged at all, although Ben realizes that the last time he saw her, he wasn't even a teenager yet. To an eleven-year-old kid, she could have been twenty-five or she could have been a hundred and all he would have registered was that she was *old*.

"Are you . . . well?"

Ben gestures to his face with the remains of his hand. His plastic surgeon was extremely proud of the work he did on Ben's eyelids. "The grafts went well," he says. Ben avoids mirrors, as much as he can. He wears dark glasses, if only to keep people from staring. "It's good to see you," he says.

It surprises her, as an opening gambit, and she takes a deep breath before rushing all of her words out in one quick burst. "I wanted to say that I'm sorry for what I did to you. I thought I was doing the right thing, but all I did was hurt you."

"It's okay," Ben says. The immediacy of her confession makes him feel uncomfortable. It's probably something she has wanted to say for a long time, but it is also putting him on the spot to respond.

"You were in my care, Ben, and I failed you."

"You had your reasons."

She catches his hesitation—that he doesn't forgive her, not entirely—and pulls up short on whatever she was about to follow up with. "You look good, Ben. For all that you've been through."

"Thank you." He doesn't mention his hand, not when he can help it, but the fingers he can move twitch of their own accord, and he feels her gaze shift to them.

"Do you feel good?" she asks.

Ben takes a breath, holds it, and lets it out again. Taking down the walls he has built is an effort. Every brick has to be worked loose before he can lift it out of place and give himself enough room to speak freely.

"Not in the slightest," he says. "I was hoping that we could talk."

He can see the change in her, the shift that she tries to mask with her poise and her careful stillness. It's like a weight being lifted: she shakes it free and stands taller. Ben feels a stab of envy that it could be so easy to do. But that's why he came back: he can't do it alone, and he can't imagine doing the work with someone who hasn't already gone part of the way down that road already. Guilt and shame are all that remain of his father's legacy, all that he has left to get rid of.

"I'd like that, Ben," Doctor Hardy says. She looks back at her desk, at her notepad and files arranged neatly on there just like the first day Ben met her, and she seems to think better of it. "There's a coffee shop on campus near here. It's not too busy at this time of day. Why don't we go get some coffee and we can take a walk in the park? Talk things over."

"That sounds like a plan," Ben says.

She smiles. "Then let's get started."

ACKNOWLEDGMENTS

There are a lot of people who deserve thanks in bringing this book to life. First and foremost among them is my agent, Juliet Mushens. Tireless, considerate, and insightful, she has always believed in my writing. Even if I had never been published, then that would be enough.

Thanks to Jenny Bent for representing me in the US, and Mushens Entertainment and The Bent Agency respectively for their support.

Thanks are due to Keith Kahla, my editor, not just for his guidance but also going the extra mile to scout locations, and to Grace Gay and rest of the team at Minotaur for all of their hard work.

To Alistair, my brother, for being a constant sounding board for every dumb idea I have, and all the suggestions for far better ones that I invariably steal from you.

To Jen Williams and Den Patrick, my best and saltiest friends, for always lending an ear.

To Mac, Katie, and the Hades crew for giving me a ready excuse to procrastinate, and a huge thanks to Jan, Pedro, and Max for making me feel well-adjusted.

Thanks to Emily Pernling and all of the staff at the IES Enskede for their support and encouragement. It means a lot to work with such an excellent team.

To Toshihiro and Eva-Britt for their support and encouragement (and also the bottomless supply of apple cake and coffee), and to the whole family Morota for putting up with me.

To my mum and dad, my first and biggest fans.

To my girls: Aoife, Eilidh, and Iona. You mean the world to me. Please stop yelling.

And, finally, to Lisa. None of this would be possible without you. I love you.

Born in Scotland, **Andrew Reid** worked as a research scientist for almost a decade on projects including DNA synthesis, forensics, and drug development. He now teaches science and lives in Stockholm with his wife, three children, and two cats.